CALL TO ARMS

Book Two of the Black Fleet Trilogy

JOSHUA DALZELLE

D1533942

Prologue

Cape Canaveral, Florida
Year: 2054 AD

The press pit was packed with jostling, shouting, and generally inconsiderate correspondents from every major news outlet on the planet. On such a momentous occasion, Steven would have thought the Tsuyo Corporation would have sprung for a bigger, more luxurious area for the world's press. Even with their wealth and considerable influence over most governments, they could use some good publicity, given the astronomical losses they'd taken in the recovery effort.

"So, do you think it's actually going to happen this time?" a voice asked from beside him. Steven recognized her as the attractive afternoon anchor for one of the myriad subscription news channels, but he couldn't place which one.

"It's hard to say." He shrugged. "One more abort, and I think people are going to start losing interest."

She gave him an annoyed glare and pressed her earpiece further into her ear. Guess she hadn't been talking to him.

Steven shrugged again and continued to make his way up as close to the raised platform as he could. As a freelance journalist, providing content to as many websites as he could, he was on a rapidly sinking ship, given the public's demand for a more interactive experience with their news. When he was at his most cynical, and least sober, he also had to admit that the professional journalist was itself a dying breed, supplanted by beautiful, augmented presenters that simply introduced clips from public relation firms or peoples' cell phones.

Steven kept pushing and sliding between people until, three rows back from the edge of the barrier, he could go no farther. He patted the pockets of his cargo pants to make sure his camera was in the right thigh pocket and his backup in the left. From the angle he was at in relation to the stage, he could see behind the curtain and to a group of people in expensive suits all toasting with champagne.

To his right, two immense launch vehicles stood on their respective pads, hissing from fuel boil off. He'd seen the dog and pony show twice before. Only when the rockets were blasting off from Cape Canaveral would he believe that the mission had actually started. His musings were interrupted by the hush that fell over the press pool.

A short Japanese man in a stylish blue suit walked confidently to the podium. Diachi Katsu, chief operating officer of the largest aerospace firm on the planet—a multinational conglomeration of the flagging military industrial complex of the United States and the resurging industrial power of Japan. If it flew, shot, blew up, or launched into space, it was almost certain that the Tsuyo Corporation had something to do with it.

"My friends," Diachi began in flawless English, with just a touch of an accent, that gave proof of his Ivy League education and practically none of his birthplace. "Today is certainly a great day." He smiled widely, seeming to savor a moment he'd probably envisioned in his head a thousand times.

"This is a day we've been building up to for fifteen years. When we discovered a derelict ship from the stars crashed on the surface of Europa fifteen years ago, rather than burden the governments of the world to mount an exploratory mission, Tsuyo answered the call and not only surveyed the site, but built the machines necessary to recover the priceless artifact."

"The exclusive rights to the technology didn't have anything to do with it, I'm sure," another reporter snorted.

Steven had to admit that he had a point. When the alien ship had been discovered, Tsuyo had applied its considerable leverage to get the world's major powers to agree to allow them to execute the recovery effort. It had taken years to develop the technology needed to launch a robotic armada that was able to dislodge the derelict from the ice of Europa, bring it back, and put it in orbit around Earth's moon.

From there it was relatively easy for Tsuyo scientists to begin reverse engineering some of the technology they found on board. Curiously, there were no signs of a crew. Nor did the ship's interior give any specific information as to what the crew may have been like, other than that they seemed to be slightly smaller than the average human.

"The vessel still maintains many of her secrets," Diachi continued. "Who sent it? Why did it come here? How long was it on that icy moon? While we're still striving to discover the answers to these questions, no one can deny the incredible progress we've made in adapting some of the technology for use by humans. Most significantly, the means with which to prove the feasibility of faster than light travel and actually construct a working prototype.

"It is to that end we've gathered here today. On the launch pads to my left are the first twelve members of the eventual forty-eight person crew that will board the *Carl Sagan*, currently in orbit above us, and take man's first excursion beyond the boundaries of our own solar system. These brave men and women will take our first starship out to Proxima Centauri and back-a mission of exploration that will take them over four light-years away, but will only take fifteen months thanks to the Tsuyo Faster-Than-Light Drive, or T-Drive."

The corporation had been on a full media blitz to embed the term into the lexicon, but it was fighting a losing battle with the nearly universally used *warp drive*.

"But enough from me." Diachi assumed a look of humility that he must have practiced in the mirror often. "Let's hear from the real heroes of this mission before they depart. Colonel, can you hear me?"

The enormous screen behind Diachi went from showing a close-up of the two rockets to a close-up shot of an incredibly handsome man that looked to be in his late thirties.

"Here comes fucking Captain America." The cynic beside Steven laughed.

"We read you loud and clear, Mr. Katsu," the man said. "Hello America, and hello world. This is Colonel Robert Blake, U.S. Air Force, talking to you from the crew capsule of the Titan VII launch vehicle. We're sitting on the pad, waiting for our ride up to the *Carl Sagan*. The crew and I wanted to tell you how honored we are to be chosen for such an important mission and the next leap in the advancement of our species.

"Over the next two years, we will be thinking of you all as we step into the next frontier of human exploration. This is Colonel Blake and the crew of the

Carl Sagan, signing off for now. God willing, we'll talk to you again soon."

Steven almost rolled his eyes at the contrived speech the colonel had just given as the screen switched back to the view of the launch pad. It seemed a bit premature since it would take twelve rockets six more flights, before the *Carl Sagan* was fully crewed and provisioned. Add in another three weeks of planned tests and checks, and the Earth's first starship, primitive as it was, wouldn't be leaving for another two months.

"Start the countdown!" Diachi said once he'd walked back onto the stage.

Even as well choreographed as the event was, it still took another ten seconds before the clock on the stage began counting down, syncing with the master mission clock in the control room on the other side of the complex. Diachi stood placidly as the first rumbling of powerful engines igniting reached the crowd. The flash of the vehicles lifting off and roaring into the sky was clearly visible before the deafening sound washed over them. Steven didn't bother filming the two specks as they raced up into the sky. He would just link to the official, high quality video for his story. "I wonder what they'll find out there," the cynic said.

"If we're lucky, nothing." Steven turned and pushed his way back through the mob, hoping to get to his vehicle and leave before the others crowded the parking area.

Chapter 1

Year: 2427 AD

"More targets have just appeared in-system, Captain. Four in total, same configuration as the others."

"Track them and update the other ships through the Link." Captain Lee tried to keep the hopelessness out of his voice.

Edward Lee was the CO of the *TCS Brooklands*, a Seventh Fleet heavy missile cruiser. His ship had already disgorged her payload of sixty-five strategic nuclear missiles, destroying only thirty-one targets and disabling another three in the process, and was now flying the perimeter of the engagement using her more powerful radar to track and update targets for the remaining Terran ships involved in what had become the second battle for Xi'an.

The *Brooklands* had flown into the system with two full Third Fleet battlegroups, both pulled in from other parts of the Asianic Union and both comprised of ships that weren't up to the task of repelling the invaders. Out of the twelve ships making up the armada, only three remained combat capable. Two were crippled, but had survivors aboard, and the other seven were nothing more than expanding fields of debris. Of the seventy-two alien constructs defending the Xi'an System, nineteen remained, including the reinforcements that had just arrived.

These alien constructs, still called "ships" by the humans fighting them, were infinitesimal compared to the monstrous, single juggernaut that had laid waste to four systems, two completely annihilated. What they lacked in size, they made up for in toughness and tenacity, however.

It had been just over four years since that first, fateful encounter, and now, after a few years of little action, the war was really heating up, and these smaller enemy ships were quickly decimating the human Fleet presence along the Frontier.

"Prepare a com drone," Lee said. "Load all mission data from the armada, and launch it for Haven immediately. Follow randomization protocol Alpha."

"Aye, sir," the OPS Officer said. "Data loading now. Randomization protocol Alpha initialized."

Even after four years, human scientists still had little idea of what the aliens, nicknamed the Phage by a captivated public with a wild imagination, were capable of. As such, all ships and com drones flying to or from the front were not allowed to take a direct route back to Terran space, especially Haven. "Drone launching now."

"Do you think we should begin moving for a transition point ourselves?" Lee's XO leaned in to whisper. Lee just shook his head, not wanting to entertain a conversation about leaving the engagement.

There was little they could accomplish now that their missiles had been expended: the *Brooklands* didn't carry any other armament. She was a strictly strategic ship that was never intended to do anything but warp into the space just outside a system, launch all her missiles, and slip away before the light of her initial transition could be detected.

The other reason Lee didn't want to have that particular conversation with his XO was that he feared it would lead to him agreeing to abandon the Third Fleet ships still directly engaged. While he tried not to show it for the sake of his crew, he was terrified beyond all measure. This was his first time meeting the enemy. In fact, it was the first combat experience of his thirty-six year career. Despite trying to remain an island of calm for his crew, his mouth was dry as desert sand and he could feel his heart pounding in his chest. Never had he imagined it was even possible to be so scared.

"The *Taipei* is reporting the loss of two main engines." Lee's com officer intruded into his thoughts. "She's trying to clear the engagement area on the two she has left."

"She'll never make it," Lee said under his breath, as the plots of the individual ships in the battle were updated on his main display. The Phage had shown a tendency to swarm damaged ships, destroying them before they could escape. With the reactionless drive the smaller Phage ships employed, they could run down a stricken Terran ship, destroy it, and get back into the engagement before their human counterparts could even think about redeploying their formation or changing tactics.

"Phage ships are ignoring the *Taipei*," the OPS officer reported. "This doesn't hold with what we know of their tactics from previous engagements."

"No it doesn't." Lee stared at the moving plots, well aware the data he was seeing was almost two hours old at their current range. In fact, nothing the remaining Phage ships were doing made a whole lot of sense. The aliens had been waiting in the Xi'an System and had fallen upon the armada like a like a pack of wild dogs, coordinated and deadly. But now they seemed to be confused, ineffectively dividing their firepower among the remaining Third Fleet ships.

The *Brooklands* was just outside the orbit of the fourth planet in the system, her orbital velocity so minimal that she could keep the powerful targeting radar focused on the engagement near Xi'an. The Phage force changed behavior and tactics so drastically that Lee had a feeling that he was observing something vital. He froze just as he was about to order the cruiser onto a new course, torn between his duty to the Confederacy and the responsibility to see his ship and crew safely away once they'd accomplished their mission goals. What was he missing? Why were the Phage changing tactics in the middle of such a decisive victory for their side?

"Other than the *Taipei*, what ships are still operational?" Lee asked.

"The *Zhejiang* and the *Dao*," the OPS officer reported. "*Dao* is still full mission capable."

Lee frowned at that last bit. The *Dao* was easily the most powerful ship in the system, one of Third Fleet's few true battleships. If she was still full mission capable (FMC), then her captain was likely keeping her out of the engagement and letting the smaller, less armored ships take the pounding. He'd have to review the sensor logs later to be certain, but if the Third Fleet captain was holding back with their most powerful ship while sacrificing two thirds of his available fleet, it didn't bode well for Starfleet's potential effectiveness against an enemy that had no such reservations.

"Coms, message the *Dao* and request a status update including expended munitions," Lee said. "Nav, begin running an active plot from our current position to our nearest jump point... make sure the helm is always updated."

"Aye, sir," the specialist at the nav station said.

"Sir, the *Dao* is reporting no damage," the coms officer said after ninety minutes had elapsed. "They did not include weapon status despite repeated requests."

"Thank you." Lee sighed. "That tells me what I needed to know."

"And that was, sir?" the XO asked.

"The *Dao*'s captain is going through the motions, but he has no intention of putting himself or his ship in a position where they can get caught up in one of those swarm attacks."

"Sir!" the OPS officer called out. "New contacts! Fifty-two targets just appeared in-system. Initial returns indicate Phage ships."

"Signal a retreat," Lee said. He was momentarily embarrassed by the relief that washed over him as he ordered his ship to withdraw, but that was quickly tamped down by the realization that he would be taking his entire crew back to Terran space alive. "Track the *Zhejiang* and the *Dao* and let me know if the *Taipei* is able to separate herself enough to accelerate to their transition point."

"Captain, look!" The XO pointed to the main display.

The Phage were once again attacking in a deliberate, cohesive nature. All remaining Phage ships raced for the *Dao* and began blasting away with their directed plasma weapons, just as the big battleship flared on the *Brooklands's* thermal sensors, her engines going to full power in an effort to escape.

"The *Dao* is taking a beating," the OPS officer said. "She's barely fighting back. Point defense fire indicates they're operating in an automatic mode. Engines are still at full power."

"Captain Chen is panicking," Lee said to himself.

He only knew the *Dao*'s captain by reputation, but it was enough that he realized Chen's appointment likely had little to do with his actual ability to command a battleship and more with who his family was connected to within the Asiatic Union. The pride of Third Fleet attempted to flee the area while Phage ships made unanswered runs on her, looking like a swarm of hornets chasing an ungainly, lumbering beast.

"New arrivals look like they're chasing after the *Dao* as well," OPS reported. "We're still more or less being ignored."

"I would theorize that they know we're the least threatening thing in the system," Lee said, more thinking aloud than addressing his OPS officer. "All our long-range weapons are expended, and we have light armor. Other than high-energy RF from the radars, we're little more than a steel asteroid out here. Either that, or their sensors have the same limitations ours do, and they haven't detected us yet."

When Captain Chen decided to blindly flee the engagement rather than fight his way out, the fate of the *Dao* was sealed. The bridge crew of the *Brooklands* watched as the Phage ships buzzed in again and again, disabling the ship's aft weaponry and degrading the engines enough that the battleship's acceleration was drastically cut. The loss of thrust allowed the fresh Phage ships to close the distance. The only bright spot of the horrific scene playing out on the main display was that the *Taipei* and *Zhejiang* seemed to be slinking out of the system unnoticed, racing along a widening arc as fast as they could.

It was a horrific six hours, watching the ship try to flee its tormenters, especially being as helpless to intervene as the *Brooklands* was. Just as the leading edge of the Phage reinforcements came within their maximum weapons range of the *Dao*, an enormous flash completely washed out the *Brooklands's* optical sensors, but the radar images told the tale.

The *Dao* had taken a critical hit, exploding with enough force that she took fifteen attackers along with her. As the optics came back up, the thermals showed the ship had broken up into four large pieces, along with a lot of associated debris, and each was traveling roughly along the same course the battleship had been taking out of the Xi'an System.

"Fuck!" Lee shouted, causing everyone on the bridge to jump.

The loss of the *Dao* was a huge blow to the human war effort as large, powerful battleships were quite rare in the current Fleet makeup. He was simultaneously sick at the loss of human life and enraged that someone as incompetent as Chen hadn't been replaced as CO of such a vital asset.

"Any escape beacons?"

"Negative, sir," the OPS officer said. "No radio beacons from the *Dao*."

"Helm, begin accelerating us out along our escape vector." Lee forced himself to calm down. "All ahead two thirds. Let's not draw undue attention to ourselves. We'll charge to the jump point at the last minute."

"Ahead two thirds, aye."

"OPS, keep track of every enemy contact down near Xi'an." Lee watched the Phage swarm all over the wreckage of the *Dao*, already dragging the larger pieces back to the planet. "I want to know immediately if they even begin to sniff in this direction."

"Aye, sir."

It was another four hours of steady acceleration until Lee began to feel that they just might make it out of Xi'an alive. It was another ten minutes after that when his OPS officer dispelled that optimism.

"Phage formation is splitting up," he said. "Ten are continuing to push the remains of the *Dao* to Xi'an. The rest have divided into two forces—one pursuing the *Taipei* and *Zhejiang*, the rest moving onto a direct intercept for us and accelerating."

"Helm, all ahead full," Lee ordered, eyes glued to the updated tracks. The Phage ships were pushing ahead at three hundred G's of acceleration, but the *Brooklands* had an almost insurmountable lead. They'd hit their jump point long before the enemy came into range.

"All ahead, aye," the helmsman reported.

"Updating our jump point plot," the nav specialist said.

Lee just nodded, watching the clocks on the main display adjust to show time to warp transition, time from enemy weapons range, and total mission time.

The *Brooklands* was not built with speed in mind and was never supposed to venture down too far into a system during a battle or be required to escape. She was meant to carry a high relative velocity from the time she warped in, fired her missiles, and warped out. As such, her engines were a bit on the underpowered side, and the Phage had an outside chance of catching them given the acceleration profiles of the small attackers that had been documented in previous engagements. From what he could see so far, however, the small force seemed content to just chase them out of the system.

"New contacts!" OPS said in alarm. "From the other side of the system, closest to us."

"Resolve!" Lee practically shouted.

As Xi'an was on the Frontier, there were definite battle lines drawn with the Phage incursion coming from the far side and the Terran defenders usually warping in from three available vectors on the opposite side. That didn't mean, however, that Lee discounted the possibility that the enigmatic enemy couldn't move beyond Xi'an and push in from the other side, cutting off their retreat.

"Confederate ships!" the OPS officer exclaimed in relief. "Transponder data coming in now... Black Fleet, Ninth Squadron, five ships in total, all *Starwolf*-class destroyers. Lead ship is the *Ares*, sir!"

"Thank God." Lee exhaled in relief. "Send the *Ares* all the battle data we have, and tell Captain Wolfe his timing could not have been better."

****

"Data packet coming in from the *Brooklands*, Captain," Lieutenant Davis said. "Looks like a raw dump of their entire sensor feed."

"Archive it, Lieutenant," Captain Jackson Wolfe said to his OPS Officer. "We don't have time to analyze it just now. Tactical, what are we looking at?"

"We have twenty-nine hostiles closing on the *Brooklands*," Lieutenant Commander Barrett said. "Still waiting on the computer to resolve the rest of the system, but we received some preliminary data over the Link from the other Fleet ships."

The shared data link, or "Link," had been a relatively simple upgrade, but had proven its worth at every engagement. Essentially, any ship in the area would broadcast their sensor telemetry so that it could be networked with the others and redistributed among the rest of the fleet. It eliminated the need for individual ships to wait twice as long for a valid radar return over long distances.

"Coms, tell the *Icarus* and *Atlas* to adjust course and accelerate toward the *Brooklands*," Jackson ordered. "Tell them to engage and destroy all twenty-nine targets."

"Aye, sir."

"Have the *Artemis* and *Hyperion* break off and pursue the formation chasing the remnants of the Third Fleet armada," Jackson continued. "Nav, plot me a course down to Xi'an, maximum performance. I want to catch those units before they're able to deorbit the remains of the *Dao*."

"What if there are more ships than just the ten defending Xi'an?" Wolfe's XO asked.

"Then we'll deal with them, Commander Wright," Jackson answered. "I'm more worried about why they've decided to try and establish another beachhead on Xi'an. What's so special about that planet? They've already stripped the crust of any usable material."

"OPS, prep a drone for atmospheric flight," Celesta called out. "Set flight profile for high-altitude surface scans, full instrument suite."

"Yes, ma'am." Lieutenant Davis keyed her headset to send the command down to Flight Operations.

Jackson smiled slightly as his XO correctly predicted his next command. After the dust had settled from the initial attack of the Phage, Jackson had pushed CENTCOM to give Celesta Wright a command of her own. Surprisingly, she'd declined and requested to remain as his executive officer. Her rationale had been that the mission that had resulted in the destruction of the *Blue Jacket* had opened her eyes to how unready she was for a ship of her own. Jackson completely disagreed with her self-assessment, but he was more than happy to keep her on his crew, and if she felt she wasn't ready, it would negatively affect her ability to command.

"Nav! Where's my plot?" Jackson asked.

"Coming up now, sir," the young specialist second class at the nav station said. Unfortunately, he hadn't been able to overcome his nervousness about working on the bridge of the *Ares*.

Based on the look Celesta gave the hapless spacer, it would be his last watch at the nav station.

"Let's look alive!" Jackson didn't let up. "There are at least seventy Phage combat units in this system and no Confederate assets within range to provide relief."

Three possible courses down to Xi'an appeared on the main display as the specialist finished his calculations. The *Starwolf*-class ship was far more capable than his previous *Raptor*-class vessel, and the navigation plots reflected that. Each of the courses showed an acceleration profile far more aggressive than the *Blue Jacket* would have been capable of and would put them in orbit over Xi'an in just over twenty-hours from their current position.

Jackson considered each for a few seconds. "Helm, come to course Charlie... all ahead full."

"Ahead full, aye."

"I hate splitting the squadron up like this," Celesta said quietly from her seat on Jackson's right. "Even with the Link, we're still waiting hours for updates from the other ships."

"Nothing for it this time," Jackson said. "We need to protect the *Brooklands,* and it looks like those Third Fleet battlegroups were decimated. If we can save the last two, maybe this won't be a total loss."

"All for a planet that can no longer even support human life," Celesta said, seeming to catch herself in mid-eyeroll.

"But also a system that's a strategic jump point into three other Terran systems," Jackson reminded her. "Even though we have no idea how the Phage navigate, they seem to be more than happy to use our own warp lanes against us."

"This is the third incursion in the last six months," she said. "Do you think they're finally gearing up for a major offensive?"

"I truly hope not," Jackson said. "We've not come along nearly as fast as I'd hoped the last few years. We're nowhere near ready to meet this enemy head on."

"I can't argue there," she said. "Shall we remain on normal watch schedules?"

"Yes." Jackson checked the mission clock and compared it to ship's time. "Stand down from general quarters for now since we're skirting well around the two major engagements. That puts first watch back on duty four hours before we begin braking for our Xi'an orbital insertion. It also means I want you to split your time on second watch with Lieutenant Davis."

"Yes, sir." She logged off her terminal and stood to leave the bridge. The pair had become much more comfortable around each other during the manic pace the previous three years. From having to train on an entirely new class of ship, to working at rebuilding a crew around the survivors from the *Blue Jacket*, they had been around each other almost constantly. While they still maintained a strict professionalism between them, they had become much more efficient at commanding a starship as a team and not just two ranking officers.

"Lieutenant Davis, work with Lieutenant Commander Barrett to break down the data the *Brooklands* sent over," he ordered. "Alert me if you find anything in there that will affect our current tactics."

"Yes, sir," the pair said, nearly in unison, as each pulled up the data packet and began dividing the work between them.

The bridge crew efficiently went about their tasks as Jackson leaned back in his seat, debating whether he needed another cup of coffee or not. He looked around the bridge of the *Ares*, the second *Starwolf*-class ship to come out of the yards and the first put into active service. She still had the "new ship smell" as the new upholstery was still outgassing from the adhesives used, and the crew hadn't had time to fully break her in.

The bridge required significantly less people than the old *Raptor*-class destroyer did. In fact, there were usually only seven people on the bridge at any given time. It made for a much less chaotic environment once his crew became accustomed to passing tasks down to their respective shops and then funneling the information back to him.

"Captain, we're getting returns from the far side of the system," Barrett said after another hour of relative silence. "The last known target data from the *Brooklands* is still accurate, we should only have ten individual targets over Xi'an when we get there."

"That's assuming they don't have forces on the surface they can call on," Jackson reminded him.

It hadn't taken them long to learn that with their reactionless drives, the Phage could land significant forces on a planet and give a Terran fleet a nasty surprise if they came barreling into orbit thinking they had an advantage.

"Keep updating the existing target tracks, but have the long range radars sweeping in high-power mode. They know we're here and roughly where we are already, so I want to favor intel over stealth."

"Yes, sir."

Jackson wasn't overly concerned with the ten targets heading to Xi'an. The *Ares* would make short work of them before they could even get close to within weapons range. Beyond all else, Jackson was worried that in what appeared to be the early stages of a full out war, they'd yet to see any tactical assets from the enemy other than the small, easily defeated attack craft CENTCOM had unoriginally named *Bravos*. There were also a smattering of sightings of what appeared to be enormous cargo haulers, but so far, there hadn't been anything even remotely like the monster, or the *Alpha*, that he'd fought across four-star systems.

Was that because they were so rare and difficult to produce? Or had humanity not demonstrated itself to be a great enough threat to warrant sending more? The absence of accurate information made him want to scream in frustration, and the apparent lack of movement on the part of CENTCOM made him want to do physical harm to an inanimate object.

"*Icarus* and *Atlas* have reported in." The young ensign at the coms station interrupted his thoughts. "All Bravos chasing the *Brooklands* have been destroyed, thirty-two Hornet missiles expended between them."

"Excellent," Jackson said. "Order the *Icarus* and *Atlas* to begin their push toward Xi'an. Inform Captain Lee that he may fly the *Brooklands* at his own discretion... He can depart the system or wait until we've cleared out all the Bravos."

"Aye, sir. Transmitting now."

"Are we overdue for a status from the *Artemis* and *Hyperion*?" Jackson eyed the mission clock.

"Negative, Captain," Lieutenant Davis said. "They will not engage the enemy for another three hours."

"Very good," Jackson said. "Keep me updated if we get anything from them or the Third Fleet ships."

The bridge fell into an eerie silence. The Tsuyo engineers had made the ship too comfortable, too sterile. He could barely hear or feel the main engines that were currently at full power, and the acoustics of the bridge had been so carefully planned that he was unable to hear the chatter between his bridge crew and their backshops. He didn't like the isolated feeling or the false sense of security it induced. A warship should feel like what it was: an instrument of destruction, with all thought of crew comfort coming in a distant second.

Four more hours of the cursed silence slowly ticked by.

"Bravos have abandoned the pieces of the *Dao* and are now coming out to meet us," Lieutenant Commander Barrett finally reported.

"Sound general quarters. Set condition 1SS." Jackson ordered. "Are you still tracking ten Bravos, Tactical?"

"Yes, sir," Barrett said. "Updating tracks and sending targeting info to the forward missile batteries."

"Activate port battery, tubes one through twelve," Jackson said. "Keep five more on ready reserve."

"Aye, sir," Barrett confirmed. "Missiles one through twelve now linked and updated with target package. We will be in optimum launch range within six hours."

"Very good, Lieutenant Commander." Jackson stood up to pace a bit. "Bring the forward laser projectors online as well. Lieutenant Davis, give Engineering a courtesy call that we're bringing the tactical systems to full power."

"Yes, sir." Jillian Davis turned to make the call to Engineering. She seemed to be mouthing the words silently into her headset as the clever acoustic panels absorbed all the sound.

Jackson made a mental note to ask his Chief Engineer, Daya Singh, if it would be possible to replace or remove all the panels so he could hear what the hell was going on. Commander Wright and Lieutenant Keller rushed onto the bridge, the former looking like she'd been waiting for an alert and the latter looking like he'd been sound asleep.

"Bravos accelerating hard and splitting up into two groups," Barrett said, his voice strained. "It looks like they're going to try a pincer movement."

"Helm, braking thrust, all reverse!" Jackson nodded to Celesta as she pulled up her own terminal to get caught up. "Cut our relative velocity by seventy percent, and then go to no-thrust."

"All astern full, aye," the helmsman called out, suddenly very alert. "Helm answering braking maneuver, reducing closure velocity by seventy percent."

"Tactical, fire the Hornets just outside the optimum range."

"Aye, sir," Barrett said. "Updating firing solution now."

The plots on the main display now updated much more quickly as the range between them and the Bravos decreased. The computer interposed a blue line between them that was his optimum firing range. Another line, this one flashing red and further from the enemy's position, indicated where Jackson wanted to fire his missiles. The computer's passive aggressive jabs at the perceived errors in his commands were a bit more tolerable than his old ship's habit of simply not performing any action its computer deemed outside acceptable limits.

Now that the enemy had reacted to their presence, the tension on the bridge was palpable, even with contact hours away. The crew of the *Ares* was one of the most battle hardened groups in the Fleet, but there was still no way to ever be comfortable or complacent when barreling toward an engagement with this terrifying enemy. Three and a half tense hours passed slowly until they were nearly in range.

"Hornets away," Barrett reported. "All twelve birds are away clean and tracking true."

The icons representing the missiles split up into two groups, deciding between them which target each would pursue and accelerating toward the Bravos that still looked like they wanted to flank the *Ares* and catch her in a crossfire.

"Helm, all ahead full," Jackson said calmly. "Maintain course."

"Ahead full, aye. No course deviation."

The reaction was almost immediate. As the *Ares* shot between the two groups of Bravos, they decelerated quickly, turning hard to come about and pursue the destroyer after the unexpected maneuver. They also slowed and actually flew back directly into the paths of the incoming Hornets. The missiles slammed into their designated targets, the hardened nose cones punching into the organic armor of the Bravos before detonating. Unlike the Alpha Jackson had battled before, the Bravos didn't seem to have the ability to heal after taking heavy damage. The warhead from a single missile was enough kill or disable it.

"Ten for ten!" Barrett whooped. "Sending the self-destruct signal to the remaining two Hornets."

That had been easy. Maybe too easy. "Still no new contacts?"

"None we can see," Barrett confirmed. "High-power scans have been active since entering the system."

"Very well," Jackson said. "Helm, all engines zero thrust. We'll just coast the rest of the way to Xi'an without lighting up the sky. OPS, are the pieces of the *Dao* going to miss the planet?"

"Engines answering zero-thrust."

"Standby, sir." Lieutenant Davis calculated possible trajectories from where the Bravos had abandoned the four enormous pieces of the destroyed battleship. "Affirmative. They'll be turned in by the planet's gravity but should continue on past it. We'll overtake the prow section before it crosses Xi'an's orbit."

"Identify each of the four pieces and report back to me which sections of the ship are still intact," Jackson ordered. "I need the information before we start braking for orbital insertion."

"Yes, sir." Davis turned back to her station and took control of the tactical sensor array.

"It seems odd that they would try an assault with only ten Bravos," Celesta said as the post-battle excitement settled down.

"I think they may have been sent as a distraction," Jackson said. "There was no logical reason for them to abandon their prize when they could have easily gotten the *Dao* pieces to Xi'an before we could have closed the range to stop them."

"But to what end? Deorbit them?" she asked. "As far as we know, they haven't reestablished their operation on the surface since the CIS Prowlers nuked the slicks from orbit."

Jackson shuddered at the mention of the Phage "slicks," enormous tracts of a viscous substance that was essentially digested material, organic and inorganic, that they used to build their ships. During his only encounter with one, he watched it eat one of his crewmen.

"And between the nuclear fallout, the debris cloud, and the atmospheric damage the Phage did, we can't get a clear picture of the ground," he reminded her. "Either way, Commander, we'll need to get over Xi'an and ascertain exactly what they were so interested in that they would risk an engagement with thirteen Fleet ships."

"Of course, Captain." She nodded.

Jackson could tell she wanted to argue for a quick flyby of the planet and a fast flight back out to their jump point, but she had worked with him long enough to know when he wasn't open to debate.

"Xi'an orbital insertion in three hours," the chief now manning the nav station called out. "Braking maneuvers in two."

"Confirmed, Nav," Jackson said. "Helm, you're clear to execute course and speed corrections from Nav."

"Aye, sir."

"You have the bridge, Commander," Jackson said, standing up. "I'm going to grab a couple hours in my office before we begin decel."

"Yes, sir." Celesta transferred her terminal over to the command chair and sat in the vacated seat almost before he could get out of the way.

While it was a great comfort to have an XO who was maturing rapidly and showed all the necessary aptitude for command, Jackson often wondered if she regretted her decision not to take a ship of her own when it was offered.

Chapter 2

"Captain Wolfe! Report to the bridge immediately!" The harsh call over the intercom was immediately followed by a klaxon calling everyone to general quarters and the subtle but distinct rumble of the engines coming back up from idle.

Jackson rolled off the small couch in his office and sprinted back to the bridge through the open hatch, his prosthetic leg whining in protest. It was only about a twenty meter run, but before he could make it, the *Ares* bucked under the unmistakable impact of enemy fire.

"Report!" he yelled as he ran onto the bridge.

"Indirect plasma fire coming from the surface!" Lieutenant Davis said. "We were clipped by the last one, but I don't believe we're being specifically targeted. No significant damage reported."

"She's right," Celesta said, looking at her display. "It looks like they're shooting up out of the atmosphere indiscriminately. I can't tell if they even know we're here or not."

"Can we penetrate that cover now that we're closer?" Jackson asked.

"Negative, Captain," Davis said. "There's too much particulate matter suspended in the upper atmosphere. The long-wave thermal optics are useless, and radar is completely ineffective below thirty kilometers."

"Understood." Jackson took his seat. "I assume we're accelerating off course to avoid our original orbital path since it was full of incoming?"

"Yes, sir," Celesta said. "Sorry, sir. I'm sending you our course corrections now."

Jackson looked over their new course along with the path of the enemy fire, trying to find some correlating pattern. It looked like his officers were correct in their initial assessment, and the enemy was firing blindly into the sky, but for what purpose?

"Nav! Get me a course correction that puts us over Xi'an at seven hundred and twenty-five kilometers at thirty-two degrees inclination," Jackson ordered. "Helm, execute immediately."

"Yes, sir!"

"What are your thoughts, Captain?" Celesta asked.

"I want us coming over the planet as far away from that incoming fire as we can manage, but we still need to see what they're protecting," Jackson said. "Is that drone ready to fly?"

She confirmed the status quickly on her terminal. "Yes, sir.".

"Good," he said. "Launch it as soon as we're in range. I have a bad feeling they're either protecting something on the surface we don't know about or clearing the way for something coming up."

"That's ominous—"

"Contact!" Barrett called out, interrupting Celesta. "*Big* contact! Something is coming up three kilometers across, roughly hemispherical."

"Helm, hard to starboard!" Jackson barked. "Get us away from this planet, ahead full!"

"Engines ahead full, steering away from the planet, aye!" The helmsman angled the *Ares* over sharply, so she was pointing almost perpendicular to their previous course, and thrust hard away from Xi'an.

They were still being influenced by Xi'an's gravity, so their course flattened out from a steep orbital insertion to a shallow arc that would send them over the northern hemisphere on their way past the planet.

"Another contact! Identical to the first, coming up five hundred kilometers south of the first contact," Barrett said.

"OPS, get optics on the new contacts, and put it on the main," Jackson ordered.

"Optics coming up." Davis worked on controlling the *Ares*'s external optical sensors.

The image of Xi'an was soon on the main display, slightly blurry as the computer searched for the new contacts and tried to focus on them. The results were terrifying.

"Tactical, confirm what we're seeing." Jackson didn't want to believe what he was looking at.

"Confirmed, Captain." The blood drained from Barrett's face. "Two Alphas are coming up from Xi'an, stern-first."

"OPS, display our orbital track," Jackson said. "I need to know how close we'll pass. Coms! Broadcast a warning to the rest of the fleet. Tell the *Brooklands* to get the hell out of this system."

"We'll sling around Xi'an well away from the Alphas thanks to our steep orbital inclination, but we've decelerated so much that we're still at risk." Celesta pointed out their projected course as Lieutenant Davis put it on the main display.

"Nav, correct course to straighten us out, and sling us around the primary," Jackson said. "Helm, full acceleration when you get the new course. OPS, give me a location for the squadron to rally away from Xi'an and broadcast a recall order to the fleet. Tactical, bring all weapons online."

Jackson took a moment to compose himself and not make any rash decisions. He was now looking down the barrel of two ships like the one that had torn through this region of space unopposed some four years ago. He had a much more powerful ship at his disposal, and four more just like it fully armed and in the system, but he held no illusions about standing toe-to-toe with either of the leviathans pushing up slowly out of Xi'an's murky atmosphere.

"Now we know what they were protecting," Celesta remarked as the *Ares* groaned under heavy acceleration.

"We also know those Prowlers weren't as thorough as we'd originally thought." Jackson's voice was bitter. "We've left this planet alone for a few years while they built two more of these monsters."

"Captain, we've ordered the squadron to form a heliocentric trailing orbit behind the sixth planet," Lieutenant Davis said. "The *Artemis* and *Hyperion* have checked in—all Bravos destroyed, no casualties. Third Fleet units are exiting the system."

"Very good, Lieutenant." Jackson stood. "Tactical, I don't want you to take your eyes off the Alphas other than to blink, understood?"

"Understood, sir." Barrett's eyes didn't come off his displays.

"We're now in optimum range to deploy the surface drone," Celesta said.

"Deploy," Jackson said. "Have it broadcast real-time, since we may not be able to come back and pick it up, assuming it even survives its mission."

Celesta sent the command down to Flight Ops. "Drone away. Lieutenant Davis, I'm sending the telemetry feed to you."

"Yes, ma'am." Davis didn't up from her station as she controlled the flow of information to and from the bridge.

"What's the plan, sir?" Celesta lowered her voice. "Can five *Starwolf*-class ships take on two Alphas?"

"It's possible," Jackson said. "It would take some inspired tactics and more than a little foolhardiness. Unfortunately, we've had such little time with this ship, I'm not inclined to push it to the edge of its performance envelope just yet. This is a disputed system with zero civilians and zero strategic assets. There's nothing to be gained by taking on such an overmatched opponent. We'll regroup further out, observe as long as possible, then report and withdraw."

"Very good, sir." Celesta kept her voice completely neutral. While she didn't directly say it, her relief at his plan was obvious.

Jackson couldn't blame her. There wasn't a single crewmember that had served on the *Blue Jacket* currently in the Xi'an System that ever wanted to engage an Alpha again, much less a pair.

The *Ares* quickly accelerated away from Xi'an, angling up and away to swing around the primary star and fly out to the rally point with the rest of the Ninth Squadron ships. Capable of over seven hundred G's of acceleration, the new destroyer would be able to make the rendezvous on the other side of the system in thirty hours without even taxing the engines.

Their best intel on the Alphas, mostly extrapolated from the *Blue Jacket's* recovered sensor logs, have their best acceleration at significantly less than the new ship was capable of. The issue, however, was that the giant killing machines weren't hampered by Newtonian physics and were able to accelerate to any point within the system in a straight line, completely ignoring the gravitational pull of the star and its planets.

"Coms, message the rest of the squadron and order them to go silent," Jackson said. "Thermal and radio emission protocols are now in place until otherwise stated."

"Aye, sir," Lieutenant Keller said from the com station.

Jackson, now technically a senior captain, was in charge of the Ninth Squadron when it was deployed on its own. The Confederate Senate, with the intent to show their constituents they were taking the threat seriously, tried to make him an admiral and put him in charge of the Fleet response to the Phage. After the initial shock and horror of the idea wore off, he'd appealed directly to CENTCOM Chief of Staff Marcum and asked to be put back on the bridge of a starship. After some back and forth, a compromise was reached to promote him to senior captain and give him the first operational *Starwolf*-class ship off the line: the *TCS Ares*.

A few well meaning officers and ranking Senate members had lobbied to have the new ship christened the *Blue Jacket*, but Jackson had steadfastly refused. His previous command would be remembered for her crew's bravery and sacrifice. Resurrecting the name wouldn't bring them back and could only diminish their legend. Besides, he rather liked the name of his new ship. *Ares*: God of War.

While he felt a burning need for vengeance, his hard-won experience told him the current situation in the Xi'an System was a fight he probably couldn't win, and wasting ships and lives to spit in the eye of the Phage would be the height of foolishness. One of the main reasons he had stopped watching the news, and most broadcasts from Haven in general, was because much of the programming these days still centered around the initial Phage incursion into Confederate space and his ship's efforts to stop it. The highly dramatized propaganda about his "victory" couldn't be healthy, and he was worried he might begin to believe the bullshit about the "implacable Captain Wolfe" and get more good men and women killed in the process.

Deep down, he felt like a fraud. His risky gambles borne from desperation and fear were being portrayed as strokes of genius, cunning, and courage. The fact that so many people were looking to him, their eyes gleaming with hope that he would save them, terrified him more than the two Alphas just breaking out of Xi'an's ruined atmosphere.

****

The bridge remained tense as the *Ares* continued to pull away from Xi'an and the two Alphas that were now sitting in low orbit. The destroyer was still running her engines at full , and they were painfully aware that they were lighting up the sky with an impressive thermal plume, should the two alien ships decide to give chase.

"Captain, you'll be interested in this." Lieutenant Davis had been analyzing the sensor logs of these new Alphas, the first to be seen since the initial encounter the *Blue Jacket* had. Jackson climbed stiffly out of his seat, put weight experimentally on his prosthetic left leg, and walked over to her station.

"What do you have, Lieutenant?"

"I'm not sure these Alphas are even combat capable." She pulled up some high-resolution optical scans and overlaid them with the radar picture and thermal spectrograph images that showed the ships in multiple wavelengths.

"You have my complete attention, Lieutenant." Jackson leaned in to look at her monitor. She took a breath before continuing.

"If you'll look here at the stern and see that I've divided the view into quadrants, the radar is showing that the areas under the hull, where the plasma charges originate, are hollow spaces," she said. "The thermal scans back this up—the four areas are significantly colder than the flanks. In fact, visual spectrum shots seem to show the hull material is very thin, almost translucent."

"This is quite interesting," Jackson said. "Conclusions?"

"Impossible to reach any with this small amount of information, sir," she said. "But when taken in the context of the wild shots fired from the surface and the fact that they haven't pursued us, I would have to say that we've interrupted the construction of these two, and they're pulling them off the planet before another nuclear bombardment."

"I'm inclined to agree with your assessment," Jackson said. "But let's do this right. Send all this down to the engineering and science sections, without your own conclusions attached, and let's see what they come up with. I'm willing to bet they'll agree with you as well."

"So what can we do with that information?" Celesta had walked up behind them while Davis had been talking, the acoustics making it impossible for her to hear the conversation from her seat.

"For now, nothing," Jackson said firmly. "I won't turn and attack with a single ship while they're in orbit over Xi'an. They've demonstrated already that there's *something* down there capable of lobbing high-energy plasma bursts into orbit. I'd rather not find out the hard way that the new outer hull armor can't withstand what the Tsuyo engineers say it can. We also have no way to determine if the entire ship is unarmed or if it was just the stern that didn't have plasma weaponry installed… or however the hell they put them together.

"For now, the plan remains the same. Meet up with the rest of Ninth Squadron and reassess the situation then. It's possible that we can gather more data from the drone and make a run at these two. Taking down two Alphas would be a huge victory but not at the cost of five of our most advanced starships."

"Yes, sir," Celesta acknowledged while Davis just nodded.

"Keep at it, Lieutenant," Jackson said. "Commander Wright, let's stand down first watch and get everyone rested and fed now that we have a good idea that those two Alphas won't be pursuing us anytime soon."

"Aye, sir."

Jackson took the time to grab a proper meal from the wardroom and go to his quarters for a shower and a change of uniform. Before entering the shower, he sat on a seat he'd had installed in the head and carefully detached the prosthetic leg from what was left of his real leg below, about four inches below the knee. He set the mechanical apparatus aside and began carefully cleaning the connections on the metal cap that was surgically attached to his leg.

The cap had a locking socket on it that the prosthetic snapped into as well as inductively coupled electrical connections that allowed it to send nerve impulses so he could control the actuators. In a lot of ways, it was as good, if not better, than his real leg had been. There were much more advanced procedures available that would allow him to have a real leg grafted back on at the knee, but the rehabilitation was far too time consuming for him given the seriousness of the challenges he'd faced after they'd fished him out of the *Blue Jacket's* wreckage.

The mechanical prosthetic might not be pretty, and certainly made people uncomfortable to look at it, but that actually made him like it all the more. Despite the accolades that had been heaped upon him of late, he still felt like an outsider looking in, the dirty Earther who was being tolerated as long as he was useful. After performing a few maintenance tasks on the leg, he climbed into the shower and reveled in one of the luxuries the brand new ship afforded him: unlimited hot water in Officer Country.

He didn't come out of his quarters for another five full hours, and when he did, he was rested, clean, and ready to look at the problems from a new angle. The reassuring thrum of the engines and the calm demeanor of the crew he passed were also welcome as he nodded to the Marine sentry and walked onto the bridge.

"Captain." Lieutenant Davis nodded to him as she vacated the command seat. "Nothing of note to report. We're getting ready to lose line of sight contact with Xi'an as we cross behind the primary star. As of forty-six minutes ago, the Phage Alphas were still in low orbit over the planet and showing no unusual thermal activity."

"Very good, Lieutenant." Jackson took his seat. "You're relieved. Get below deck and grab some rack time."

"Yes, sir," she said. "Here's to a quiet watch."

"Indeed."

Jackson pulled up the ship's status on his terminal and checked specific details from each department. He sent a quick message to Commander Singh, his Chief Engineer and best friend, about meeting up for dinner before their rendezvous with the rest of the squadron. He answered another dozen messages to different department heads, mostly about mundane ship's operation, and marveled at how calm the atmosphere aboard was as they had two ships of a planet-killer class sitting nearby. Maybe they really had come a long way in a short time.

"Nav! How long until we reach the rest of the squadron?" he called out.

"We'll reach the rendezvous coordinates in seven hours, forty-five minutes," the specialist at the station answered immediately. "The *Artemis* and *Hyperion* will arrive approximately three hours after us." Jackson already knew all this from looking at his status board, but he'd never seen the specialist second class on the bridge and wanted to see if the young man was paying attention to his surroundings.

"Thank you, Specialist." He pretended not to notice the thumbs up the com officer gave the young enlisted spacer.

They were now cold-coasting. Having burned hard to change orbits and slingshot around the star, they were now able to fly purely on momentum, virtually disappearing into the surrounding space to anyone who was looking for them.

"Tactical, have we reacquired the Alphas after coming around the primary?" He looked over the telemetry data from the drone that, miraculously, was still flying over the planet's surface.

"Yes, sir," the ensign sitting at the tactical station answered. Her name was McCollum, and she'd scored especially well during training when they were all coming up to speed on how to operate the new ship.

"And?"

"Uh... they're still orbiting over Xi'an, sir," she said with uncertainty.

"Make sure you give me all the information you have, Ensign," Jackson snapped. "Don't make me drag each detail out of you."

He wasn't deliberately harassing the tail end of second watch, but he knew from his own experience as a young officer that things tended to fall into a comfortable routine. They needed to be able to do their jobs no matter who was on watch and who was giving the orders. He keenly felt the pressure to make sure they were ready for what was coming... and the fact the Phage had now begun pushing into Confederate space in earnest meant he was running out of time.

He passed the last few hours before they needed to reengage the engines by drilling his bridge crew before their first watch counterparts came on duty. When Lieutenant Commander Barrett walked onto the bridge, Ensign McCollum practically flung herself out of the seat to give turnover as fast as she could and escape. Barrett gave his captain a questioning look but said nothing as he slid into the seat and began reconfiguring the station to his preferences.

"You're on duty early, sir." Celesta walked onto the bridge and began taking inventory of the ship's status and personnel.

"Wanted to get a feel for the new spacers we picked up when they turned the ship over to us." He left it hanging.

"How do you feel they performed?" Ship's personnel was her responsibility, and she took it as a personal affront when they didn't meet expectations.

"They're trying," he said diplomatically. "They're young and inexperienced, but they take their jobs seriously and don't repeat mistakes. It's hard to ask for much more than that."

"Perhaps, sir," Celesta shrugged noncommittally. "I'd prefer they were a little better trained before we got them, but I suppose circumstances didn't permit that."

"They'll be fine, Commander," Jackson insisted. "We're about to fire the engines and begin our final braking maneuver. Hopefully the *Atlas* and *Icarus* are there waiting for us like they're supposed to be."

"How long until the *Artemis* and *Hyperion* make the rally point?" she asked.

"A few hours after us unless they pushed a little harder than originally planned," he said. "Once we're there, we can have a conference with the other command crews and figure out how we want to handle our two interlopers."

"I went below after my watch. Commander Singh is itching to try out some of the new weapons," she said. "Specifically the rapid-fire mag-cannon."

"He turned out to be a lot more bloodthirsty than I would have imagined," Jackson deadpanned.

Celesta's willingness to disobey orders for the greater good and back up Jackson as captain of the *Blue Jacket* instead of removing him from command had brought her into the fold with Daya Singh. During his own recovery and the shakedown of the *Starwolf*-class prototype, the pair had cemented their friendship. Jackson sometimes worried that it led to some lapses in professionalism, but the tradeoff was worth it, and his own interactions with the Chief Engineer were often far more personal than Fleet customs and courtesies would dictate.

"There'll be plenty of fighting to go around before this is all over. Right now we have a real opportunity to learn something rather than charge in and start peppering those two Alphas with cannon shells and nukes."

"No argument here, sir," she said.

****

Ninth Squadron made their rendezvous without incident. All five of the destroyers moved into a loose formation and initiated a tight-beam com laser connection with the ship on either side to allow two-way communications between all the vessels. At the request of the other COs, Jackson allowed for a five-way conference, despite his suspicion that it would be a complete waste of time. After the *Ares* had stabilized in her holding position, he, Commander Wright, and Lieutenant Davis were looking at each of their counterparts on the divided screen in the command deck conference room.

"Our best information indicates that both Alphas are still orbiting Xi'an and making no move to leave the system." Jackson opened the meeting with no preamble, wanting to get it over with and get his people moving as quickly as possible. "The drone we launched during our flyby has been destroyed, but before that, it was able to transmit images of what look to be the shipyards, for lack of a better term, where these two Alphas were constructed and launched. It also confirmed that the weapons fire that cleared the path to orbit originated there." He looked around to gauge the response of his audience.

"So our options are to continue observations from far orbit as we are now, or take this opportunity to destroy the two Alphas that we have surmised are incomplete and possibly without armament."

"I think the choice is obvious," Captain Levitt said from the *Icarus'* conference room. "Observation and reporting is grand for a scientific expedition, but taking the risk that those two Alphas could leave the system and be completed elsewhere, only to return to Confederate space, is unconscionable. They must be destroyed here. Now." "Captain Wolfe, while we all respect your experience with this type of enemy ship, could your hesitation to attack be overcautious given the current circumstances?" Captain of the *TCS Hyperion,* Olivia Forrest's voice dripped with disdain.

"What hesitation would you be referring to?" Jackson kept his face and voice neutral. "This is simply a forum for you to voice your opinions as we regroup. A meeting called at your request, I would remind you. I may, or may not, follow the consensus reached here depending on what I feel is the best course of action."

"Nobody is suggesting that we're hesitating," Levitt said quickly, despite the fact that Forrest had said just that only moments ago. "But... we do need to figure out fairly quickly what we're going to do."

Jackson suppressed the urge to yet again point out that it was their desire to talk the issue to death that was the cause of the delay. He held his tongue as he recognized it for what it was: they were all scared. More accurately, they were shitting-their-pants-terrified. They wanted to save face by letting him be the one to order the withdrawal.

The conversation continued for the next twenty minutes with Jackson more or less staying in the background. He'd already made his decision, but it wouldn't hurt to get a read on his other captains and allow them to feel like they had a say in the plan. Thankfully, the four were divided down the middle, so Jackson could decide either way and only piss off half his subordinates.

"I think I've heard all I need to hear." He interrupted Forrest just as she was launching into another long-winded attack on Captain Caruso, CO of the TCS *Atlas*. "After this meeting, we will prepare the squadron to make an attack run on both Alphas currently orbiting Xi'an. The trip back down into the system will take at least twelve hours, and in that time, I want at least three possible strategies for deploying the squadron against both targets simultaneously. As we approach, and the sensor delay lessens, we'll commit to one of those and press the attack. Any questions?"

Captain Levitt looked like he wanted to say something, but fell silent and shook his head when Jackson looked directly at him.

"Good. Get your ships and your crews ready," Jackson said. "We'll begin flying back down the well in exactly fifteen minutes. Dismissed." He waited until all the monitors blanked, displaying each ship's crest in place of the video feed, before standing up and turning to leave.

"Commander Wright, please ensure the *Ares* is ready to fly and fight," he said. "Lieutenant Davis, begin working with Lieutenant Commander Barrett to devise an assault plan on both Alphas, keeping in mind that we'll be attacking with the entire squadron."

"Aye, sir." Davis turned on her heel and left immediately.

"Was there something else, Commander?" Jackson said as Celesta stood but made no move to leave.

"Yes, sir," she said. "If I may… why allow them to bicker amongst themselves? It was fairly obvious that none of them wants to attack the enemy despite all the bluster."

"We had to regroup at a logical place if we wanted to hit those two Alphas with the combined strength of all five ships," Jackson said. "We've lost a little time by moving back out into the outer system, but it's given us an opportunity to make sure we're not being baited into a slaughter. This will be the first real taste of combat for the rest of the Ninth. For the last year, all they've done is warp into a system, dispatch a handful of Bravos with the new Hornets, and warp out. Depending on what we find down there, this could be the first real battle *we've* faced since that first Alpha incursion. I think the reality of it might be sinking in."

"I understand, sir." Celesta's tone indicated that she was not fully convinced. "If that'll be all…?"

"Dismissed, Commander," Jackson said.

He took his time walking back to the bridge, stopping by the wardroom for a fresh mug of coffee and a quick bite to eat. Had his conversation with Commander Wright been inappropriately candid? His own misgivings toward his fellow captains was one thing, but voicing them to a subordinate, even one as trusted as his XO, was another entirely.

His frustration with the lack of progress by the Confederate military machine was reaching critical mass. Did they truly not comprehend how grave the threat was? He shook his head, as if the action could actually clear out all the extraneous thoughts, and tried to bring his focus entirely on the matter at hand.

While commanding a starship during combat operations was becoming part of his normal routine, he was still never fully comfortable with it. There was never a moment when he was flying toward an engagement, even against the comparatively weak Bravos, in a starship weighing hundreds of thousands of tons that he wasn't painfully aware of the hundreds of lives within the hull that were trusting him to keep them alive. It ate away at his insides like a cancer, and it seemed to have a cumulative effect as the ghosts of the crewmembers lost on the *Blue Jacket* would still haunt his sleep, each of them silently accusing him of betraying that trust and leading them to their deaths.

When he reached the bridge, Celesta had all departments already checked in for departure, and his OPS and Tactical officers were hard at work trying to figure out how best to deploy five destroyers against two targets as large as an Alpha. It was a unique challenge as every recent engagement, including his own initial battle with the Phage, usually pitted a single Terran ship operating autonomously against anywhere from one to fifty Phage ships.

"All departments have checked in, and Engineering has cleared the ship for flight," Celesta said.

He sat down and checked over his monitor himself. "Coms! Signal the squadron. We're breaking orbit in five minutes," Jackson said. "Trailing wedge formation, all ships form up on the *Ares*. We'll be accelerating at five hundred G's until we break for the targets."

"Aye aye, sir." Lieutenant Keller pulled his headset back on fully.

The instructions to the rest of the squadron were out of habit but unnecessary. The Link would send out a burst transmission of the *Ares'* navigational data to the other ships as soon as she began thrusting out of her current orbit.

Jackson leaned back in his seat and rubbed his chin, trying to quell the nerves that had started as soon as he'd decided they would attack the two Alphas with a handful of destroyers. Despite the advancements in technology found on the *Starwolf*-class ships, he couldn't help but marvel at the disparity between them and the enormous Phage units. As he felt the soft vibration through his seat of the engines coming to life, he hoped the two ships orbiting the former human colony were as helpless as they appeared.

"Helm! Ahead two thirds until we reach our target velocity," he ordered. "Take us down." "Engines ahead two thirds, aye."

Chapter 3

The short burst of acceleration had pushed the *Ares* to .07c, or seven percent of the speed of light. The rest of the squadron timed their own acceleration maneuvers so that they fanned out behind the lead destroyer, separated by around fifteen thousand kilometers. They were now cold coasting toward Xi'an, listening and watching with their passive sensors as they approached the planet in as stealthy a manner possible.

As they closed the gap, the tension on the bridge of the *Ares* climbed proportionally. Commander Wright had set up a supplemental watch schedule that would put first watch back on the bridge four hours before they crossed the orbit of Xi'an's furthest moon without keeping the ship at general quarters. She sat pensively in her seat next to Jackson as the mission clock ticked up and the distance ticked down.

"Make the call, Commander," Jackson said quietly. "Let's get ready."

"General quarters, general quarters," she called over the ship-wide PA. "All hands, man your battle stations. Set condition 2SS and prepare for imminent contact with enemy ships."

Condition two, ship to ship, 2SS, let the crew know there would be combat between ships in space, and they were part of a larger force. Since the *Ares* was officially handed off from Tsuyo shipyards to CENTCOM, Jackson had been running them through drills until they knew the difference between ship configurations like the backs of their hands.

"Tactical! Go active, and paint the targets," Jackson ordered. "OPS, put our sensor telemetry on the Link and make sure the other ships stay silent until they're ready to engage."

"Yes, sir!" Lieutenant Commander Barrett said.

Instantly, the threat board began to populate, showing the two Alphas, now sitting in a high transfer orbit, and the other four ships from their own squadron.

"Plot a firing solution for the Shrikes," Jackson ordered. "Two missiles to each target."

"Targets reacting to active radar," Lieutenant Davis reported. "Alpha-One is accelerating around the planet. Alpha-Two is pushing away and coming onto an intercept course."

"That's unexpected," Celesta said.

"Indeed," Jackson frowned. "If they're really toothless, why risk coming out to meet us? OPS, how long until Alpha-One crosses the horizon?"

"Fifty-one minutes," Davis reported.

Jackson confirmed their range on the main display before. "Tactical, firing solution for Alpha-Two only, two missiles," he said. "OPS, tell the *Icarus* and the *Atlas* to break formation and engage Alpha-One as it comes around, nukes are authorized."

"Solutions plotted and missiles are updated," Barrett said tightly. "Armament has confirmed both birds ready to fire."

"Standby," Jackson said.

Alpha-Two slowed its approach, almost coming to a full stop between them and the planet. The behavior was all wrong for a target that was supposedly unable to defend itself while looking at multiple heavily armed hostiles bearing down on it. The *Icarus* and *Atlas* were now veering off away from their formation to catch

Alpha-One as it came around Xi'an, both ships accelerating hard.

"Sir?" Barrett said.

"Fire both birds, five hundred millisecond stagger," Jackson said. "Helm, all reverse one quarter. Let's shed some of this speed. Tactical, get the auto-mag ready to fire... high-explosive penetrators, twenty-five round burst."

"Missiles one and two are away, time to impact... one hundred and sixty-three minutes," Barrett said. "Auto-mag is online, and power-bank is fully charged. Twenty-five round burst will be available in two minutes."

"OPS, tell the *Artemis* and *Hyperion* to bear starboard and shallow out their insertion angle," Jackson said. "I also want them cutting their velocity by a third, and to be ready to hit Alpha-Two's flank if needed."

"Yes, sir," Davis said.

"What's worrying you, sir?" Celesta asked quietly, once he'd forced himself to walk back to his seat and sit down.

"Something's wrong," Jackson whispered. "I don't think this thing is as defenseless as our analysis indicates. A lot of our assumptions are based on what CENTCOM's scientific staff was able to glean from the pieces of that first Alpha... but we've had no independent verification of that. I think we could be looking at an entirely different class of Alpha. Their rough dimensions are the only method we've used to classify them up to this point."

"And the speed reduction and formation change?"

"I'm trying to keep us from overextending and being unable to withdraw," Jackson explained. "With the other four ships dispersed, we also aren't so bunched up and presenting such an easy target."

"Missiles are past the halfway mark, sending the final arming command," Barrett said, a little over an hour later as their missiles continued to streak toward the now fully stopped Alpha-Two.

The new generation Shrike tactical missiles, now sporting nuclear warheads, were designed specifically as Alpha-busters. They had considerably higher yield than the typical tactical nuke, almost as much as a strategic weapon, but it was designed with a unique delivery system that would maximize the payload's destructive potential.

Nuclear weapons in space were a dicey proposition due to the characteristics of the blast. The nasty stuff, like gamma and neutron radiation, was still there and propagated from the detonation unimpeded, but the lack of an atmosphere meant the pressure wave and thermal radiation were nullified. The Shrike was therefore given an ultradense, extended nosecone that would pierce the organic hull of an Alpha before a final rocket stage would blast the warhead as deep as it could into the monster, where the pressure wave and thermal radiation would be devastating.

"Still no response from the target?" Jackson asked.

"No, sir," Davis said. "No thermal buildup on the leading edges or on the nose."

They waited tensely for another thirty minutes for the Alpha to make a move so they could counter it. That it just sat there motionless in space, waiting for the two missiles, was unnerving. Jackson couldn't even be sure the damn thing could see the projectiles. The first Alpha he'd tangled with had no problems finding the *Blue Jacket*, no matter where he was, but it had never seemed able to detect their expendable munitions unless they were fired at extreme close range.

"Movement!" Davis called. "Alpha-Two is now accelerating toward us... wait... It's changing course and climbing above our missiles."

"Birds are correcting course," Barrett said. "No joy. Target has closed the range too quickly, they won't be able to pitch up steeply enough and maintain velocity for penetration."

"Send the abort signal." Jackson gripped his arm-rests as the Alpha came at him on the main display. "Put them in orbit over Xi'an, and we'll recover or repurpose them later. Start tracking for an auto-mag shot, and prep two more Shrikes and a full spread of Hornets."

"Yes, sir." Barrett's hands flew competently over his controls. "Auto-mag firing solution in ten seconds, targeting the nose—"

"Incoming flash message from the *Atlas*!" Lieutenant Keller, the *Ares*'s coms officer called out. "Alpha-One opened fire on them before they could come fully around Xi'an and acquire a target lock. Unknown weapon. *Atlas* has degraded hull armor on the prow."

"What about the *Icarus*?" Jackson said.

"Unclear," Keller said. "I believe they're saying she's withdrawing."

"What?" Jackson nearly shouted. "Lieutenant Keller, you get a hold of that ship, and you find out what's going on. Now!"

"Yes, sir!"

"Captain! The hull of Alpha-Two is opening on the leading edges," Davis called out.

"Explain." Jackson turned away from the coms station and refocused on the main display.

"Six openings, four port, two starboard, irising open along the centerline." Davis put the enhanced image up for him to see. "Helm! Pitch down thirty-five degrees, full emergency acceleration!" Jackson called out as he realized what he was looking at.

"Sir, what—"

"Incoming fire from Alpha-Two!" Davis shouted, cutting off Celesta. "Thirteen projectiles accelerating toward us at over eight hundred Gs. They seem to be unguided."

"Helm, pitch us down another five degrees," Jackson said as the bridge began to shake from the *Ares's* powerful main engines running past their accepted limits. "Are the enemy missiles tracking?"

"Correction, missiles are now angling down toward us, but it looks like they'll still overfly us," Davis said.

"We're going to pass almost directly under Alpha-Two," Celesta reminded them. "OPS, watch for any weapons deployment on their ventral surface."

"Nothing yet, ma'am," Davis said.

"Coms! Tell the *Artemis* and *Hyperion* to attack from the flank," Jackson ordered. "Wait until we're out of range before they lob any nukes in. We don't want to get caught up in the blast if they manage a direct hit. OPS, how long until we pass underneath?"

"We'll be directly under the target in thirty-six minutes at a range of five thousand two hundred kilometers," Davis said.

"Tactical, update your auto-mag solution," Jackson said. "I want to stitch all twenty shells along the target's ventral surface. Helm, prepare to go to zero-thrust and surrender attitude control to the tactical computer."

"Yes, sir." Barrett drowned out whatever affirmation the helmsman offered.

The auto-mag, a single barreled mag-cannon capable of rapidly firing fifteen hundred millimeter shells like a machine gun, was a hasty addition to the *Starwolf*-class ships. As such, it was hard-mounted in the belly of the ship with the muzzle of the gun coming out just under the pointed nose of the ship.

Since it wasn't installed in an articulated turret, the entire ship had to be precisely aimed to fire the weapon. It was far from optimal, but it was better than nothing, and it had been a hard-fought battle on Jackson's part to even have the weapon installed at all.

"The *Artemis* and *Hyperion* are on their way in," Lieutenant Keller reported. "They're asking for permission to go to active sensors."

"Granted!" Jackson barked, mildly annoyed. Apparently both captains had forgotten that standard operating procedure cleared them for all tactical systems when actively engaging an enemy target. "What's the status on the *Icarus*?"

"They're clearing the engagement area," Keller said. "There appears to be some confusion on the bridge, sir. I'm unable to get confirmation that they've been damaged or had any malfunction."

"OPS, get me a position on our wayward destroyer, if you can," Jackson said. "Coms, tell the *Atlas* that we'll be coming around the planet shortly after passing Alpha-Two… What is the status of Alpha-One?"

"Firing solution is locked in, Captain," Barrett said. "We'll be within range in under five minutes."

"Helm! Zero-thrust," Jackson ordered.

"Engines answering zero-thrust," the helmsman confirmed.

"Tactical, you're clear to assume attitude control."

"Yes, sir." Barrett began his targeting scripts that would pitch the *Ares* back up so her nose was leading the target as the two ships screamed past each other at almost thirty thousand kilometers per second. "Pitching up and authorizing fire control computer to engage the weapon. Waiting on command authority."

"Authorized." Jackson pressed his thumb against the display of his terminal to give the final go-ahead for the computers to assume control of the ship's offensive systems.

"We've got five more ports opening up on the ventral surface," Davis warned.

"Five seconds," Barrett called out. "And... firing!" The auto-mag was an enormous, powerful machine, and when it began firing, it was not a subtle thing. Capable of one hundred and fifty rounds a minute, the cannon began belching out high-explosive shells at a rate of five every two seconds. The deck shook violently as the ship continued to pitch up, the attitude thrusters struggling to walk the line of fire down the line Barrett had programmed.

The auto-mag pulled so much power from the main bus that the lights on the bridge dimmed slightly as the power plant struggled to keep engines and weapons fully operational. "All shells away! Cannon clear and safe, releasing helm control," Barrett called out.

"Helm, pitch us back down on our original course, and bring the mains back up, ahead one half," Jackson said. "OPS, track our hits."

"Recording impacts now, sir—Whoa!" Davis exclaimed. "Two shells hit one of the open ports. Secondary explosions visible along with multiple hull breeches, sir. Target is now moving off and no longer turning to pursue."

"Tell the *Artemis* and *Hyperion* to try and finish it off. They may attack at Captain Forrest's discretion," Jackson said. "Coms! Where's my update on Alpha-One?"

"The *Atlas* is no longer answering requests for updates, Captain," Keller said.

"I'm trying to reinitialize their Link remotely, sir," Davis reported, sounding harried.

"As quick as you can, Lieutenant," Jackson said, completely unsympathetic. "We'll be coming around the terminator blind if the *Atlas* can't get us a good position for the enemy ship."

Xi'an loomed large in the main display, her ravaged atmosphere swirling with angry stripes of brown and red, but Jackson was only paying attention to the overlaid tracks of all the ships on the two dimensional representation of the star system. Next to each ship was a number that denoted the ships "altitude" in relation to the ecliptic so that, with practice, one could almost visualize the scene in three dimensions.

The data for Alpha-One was flashing red, telling him that it was old and unverified. The fact both ships he'd sent around the planet had yet to either report back or update their status weighed heavily on his mind, but not as much as the fact the enemy ship hadn't come back around Xi'an. Even at a leisurely orbital velocity, it should have reappeared before the *Ares* had opened fire on its twin.

"Link connection re-established with the *Icarus*," Davis said. "*Atlas* is still unresponsive. Data coming up now."

Jackson leaned forward. The position for Alpha-One changed very little. It had drifted up to a higher altitude, but it was still hanging over Xi'an and looked for all the universe like it was waiting on them.

"Can the *Icarus* verify the target's orientation for us?" Jackson asked, not directing his comment at anyone in particular.

"*Icarus* is still not answering coms, Captain," Lieutenant Keller said.

"Link connection just dropped again," Davis said. "I can't get it back, but from the last radar image, I'm able to determine the target's orientation in relation to the planet. Putting it on the main now."

Jackson studied the rough representation of the target, his fears confirmed. "Helm! Roll ninety-six degrees to starboard and pitch down thirty-two degrees," he ordered. "Standby for throttle up."

"Sir—"

"I'm overriding the safety locks," Jackson said. "Carry out the order."

"Aye aye, sir," the helmsman said, hesitation still evident in his voice. "Rolling over and diving toward the planet."

Jackson continued to look over the calculations he'd been working out on his own terminal, ignoring the concerned looks around him.

"OPS, retract forward optics and antennas, and secure outer hatches," he ordered. "Helm, continue your dive, and level out at twenty-five thousand, three hundred meters above the surface of Xi'an."

"Captain, that will—"

"In a moment, Commander." Jackson cut off his XO. "Nav, verify my numbers." He bracketed his calculations with his two hands on the display and sent them over to the nav station where the chief on duty plugged them into his system.

"Course verified, Captain," the chief said. "We are currently flying too slow for it to work."

"Thank you, Chief." Jackson's eyes were glued to the outside view on the main display until it disappeared once the optical sensors had been retracted. "Helm, ahead full. We need at least twelve thousand, five hundred and seventeen meters per second forward velocity."

"Ahead full, aye," the helmsman said, sounding confident with the more specific command.

The *Ares* rolled and descended rapidly toward the opaque atmosphere, her two main engines spewing white hot plasma at full power. Once the ship began to rub up against the thermosphere-mesosphere transition, it began to shudder as the hull temperature rose.

"OPS, keep an eye on our hull temp," Jackson said. "Helm, when I give the order, I want you to pull us up into a climb, fifteen degrees nose-up. Lieutenant Davis, as soon as the hull temps begin to drop again, redeploy the sensors and get me a fix on Alpha-One. Tactical, be ready to snap fire three Shrikes. You'll have to be ready to acquire the target and fire very quickly."

There was a chorus of affirmations as the *Ares* really began to rock and buck deeper she flew into Xi'an's atmosphere.

"Sir?"

"I have a hunch, Commander," Jackson said to Celesta. "It looks like the pair are talking to each other, as we'd suspect, and this one is waiting for us to appear over the horizon at any moment."

"Agreed." Celesta raised her voice over the harsh rumbling now that the ship was pushing even deeper into a place it was never meant to go.

"At the altitude it's sitting at, I think we have a good chance of coming up underneath it while its concentrating on where we should be from what they've observed of our normal orbital flight profiles," Jackson said.

"I feel I must point out that if it isn't fooled, and we take a serious hit while so low in the planet's atmosphere..." she left her sentence unfinished.

"I'm well aware of the risks," Jackson assured her. Any faltering in either main engine meant the ship would decelerate and simply fall to the surface of the planet. "But I'm confident in the strategy. They learn quickly by observation, but no other Terran starship is capable of this maneuver, so I doubt they'll be expecting it."

"Commander Singh will not be happy." She pointed to the spiking hull temperatures now displayed on the main in flashing red.

"I wouldn't think so," Jackson agreed. "Helm, standby!"

"Standing by, sir!" the helmsman said.

Jackson would have chuckled at the young man's high-pitched voice if he wasn't feeling the same fear himself. He said a silent prayer that the *Ares's* internal sensors were as accurate as he needed them to be before giving his next order. "Helm, pitch up! OPS, Tactical... get ready!"

If anything, the violent buffeting increased as the attitude jets struggled mightily against the slipstream to raise the *Ares's* nose. The computers took note of this and angled the "nozzles" of the main engines up ten degrees to compensate. After that short, ass-clenching moment, during which Jackson thought he may have killed his entire crew and lost his ship without taking a single shot from the enemy, the destroyer pulled her nose up and began to climb rapidly out of Xi'an's upper atmosphere.

The hull temperature started to drop just as quickly as the warship was gaining altitude, the advanced material shedding off the heat now that the friction was removed. Once it dropped below seven hundred and fifty degrees Centigrade, he knew they were out of immediate danger... and flying into a worse one.

"Outer hatches opening, sensors redeploying," Davis called out. "Radar and optics searching for target."

"Target acquired!" Barrett nearly shouted.

"Fire at will!" Jackson was equally excited as the image of the Alpha appeared above them and slightly to starboard... still diligently pointed toward the horizon where it expected them to appear.

"Birds one, two, and three are away," Barrett said, after he fired off three tactical nukes. "Flying hot and clean. Time to impact, four minutes."

"We rarely get a shot this close," Jackson said. "Helm, shallow out our climb. Two hundred and fifty kilometer altitude, maintain inclination."

"Aye, sir."

The *Ares* flattened out in her climb, passing rapidly under the Alpha and continuing along toward the far horizon and the battle against the Alpha-Two.

"We've been spotted," Davis said. "Alpha-One is rotating around, bringing its nose to bear. Weapon ports opening along the leading edge."

"Range?"

"Thirty-four thousand kilometers and increasing."

"First missile impact in fifteen seconds," Barrett said, silencing all conversation on the bridge as everyone held their breath. They were so close, they didn't need to wait for the light to reach them before they knew the first missile had found its mark. The *Ares's* optical sensors were attenuated enough that Jackson could actually see the distortion ripples as a nuclear shockwave propagated across the Alpha's organic hull.

"Impact!" Barrett broke the silence with the unnecessary update.

The next two missiles hit in quick succession, burying their warheads deep as they flew unimpeded through the gashes opened up in the hull from the first missile. The detonations of the last two warheads shredded the insides of the Alpha. The tough organic hull undulated and bulged as the waves of energy bounced around, completely destroying the inner workings of the massive ship until it could no longer hold and burst open like a seedpod, sending the smoking ruins of the Alpha's guts streaking off into space.

"Yes!" Lieutenant Keller pumped his fist in the air. The rest of the bridge crew cheered and clapped as the *Ares* flew away unscathed, save for a discolored hull. Jackson let them carry on a moment longer before reasserting control.

"We are still engaged, people," he said sternly. "Get me status updates on the rest of the squadron, and prepare the ship to face Alpha-Two when we come around the planet."

Davis checked her Link statuses. "*Atlas* is unresponsive. *Icarus* is unresponsive. *Artemis* has taken damage, but nothing critical, and *Hyperion* is FMC. *Artemis* is reporting that Alpha-Two has departed the system."

"Coms, find out where in the hell my other two destroyers went," Jackson said. "Tactical, begin scanning for debris along their last known flight path." His insides twisted at the thought of losing forty percent of his force in the first real battle of what was becoming an inevitable war.

"Plasma fire coming up from the surface!" Lieutenant Davis shouted. "Impact in seven seconds!"

"Helm! Full emergency stop!" Jackson ordered. "Roll to port seventy degrees!"

Even with the cutting edge artificial gravity generators, the crew was still thrown forward as the main engines reversed thrust and pushed mightily against *Ares's* inertia. Jackson climbed quickly to his feet, having been tossed from his seat, and saw the nine plasma shots intended to destroy them streak past just off the port bow as the ship completed her roll maneuver.

"All shots missed... barely," Davis said.

"All ahead full!" Jackson ordered. "Nav! Get me an orbital transfer and a path away from this damn planet. OPS, use our drone data, and coordinate with Tactical for a surface strike, use the two Shrikes we left in orbit."

When the *Ares* shot around the horizon at full power, she'd already climbed up to a transfer orbit in order to reach the altitude the *Artemis* and *Hyperion* were sitting at. Jackson had been more than a little shocked when he'd looked over the damage report for the *Artemis*. The destroyer had taken quiet a beating, including a direct hit with one of those Alpha missiles, but had managed to stay in the fight. Captain Forrest had requested permission to withdraw to a safe distance from Xi'an to begin effecting repairs. Jackson immediately approved and sent the *Hyperion* along with her as an escort.

"How are we looking, Tactical?"

"New flight profile has been sent to the Shrikes, Captain," Barrett said. "They've got enough fuel left for a deorbit burn, and then they'll freefall the rest of the way in."

"Air burst detonation?" Jackson asked.

"Yes, sir."

"Very good." Jackson sat back in his seat. "How long until they're in position?"

"Deorbit burn will happen in another seventeen minutes," Barrett said. "After that, it'll be another six minutes to detonation."

"OPS, launch another drone," Jackson said. "I want it loitering outside the impact zone at a safe distance, and when the blast subsides, let's get some data on what's left on the ground. Have it transmit the data as a burst and then self-destruct."

"Aye, sir," Davis said. "Drone launching momentarily."

"Self-destruct?" Celesta asked.

"We're going to be steaming away from Xi'an by the time the area is safe for it to get in there," Jackson explained. "While it's true, we could put it back in orbit or land it on the surface for a potential later pickup, I don't see a point in leaving it intact for the enemy to find if they come back. A lot can be learned about our level of technology and engineering methodologies by studying something as mundane as an automated drone, not to mention exactly which part of the EM spectrum we communicate on and how we perceive the universe around us."

"Of course, sir," Celesta said. "I should have thought of that."

"Don't worry, I have something more important for you to think about," Jackson said. "I need you to find my missing ships. I can't leave this system without knowing where two fifths of my squadron disappeared to. You're authorized to pull from any departments and utilize any equipment you need, including long-range coms and high-power radar."

"Right away, sir." She shot to her feet. "I'll be in CIC."

"Missiles are entering the atmosphere now," Barrett said after a few more minutes of relative calm on the bridge. "Standby for confirmation of detonation."

It was another tense few minutes before they saw evidence of the nuclear detonation on the surface. The *Ares* was just coming around the terminator, crossing into the night side, when the horizon lit up with a tremendous flash. The light from the explosion diffused in the polluted atmosphere so it appeared to be a glow that encompassed half a continent.

"Detonation, both missiles," Barrett still reported, even though everyone had already seen it with their own eyes.

"That's it until the drone confirms the ground site has been eliminated," Jackson said. "Stand down from general quarters. Nav, plot a course to rendezvous with the *Artemis*. Helm, you're clear to engage... ahead two thirds. Let's leave this godforsaken planet behind us."

Chapter 4

"So, Captain, please show me the supplemental technical data you received from Tsuyo that led you to believe that a *Starwolf*-class starship was capable of being flown within a planet's atmosphere." Daya Singh pasted an obviously forced smile on his face.

"Well, Commander, it was simple supposition based on first year academy physics." Jackson took a sip of water. "She's two thirds the weight of the old *Raptor*-class ship with over four times as much available engine power. Not only that, but with all her antennas and sensors retracted, she has a fairly slippery shape. I will admit it was a tad unnerving though."

"Seriously, Jack." Singh dropped all pretense of joking. "What in the hell were you thinking?"

"I was thinking that I was once again leading a woefully inadequate ship against a Phage Alpha," Jackson said. "It was a calculated risk just slightly less insane than blindly flying around a planet directly into the damn thing's field of fire."

"That's why you're a captain and I'm an engineer, I suppose." Singh shrugged.

The pair was sitting in the Captain's Mess enjoying some down time and an evening meal while the *Ares* continued her leisurely flight back to the rest of the squadron where the *Artemis's* crew was scrambling to get field repairs complete before they departed the system. Commander Wright was still trying to find the *Icarus* and *Atlas* and hadn't taken a break since Jackson had tasked her with the project.

"I'm going back to the bridge." Jackson stood suddenly. "I want to be there when we meet up with the *Artemis* and *Hyperion,* and I'm not going to be able to relax until we find out what happened to the other two ships."

"I should probably get back to my work center as well." Singh also stood. "Your little joyride through the Xi'an sky wasn't without consequences. The external heat exchangers have dropped in efficiency since the engagement."

"Sounds relatively minor," Jackson said. "Let me know what you find."

Even after trying to sit for a meal and calm himself down, Jackson was still wired, buzzed on adrenaline and fear. He'd left the bridge shortly after the *Ares* had broken orbit for the outer system, so the crew wouldn't see that his hands were shaking after the encounter with the Alpha. They seemed to have all the confidence in the universe in his ability to get them through alive. Some of the crew aboard that had served on the *Blue Jacket* even seemed to look forward to the chance to kick some more alien ass.

But the truth ate at him: eventually his luck was going to run out. The Phage adapted and learned from each encounter at a frightening rate, and he still relied on panic-fueled inspiration to find workarounds for the inadequacies of human weaponry against the Phage's true big guns like the Alphas. To make matters worse, even after four years, much of what they thought they knew about their enemy was just best guess. Destroyed Phage ships offered little in the way of useful intel, other than that they were all crewless and were either a form of automaton or, more terrifyingly, were some sort of living machines.

Jackson left that sort of speculation for the egg-heads at Fleet Science and Engineering. He'd worked with CIS and CENTCOM to develop a set of tactics and standard operating procedures when engaging the Phage based on his own experience, but it all went out the window with every battle as they seemed to demonstrate a new ability or completely different behavior. The fact that the two Alphas seemed to have been mimicking Terran missiles and kinetic weapons instead of their usual directed plasma bursts was yet another wrinkle in trying to understand the Phage.

His comlink chirping made him stop midstride, just before he got to the hatch leading onto his bridge, a soft whine of protest coming from his left leg as he planted all his momentum on the prosthetic. The screen on the unit was a text only message informing him that Captain Forrest wanted to debrief him as soon as possible. He debated making her wait, but he had nothing pressing going on other than trying to come up with a plausible story in his head to explain to his superiors how in the fuck he lost two irreplaceable, top-of-the-line warships in their first real engagement with the enemy.

He spun on the ball of his right foot and quickly made his way back to his office, confirming the request on his comlink and letting Captain Forrest know he'd be available within the next five minutes.

"Senior Captain Wolfe." Captain Olivia Forrest nodded respectfully, her entire demeanor much changed from all the other interactions Jackson had ever had with her. "Thank you for taking my request on such short notice, sir."

"Not a problem, Captain." Jackson shifted in his seat. "Is there a particular reason you wanted a face to face? We'll compile all of the *Artemis's* mission data with our own when we submit the final mission report to CENTCOM."

"Yes, sir," she said. "I wanted to apologize for allowing the Alpha to escape the system and for allowing my ship to be so badly damaged."

Jackson was surprised for a second time in as many minutes. Olivia Forrest apologized for nothing, especially her own mistakes. The more at fault she was, the more aggressive she became.

"I think we were all taken by surprise, Captain," he said carefully. "I'm not ascribing blame to anyone in particular for any of the missteps we made from the time those two Alphas appeared. We'll parse through the data with a dispassionate eye and make adjustments so next time we don't repeat our mistakes."

"That is very gracious of you, sir," she said with no hint that she was being anything but sincere. "Your tactics against the other Alpha were inspired, if I may say." She seemed to hesitate a moment before she continued, looking at each of the other captains before she did. "I also wished to speak with you so I could request permission to withdraw the *Artemis* back to uncontested space."

Jackson leaned back in his chair as he considered her request. The *Artemis* was banged up but still combat capable. Having her pull out of the system before he knew what had happened to the *Icarus* or *Atlas* might be foolish on his part.

"Request denied, Captain," he said. "We're still missing two ships, and I'd rather keep the *Artemis* here in case we need her resources in the search... or the recovery. As soon as we locate them and ascertain their condition, I will revisit your request."

"Understood, sir." Forrest's mouth pinched. "*Artemis* out."

Jackson reflected on the exchange for a moment as well as the unexpected request. The crucible of combat, even the sterile type of combat done from the bridge of a starship over vast distances, tended to change a person... and change them almost immediately. It wasn't that he was unsympathetic. He understood her desire to leave after surviving a firefight, but he didn't have the luxury of indulging her discomfort.

"*Captain Wolfe to the bridge.*" Celesta's voice came over the intercom speaker in his office and from his comlink.

"On my way," he said, climbing out of his seat and slipping his comlink back into his pocket.

****

"The *Atlas* has checked in, sir," Celesta said as soon as he walked onto the bridge. "Systemic failure with main power is what they're telling us. Apparently it killed everything: coms, propulsion, steerage... the works."

"I'm going to assume Captain Caruso didn't activate the emergency beacon because he wasn't sure if the enemy was still out there or not." Jackson stared at the bright green dot representing the *Atlas* on the main display.

"Correct, sir," Celesta confirmed. "They informed us that they were ready to fire the mains and would be coming our way as soon as they were under power."

"And the *Icarus*?" Jackson asked.

Celesta motioned for him to approach the terminal she was using at the back of the bridge. Wordlessly, she pointed to a message that had been sent to the *Ares* from Captain Jonathan Caruso, CO of the *Atlas*.

Captain Wolfe,

I am sending this message separate from our official communications regarding the Atlas's *power plant failure, as I am not sure how you will want to handle it. While I cannot tell you where the* Icarus *currently is, I can tell you that she is likely still in one piece. When we split from the formation to intercept the Alpha circling around Xi'an, the* Icarus *began to lag back slightly. We sent a message requesting that they get back on the line, but we were engaged by the enemy before we received an answer.*

The Atlas *took a glancing blow from two of the Phage missiles, something I was unaware they even had, and when we tried to energize the forward laser projectors for point defense, the main power bus failed to the forward sections. We accelerated out and past Xi'an and requested that the* Icarus *cover our withdrawal until we could fix the problem. They never answered. A review of the sensor logs shows that as we were fired upon, the* Icarus *turned from the engagement and accelerated away from Xi'an at max burn. Our power plant went into safe mode and shut us down before we could track their trajectory.*

I do not know where Captain Levitt and his ship are. All I do know is that he abandoned us as soon as the shooting started. As I said, I am not sure how you will wish to handle this, so I am keeping it off of official records for now.

Captain Caruso
CO, TCS Atlas

"Oh, this isn't fucking good." Jackson muttered under his breath, running a hand through his short, dark hair.

"Indeed," Celesta said just as softly. "Right now, we're the only two people who have seen this, and I'm sending it to your personal directory."

"Thank you," Jackson said. "First, we need to find the damn ship. Once that happens, I can figure out what I'm going to do. Obviously we can't just let him keep it but I don't know who I can stick in the chair for the duration of the mission." Despite the seriousness of what Levitt was being accused of, Jackson couldn't help but feel enormously relieved that the *Icarus* was intact and not destroyed or captured.

"I'm scanning the entire system with the high-power array," Celesta said. "Even if they're running silent, we know exactly what sort of return to look for from the ship's hull material. It may take a bit, but we'll find her."

"That's assuming she hasn't already warped out of the system while we were engaged," Jackson said quietly. "Keep looking, and update me with every detail on my comlink if I'm not on the bridge."

"Yes, sir.".

As it turned out, it didn't take them nearly as long to find the ship as they'd feared it would. It was less than an hour after Jackson and Celesta had spoke when the com beacon for the *Icarus* lit up on their display, chirping out the destroyer's position and status loud and proud. The beacon was followed shortly by a terse com message from a terrified looking lieutenant commander.

"This is Lieutenant Commander Nimski, tactical officer of the *TCS Icarus*." His voice shook. "I've assumed command of this ship and have had Captain Levitt and Commander Carlton taken into custody. I would like to speak with whoever is currently commanding Confederate forces in the system."

"Coms! Tell Commander Nimski to rendezvous with the rest of the squadron." Jackson leaned forward, vigorously rubbing his temples with the heels of his hands. "Provide coordinates. Let him know if he needs assistance we can help him further."

"Aye, sir," the young ensign at the com station said.

"You have the bridge, Commander Wright," Jackson said. "I'll be in my office. Just get that ship back into the formation so we can get the hell out of this system."

"Yes, sir." Celesta slid into the command seat.

****

The single knock at his door made Jackson jump as he was so focused on his task. "Enter!"

"Sir, the *Icarus* has rejoined the formation." Celesta stepped in through the hatchway. "The *Artemis* has sent over two requests to withdraw since... are you well, sir?"

"Yes, yes." Jackson waved her off. "Just trying to stitch together all the sensor logs from the squadron into a cohesive picture of the encounter."

"We have an entire team of analysts down in CIC doing just that." Celesta frowned. "Is there something in particular you're looking for?"

"I want an unfiltered view," Jackson said. "The analysts are always trying to be helpful by excluding what they deem to be extraneous, but you and I both know a small detail that seems unimportant can actually be the key to understanding the thing as a whole."

"You're worried about something specific." She walked in and closed the hatch.

"I had a suspicion," Jackson said. "I didn't know for sure until I synced up all the time codes and played the logs from the *Ares* and the *Artemis* simultaneously.

"The reason the *Artemis* never got a killing shot in on their target is that at the exact instant our missiles impacted the first Alpha, the second wheeled and fled at what I previously would have considered an impossible rate of acceleration for that type."

"Our target warned the other we had new weapons and tactics," Celesta offered.

"And the other ship fled back beyond the frontier, likely to warn its... people... and analyze the information from the battle the same as we are." Jackson said with a scowl. "I have a feeling the next Alpha we face will already have modifications to defend against what was observed over Xi'an."

"Are you certain?" Celesta asked. "Our kinetic weapons were still largely effective."

"Not entirely." Jackson spun his monitor. "Watch."

Celesta sat in one of the unoffered seats and watched the high-resolution thermal imagery of their auto-mag shells impacting the first Alpha they'd engaged. Some obviously punched through the tough organic hull, but just as many smashed against it, exploding against the surface and not penetrating. Jackson had filtered a lot of the flashes out so they were able to clearly see that had two of the shells not flown unimpeded into one of the missile ports, their first salvo wouldn't have caused near the amount of damage it had.

"Maybe we're looking at a coincidence?" she asked after watching the opening shots of the engagement multiple times. "We did inflict a lot of damage to that ship before handing it off to the *Artemis* and *Atlas*."

"Besides the fact that I don't believe in coincidences like this, we didn't cause *that* much damage with those two lucky shots." Jackson shook his head. "It's certainly something to think about. This is just some preliminary looks at the battle... We'll do a more comprehensive debrief once the backshops get done with their own analysis."

"Of course, sir." Celesta stood and smoothed out her utilities. "What should I tell Captain Forrest?"

"Tell the squadron that they are clear to withdraw," Jackson said. "They are to follow all randomization protocols with Captain Forrest in overall command. I want them to fly to Neatlantia and wait for us there. Inform Captain Forrest she may replace the *Icarus's* current CO at her discretion but that Levitt and his XO are to remain in custody."

"Sir?"

"We're going hunting, Commander." Jackson's eyes stayed locked on the video of the nuclear blasts ripping apart the other Alpha. "There's a reason that other ship ran from two Terran destroyers and there's a reason the Phage keep coming back to Xi'an. We're going to find out what that is. Let Commander Singh know that we'll be departing within the hour."

****

The four remaining ships of the Ninth Squadron broke out of their orbit around the sixth planet, an impressive Class II gas giant, and began accelerating for their jump point. Jackson had declined Captain Forrest's request to accompany him once she found out that he intended to track the escaped Alpha. Despite the fact that she had made it clear how much she disliked him since their first meeting nearly ten years prior, he had to grudgingly concede that she'd handled herself very well in her first foray into battle.

She quickly got over her initial shock and was willing to fly into potential combat with him again as well as having stood toe to toe with something as overwhelming as a Phage Alpha. He'd looked over the *Artemis's* logs, and Forrest hadn't backed down or retreated. In fact, she'd driven her ship forward to make sure her point defense overlapped with that of the *Hyperion* after they'd taken that first volley on the chin.

Conversely, Captain Levitt, one of his long time allies, had completely fallen apart. Jackson couldn't have been more disappointed and disgusted with the man's behavior. There would be no saving Levitt's career, nor should any attempt be made. Had his actions resulted in the loss of the *Atlas* and her crew, Jackson would have been more than tempted to toss his ass out the nearest airlock and save CENTCOM the trouble of a general court martial.

"They're on their way, sir," Celesta said. "Chief Engineer has cleared the *Ares*. We can get underway at your discretion."

"Thank you, Commander." Jackson stood. "Helm! Prepare to break orbit. Nav, get me a destination to Jump Point X-ray. Use any gravity assists if they're available, but don't make a special trip around a planet just to save a few thousand pounds of propellant."

"Aye, sir," the helmsman said. "Main engines coming online now."

"Course laid in and sent to the helm," the specialist at nav reported.

"Very well." Jackson sat. "Let's not keep the Phage waiting... Helm, at your discretion, all engines ahead full."

"All ahead full, aye!" The helmsman gave a small, tight-lipped smile.

Jackson let them all enjoy the moment. For many of them, this was the second Alpha they'd killed. Why should a third that's already been wounded be any different? As the engines ran up, the mild surge pressed them back slightly until the gravimetric generators could catch up. The swirling clouds of the gas giant blurred as the destroyer accelerated hard to slingshot around and pull out of orbit.

"Jump Point X-ray?" Celesta asked. "I don't recall seeing that on the latest star charts, sir."

"It won't be on the official one," Jackson said. I have a set that Agent Pike gave me before we departed Jericho Station. once the *Ares* was cleared for duty."

"*Pike*," Celesta said as if the name caused her pain. "If I may, sir... what is beyond Jump Point X-ray?"

"The warp lane that leads to the system the AU had been colonizing in secret, the one we think tipped the Phage off to our existence," he said. "If they pushed back into Xi'an and gathered enough raw material to create another slick big enough to spawn two Alphas, I have to believe this next planet will be their logistics hub for the operation."

"I would expect it to be fairly well guarded then," Celesta said.

"Maybe," Jackson said. "There's another world beyond that one that could be the real target. Either way, we're going to transition out of warp well short of the system and begin gathering intel as we go. This is more of a fact-finding mission than anything else. If we can take out the wounded Alpha, so much the better, but what I really want is to know what's happening just outside of Terran space."

The *Ares* charged hard down into the system, altering course only slightly to swing around the primary star in as efficient an arc as they could before spiraling back up the other side of the well. They were only five hundred kilometers from their jump point when Jackson ordered the main engines killed and the warp drive deployed.

The *Starwolf*-class was sporting a seventh generation warp drive that utilized four fast-deploying nacelles, two fore and two aft that were always charged. The ship had no sooner locked the nacelles into place and turned them into position when the capacitor banks poured the power into them, and the *Ares* transitioned out of the system with barely a flash to mark her passing.

Chapter 5

The trip out to the next star system—simply called X-ray by the crew, as the Asianic Union was still trying to pretend they didn't have any knowledge of the planet or its previous human colony—was shaping up to be as boring as Jackson had hoped it would be. Since the ship was more or less brand new, there was little in the way of maintenance to be done, so Singh tried to fill his crew's days with near endless drills and training on the intricacies of the new ship. By the end of the first week, there were more than a few grumbles and hostile looks shot his way as he walked the corridors.

If Singh was getting dirty looks, Major Ortiz's Marines looked at him with expressions that promised violence if he ever turned his back. The Marine officer was making sure his charges didn't have the chance to get bored and start causing trouble on a ship that, oddly, was slightly more cramped inside than the *Blue Jacket* had been.

For his part, Jackson let Celesta train the bridge crews undisturbed. Instead of hovering and generally being a pain in her ass, he took the opportunity to walk around to all the different work centers, meet his new crewmembers, and reacquaint himself with those who had come with him from his last command. By his side, whenever he descended into the lower decks, was Master Chief John Green, an imposing man of early middle age whose physical presence was only eclipsed by a voice that could be heard echoing ten compartments away. Jackson had met the man when he'd first taken command of the *Ares* and, remembering the last pile of shit he'd had as a senior enlisted advisor, had accepted his transfer with a certain amount of resignation.

But, joy of joys, Master Chief Green was a no excuses, no bullshit, real deal senior NCO that kept his finger on the pulse of the crew and was an invaluable conduit of information to and from the captain. The more Jackson got to know him, the more he began to have a genuine fondness for the foul-mouthed man from New America and looked forward to the Chief's visits up to Officer Country, where he would inevitably blister the paint and cause more than a few officers to blanch with a string of obscenities so creative that it would leave Jackson mesmerized. Was he really that quick on his feet, or did he have them memorized and chambered, just waiting for a chance to unload?

"Things are looking good, Chief," Jackson said, as they walked along the central access tube. "The ship is spotless, and it seems like the crew is really getting their proficiency dialed in on the new systems."

"They're marginally better than they were a fucking year ago," the Chief growled. "But calling them *proficient* may be a tad too generous, sir."

"Maybe," Jackson said. "But please tell them that overall I'm pleased with what I'm seeing."

"Will do, Captain," Green said.

"I'd also like to make sure they're getting some downtime," Jackson continued. "I'll speak about it in the next meeting with the department heads, but it's something I think I'd like to see you take charge of."

"Downtime," Chief Green repeated, as if trying out how the word felt in his mouth for the first time. "Are you certain you want them having too much time with nothing to do? There's always something that needs cleaning—"

"I'm sure, Chief." Jackson tried not to laugh. "They've earned a bit of a break after the excitement of the last few weeks. I need them rested and sharp when we hit the X-ray System."

"I'll make sure it happens, Captain." Green's tone indicated he didn't fully agree with his boss's assessment. Like most NCOs, he seemed to feel the best way to keep a crew sharp and happy was to keep them too busy to worry about anything but doing their jobs.

"Thanks, Chief," Jackson said. "I'm heading back to the bridge. Let me know if anything comes up."

"Of course, Captain."

"Captain's Mess tonight at 1830, Chief," Jackson said, watching the Chief closely. "I expect to see you there."

The Chief tensed up, not turning around and not saying anything, before stalking off around the corridor. Jackson noticed that the man loved to skirt the edge of disrespect when dealing with officers on the *Ares* almost as much as he despised the forced social interaction in which he would have to get into his dress blacks and nod politely while some lieutenant junior grade prattled on about what they thought the keys to leadership were.

****

The conversation at the semi-formal evening meal was mostly compartmentalized, with people talking to those in their immediate vicinity while Jackson and Chief Green both held themselves apart from the individual groups. One conversation, however, was becoming decidedly more animated, even heated, and began to absorb those around it as more people entered the fray to voice their opinions.

"I simply can't understand how you can be so enthusiastic about a war that's already cost billions of human lives before it's even really started," Commander Owens, the *Ares's* Chief Medical Officer, was saying, his tone full of righteous indignation.

"You're twisting my words, Doctor," Major Ortiz said calmly. "*Enthusiastic* would be a gross mischaracterization of what I said. My only point was that if we are to fight an inevitable war, I hope my men and I are able to participate as more than starship ballast. But let's examine your premise... humans are mortal creatures. We *all* die. In the grand scheme of things, how is death by alien invasion different than death by influenza or exposure?" The last sentence silenced Owens but only because he was gaping in shock.

"Major Ortiz, are you seriously suggesting that a Phage invasion is simply nature running its course?" Lieutenant Davis asked.

"Of course," Ortiz said. "It's simply nature on a far larger scale than we've ever experienced. For millennia, humans have stood outside of the natural order of things, our tools allowing us to observe without truly being a part of the cycle of life as evolution intended it. Our tools are now nuclear fission missiles and starships, but the underlying principle is the same."

"I can't understand how you can be so cavalier about what could be the systematic annihilation of the human species," Commander Juarez said.

"Accepting reality on reality's terms and having a cavalier attitude are two different things." Ortiz still didn't break his calm, relaxed demeanor in the face of a multi-pronged assault.

The flight operations officer frowned at the answer, but remained silent.

"Are you really so enthusiastic about fighting the Phage, Major?" Celesta Wright asked. Jackson watched the conversation with interest, but sat silently. The Major's words had struck a chord. Where did he stand on this war? It had been thrust upon him before, but did he agree with Ortiz that it was a chance for humanity to prove their worthiness?

"Again, enthusiastic would incorrectly label me as a warmonger or battle junkie," Ortiz said. "I am a warrior and a soldier. If there's to be a knock-down drag-out match for our right to exist, then yes… I want to be at the tip of the spear.

"Can none of you see it? Win or lose, we're living in legendary times. Our actions will determine the fate of our entire species, and the choices we make, or don't make, will ring through history for centuries. So no, I am not enthusiastic, but I *am* willing to accept the challenge that's been given us. What is the point of being alive if only to exist and consume? The universe has asked if we are worthy. How will we answer that question? That's all I'm saying."

The short speech left the rest of the room stunned. Nobody offered a rebuttal, and there were a few uncomfortable throat clearings before Jackson raised his glass.

"To accepting the challenge." He nodded to Major Ortiz.

"To the challenge!" came the ragged chorus from the rest of the Fleet officers in the room, some looking a little shamefaced after the Marine major's impassioned words.

"I'm glad I came to mess tonight, Captain." Chief Green smiled from his place on Jackson's left.

"I'm thrilled you're so entertained, Chief," Jackson deadpanned, sipping his water as the conversation began to subside into its previous, smaller groupings.

He sat and contemplated Jeza Ortiz's words, not entirely sure he was comfortable with their implication. So far, he'd been concentrating on the small, immediate targets in front of him. The single Alpha invading Terran space, the single challenge of getting the *Starwolf*-class ships tested, the single challenge of getting his new crew up to speed... Never did he sit and fully try to comprehend what implications his actions could have on his entire species.

After another thirty minutes, people began to excuse themselves and file out of the officer's mess, Chief Green leading the charge, until Jackson was sitting alone with Daya Singh and Celesta Wright.

"That was a hell of a speech Ortiz gave," Singh said as Jackson went to pour himself another coffee.

"I wasn't aware our Marine commander was such a philosopher," Celesta said. "I have a feeling Owens underestimated him before starting that little spirited discussion."

"It was good for him." Jackson checked to see that the hatch was fully closed before continuing. "Humility and Commander Owens aren't always on speaking terms, and I'm sure he thought a Marine major to be well beneath him when he opened his mouth. I'm just glad Chief Green stayed out of it."

"It's certainly something to think about." Celesta pushed back from the table. "If you gentlemen will excuse me, I need to relieve Lieutenant Commander Barrett for the remainder of second watch."

"I'm right behind you," Singh said as he finished his tea. "I want to get some sleep before we transition into real-space tomorrow."

Jackson filed out with them and headed to his quarters, even though he knew sleep would be elusive. He was destined to spend a fitful night as nearly every other ship's captain did the night before an imminent battle. Even the act of flying to system X-ray was dangerous, as the warp lane hadn't been officially cleared and vetted by CENTCOM, but the fear of running into something with enough mass to collapse their warp distortion fields was a distant second to flying in and meeting an entire fleet of Phage ships with his lone destroyer. The words of his Marine detachment commander came back to him as he closed and locked his hatch.

Legendary times indeed.

****

"Standby for warp transition!" the chief at Nav practically bellowed. After a sharp jolt, the main display came back up, and they were all staring out at unfamiliar stars and little else.

"Tactical and OPS, start a full passive sensor scan of the surrounding space," Jackson ordered. "I want everything capable of receiving on this ship listening and recording with the computer sifting through for anomalies. Leave the warp drive deployed for now... We're going to cold coast while we listen. XO, please tell Engineering that I want to run in low-power mode until otherwise ordered."

"Yes, sir." Celesta sent the direct message to Singh.

They'd transitioned in 35.27 astronomical units from the X-ray System's primary star, placing them well outside the boundary of the debris which was all that remained of the accretion disc that formed X-ray's planetary bodies. Jackson's plan had been to pop in on the outer edges of the system, collect as much data as possible, and either move into the system or bug out as quickly as he could.

After six straight hours of listening and detecting nothing of note, it became obvious that the limitations of their passive sensors, coupled with an infuriating lack of understanding about their enemy, meant that no matter how long they sat outside of X-ray, they'd never learn a damn thing.

"OPS, prep one of the Jacobson drones for flight." Jackson carefully weighed his options. "I want a decaying orbit toward the primary at maximum acceleration. Full active package including high-power radar, and I want it chirping in constant telemetry mode."

"Aye, sir," Davis said. "Drone is being prepped now. Flight OPS say it will be ready for launch in fifteen minutes."

"Very well," Jackson said. "In the meantime, retract and stow the warp nacelles and prepare to fire the mains. We'll be creeping up a little closer once the drone gets in there and starts raising hell."

"I take it we're abandoning subtle, sir?" Celesta asked, leaning in as she spoke so that the rest of the bridge crew couldn't overhear.

"Partially, Commander," Jackson said. "We'll keep the *Ares* hidden as long as possible, but any intel we gather by letting the light and radio waves trickle into the passives will be useless by the time we get it. If there's anything actionable in this system, we need to know now."

"I'll be down in CIC monitoring the telemetry stream." She grabbed her coffee and stretched her legs.

"Excellent idea," Jackson said. "Go ahead and firewall the raw feed there, and only send anything of interest to the bridge."

"Yes, sir." She hustled off the bridge in order to get to CIC and settled by the time the drone was launched.

"Flight OPS reports drone is in the forward launch tube and ready for launch, sir," Davis said after another ten minutes had passed.

"Launch the drone," Jackson said.

A few seconds later, the bright flare of the drone's plasma engine streaked away from the *Ares*, disappearing within seconds among the background light of the stars. The Jacobson drone, named for someone important that Jackson had never bothered to learn about, was the most advanced unmanned vehicle the Tsuyo Corporation had available to put on the *Starwolf*-class ship when they'd launched. They could be configured per use with mission modules that allowed him to cater to whatever need he had, including weapons delivery. All in all, not a bad bit of tech to have.

"Drone is away," Davis said. "Telemetry stream expected in another ninety minutes. Active sensors will come on shortly after."

The drone had been programmed to delay reporting back until it was well within the system. It didn't do a whole lot of good to try hiding when the drone transmitting from their position would basically roll out the welcome mat.

"I want everyone rotating out to get something to eat and stretch their legs," Jackson said. "You have one hour before I want all of first watch back on duty and ready to begin receiving data from the drone."

There was a burst of hushed conversation as some specialists called up their backups while others, like OPS and Tactical, negotiated who would go for the first thirty minutes, as their positions were somewhat interchangeable.

Jackson forced himself to remain calm as the clock on the main display counted down to when they should begin receiving data from the drone. If there was anything in the X-ray System, and if the drone was able to find it, it probably wouldn't be in the first few minutes of the radar being powered up.

Lieutenant Davis walked back onto the bridge after being gone for less than twenty minutes, handing him a fresh coffee before relieving Lieutenant Commander Barrett. Jackson nodded his thanks, noted from the smell that she'd correctly guessed which of the coffee brands stocked on the ship he preferred, and continued watching the clock and listening to the hushed voices of his crew.

"Mark!" Lieutenant Davis said as the clock reached zero and began counting back up. "We should begin receiving data any minute."

The bridge remained deathly silent as the clock ticked up past one minute, then two, and eventually five minutes with still no telemetry signal from the drone. Worry began to gnaw at Jackson's stomach lining until, eight minutes past when it should have began transmitting, the status light next to the drone's name on the main display winked from red to flashing yellow, then went solid green to indicate they were getting a valid signal.

"CIC confirms we're receiving valid data," Davis said. "Signal strength is excellent, and the drone's active sensors are already transmitting."

"Tell Engineering to prep the mains for restart," Jackson said. "Send the drone's course through the outer boundary debris to Nav so we can get a course plotted into the system."

"Understood, sir," the specialist at Nav confirmed without having to be specifically ordered.

Jackson looked up his name and made a note to commend his attentiveness to his department head.

"Nav, once you have a course that lets us fly up through all this, send it to the helm," he ordered. "We're going to begin a nice, slow creep into the system and wait to see if the drone sees anything worth investigating. Settle in, everyone... This may be a long, boring watch."

****

"Two more anomalies detected," Davis said. "Analysts are scrubbing the data now."

Jackson didn't bother to respond. It had been nearly nine hours since the drone had begun actively scanning the system, and there had been an average of ten anomalies an hour. So far, none had resulted in anything more interesting than an asteroid that was flying against the orbital direction of its neighbors. He'd known it was going to be a long watch, but now he was faced with a choice: rotate personnel out and hope that the drone continued on without finding anything, or keep first watch on duty and risk them being utterly exhausted if it did find something.

"Contact!" Davis barked, almost causing him to jump. "One of the last anomalies is an eighty-five percent match for an Alpha and a sixty percent match for the one that fled Xi'an."

"OPS, tell Engineering to prepare the *Ares* for normal flight mode," Jackson said. "Coms, call down to Flight OPS, and have them redirect the drone for a closer look at this anomaly."

As the crew shook off the lethargy that had settled in during the long watch, Jackson pulled up the raw data from the drone on his terminal and looked at the radar returns. He had to admit, it did look a lot like the stern quarter of an Alpha, but after looking at the feed in continuous frame mode, it appeared the anomaly was in a slow tumble. He frowned, trying to make sense of what he was seeing.

"Engineering has cleared the *Ares* for normal flight, Captain," Davis said.

"Helm, engage along the prescribed course. All ahead one half."

"Ahead one half, aye."

"Nav, plot a series of contingency courses for the anomaly," Jackson said. "One standard approach, one stealth approach, and one max performance. I also want an escape course back to our jump point being constantly updated."

"Aye, sir," Specialist Accari said.

"The drone is being backtracked along its original course to get updated data on the anomaly," Davis said. "It will be a full burn, sir. If anything out there is looking, it's going to light up like a beacon."

"It's been thrusting into the system the whole time while broadcasting on multiple bands, Lieutenant," Jackson said. "If something were going to take notice of it, I would think we'd have seen it by now. Tell Commander Juarez to proceed with his current flight profile."

"Yes, sir," Davis said.

It didn't take long for the lightweight, overpowered drone to come around and accelerate back to where it had last had contact with the anomaly. Jackson was well aware that the data he was seeing was over two hours old, but it didn't stop him from tensing up as the high-resolution optics of the drone clearly picked up a Phage Alpha, spinning in the space between the orbits of the fifth and sixth planets in the system.

"Which planet was the AU colony on?" Jackson asked.

"First planet, sir," Davis said. "Does CIC concur with what we're seeing from the live feed?" Jackson asked her. "Thermographics appear to be showing no activity. All the visible regions of the hull are uniform in temperature."

Davis spoke quietly into her headset. "Confirmed, sir."

"Have the drone get close enough to open fire on it with its point defense lasers," Jackson said.

"Sir?"

"You heard me, Lieutenant." Jackson leaned, watching the spinning behemoth resolve in greater detail as the unmanned probe continued on its course.

"Updated commands sent, sir," Davis said. "Might I ask what you're hoping the results are?"

"My hope is nothing, Lieutenant," Jackson said. "If it allows the drone to get in close and pepper it with laser fire without any response, we can conclude that it's likely dead. If it comes about and destroys the drone, we're still far enough away to prepare ourselves for engagement."

She didn't look particularly relieved at his answer but didn't question him further.

The speedy Jacobson drone closed the distance to the Alpha in less than three hours, decelerating to a full stop relative to the spinning hulk of the Phage ship. Jackson held his breath as the thermal optics showed the drone's point defense lasers heating up sections of the hull, inflicting absolutely no damage. Part of the problem was the hull was incredibly resilient to thermal energy, and another was the tepid lasers on the drone couldn't maintain fire on a single spot for very long due to the enemy ship's tumble. Inflicting damage wasn't the point of the experiment, however.

"There!" Jackson said as the bottom of the Alpha came into view. "Roll that back a bit and enhance the damaged portion of the hull."

Davis split the views on the main display, the left jogging backward to the point the captain wanted and the right showing the real-time feed of the drone, still merrily blasting away at the enemy.

"Here, sir?"

"Yes," Jackson waved. "Have CIC confirm that the area we're looking at matches up with where our auto-mag shells hit."

"Confirmed," she reported quickly.

"Interesting," Jackson murmured. "Command the drone to cease fire and take up station, keeping near the Alpha. Prepare a com drone with the data we've just collected, and send it back to CENTCOM. Flag it priority one-alpha. Make sure to include the drone's command codes in the message."

Flagging it at such a high priority would automatically bring it to the attention of the person he most wanted to see it, while keeping within protocols and alerting command of any noteworthy developments on the frontier.

"Com drone ready, sir," Davis said. "New instructions to the drone are being updated by Flight OPS."

"Nav, I'm sending you coordinates for a jump point in this system." Jackson accessed a secure directory on the command server. "I want a course plotted there, best possible speed. Coms, tell Commander Wright I need her back on the bridge as soon as possible."

"New course laid in, sir," Accari said, "But I feel I should point out that this jump point does not correspond to an approved warp lane."

Barrett shook his head as Jackson gave the young specialist a flat stare.

"I am well aware of that, Specialist Accari," Jackson said. "Helm, engage on new course, ahead full."

"Ahead full, aye," the helmsman said.

The *Ares* turned off her course leading to the inactive Alpha and accelerated toward the jump point across the system, her main engines pushing her along at over seven hundred Gs.

"Change of plans, sir?" Celesta asked as she hustled back onto the bridge. "We're not checking out the Alpha?"

"It's dead," Jackson said. "We're leaving the drone here, and CIS can come collect it."

"Dead?" She grimaced, seeming to still be uncomfortable with using terms like "dead" or "alive" to describe the Phage ships. "Might it not be prudent to use one of our Shrikes to be sure before we leave, sir?"

"Normally, yes," Jackson said. "But I'm more than convinced that I'm correct, and this is an irreplaceable chance for Fleet Science to get their hands on a mostly intact Phage unit."

"Yes, sir," Celesta said, dropping her argument to fire upon the Alpha. "What to you think killed it?"

"Another lucky shot," Jackson said. "Those shells we managed to get up inside the missile ports must have hit something vital. Not only was the thing cold as space, none of the hull damage had begun to heal. It must have limped this far and died. So, since we know it was unlikely this was its ultimate destination, we're going to find out what's hiding beyond this system.

We're not steaming full bore toward the Zulu jump point."

"I see," she said noncommittally. "The AU has been evasive about their colony in this system, but they've been adamant that they've never explored past this point."

"And yet our mutual friend has found otherwise." Jackson gave her a tight smile. "While Agent Pike was never able to confirm that the AU had used the Zulu warp lane, he *was* able to verify the coordinates. It's going to be the same drill: hop in, take a peek, hop out."

"I'll prepare a brief for the command section." Celesta pulled her terminal around.

"Prepare a general brief for the entire crew as well, if you would," Jackson said. "The information is highly classified, but they need to be ready for the worst."

"Yes, sir."

Chapter 6

The *Ares* transitioned back into real-space after warping 14.7 light-years from the X-ray System. A quick star fix by Nav verified that they'd arrived in the Zulu System, but they'd transitioned in far closer than Jackson had wanted. They were actually within the orbit of the outermost planet.

"Nav, get with CIC and find out why we're so far into the system," Jackson ordered. "OPS, get the main engines up, and stow the warp drive. Tactical, begin passive sweeps of the system."

"Any idea why we missed our target so badly?" Celesta asked quietly.

"My first guess would be that we had faulty intel from CIS as to the precise location of this system," Jackson said. "We'll update our position here so the trip back won't have a repeat."

"Contact!" Barrett said sharply. "Captain, we have a multitude of thermal contacts, some quite massive, moving about within the inner system."

"Any chance they're natural phenomenon?" Jackson asked.

"There's a chance, sir, but the computer is giving a seventy-eight percent probability that they're artificial constructs," Barrett said.

"Phage ships don't normally have such dramatic heat signatures." Celesta looked over Barrett's shoulder.

"No they don't," Jackson drummed his fingers on the armrest of his chair. "At least not when they've been actively trying to hide, but I don't think that's what we're seeing here. Look at these three larger contacts... The scale is off the charts. I think we're getting our first look at a Phage base of operations. I'll bet those larger contacts are production facilities."

"You're not going to like this, Captain," Barrett said. "I'm now able to roughly determine size and mass for the other, less pronounced contacts... In addition to the three suspected production facilities, the computer estimates twenty-one Alphas and over three hundred Bravos. The smaller contacts are harder to track because they're interacting too closely with the larger ones."

Jackson tried to respond, but his mouth had gone completely dry. There were over three hundred Phage units—twenty-one of them Alphas, and three of unknown specifications other than enormous on a scale that defied logic. This was not good. He had flown his ship right into the lion's den.

"Okay," he managed to say eventually. "We came out here to find what the Phage were up to, and I'd say we've done just that. This might be the beginnings of a full invasion force. They're staging up right outside of Terran space, and we need to accomplish two very important goals: gather as much detail as we can about what's here and then get the hell out of here without being spotted... if we haven't been already."

"How would you like to go about this, sir?" Celesta said, her voice and posture tense.

"That is a very good question, Commander," Jackson said. "Nav, what's our position and relative velocity?"

"Thirty-one point six astronomical units from the primary star, fourteen degrees declination off the ecliptic, ninety-eight thousand, four hundred meters per second forward velocity carried over from transition," Accari said.

"I'm open to suggestions, everyone," Jackson said. "This is a situation without precedence, and we've got a little time before we need to light the mains and then likely be detected."

"Given the acceleration those Bravos have demonstrated in past engagements, I don't think it's realistic to try and stop and accelerate back out to the jump point." Celesta kept her eyes trained on the computer as it began to populate the threat board with the best extrapolations it could manage, given the very limited information it had so far. "These are just the units showing high heat signatures. There could be hundreds, even thousands, more sitting cold in this system."

"That's a disturbing prospect, ma'am," Barrett said. "If they have any deep patrols running cold, we could be crossing their paths very soon if we haven't already."

"OPS, I want this ship as cold as possible," Jackson said. "Tell Engineering I want the lowest power mode they can manage while keeping in mind we may need to bring the engines and weapons up very quickly if we're spotted."

"So turning and running is out," Celesta said. "We're also now quite possibly the farthest beyond the frontier that any human ship has ever been, so there's no vetted and cleared jump point waiting for us somewhere else in the system."

"Engineering is running both reactors down to twenty-one percent, sir," Lieutenant Davis said. "Commander Singh said he'll need three minutes to bring them back up to full power and another five to get the mains started."

"I'm still not used to such short reaction times from the primary flight systems," Celesta said. "This will be a significant advantage."

"Gotta love a new fucking ship, ma'am," Master Chief Green said from where he was leaning against the bridge entry hatchway, his thick arms crossed over his chest. "If you don't need me, Captain, I'm going to take a walk and settle the crew a bit... Don't want 'em pissing themselves before the fighting even starts."

"Thank you, Chief." Jackson felt slightly guilty at how much he enjoyed Celesta's reactions to Green's casual profanity.

"As I was saying," Celesta said loudly, "running so cold and being able to react so quickly should help tremendously, but then the real question is how long do we keep this up? We can't cold coast out to the other side of the system. We don't have enough food aboard for a trip that long, and there's nothing on the other side but more unexplored space."

"Not only that, but we need to get the information about this Phage fleet back to CENTCOM," Jackson said. "They'll need to deploy a response force to the frontier as fast as they can manage it... probably sooner."

"What are your orders, sir?" Celesta asked after the impromptu strategy meeting fell silent.

"Tactical, continue collecting data with the passive sensors and begin building a computer model of the Phage fleet composition," Jackson said. "OPS, I want you utilizing the same data, but I need to know anything you can tell me about the individual configurations. We've already seen two distinct Alphas so far. I can't imagine that's all they have. Nav, use any and all information on this region of space we have on the servers, and figure out the most logical way out of here given our current position and speed. All of you pull heavily from your backshops and coordinate any additional resources you need through Commander Wright. Any questions? Good... Let's get to work."

The *Ares* continued to glide silently through the void, her course angling down and away from the ecliptic, but already they were detecting the pull of the primary star's gravity with their instruments. If they continued on, they would begin to shallow out in relation to the orbital plane and begin moving back toward the Phage formations clustered near the inner planets, but not before they passed underneath the three larger constructs orbiting one of the system's two gas giants.

Jackson's crew went about their jobs in a sort of quiet panic, working diligently but always with an eye on the threat board. He had an idea in his mind about how he wanted to egress the system, but it wasn't the time to tell his crew about it yet and give them one more thing to worry about.

It was some hours after entering the system when their fear of wide-ranging Phage patrols was realized. A nine-ship formation of Bravos came within range of the passive sensors and flew within two hundred thousand kilometers of the nearly powerless destroyer. They gave no indication that they noticed them at all as they streaked by without slowing. Jackson had Barrett and Davis write down their impressions of the encounter for the official log that would be attached to the raw data, as it may give some clue as to how they detected Terran ships. The fact there were nine ships in the formation might even hold some insight into the aliens' thought processes.

"We're getting a good picture of the ships in the inner system and the patterns they follow," Barrett said the next day. "What looks like utter chaos at first is actually a carefully choreographed dance. The computer has been able to begin building predictive models based on what the different Phage ship types are doing."

"What about our giant friends in the outer system?" Jackson asked.

"They don't move much," Barrett said, "But everything else has been moving toward them. The Bravos all take turns flying from the inner planets and then back out to one of the three constructs. I can't tell if they're picking up or delivering during these visits."

Jackson took a closer look at his tactical officer's bleary eyes. "Lieutenant Commander, while I'm very intrigued by what you've been observing, is there some reason you haven't left your post since yesterday?"

"I didn't want to try and turn over how I was running the tracking algorithms to the relief watch, sir," Barrett said. "I have everything more or less automated right now. I'll grab some rack time on the next rotation."

"You'll call up a relief before that." Jackson ordered. "I want you out of that seat within the hour."

"Yes, sir."

"Captain, do you have a moment?" Lieutenant Davis called from her station.

Jackson patted Barrett on the shoulder before walking over to the OPS station. "What have you got, Lieutenant?"

"Do you agree that one of our main priorities should be to get a better look at the three constructs orbiting the seventh planet?"

"I do," Jackson said. "Please get to the point quickly, Lieutenant."

"Yes, sir." Davis looked a little stung at the rebuke. "I think I can get us a closer look, but it's going to cost us another Jacobson drone and require you to tell me exactly how you intend to get us out of this system."

Jackson thought about lying to her and saying he hadn't decided on a method of escape yet, but Davis seemed to always be able to tell when he was shooting straight and when he was just mouthing platitudes for the sake of the crew.

"It's fairly simple, Lieutenant." Jackson looked around before continuing. "When we begin to get pulled back up by the star's gravity, and while we still have a healthy amount of forward velocity, I'm going to order a blind warp transition out of the system without firing up the mains."

Davis swallowed hard at the idea and actually seemed to pale a bit. A blind jump, within an unknown system, and into unknown space was an enormous risk to be taking. Some would dismiss the idea out of hand as being too much like attempted suicide with a fair chance of accidentally succeeding.

"That will still work with what I want to do, but the coordination will have to be perfect," she said. "Let me show you."

Over the next hour, they went through the details of her plan, called over Specialist Accari to make sure her astronavigation was correct, and checked the *Ares's* manifest to make sure all the required equipment was aboard.

"Go. Now," Jackson said after they'd settled most of the details. "Don't send this down to Flight OPS. I want you to physically go down and supervise the modifications to the drone. Don't withhold details about your plan, but let's keep the part about our pending departure from this system classified for now."

"Yes, sir." She hopped up from her station and practically ran off the bridge.

Jackson watched her go before pulling out his comlink and typing out a quick message for Commander Singh to join her and ensure the techs down in Flight OPS weren't too flummoxed by the unusual modification requirements.

****

"Flight OPS has cleared us for launch," Lieutenant Davis said. "Our window is open for the next thirty-eight minutes."

"Launch the drone," Jackson said.

Down in the forward launching tube, a specially modified Jacobson drone nudged its way out of the *Ares* on few small puffs of compressed gas. As per the plan, the drone paced ahead of the destroyer for a bit to ensure it wasn't emitting any unforeseen thermal energy. They'd cooled the drone's fuselage with liquid nitrogen before putting it into the launch tube and were letting it sit to normalize its external temperature with surrounding space.

Even at only a few hundred meters away, Jackson was impressed at how indistinct the drone was on their thermal optics. It barely registered, even when firing its compressed-gas maneuvering jets.

"Drone thermal signature is well within the accepted limits." Davis looked at the tiny automated craft with multiple imagers.

"Mission is a go," Jackson said. "Send it."

Davis reached over and executed a command that would send a single, two millisecond pulse from a low-powered com laser, telling the drone that it was clear to begin its mission. It immediately began a slow, steady climb away from the *Ares*, sparingly firing its jets as it utilized the velocity it had inherited from the destroyer. Within minutes, it was no longer visible on their passive sensors.

"Impressive," Celesta said. "Depending on how the Phage 'see,' I imagine the drone will be able to get quite close."

"It's thermally shielded and stealthy against RF emissions, and we've removed its plasma engine," Jackson said. "I would assume if the *Ares* can sneak by as she is now, then the drone shouldn't have much trouble. I'll be honest though, other than a few random patrols, it doesn't look like security is a big concern in this system."

"Would *you* be overly concerned if you had twenty-one Alphas backing you up?" she asked.

"We've proven to them that we're willing and able to kill them." Jackson shrugged. "That alone would make me a little more cautious."

With the excitement of the drone launch past, the bridge of the *Ares* calmed back down to the monotonous routine of observing the passive sensors and keeping track of all the Phage traffic flying about as the destroyer continued gliding well below the ecliptic. The work was so mind-numbing when nothing was happening that Jackson ordered a third watch propped up on the bridge, utilizing junior spacers and dispersing his seasoned operators among them.

Jackson pulled in several of his senior staff and let them in on the plan to exit the system. Predictably, they were less than enthusiastic about something that their training told them was tantamount to certain death, but after the protests had died down he was able to make them see that there while there was nothing that could be done without significant risk, the data gathered about the Phage fleet had to make it back to Haven at all costs.

"Captain, we may need to fire the mains for at least a short burn just before we transition," Singh argued. "While we're carrying enough relative velocity, I'd be more comfortable getting on a course moving well away from the primary before attempting to engage the warp drive."

"What are the no-bullshit odds of the star's gravity interfering with our warp distortion fields?" Jackson asked.

"Off the top of my head, I'd have to say better than ten percent, which is significant," Singh said.

"Even with the proposed flight parameters?"

"Especially so," Singh said. "You're wanting a short burst, in your words, but it doesn't really work that way. By the time the distortion fields stabilize, and the ship has begun her transition, we will have already moved quiet close to the star. It wouldn't be much of a stretch to imagine it could collapse our field and leave us stranded in the corona or upper chromosphere for the short time it would take for us to be incinerated. I'm sorry, Captain, but I just can't sign off on the risk you're asking us to take. Even without our proximity to the star, there's a significant risk."

"Well, then," Jackson said, sighing as he looked at the ceiling. "That's why we're having this meeting. What other options can you give me that don't include lighting off a large thermal bloom in the system by firing the main engines?"

"The short answer is none," Singh said. "Not without exposing the ship to shear forces she was never designed to handle. If you give me some time, we can work to minimize the thermal signature of the mains, but we won't be able to hide it entirely, and it'll require a significantly longer burn than you would like to get us moving along on the new course."

"But with the mains already online, if we're spotted, we can just make a break for it," Celesta said. "We should have plenty of time for a full burn and warp transition before they can get any of those Bravos close enough for a shot."

"I don't doubt that, but I was hoping to get out of this system without them knowing we were here," Jackson said. "They'll know about the drone, of course, but if nothing leaves the system that they're aware of, it might not cause a reaction. The last thing I want is to force them to step up their own schedule and take this fleet to Terran space long before we're ready."

"I hadn't considered that," Commander Juarez said quietly. "I apologize, Captain. This entire time I thought you were simply trying to exit the system without risking an engagement for our own sakes... I didn't full understand the ramifications our actions may have for the frontier worlds."

"A fleet this big and diverse... They're not gunning for a few under-defended colony worlds at the edge of Terran space," Celesta said. "This is a full invasion force. So the question is this: do they have more knowledge of where our planets and colonies are than we're assuming they do?"

"Let's keep the speculation to a minimum for now and keep our focus on the task at hand," Jackson said. "Commander Singh, I want a proposal for a main engine burn sent to me within the hour. If there's nothing else, you're all dismissed."

It only took Singh twenty minutes to give Jackson a very thorough report of his proposal to light the mains and give them the nudge they needed to get on the correct course. He'd done his due diligence, and there were actually three separate proposals, each with varying degrees of risk, with all the necessary data he'd need to make his decision. He looked at the clock on the wall of his office. He had just under ten hours to finalize his decision before it was taken out of his hands completely by virtue of the Jacobson drone completing its mission.

By the time he'd decided, had a short sleep in his office, and made his way back to the bridge by way of the wardroom for a quick bite, the excitement was palpable. Sometime during the current watch, they'd get confirmation that their drone mission was either a success or a failure. They would be forced to leave the system no matter which it was, but the outcome would determine if it was sneaking out unnoticed or being chased by an enormous Phage armada.

"OPS, tell Commander Singh that he's clear to begin prepping the main engines for his low-profile burn proposal," Jackson said. "He is not to begin heating the plasma chambers without my command."

"Yes, sir," Davis said.

"I also felt that method gave us our best chance at accomplishing all of our goals," Celesta said as he sat down.

"I'm not fully convinced, but nor do I have any better ideas, and we're against the clock," Jackson said. "No matter how many tricks you can play with the nozzle restrictors, we still need enough thrust to overcome inertia and get a few hundred thousand tons of starship moving in a different direction."

"Standby!" Davis called out sharply, cutting off whatever Celesta had been about to say. "Data transmission coming in from the drone."

"OPS, compile and archive the data," Jackson said. "Coms! Tell Engineering they're clear to ramp up reactors one and two and start main engines."

"Nav! Make sure the helm has the corrected course for warp transition," Celesta said.

"Yes, ma'am," Specialist Accari said.

At Jackson's request, the young spacer had been moved to split first and second watch for additional mentoring.

"Transmission has stopped," Davis said. "Confirmation of detonation. Jacobson probe is destroyed."

"Helm, engage new course," Jackson said. "Modified acceleration profile delta. Tactical, what's going on with our friends?"

"It looks like the detonation has gotten them stirred up, sir," Barrett said. "We're still being ignored, but all the Alphas are converging on where the probe was, and the three large constructs are accelerating away from the planet at a surprising rate."

"Fuck."

"Sir?" Celesta asked.

"I'd been hoping those three big ones were nothing more than stationary production facilities," Jackson said. "But with that sort of acceleration, it looks like we're seeing a new class of Phage ship."

"I hope they're logistical assets and not strategic," Celesta said.

"As do I," Jackson said. "Nav! How are we doing?"

"We're accelerating away from the system within the predicted envelope, sir," Accari said. "We'll be clear of potential gravimetric interference from the star in less than two hours at current power levels."

"Let me know the instant we are," Jackson said. "Tactical?"

"Phage units are now fanning out away from the planet," Barrett said. "The big boys have broken orbit and are moving toward the inner system at an impressive clip... around two hundred and fifty Gs."

"What does your predictive model say about their behavior?"

"Not a whole lot as this is something completely new, sir," Barrett admitted. "But both the computer and I agree that they seem to have started a systematic search pattern that's progressively moving away from where our drone exploded."

"That was a forty-thousand terajoule warhead we loaded on it," Celesta said. "There won't be anything left for them to analyze."

"The byproducts of the nuclear explosion itself will linger," Jackson said absently as he watched the main display. "If they have a complete profile of Terran weapons used against them so far, they might be able to figure out it was us that took a shot at them. All of our fissionable material comes from the same source in the New European Commonwealth right now."

"We should be long gone by the time an analysis like that can be completed." Celesta's voice was full of uncertainty.

"That's the idea, but we have no way to know that for sure," Jackson said.

Time seemed to slow to a standstill as the destroyer continued to slink away from the enemy hoard. The mood aboard was tense, but Jackson could sense that in spite of this the crew wasn't panicked or otherwise unable to perform.

"Course correction complete," Specialist Accari called out just over two hours later. "We're now moving away from the primary star at a declination of thirty-nine degrees off the orbital plane and at an acceptable forward velocity for warp transition."

"Engines zero thrust," Jackson said. "OPS, tell Engineering to shut down and secure the mains as soon as they throttle back."

"Engineering is securing main engines from modified flight mode," Davis recited off her display. "Commander Singh wants permission to deploy the warp nacelles."

"Deploy," Jackson confirmed. "Do not apply power until I give the word."

He watched the status on the main display change as *Ares* was reconfigured for warp flight. Unlike on the *Blue Jacket*, where the forward warp emitters were visible, the small warp nacelles used on the *Ares* deployed from both flanks and couldn't be seen from the bridge "view." Since the emitters weren't exposed in this new design, there also wasn't any visible light emitted, but Jackson wasn't taking the chance that the Phage might detect the minute gravimetric distortion they created while charging.

"Captain, all detectable Phage units are now heading back toward the inner system," Barrett said. "They seem to be crowding in around the three unclassified constructs between the orbits of the second and third planet."

"It's too bad we don't have any recon drones capable of warp flight," Jackson said absently. "OPS, tell Engineering I want the warp drive charged and online. Nav, when you get a green indicator on the drive you are clear to transition out of the Zulu System."

"Aye, sir." Accari kept his focus on his displays.

A few moments later, the ship shuddered slightly as the warp drive engaged, and they left the Phage fleet behind. A short twenty minutes later, the ship shook and bucked again as she emerged back into real-space.

"First warp transition complete," Lieutenant Davis reported. There were some hushed celebrations on the bridge that Jackson allowed as his crew was elated they'd survived the "warp hop." Though he would never show it, he was as relieved as they were.

"Okay, everybody." Jackson stood and raised his hands to get them back on task. "That was the dangerous one. Now that we're clear of the Zulu System's boundary debris, we can more carefully plot our course back to Terran space. OPS, tell Engineering to bring all primary and redundant systems back online and fire the mains. Nav, begin calculating our exact position and start plotting me a course back to the Xi'an System from here. Commander Wright, you have the bridge."

Chapter 7

"Position confirmed," the chief sitting at the nav station reported. "We're now in the Xi'an System."

"Tactical, start full active scans of the system," Celesta said.

"Ma'am, we have three CENTCOM transponders squawking in-system," Lieutenant Keller reported from the com station. "Generic codes, no ship registry or unit designation."

"Can you determine ship type?" Celesta asked.

"No, ma'am."

"Activate our transponder, standard hail," Celesta ordered. "Tactical, try to get me at least a class type on those ships, and continue scanning the system. OPS, have the *Ares* configured for normal flight."

"Ma'am, we're getting a request to stop active scans," Keller said after they'd been in the system for a little over an hour. "The message came in on standard encryption with the correct time increment."

"Tell them we will comply when they provide command authority," Celesta said. "Until then, keep scanning."

"I'm getting the initial returns on two of the ships, ma'am," Barrett said. "Eighty percent certainty that they're CIS Prowlers. The third seems to have disappeared."

"Which means it has active stealth capability," Celesta said. "Cease active scans—low-power anti-collision radar only. Coms, let me know if they bother replying. I'd still like to know exactly who we have in this system with us."

"Ma'am, incoming message coded for you," Keller said.

"Is it addressed generically to the CO? Or did they ask for Captain Wolfe by name?"

"No, ma'am... it's an encrypted message specifically to Commander Wright," Keller said. "Forwarding it now."

Her interest piqued, Celesta entered her credentials and pressed her thumb to the display so that the computer could get a biometric reading. As she read, she could feel her expression morph from one of mild surprise a blushing red anger, her fists clenching tightly at her sides.

"Helm, stabilize our flight." She worked to unclench her jaw. "Attitude thrusters only. Maintain zero thrust, and heave to... We will have a ship coming alongside to dock shortly. OPS, please inform Commander Juarez to expect a CIS Broadhead at our starboard airlock, and send a runner to wake Captain Wolfe and inform him he will have a visitor."

"Aye aye, ma'am," Davis said.

****

"Do you wake up every morning and think of new and interesting ways to fuck up my world, Wolfe?" Agent Pike stomped across the flexible gangway from his small Broadhead and onto the *Ares*.

"Nice to see you too, Pike." Jackson crossed his arms. "To what do I owe the pleasure?"

"We should probably speak in your office... alone." Pike's face showed none of the sardonic wit Jackson had come to associate with the man when he was in his real persona, or at least what he assumed to be his real persona.

"Follow me." Jackson nodded his head toward the hatch.

He led the CIS spook through the ship, until coming to a lift that would take them straight up to Officer Country and the command deck. The *Starwolf*-class ship was mercifully shorter in both length and height than the *Raptor*-class had been, so they were stepping into the well-appointed office mere minutes after leaving the starboard airlock.

"Just so you know, I've got two more Prowlers in the X-ray System trying to figure out what to do with your dead Alpha." Pike closed and locked the hatch. "Hell of a shot."

"Lucky shot," Jackson corrected, indicating to one of the chairs, but Pike had already flounced into one. "Somehow I doubt you've brought four CIS Prowlers out to the Frontier just to collect a carcass that isn't going anywhere."

"No," Pike said, "I came to find out where the hell one of the Fleet's brand new destroyers had flown off to by itself. Nice job sending the rest of the squadron back in complete disarray. Three of the four COs were relieved of duty."

"Who survived?" Jackson wasn't necessarily surprised. Maybe Pike was here to relieve and take *him* into custody.

"Forrest."

"Good."

"Really? I thought you two hated each other," Pike said.

"We still do on a personal level, I'm sure," Jackson smiled. "But she showed real courage and skill when that Alpha charged. So... aren't you going to ask me what I found out past X-ray?"

"Don't. Just... don't." Pike removed a flask from his jacket. "I'm not listening to this story sober. Knowing you, there's probably a whole new species out there you managed to declare war on." He took a long pull off the flask and offered it to Jackson, who shook his head. "Really?"

"Haven't touched the stuff since that one last drink in Marcum's office." Jackson tried not to let his discomfort at the subject show. "I had to go through a pretty intense detox program when they weaned me off all the pain killers during the physical rehab. I figured as long as I was already sober, might as well try and stay that way."

Pike seemed to consider that as he took another long drink. "So if you weren't drunk when you went chasing the Phage out beyond the Frontier by yourself, what were you doing?"

"I was just trying to gather information while the trail was hot," Jackson said. "I had no intention of engaging the enemy without support. We even managed to pull it off, and trust me, when you see what we found, you'll be thanking me."

"Don't hold your breath," Pike said. "Show me what you've got."

Without any preamble, Jackson played him some of the sensor logs he'd stitched together into a single file that he'd intended to put as the header to his report. Pike watched the whole thing silently, his eyes narrowing as he took it all in. As soon as it ended, he played it again in its entirety before leaning back in his chair and pawing at his jacket for his flask again.

"We are so fucked."

"Their most logical point of ingress will be the Xi'an System again," Jackson said. "Every one of their incursions has come through here. If we can get the Ninth back along with both Black Fleet battlegroups, we might be able to hold long enough Pike assumed a pained expression at the mention of all the Fleet assets he was listing. "What?"

"Black Fleet has been recalled to Haven," Pike said. "They won't be coming to this system for some time."

"What are you talking about?" Jackson asked. He wasn't completely sure the squirrely CIS Agent wasn't just screwing with him for fun. "Haven?"

"There've been some... developments... since you departed and came back out to the Frontier," Pike said. "Since there hasn't been any real action along this front until recently, the sense of urgency has been all but lost. In fact, some of the enclaves don't feel the threat is worth the risk and are withdrawing their support for the campaign." Jackson stared at the spy as if he'd grown a second head.

"All of that aside, why has the Seventh been recalled?"

"CENTCOM feels there is a genuine threat to the Confederacy as New America and Britannia have both made declarations that they would refuse any demands they participate in a war they're now accusing you of starting," Pike said. "Not their exact words, of course, but you get the point. They've even insinuated that their respective numbered fleets would be used to enforce their policy decisions."

"New America and Britannia have threatened to attack Haven?" Jackson leaned back, reconsidering the offer of Pike's flask. "This is insane. We've only been gone for three months! How the hell does this happen?"

"It's been simmering for a couple of years," Pike assured him. "This is all posturing and empty threats… I think. The real reason for the lack of cooperation is that the two enclaves aren't willing to let the First and Fourth Fleets make way for the Frontier and leave them open. In the minds of a lot of people, this is a problem for the AU and the Alliance."

"They're really blaming me for starting the war?" Jackson asked, for some reason finding that important.

"You know how news media is." Pike shrugged. "They don't know about the AU's illicit colony building, and they have to have someone to pin it on. The politicians recognize an easy out when they see one, so they've elected not to correct them."

"It's not as if you were universally loved anyway," Pike offered. "Pinning the pending war on an Earther is almost comforting for a lot of the population on Haven."

"Careful," Jackson warned.

"I don't care where you're from." Pike waved him off. "The point is that I think we have to face the reality that we're going to surrender the Xi'an System to the Phage. We don't have sufficient forces available to hold here, especially with what you've just shown me."

"I haven't even shown you the best part," Jackson said with a grim smile.

He reached over and played the queued up footage of the high-resolution optical and radar scans of the three enormous constructs the Jacobson drone had transmitted before self-destructing. Pike just stared at the screen once the video had played.

"I'll need to send all this to CIS," he said hoarsely.

"Lieutenant Davis is already packaging everything into a com drone," Jackson said. "I stopped her from launching when I heard you were in the system, in case you wanted to add anything to it before it hits CENTCOM and CIS."

"I think I will," Pike said. "May I use your terminal?"

"There is no way in hell I'm giving you unfettered access—"

"Captain Wolfe to the bridge!"

Jackson locked out his terminal before rushing out through the hatch, not bothering to see if the CIS operative was behind him.

"Report!"

"Two Prowlers just transitioned into the system and ordered a full withdrawal," Celesta said. "They're reporting that three Alphas and an indeterminate number of Bravos are likely inbound. They left the system just as the Phage arrived in the X-ray System and began cannibalizing their dead comrade."

"They're already coming back in to establish a beachhead in this system," Pike said from behind Jackson. "Our ships are designed for quiet interdictions, we can't stand and fight a Phage force this big."

"We're not staying," Jackson said. "Lieutenant Davis, allow Agent Pike to append a message onto the com drone package, and then launch it. We'll be following shortly behind it."

"Commander Wright, would you be so kind as to order the Prowlers out of the system," Pike said with a wide smile. "They know I'm over here, so just use my name as the authorization. Tell one of them to drop the usual drone package before hitting their jump point."

Celesta said nothing to the CIS agent but walked around behind the command dais and gave the com officer her instructions.

"Captain, we need to get to Haven as quickly as possible," Pike continued. "It pains me to say this, but your ship is significantly faster than mine. If you wouldn't mind, I'd like to hitch a ride with you."

"You're going to leave that Broadhead here for the Phage?" Jackson asked.

"And lose my baby? Not on your life." Pike snorted. "It can fly itself back home and even be docked and fueled by the time I get around to retrieving it. I'll just grab some things and send it on its way back to Haven."

"Commander, how long until those Alphas reach Xi'an?" Jackson asked as Pike jogged off the bridge.

"The Prowler captain we spoke to wasn't sure," she said. "She did say that they made their way across to that dead Alpha at a fairly leisurely pace and didn't look to be in any hurry. They got away clean, no pursuit, so it could be hours, or it could be weeks."

"This could all just be according to their own internal schedule and has nothing to do with us, sir," Davis said.

"Or they could have gotten word somehow that an Alpha died in the X-ray System and were just now getting around to retrieving it," Jackson said. "Either way, we're operating under the assumption that their ultimate goal is Xi'an... again. Let's get everything buttoned up and get out of here. Let engineering know we'll be starting main engines as soon as that Broadhead is detached."

"Captain, Flight OPS is reporting that our starboard airlock is secure and the Broadhead is ready for departure." Lieutenant Keller relieved an ensign at the com station.

"OPS, disengage the mooring clamps," Jackson said.

"Clamps disengaged and supports retracting," Davis said. "Broadhead is thrusting away to starboard."

"Start main engines," Jackson said. "Prepare for departure. Nav, plot a course for the Haven jump point, best possible performance. We need to transition out of this system before the Phage make it here. Otherwise, it's the long way around."

"Main engines are up."

"Course is plotted and locked."

"Helm, engage on new course," Jackson said. "Ahead full."

"Ahead full, aye."

****

Nothing they'd observed so far led CENTOM to believe that the Phage had any way to track a ship once it transitioned to warp, other than extrapolating a destination based on the last known trajectory. Jackson felt reasonably justified in taking a direct line to Haven, rather than bouncing around the Frontier when an entire armada of CIS ships had just cleared the system. Still, there was a nagging doubt at the back of his head that made him wish he'd at least bounced through Neatlantia before heading for home. Singh had theorized that they might be able to detect the warp lanes by the expanding interstellar particles the passing of each ship continued to push out and away, but if that were the case, there was little he could do to keep the Phage ignorant of the core worlds.

He'd set Pike up with a terminal in his quarters and, against his better judgment, allowed him access to the *Ares's* servers so the spy could go over all the raw intel they'd gathered in the Zulu System and he could do his own analysis on the flight back. In return, Pike had provided him with information on the current political discord so that he could be prepared when they got back to Haven.

From what he could tell, it seemed to be an acute case of war-fatigue that had set in before the war had even actually started. The citizenry had been getting hit over the head for over three years about the pending threat with nothing really happening. As the media was wont to do, their reports became more and more hysterical and fantastical, in an attempt to keep their audience interested, until people were no longer paying any attention. In fact, many believed it was just a ploy by the Confederacy to tighten its grip on the enclaves.

Now that the threat was presenting itself again, people were no longer willing to be frightened into action. Jackson's name did appear in many reports, but more as a bumbling rube than the hothead captain who kicked off an interstellar war. He wasn't actually sure which he preferred.

He eventually became disgusted at all the political wrangling over an issue that shouldn't be political at all and closed all the files. He tried to delve into the CENTCOM after-action report on the three demoted captains from Ninth Squadron and, if anything, became even more disgusted, finally switching off his terminal to take a walk and clear his mind.

****

"Is this seat taken?"

Celesta looked up from her tile and narrowed her eyes slightly. "If I said yes would you leave?"

"Probably not." Pike set his tray down and sat across from her. "I think maybe we got off on the wrong foot, Commander."

"Maybe we got off on the right foot," she said. "Did it ever occur to you that I just don't much care for your company?"

"Well to be fair, we really don't know each other," Pike said. "You met Aston Lynch, political aide. Not me. "

"Aren't you Lynch?"

"I can't stand the man, if I'm honest," Pike said. "But he's necessary for me to do my job."

"It gives me a headache to hear you talk about your alter ego in third person," Celesta said. "So what is it you want, Pike? What is your first name, anyway?"

"It's just Pike. I don't want anything, Commander, other than a friendly conversation."

"Couldn't you chase after Lieutenant Davis or any of the other attractive young officers aboard?" Celesta closed down her tile and set it next to her food tray, an encouraging sign if someone was as good at reading people as Pike was.

"Davis has her sights set a little higher than a lowly lieutenant colonel in the intelligence service," he chuckled. "But I think you still misunderstand my intentions… this is not a play to get you to invite me to your quarters."

"Then I'll ask again… what are you after?" A lot of the rancor had ebbed from Celesta's voice as Pike showed himself to not be the leering jackass she had first thought.

"I spend most of my life either by myself in a small ship, surrounded by the most vile scum in the Confederacy, or stuck listening to preening politicians congratulating themselves on their own greatness." All the humor dropped from Pike's voice. "An opportunity to just talk with a beautiful, educated, and interesting woman isn't something I would pass up without at least trying."

Celesta let her scowl slip a bit now that it was apparent he wasn't leaving. Even though he was probably still trying to play her, at least he was doing it in an interesting way.

"Ok, Lieutenant Colonel Pike." She leaned back. "Why don't we talk about what's happening in the core worlds and why CENTCOM doesn't have three full task forces sitting in the Xi'an System?"

The pair talked for a few hours about a variety of subjects, the agent even thawing the Fleet officer's professional stoicism enough to elicit a few laughs, a sound that startled most of the junior officers eating nearby.

****

The rest of the flight to Haven passed uneventfully. As Pike had asserted, the *Ares* beat the Broadhead to Jericho Station by more than two weeks, despite the smaller ship's head start. It was a feat that had all the Tsuyo engineers buzzing with excitement as they met the destroyer at the dock to pull all her telemetry logs and get a performance report from the crew. They cheered and clapped each other on the back when Celesta told them the *Ares* had killed two Phage Alphas without sustaining any damage.

She then sucked all the joviality out of the conversation when she casually told them how they'd flown the ship through Xi'an's atmosphere at high velocity. As the command crew walked away, the Tsuyo team looked at Wolfe as if he were criminally insane.

"You could have left that last part out, Commander," Jackson complained as they climbed onto the moving walkway.

"They'd have found out anyway when they reviewed the logs of the engagement, sir." She shrugged. "Throwing out something like that shocks them enough to allow us to escape the conversation. Otherwise they'd have followed after us, asking about every aspect of the ship's performance."

"Ruthless." Jackson smiled with approval. "You're very quickly learning what it takes to be a captain."

The Tsuyo engineers ended up being only the precursor to a whole series of people waiting to greet the hero crew. Pike, dressed in his role as Aston Lynch, made outrageous claims about the bravery of the crew as he greeted his "boss," Senator Augustus Wellington, and six other members of the Confederate legislature. Now that he knew what to look for, Jackson could see Wellington's jaw clench at Lynch's ridiculous embellishments and foppish demeanor.

Jackson let Celesta run interference as people came up to greet and question the command crew, a task she had taken to naturally and was quite good at. She was not only more personable but was far more diplomatic than he could ever hope to be. Not only that, but her crisp Britannic accent didn't offend sensibilities like his very obvious Earther dialect.

As they escaped the greeting parties and rode one of the transparent tubes to billeting, Jackson looked down at Haven. It was the first time he'd been back since leaving, after his exoneration in the loss of the *Blue Jacket* (and weeks of intense physical therapy), for a secret Tsuyo shipyard to take command of the *Ares* some forty months ago.

For some reason, whenever he saw Haven from space, it gave him an intense longing to see Earth again. Maybe he'd talk Pike into taking him back there when things settled down since flights to and from the birthplace of humanity were few and randomly scheduled. He figured the agent might enjoy a trip back as well, as he'd begun to have suspicions about the man's carefully guarded origins.

****

"Enter!" Jackson called out when he heard the chime.

While he'd been in command of the *Blue Jacket*, he always consoled himself during trips to Jericho Station with the fact that Officer Billeting was far more luxurious than his sparse ship's quarters. Tsuyo ship designers had addressed that disparity, however, and compared to his suite aboard the *Ares,* the quarters on Jericho now looked rather dated and worn.

"I was going to go grab dinner." Singh walked in and keyed the door shut. "You want to put your leg on and join me?"

Jackson gave him an unfriendly glare as he reached over and grabbed his prosthetic. "You're actually going to spend time on the station and not watch over the shoulders of the Tsuyo techs as they crawl all over your ship?" He engaged his leg into its socket with a metallic *clack* and waited for the nerve sensations to come alive. The strangest part was that it genuinely felt like he'd sat on his leg wrong, and the circulation was coming back—pins, needles, and all.

"If you must know, they're digging into some parts of the power plant that I don't have clearance to see," Singh said. "We were all asked to disembark in no uncertain terms."

"I still can't believe they're playing these games with their technology, all things considered." Jackson stood and smoothed his pant leg over the metal of his prosthetic.

"Old habits, I guess." Singh shrugged, trying very hard to pretend that the snub didn't bother him. "The more irritating part is that I don't even think it's a matter of security clearance. I think they view Fleet engineers as little more than over-qualified machine operators. The insinuation was that it served no purpose for me to be there since they'd brought their own techs to fetch tools and parts, and I'd just be in the way."

"Ah, the forever-running cold war between scientists and engineers." Jackson managed not to laugh as he ushered Singh out into the corridor. "I think maybe you're being a little oversensitive about it."

"I'm being nothing of the sort." Singh sniffed.

"You heard the one about the scientist and the engineer who were locked into separate workshops and told they weren't allowed to come out until they'd built a simple radio receiver?" Jackson asked as they walked down the near-deserted corridor.

"Why do I have a feeling this joke will be at my expense?"

Jackson ignored him and pressed on. "So a scientist and an engineer are tossed into separate rooms, stocked with tools and parts, and told that they aren't allowed out until they've produced a working prototype for a radio receiver. After two days, the scientist has covered the walls in scribbling and looks like a mad man, raving about how not only is it impossible to build a receiver with the parts given but that he's proven that radio is theoretically impossible anyway.

"When they check on the engineer, they find that he'd built the receiver in less than a day, fashioned a crude speaker and antenna, and had found a radio broadcast he liked and hadn't bothered to tell them he'd finished."

Singh chuckled at the anecdote despite himself. "I'm assuming there's a point to this anecdote?"

"The point is that you do your job, and you do it very well," Jackson said. "Try not to worry about how they do theirs. The old dividing lines are falling, but it seems Tsuyo Corporate isn't about to hand over the keys to the kingdom over something so petty as an interstellar war that threatens to wipe out the human species."

"So clever," Singh deadpanned. "I hope they have something with a little more zing than the *Ares's* officer mess serves."

"Not everyone likes pain-flavored food," Jackson said to his friend as they walked into the beautifully decorated mess hall.

Singh's strong South Asian lineage—an archaic Earth term for what used to be India—meant that he normally preferred food with a level of heat that made it almost inedible for someone like Jackson, who grew up on the much milder North American-style fare.

"It toughens you up." Singh walked up to the line and checked out the menu.

"My stomach lining would disagree."

They had no sooner sat down and began eating when a fresh-faced ensign walked into the hall and walked up to their table, snapping to attention.

"Senior Captain Wolfe," he said, "Your presence is requested on the surface of Haven at Chief of Staff Marcum's home."

Jackson settled his napkin on the table. "When do I leave?"

"Your shuttle departs in sixty minutes, sir. Details of your departure will be sent to your comlink momentarily."

"Thank you, Ensign." Jackson pushed his tray back. "I suppose I'll need to change into dress blacks if I'm heading down to the surface."

"I wouldn't presume to know, sir," the ensign said, mistaking the rhetorical question for a literal one. "If I may say, it was an honor to meet you, sir."

Before Jackson could respond, the young officer spun on the ball of his foot and marched out of the mess hall.

****

After a bumpy shuttle ride from Jericho Station to an air base on the coast of Haven's northern continent, Jackson was met by another aircraft that whisked him away to the residence of the CENTCOM Chief of Staff. He tried to ignore the electric turbines whistling outside the window as the lush, green landscape of Haven's northern hemisphere in summer streaked by. His agitation at being called off of Jericho began to morph into a simmering anger as he suspected that he was heading for some formal dinner with a group of dignitaries instead of getting his ship ready to head back out to the Frontier.

It was like a low-grade headache, the constant buzzing just on the edge of his awareness that kept reminding him that every hour wasted was another hour they'd never have back to prepare for the Phage when they decided to come full force. And come they would.

Unlike a lot of the CENTCOM brass who had the luxury of speculation, Jackson believed down in his core that the clock was quickly running out until their enemy did something even more horrifying than sending in a single Alpha to attack a handful of frontier planets.

The pitch of the motors changed and they descended rapidly for an open patch of lawn just north of the sprawling home that was the traditional residence of the Chief of Staff for the last seventy years or so. The pilot goosed the power on the down-canted turbines just enough to flare the small craft before it bounced gently on its landing gear and rolled forward.

"Sorry for the aggressive descent, Captain," the pilot said through the intercom. "We were told it was urgent to get you here quickly."

"I've been through worse, Lieutenant Commander." Jackson waited as the crew chief popped open the hatch and stepped aside so he could disembark.

As soon as his feet hit the grass, a small, open air vehicle tore across the lawn toward him. A bit of curiosity peeked through the anger he'd been carrying from the air base. He had a hard time believing something like another dinner with politicians would be treated with so much urgency.

"Senior Captain Wolfe," the Marine corporal driving the vehicle managed to sit at attention as it slid to a stop. "If you'll please come with me, sir, it's urgent you join the Chief of Staff as quickly as possible."

Jackson slipped into the passenger seat and hung onto the armrest as the corporal stepped on the accelerator hard enough for the tires to chew up the manicured turf.

Jackson was ushered inside, and his stomach growled at the remnants of what had obviously been a lavish buffet that had hardly been touched. As he watched the servants put away the food, he wished he'd been able to eat on Jericho before being summoned.

As someone who had lived most of his life on a starship, he didn't understand the need dirtsiders had for face-to-face communication. It was far more efficient to talk over a secure video channel, especially at such close range where there wouldn't be any lag.

He was led past the reception area and through a heavy security door where he was scanned by three Marines with handheld devices, each looking for separate threats. His prosthetic leg caused them some consternation until the ranking Marine's comlink chirped. When he answered it, Jackson could clearly make out the voice of Marcum shouting to let him in. Unruffled, the sergeant pocketed the comlink and gestured for his subordinates to stop.

"Sir, if you'll just enter the first lift on your right, it will take you to where you need to go." He indicated down the bleak hallway with his right hand.

"Thank you, Sergeant." Jackson walked toward the lift quickly, having a very bad feeling about what he would find when its doors opened again. The lift accelerated downward rapidly enough to make Jackson's stomach do a flip. As a lowly captain, he wasn't privy to the secrets of the Chief of Staff's home, but he'd never even heard any rumors about such extensive underground levels.

When the lift braked to a stop, and the doors opened, he was even more surprised. The large, dimly-lit room could have been mistaken for the CIC aboard a *Tundra*-class fleet carrier. Computer terminals ringed the perimeter while the center of the room was dominated by a large, circular table that looked to be a newer generation holographic display. Tsuyo had originally fitted such a display on the bridge of the *Starwolf*-class prototype but removed it after Jackson complained loudly and often that it was an unnecessary distraction.

"Wolfe! Get your ass in here!" Marcum shouted from the far side of the table. He was wearing his formal dress uniform, jacket hanging unbuttoned and the tie half torn off in a testament to the hasty nature of his departure from the planned dinner. "This is a fucking disaster!"

"What's happened, sir?" Jackson stepped up to the table and tried to figure out what he was seeing in the three dimensional display.

"CIS com drone came in while your shuttle was descending," Marcum said. "The Phage have retaken the Xi'an System, and it looks like they were trying out some new toys."

"Retaken?" Jackson said. "We conceded the system to them."

"Yeah... well they've made sure we have no reason to go back," Marcum said. "They've destroyed Xi'an."

"Destroyed—"

"Yes, goddammit! Keep up, man!" Marcum shouted. "They moved in with those new Charlie constructs you found near Zulu and completely destroyed the planet. Look." As Jackson's mind reeled from the impossibility of the statement, Marcum replayed the high resolution optical feed from the automated drones they'd left in the Xi'an System. What he saw chilled his blood and made him grip the edge of the table in case he fainted.

"That's impossible."

"I'd suggest you forget you even know what that phrase means, Captain," Marcum said, as the video repeated again. "Watch it a few more times, and then snap out of it… we've got a lot to talk about."

Chapter 9

The evidence on the drone feed was beyond conclusive. The Phage "Charlie" units, as they were blandly designated, were planet killers in every sense of the word. Jackson's mind simply wasn't prepared to accept that something built by intelligent beings would have the power to make an entire planet cease to exist.

From the vantage point of the stealthy CIS drones, he watched the Charlies appear in the system and maneuver themselves in a low orbit around Xi'an, equidistant from each other and in crossing orbits that allowed them to maximize their coverage over the planet. Each Charlie then accelerated along their orbital paths and unleashed a veritable hell upon Xi'an. The superheated plasma streams from the three moon-sized Phage units blasted away the atmosphere and began boiling the bedrock of the planet's crust.

The details of the process were quickly obscured as Xi'an became nothing more than a slow moving comet on the drone sensor feed. The tech controlling the feed sped it up so that when the image showed only the cooling molten core of the planet surrounded by three lifeless Charlies, nearly thirty-two hours had elapsed. The fact that they could sustain that level of firepower for that long seemed implausible, but there was no denying what he'd seen on the sensor feed.

"Feel free to throw up, Captain," a deep voice said from the direction of the lift.

Jackson turned and saw Fleet Admiral Jorenson Pitt walking toward him, as always in his impeccable dress black uniform.

"We'd arranged this meeting when the *Ares* made orbit to discuss new developments and a generalized strategy for the Frontier. But we are now in crisis management mode after this recording came in. What do you make of it, Captain Wolfe?"

"Beyond the sheer horror of this new weapon, this attack made little sense, Admiral," Jackson said. "We'd withdrawn from the system, and they'd already rendered Xi'an incapable of supporting human life. Why spend the resources to obliterate what they'd already essentially made useless to us?"

"Why indeed," Admiral Pitt said. "But the damnable hell of it is that despite the servers full of data our geeks have collected, we're no closer to understanding what these things want than you were when you found the one over Oplotom."

"Could this have been a warning?" Marcum walked around the table. He was technically the highest-ranking officer in CENTCOM, but he was viewed more as outside the official chain of command—more of a liaison with the Confederate government. Pitt was the man who gave the Fleet its marching orders once all the political considerations had been settled.

"I don't think so, sir," Jackson said. "A warning would indicate a desire to communicate on some level, something the Phage have never shown any indication of."

"What are you thinking, Captain?" Pitt asked.

"Since we can agree that there was no strategic or symbolic reason to destroy Xi'an, the only other thing that makes any sense is that this was a weapons test," Jackson held up his hand as both his superiors attempted to argue the point. "I know that there were two other rocky planets in the Zulu System, so what we don't know is: why drag three Charlies all the way to Xi'an for a live fire exercise."

"That's quite a lot of unknowns, Captain," Pitt said sourly. "Let's put the conjecture aside for a moment until the rest of the science team gets here. What we need to do immediately is determine what our answer will be."

"Admiral, perhaps I'm not the person most qualified to be in on discussions of—"

"Wolfe, your modesty might be a big hit with the review boards, but right now, I need you to shut up and get to work," Pitt growled. The man was not known for his subtlety.

"Yes, Admiral," Jackson said. "Can we get a clear view of the Charlies after the debris cloud had dispersed a bit more?"

"At once, Captain," the specialist working the terminal said. "The drone stopped recording and sent it to Haven soon after the attack, so it won't be much."

"Just give me what you have." Jackson leaned in on the table.

The best he could get from the truncated sensor feed was a few thermal stills, but it showed him that what he suspected about the Charlies was true. It also showed that Xi'an wasn't completely destroyed. While greatly reduced in mass, the thermal images clearly showed a cooling, irregular ball of molten iron and nickel that had been under the miles of crust and upper mantle before the Phage ships had blasted them away. Jackson switched through the images rapidly, going back and forth to verify his suspicions.

"Captain!" Pitt snapped.

"Sorry, Admiral." Jackson straightened up. "Two things. The first is that while Xi'an is no longer a viable planet for habitation, they weren't able to completely destroy it. Second, the effort completely expended all three Charlies. They're now adrift near what's left of the planet."

"Show me." Marcum stepped around to where Jackson was standing.

Over the next few minutes Jackson showed his superiors that once the Phage ships had stopped firing, their thermal signatures began to reduce significantly, and they appeared to be flung out from the planet, no longer able to maintain their high velocity, low altitude orbit.

"If you'll notice, sir, the Charlie units seem incapable of controlled flight after firing their primary weapon," Jackson said when he looked over and saw Marcum was having trouble picking the details out of the grainy, washed out thermal stills. "My initial assessment would be that these are actually expendable weapons or that once they've fired, they need to be recharged."

"Thank you, Captain," Marcum said absently. "Orderly! Go fetch Dr. Allrest. He'll be cooling his heels in the main briefing room."

"At once, sir!" The young enlisted spacer near the door spun and walked briskly from the room.

"Allrest was supposed to be part of this evening's entertainment," Marcum explained. "He's been heading up the discovery project that was analyzing the pieces of the Alpha you first encountered. I wanted you to be briefed in a more comprehensive manner on the things we've learned about the Phage... but that will have to wait while we handle the immediate crisis."

"Sir, even at the high-warp flight sustainable by com drones, this data is weeks old," Jackson said. "No matter how quickly we decide on a course of action, and act here today, it will likely be too late to stop whatever the Phage has planned."

"You're suggesting that we just let them have their fun in the Xi'an System, Captain Wolfe?" Pitt glared at him from across the table.

Jackson took a deep breath before answering. "No, sir. My only point is that anything we were going to do should have been done a year ago. Starfleet should have already had a regular rotation in place for a blockade on the Frontier along the known incursion points used by the Phage."

"There are some… complications with that notion, Captain." Marcum raised a hand to silence Pitt. "That was going to be another part of your briefing. We'll fill you in later, but suffice it to say that if the current political climate doesn't change, CENTCOM won't have the units to establish a blockade."

Jackson let the last remark go without further comment, despite his burning curiosity about what the Chief of Staff had meant. Starfleet was a military organization with civilian oversight, something that was necessary and appropriate, but he had assumed once the Confederate Senate had recognized the threat and authorized CENTCOM to prepare their defenses that the political wrangling would have ceased.

While they waited for the civilian scientist, Jackson played around with the different angles they had of the encounter that resulted in the virtual destruction of an entire planet. The more he looked at it, the more he was convinced that the Phage had picked this as a test run.

There was one factor that kept punching holes in that theory, however, and that was the fact that the X-ray System had a planet of similar composition that the Phage would have bypassed to destroy Xi'an. But, they were aliens. His human logic and though processes had thus far given him almost no insight as to the motivations or desires of the Phage, other than that they seemed to enjoy wiping out human colonies.

"Ah, doctor," Marcum said, causing Jackson to look up. "Welcome."

Dr. Eugene Allrest was a thin man who projected a calm confidence that Jackson found appealing. Here was a man that looked like he had some answers.

"Captain Wolfe." Allrest smiled warmly and walked over to shake Jackson's hand. "It's a genuine pleasure to meet you in person. I must confess after watching all the logs from the *Blue Jacket* multiple times, I feel like I've known you for some time. So, what do we have here?" He indicated toward the repeating clip from the intel drone.

Over the next thirty minutes, Dr. Allrest quickly absorbed the data from the drone with a clinical dispassion that Jackson envied. While the scientist completely shut out all the activity around him, the two senior Fleet officers were becoming impatient and agitated.

"It's too bad the drone stopped recording so soon after the event," Allrest said finally. "The behavior afterward would have been helpful to plug into the predictive models. By the way, Captain, the data the *Ares* collected in the Zulu System was invaluable."

"Doctor." Pitt let loose the reins on his exasperation. "Your opinion on the Xi'an incident, if you please."

"Of course, Admiral," Allrest said. "This was almost certainly a simple weapons test. We've seen them take similar action when we were first introduced to the Bravo constructs."

"Can you take a guess as to why they traveled all the way from Zulu to Xi'an?" Jackson asked.

"I'd rather not," Allrest shook his head. "I have no idea why that particular planet was picked as their test site."

"Well this was all fairly useless," Pitt growled, walking to the back of the room where the coffee urns and sandwiches were.

"Sir, we need to deploy a network of drones along the Frontier immediately," Jackson said. "Specifically the warp lanes along the AU/Alliance corridor. We have to assume they'll follow along the same path as that first Alpha, which will put them quickly over still-populated planets like Podere and Nuovo Patria."

"We have the drones ready but no way to quickly deploy them." Pitt walked back with a glass of water. "They aren't capable of high-warp flight themselves, and all the Prowlers are otherwise engaged."

"The *Ares* can get out there faster than the Prowlers, sir," Jackson said. "We can take the first load, and then the Ninth can finish the job once the CO situation is settled."

"You're not going anywhere, Captain," Pitt said. "Let's get him up to speed on what's happening in the Senate, and then we can task the Ninth Squadron with deploying the intel drones."

"With all due respect, Admiral... the Phage have just deployed and tested a new super weapon," Jackson said. "I urge you to reconsider—"

"Stow it, Wolfe," Pitt said. "You need to be made aware of the situation here on Haven. It's just as crucial we solve this as it is that we respond to the latest move by the Phage, and I can't afford to have you flying off half-cocked every time these aliens do something unexpected."

"Of course, Admiral."

The remainder of the evening, Jackson was briefed by the technical and research staff about all the developments that had been made concerning the Phage. He even managed to grab a few sandwiches in between presenters. The technical portion was impressive. Tsuyo and CENTCOM scientists had made great strides in understanding the physical makeup of Phage constructs and how to defeat them. The new Shrike penetrating nuke, as effective as it was, wasn't the only thing they were working on.

What concerned Jackson the most, however, was the obvious lack of anything remotely close to discovering who the Phage were and why they were wiping out human colonies. He was shocked to learn that they'd captured individual Bravo units alive in an incredibly daring operation by CIS, but it was to no avail. None of the units were responsive once they were brought back and interrogated in every conceivable manner.

The Bravo would just sit motionless in the holding pen. In the end, all four captured units were destroyed and studied. There was one vital breakthrough, however, and it was independently verified by the data the *Ares* had brought back from the *Brooklands* as well as recorded first hand in the Zulu System: the Phage had a hive mind.

Data from past engagements had shown that as Bravo units were eliminated from a battle, the Phage tactics would become erratic and ineffective. While this had been documented, its significance wasn't fully realized until the *Brooklands* observed the broken Phage attack in Xi'an coalesce once again the moment more units appeared.

It seemed they established a local, aggregate processing apparatus wherever they were when within range of each other. The larger the group, the more complex the behavior. When the *Ares* recorded the actions of the hundreds of constructs in the Zulu System, CENTCOM Research and Science Division was able to say unequivocally that the Phage were utilizing a shared "consciousness," for lack of a better term.

There was still some argument about what was the perfect number of Phage units that could be in such a group before it became unwieldy and unresponsive, but Jackson had begun to tune out at that point in the briefing. The horror of having to devise tactics against an enemy that, literally, shared the same mind was making his head swim. How could you hope to defend against that, much less mount an effective counteroffensive?

Even if the enemy tactics were flawed, the fact that they could execute them simultaneously and without debate or delay would always give them an advantage over Terran fleets with individual intellects and egos commanding each ship, to say nothing of the significant com delays created by distance.

The briefings mercifully ended with the technical staff promising to try and determine the range and, if possible, the method for the apparent telepathy employed by the Phage. Jackson was taken back to guest quarters that were on the grounds of the Chief of Staff's residence, eventually falling into a restless sleep that was plagued by nightmares. In his mind's eye, he saw hundreds of Phage Alphas, all of them thinking and acting as one, crossed the expanse of space, slowly erasing humanity planet by planet.

Chapter 10

Jackson was already awake the next morning when a soft, single knock at his door let him know his uniform had been dropped off. He'd given it to the orderly last night to have cleaned and pressed when he discovered he wouldn't be returning to his ship but rather accompanying Chief of Staff Marcum to a hearing in the Senate regarding the trouble in New America and Britannia.

He would have been more enthusiastic about fighting the Phage in an EVA suit and a pocket knife, but it was made perfectly clear to him that his attendance was not optional.

"Good, you're ready," Admiral Pitt said as Jackson strode into the foyer of the main building. "The shuttle will be here within the hour. I'd advise you to grab something to eat since these things tend to run over by quite a bit."

In a little under an , they were all climbing onto the military shuttle, a large, four engine affair that was purpose-built to ferry dignitaries around Haven in comfort, though none of the men and women in Fleet dress uniforms looked particularly happy. Jackson was just thankful he was going as an observer this time. Even after his exoneration by Marcum and the President himself, he had still been dragged before countless Senate committee hearings and made to dance so that the politicians could be seen taking the Phage threat seriously on the news broadcasts back home.

As the shuttle approached the Capital Jackson craned his head to get a look at the enormous domed structure of the Senate, the word given to both the building and the body it housed. It was loosely modeled after the Roman Pantheon as it was the only historical structure the original government on Haven could seem to agree on. The thought was to be inclusive of everyone by not copying the existing seats of power on Earth like the Capitol in Washington, D.C. or the Kremlin. Jackson always welcomed the sight of the Senate, since it was one of the few buildings left on Haven originally built by settlers from Earth.

"We'll be in the gallery on the main floor," Marcum warned them as the shuttle began its descent. "Please remember that you'll have a news camera on you at all times. Let's act like professionals. No eye rolling, no laughing, and for God's sake no picking in your nose or ears."

The last comment elicited a handful of polite chuckles.

"We've all been through these before." Marcum continued. "Let the politicians put on their show, and then the real power brokers will make deals behind closed doors. There are two enclaves making all the noise, and hopefully today, we'll figure out what concessions they're trying to wring out of Haven."

Jackson was only half listening since this was, almost verbatim, the exact briefing they'd gotten before the shuttle had landed to pick them up. Was Marcum so nervous because of what he knew and wasn't telling them, or because of what he didn't know?

Once they'd been ushered in through the security checkpoint and shown to the section they'd be sitting in, it didn't take long before the delegates from the five enclaves began filing in, as well as the representatives from Haven and, surprisingly, two observers from Earth. The birthplace of humanity had refused entry into the Confederacy so long ago, a choice that they were continually punished for since, as Haven made sure they never forgot their place.

Just as Jackson was about to ask if it was normal for his home planet to even have representatives on Haven, the swelling score of the official anthem of the Terran Confederacy started, and everyone solemnly stood and faced the banner hanging at the back of the immense hall. As the last notes died out, there was one final surprise for everyone as President Caleb McKellar, decked out in the crimson robes of his office, climbed the steps near the dais and took his seat. A sitting president very rarely attended a full assembly of the Senate during their tenure, if ever.

"Please remain standing as we welcome the President of the Terran Confederacy... the honorable Caleb Sasha McKellar!" the Sergeant at Arms boomed from the back of the hall.

President McKellar stood, bowed, and waved that everyone be seated. Once the crowd had settled in their seats and the murmurs had ceased, a wispy man in the traditional black robes worn by the Senate came to the podium.

"The floor recognizes the honorable Jespen Wilcox from the planet Columbiana, New America enclave." He set down a small gavel and tottered off the dais. He was replaced by a rotund, flushed-faced senator who marched up to the podium and slapped his tile down loudly, eyeing the assembly in what was unmistakably open aggression.

"This should be fucking good," Admiral Pitt muttered beside Jackson, his lips not moving.

"Thank you, Speaker Graves," Wilcox said. "Honorable delegates, esteemed guests... much of our deliberations today are to be geared toward discovery—and to pull the cloak of secrecy from the events we are being told threaten our very existence. I will not draw this out any longer than I need to. The Chair would like to call Dr. Eugene Allrest to the floor."

Dr. Allrest, not seeming surprised by the summons, walked onto the floor from a side chamber. He was dressed in an expensive, if slightly archaic, suit and looked completely at ease as he sat at the table facing the dais.

"Thank you for coming, Doctor," Wilcox said as if the summons he had issued left Allrest any choice. "I've asked you here to give your expert testimony in regards to what many are calling a *war* with the first intelligent species we've met besides ourselves."

"That's technically incorrect, Senator—"

"The first that has shown any indication that it wishes to interact with us." Wilcox corrected himself quickly, waving off Allrest's protest. "As the project leader of what the military has dubbed the Phage Discovery Project, a fairly innocuous name, you have been privy to an overview of not only the effort Starfleet has put into destroying these aliens but what we've been able to discover about them so far. Is this a fair assessment?"

"Yes, Senator."

"Very well, then." Wilcox clasped his hands behind his back. "Could you enlighten this assembly as to how your efforts have fared in making contact with the civilization we've colloquially been calling the *Phage?*"

"Senator, we have not captured a significant enough number of Phage constructs—"

"No, Doctor." Wilcox leaned forward suddenly and grabbed the podium. "I'm asking about the effort to send an envoy to the aliens and attempt direct communication. You *have* made an attempt to simply talk to them, have you not?"

Allrest now looked like a frightened animal in a spotlight. "I have simply performed the analysis required of me, Senator. I don't dictate strategy or policy to Starfleet."

"Let me ask it a different way," Wilcox said. "At any time, did Starfleet R&D or Science Section ask you to develop a plan for first contact?"

"No."

"Is it possible that this *war* is simply a misunderstanding? That a single destroyer captain of questionable character may have put our two species on a collision course with a shoot-first-ask-questions-never attitude?" Wilcox was now obviously playing to the room, barely even looking at the doctor.

"I respectfully refuse to answer the question," Allrest said. "The entire line of inquiry is speculation and, as I understood it, I was asked here to speak on technical matters."

"Of course, of course." Wilcox smirked to the delegation from Britannia.

Jackson clenched the armrests of his seat so hard his skin squeaked against the varnished wood.

"Relax, Captain," Pitt whispered, leaning over. "We were expecting this. We're going to return fire. Don't worry."

Jackson nodded and forced himself to look relaxed and unconcerned as he again became painfully aware that the news cameras in the room were likely focused on him during that last line of questioning.

Wilcox grilled Allrest for another thirty minutes, nearly all of the questions having nothing to do with scientific fact and everything to do with CENTCOM's response to the threat. More specifically, the questions were just a pretense for the senator to grandstand and insinuate that Starfleet was little more than a rogue military agency out on the Frontier starting wars for their own benefit.

Mercifully, the inquisition ended after a few half-hearted questions from two other senators, and a visibly shaken Dr. Allrest was led away from the table. A brief recess was called, and the table was set up for the next person to give their testimony.

Pitt grabbed Jackson's shoulder and pushed him back down when he tried to stand. "The press is circling like sharks out there. I'll grab you a water, but you stay put."

"Yes, sir." Jackson sat back down and ignored some openly hostile looks he was getting.

Senator Wilcox hadn't mentioned him by name, but there was little doubt in anyone's mind to whom he was referring when he accused some "Fleet hothead" of launching an unprovoked attack. The hell of it was that technically, Wilcox was right. Jackson *had* opened fire with the *Blue Jacket's* forward laser battery before the Alpha had melted them off the prow with a single plasma burst.

As far as he was concerned, that was all a legal technicality since he'd encountered two lifeless planets that used to host human colonies before he'd finally caught up to the big son of a bitch. But, governments tended to be quite enamored with legal technicalities when they served a purpose. Not for the first time, he wished he was back on the bridge of the *Ares*.

"The Chair welcomes Central Command Chief of Staff, Fleet Admiral Joseph Marcum." Wilcox's tone left little doubt as to the senator's opinion of the Fleet officer.

"Senator." Marcum nodded to Wilcox. "Esteemed delegates."

"Admiral, you heard the testimony from Dr. Allrest, did you not?"

"I did." Marcum leaned forward slightly, looking completely within his element.

"I'll get right to the point, Admiral," Wilcox said. "Many within this body have become concerned recently that Starfleet has dragged humanity into a war with another species by mistake. Some are even questioning the motivations of CENTCOM, given that the projected budget analysis begins phasing out a militarized Starfleet within the next twenty years."

"What, exactly, are you implying, Senator?" Marcum asked.

"Do I need to spell it out for you, Admiral?"

"I think, for the sake of the official record, that it would be best if you did, sir," Marcum said.

"I am giving voice to the concern that CENTCOM has taken a convenient opportunity to justify the existence of a bloated bureaucracy that supports an unneeded and generally unwanted fleet of sinfully expensive warships and their crews," Wilcox said. "With this war coming when it has—a war that hasn't threatened us in the nearly four years it's been going on, I might add—Haven and Tsuyo Corporation are now fully justified it maintaining the status quo and withholding technology and intelligence from the other Terran enclaves—"

"Objection!"

"The Senator from Haven does not have the floor!" Wilcox said loudly. "Admiral... would you care to address these allegations?"

Jackson knew politics at least well enough to realize he was watching a performance. Wilcox wasn't actually addressing Marcum, he was playing to the cameras and making sure his outrageous charges were implanted in the public consciousness regardless of their validity or even if he actually believed them. If Marcum couldn't answer with a definitively negative response, no matter how absurd the accusation, it would be spun to the people of New America as a sort of admission of guilt.

"The charges are fairly ridiculous," Marcum said thoughtfully. "But I will, of course, provide an answer to the assembly to the best of my ability."

"We look forward to your answer," Wilcox said.

Marcum waved his aide forward and whispered instructions into his ear, holding the mute button on his microphone as he did.

"If you'll indulge me, Senator, I've prepared a presentation in anticipation of this line of questioning." Marcum stood up from the table. "Please be aware that the imagery you're about to see will be highly disturbing. This will be the first time they've been declassified in order to show the general public. Even for members of the Senate Intelligence Subcommittee, a lot of these will be new as we've just received the intel ourselves."

"Please get to the point, Admiral." Wilcox looked annoyed now that Marcum had taken the initiative.

"Steward, please activate the chamber screens." Marcum ignored Wilcox. "Ladies and gentleman, members of the press... I'm about to show you a brief compilation of imagery collected during our engagements with the Phage. I will provide pertinent facts to accompany the imagery, and we'll be reviewing these in chronological order. If I may, I'd ask that you reserve all questions until I've completed the presentation."

Over the next ninety minutes, there were gasps of shock and cries of outrage as images of the Phage's path of destruction were paraded on the screens. Marcum calmly narrated the events as they unfolded, culminating in the footage of the new super weapon destroying what was left of Xi'an. Those same cries of outrage were then tinged with fear as the war finally hit home for the people who had looked at it as a "Frontier problem" for the previous few years.

When the footage from Pike's Broadhead of Jackson driving the *Blue Jacket* into the first Alpha unit played, and Marcum explained that he alone had remained on the ship to finish off the threat, the looks cast in his direction were no longer angry, but awed. Jackson simply felt ill as he again watched his old ship in her final, glorious moments.

"As you can see, the threat is very real, and it was brought to us by an inexplicable, terrible enemy," Marcum said. "Despite the insinuations to the contrary, we did not ask for this war, nor are we particularly excited to fight it… but what we want is irrelevant right now. Thank you." Without waiting to be dismissed, Marcum turned and walked away from the table as the lights came back up and showed a bewildered Senator Wilcox standing at the podium, gripping the gavel in both hands.

"These proceedings are adjourned for the day," he said when he noticed that everyone was staring at him. "We will reconvene tomorrow."

****

"Look at Wilcox... I've never seen someone so pissed." Admiral Pitt laughed quietly as they all took their seats again the next morning.

Jackson looked over at Senator Wellington. The man was positively seething. The previous night, the news coverage had not been kind to the senator from New America as Marcum's surprise presentation had pulled the rug right out from under him. Wilcox still had the floor from the previous day, so he slowly climbed the dais, watching impassively as delegates and media reporters slowly filed in.

Jackson had stayed in the capital the night before, having been met by the party of observers from Earth and begged to come and speak to the rest of their group. After dinner, he'd even been convinced to record a few interviews to be aired on Earth's various news outlets. As the evening had worn on. he'd become exceedingly uncomfortable with the adoration and lavish praise his fellow Earthers heaped upon him. At the best of times, Jackson considered himself a victim of circumstances. At worst, he felt little more than a fraud who had gotten exceedingly lucky with an impossible gamble that still ended up getting a sizable number of his crew killed.

"The assembly will now come to order!" Wilcox's booming voice shook Jackson out of his reverie as it echoed throughout the domed chamber. The delegates' private conversations tapered off, and they looked on with interest. Wilcox had been embarrassed badly the day before, and there were more than a few friendly wagers as to how he would respond.

"What I have to say today will not take long. After much deliberation, and with the authority vested in me by the New American regional government, I officially withdraw our support from the Confederacy in the war with the species known as the Phage."

The chamber erupted in loud, chaotic conversation as Wilcox stood passively, letting his words sink in.

"Furthermore," he continued once they'd settled down, "as per conditions set forth in article six, sections two and three of the Unified Defense Accords, we are not only withholding financial and material support, we are recalling all Fourth Fleet ships to enforce our own boundary defense. As such, those ships are now withdrawn from Central Command's authority and cannot be utilized for their war effort."

Now the room exploded in angry shouts and curses hurled at the Senator who, for his part, gave the oddly impassive Admiral Marcum a tight lipped smile.

"Let's go." Marcum stood suddenly, sending his aides scrambling to collect his haphazardly scattered belongings. Jackson, Pitt, and a handful of junior officers followed Marcum out as he bulldozed his way through the pack of jostling reporters squawking for a reaction or a quote. Marcum wouldn't be deterred, however, and didn't slow his pace until he was climbing into the air shuttle that had begun to start its engines at the sight of the storming chief of staff.

"The fix was in," Pitt said to Jackson as the shuttle's engines spooled up and hauled them into the air. "Wilcox had already been told to withdraw their support no matter how the proceedings yesterday had gone. He wasn't even making a good show of it... even the new generation com drones can't get to Columbiana and back to Haven in a single day."

"I just don't understand the motivation or the politics behind this move." Jackson's stomach tied in knots as he realized the mighty Fourth Fleet battle cruisers were now out of the fight.

"There's a lot you've likely missed being on a starship for so many years, Captain." Marcum seemed to have calmed down a bit as they flew back to his residence. "For over a decade, Haven has had a harder and harder time trying to keep the enclaves from splintering off into their own sovereign states. The only thing holding them back is the fact Tsuyo Corporate is still here, and they know if they want to be included in the distribution of newly released technology, they need to come and kiss the ring."

"Rather blunt, but essentially correct," Admiral Pitt said. "There's been a lot of resentment simmering under the surface for many years over Haven acting as the gatekeeper to Tsuyo R&D. They've all tried to duplicate and improve upon the tech, but without a starting point, it's been a futile effort, and none have been brazen enough to try dismantling one of their own ships for fear of taking that final step and incurring the wrath of the Tsuyo board."

"I suppose this was all just harmless gamesmanship before Xi'an." Jackson stared out the window.

"Indeed," Pitt said. "But for right now, we've still got work to do. Captain, I want you to task three ships from Ninth Squadron to begin deploying intel drones across the Frontier systems. Preferably the three ships that still have captains."

"Yes, sir," Jackson said crisply, thankful to be back in the realm he knew. "The Ninth arrived in orbit over Haven yesterday."

"Have you given any thought to who should take command of the *Icarus*?"

"I wasn't aware my input was requested, sir," Jackson said.

"You're technically in command of the Ninth," Pitt said. "Normally, command of a starship is subject to a specific approval process, involving the Senate, but given the circumstances, I think we need to take matters into our own hands. How about Captain Lee?"

"The CO of the *Brooklands*?" Jackson hesitated. He wasn't sure if he was expected to just agree with his superior's recommendation or if his opinion was actually wanted.

"Spit it out, Wolfe," Marcum snapped. "If there's a reason you don't like Lee for the position, speak up."

"Captain Lee is a fine CO and accorded himself very well during the second battle of Xi'an," Jackson said, "but the *Brooklands* is a missile cruiser. Lee deserves some recognition, but he isn't a destroyer man. I'm not sure right now is the best time to let him sink or swim on the bridge of the newest class of warship."

"Noted," Pitt said with a nod. "I assume you already have someone in mind?"

****

"Absolutely not, sir!"

"I may have given the impression I was asking, Commander." Jackson leaned back in his chair, secretly enjoying the moment. "This was not a request."

"Captain, I thought I'd been clear when I said I didn't feel I was ready," Celesta Wright said emphatically.

Jackson had called her into his office the moment he'd been ferried back up to Jericho Station and made his way back to the *Ares*. He'd already gotten the necessary approvals from Black Fleet's command authority, and he wanted to get Celesta into the *Icarus* and underway before anyone had a chance to hold up her transfer and put their second cousin's roommate, whom they owed a favor, in the chair.

"Commander... Celesta, you *are* ready for this," Jackson said firmly. "If it makes you feel any better, this is a provisional posting. You'll retain your current rank, and if the *Icarus* makes it back in one piece then, there will be a formal review board."

"I'm not sure I'm entirely comfortable with the gallows humor just now, sir," Celesta said, stood to pace the length of the office.

"Not a whole lot is changing," Jackson said. "You'll still be in the formation and taking orders from me, but you'll be doing it from the bridge of your own ship. This has been your goal since you first stepped foot on the *Blue Jacket*, and now you're being handed one of the most advanced starships in the fleet."

"Stepping on a lot of toes in the process, I'm sure." Celesta fell back into her chair.

"Not especially." Jackson shook his head. "Captain Levitt and his XO were both yanked off the ship as soon as she entered orbit over Haven. You'll have a full commander for a chief engineer, but you'll outrank everyone on the command staff. Not to mention the respect you've earned within the squadron for your role during the initial incursion."

"Who will be taking my place here?" she asked, signaling for the first time in the conversation that she understood she *would* be departing for the *Icarus*.

"The obvious choice." Jackson shrugged. "I'm moving Davis to XO, acting only since her current rank will require an exemption for that posting. The good news there is that she can still perform her job at OPS when we go to general quarters."

"I'm not sure I like what that says about my usefulness aboard the *Ares*, sir."

"You know what I mean, Commander." Jackson waved her off. "When we're at battle stations, the two of us are more of a redundancy on the bridge."

"I suppose the next obvious question is when do I report for duty?" Celesta clenched and unclenched her hands in an unconscious gesture Jackson recognized as meaning she was anxious.

"The *Icarus* is being towed into dock as we speak." Jackson smiled. "We'll be performing the change of command ceremony as soon as the airlock opens."

Chapter 11

"Incoming message from the *Ares*, si—ma'am," the com officer said.

"Send it to my station, Lieutenant Sieffert."

The message icon on Celesta's display lit up. It was the fourth day of her new command, and she felt like she was settling in nicely. The crew didn't seem too shaken up over the change of command, and she'd taken the time to try and get to know as many as possible.

As soon as she took command, CENTCOM ordered the *Ares* and *Icarus* out of the docks, and ever since, then they'd been circling Haven in an extremely high orbit to stay out of the way of the constant traffic to and from the mammoth station.

Captain Wright,

> *Standby for an intel package coming up from Admiral Pitt's office. Our orders will be included in the transmission. I've not been given any indication as to what assignments may be coming to us or if we're even flying out together. Execute your orders without any confirmation from me, no matter how unusual they may sound. Good luck.*

> *Senior Captain Wolfe*
> *CO, TCS Ares*

"Ma'am, another transmission incoming. This one is a fairly large data packet," Lieutenant Sieffert said. "It's marked as classified, your eyes only."

"Very good, Lieutenant," Celesta stood. "Send it to the terminal in my office."

"Yes, ma'am."

After the theatrics that had been played out in the Senate in the weeks prior, she'd been expecting orders to mobilize for the last two days. Three of the five Ninth Squadron ships had already departed the system, the flight under the command of Captain Forrest. She'd reached out to Celesta to congratulate her on the posting just before the *Artemis's* beacon vanished as the ship transitioned to warp.

Even though she had been told that the transmission had come from Admiral Pitt's office, she was still surprised once she entered her command codes and unpackaged all the content. There was a video message included in all the data files from the Admiral himself.

"Captain Wolfe, Captain Wright... I wish I had better news for the two of you, but it looks like the Ares *and* Icarus *will be departing Haven in the opposite direction of the Frontier. As you know, New America has declared Fourth Fleet as no longer answerable to CENTCOM. What you don't know is that they're also holding Black Fleet ships hostage at the New Sierra Shipyards.*

"Both full battlegroups still assigned to the Black Fleet had been in Sierra's docks for the last eighteen months, getting refitted with the new auto-mag cannons and upgraded launch tubes for the new generation Shrikes. Apparently when the recall order directing them to return to Haven came through official channels, the ships were seized by crews at the shipyards and the crews essentially taken hostage." The Admiral's face looked haggard and drawn compared to the short time ago when Celesta had seen him on the news vid.

"That's not the extent of the good news, either. Britannia had apparently been working with New America closely on the resolution to withhold support for the war. They've given us a preliminary warning that they have recalled all First Fleet ships. Not to bore you with the politics, but it seems the two enclaves the furthest from the fighting seem to feel this might be more of an opportunity than a risk.

"So your mission: we need those Black Fleet ships released from New Sierra. Within an hour of this transmission, intersystem cargo shuttles will be launched from Jericho to deliver the necessary personnel to both your ships. Captain Wolfe, I'm trusting your judgment. Execute your orders as you see fit. I know fighting Fourth Fleet instead of the Phage is as distasteful a notion as there is right now, but these are the cards we've been dealt. Also, be aware that not all First and Fourth Fleet captains are honoring the recall order. CIS tells us that there are more than a few rogue ships inbound to Haven. Just be aware that not every ship you face is guaranteed to be hostile.

"Good luck, Captains. You're going to need as much of it as you can muster between the two of you to pull this off. Pitt out."

****

"You can't be fucking serious!" Jackson shouted to the ceiling of his office as the video of Admiral Pitt winked out. How could things have spiraled out of control so quickly? Wasn't a hostile alien species trying to exterminate them on sight bad enough? He rubbed at his temples furiously before jabbing a finger at the button that activated the intercom.

"Lieutenant Davis, please report to my office," he said as calmly as he could manage.

"Yes, sir?" Lieutenant Jillian Davis asked as she walked in after he keyed open the hatch.

"Close the hatch and have a seat, Lieutenant," Jackson said. "How are you adjusting to your additional duties?"

"Frankly, I was a bit overwhelmed at first, Captain," she said. "But I'm adjusting. There won't be any issues when it comes time to get underway."

"I didn't expect there would be," Jackson said with a faint smile. "Watch this." He spun his monitor and replayed the video message from Admiral Pitt. Her mouth dropped open as it finished, and afterward, she simply sat there silently.

"I thought the mutiny aboard the *Blue Jacket* would be the worst thing I ever witnessed in my career," she said finally. "A civil war on the eve of a major offensive by our enemy certainly tops that... sir."

"I'm going to tell you the same thing I told Commander Wright when she first walked into my office as XO... when we're meeting privately, there's no need to adhere so strictly to customs and courtesies," Jackson said. "I'll need your honest assessment of things, and I'll need it without all the 'sirs' and 'with all due respects' getting in the way. Understood?"

"Yes, sir," she said before she could catch herself, grinning ruefully at the slip.

"We have a whole mini armada of cargo shuttles heading up from Jericho as we speak," Jackson said. "I'm going to be down at the cargo dock with Major Ortiz inspecting the incoming material and personnel. You'll be on the bridge. I want you sitting in the command seat, so call up another operator for the OPS station. Make sure you funnel me any information you think I'll need to know, just like you always do anyway. Any questions?"

"No, sir."

"Good," Jackson said. "Dismissed, Lieutenant."

****

"So who the fuck is CENTCOM sending up that they think we can't survive without?" Chief Green stood with Jackson and Major Ortiz as Commander Juarez's crew prepped the massive cargo airlock to cycle when the first shuttle made hard dock.

"It'll either be a bunch of tech weenies who aren't used to life aboard a starship, or it will be a pile of Colonial Guardsmen from Haven," Ortiz said.

"Which would you prefer, Major?" Green asked.

"Neither." Ortiz shrugged. "At least the techies keep to themselves, though. The guardsmen will be nothing but targets of opportunity to my Marines. I'll be writing incident reports from here all the way to the Frontier. By the way, Captain, why would we be taking on a bunch of knuckle draggers?"

"Where did you hear we're gaining infantry, Major?" Jackson decided to ignore the derogatory term for regular soldiers.

"I hear things," Ortiz said evasively. "We're not on com lockdown, and sixteen shuttles loading up and departing Jericho all at once tends to set tongues wagging."

"We're about to find out, sir," the chief said as the lights around the airlock cycled from green to red, and then back to green as the intermediate space between the two hatches was quickly flooded with atmosphere. When the *Ares's* inner hatch swung ponderously up out of the way, none of them were expecting what walked out.

"Fuck me sideways with a stick," Chief Green let out softly. "Are they who I think they are?"

"Indeed they are, Chief," Jackson said, enjoying Ortiz's slack jawed stare. "Starfleet Special Forces. Two full teams of NOVAs."

"Shit," Ortiz muttered as he followed Jackson to greet their new passengers. "I'll still be writing incident reports, just for a different reason."

"Captain Wolfe." One of the men in unadorned black fatigues came to attention and snapped a salute. "Lieutenant Commander Amiri Essa and NOVA Team Four reporting for duty."

Jackson afforded him the respect of coming to attention himself and returning the salute.

"Welcome aboard the *Ares*, Lieutenant Commander," he said. "This is Major Jeza Ortiz. He'll be taking care of you and your men."

"Of course, sir," Essa said. "Major, I have twenty-four men and their gear I need to get off the shuttle and clear of the area so the remaining seven shuttles can dock."

"This way, Lieutenant Commander." Ortiz shook the Fleet officer's hand before waving the rest of the NOVA team over to muster by the hatch leading out of the cargo bay.

On the *Icarus*, an identical introduction was likely taking place with equally astounded reactions. Out of the roughly twenty-one million people serving in the Confederate Armed Forces, there were only ten NOVA teams, each with twenty-five members. The best of the best of the best before even being selected, and then they were sharpened into a lethal instrument by grueling and often unorthodox training methods.

Unfortunately, NOVA were trained to fight other humans, so despite the intrigue of meeting living legends, Jackson was quite unhappy to have them aboard his ship. Their presence only reminded him that, despite the threat amassing along the Frontier, his ship was flying in the wrong direction and preparing to fight the wrong enemy.

The next two shuttles contained nothing but routine cargo for the *Ares* and the NOVA team that had just come aboard, but the fourth shuttle contained a few more surprise passengers.

"Dr. Tanaka." Jackson came forward and shook the hand of the Tsuyo scientist that had introduced him to the *Starwolf*-class starships. "Welcome back aboard the *Ares*. What brings you out here?"

"Captain Wolfe, a pleasure to see you again," Tanaka said. "I'm here to oversee the installation of some new systems that weren't ready for deployment when the new destroyers left the shipyard."

"New systems?" Jackson frowned. "Doctor, I'm not sure now would be the best time to install and test new hardware. The ship is about to fly into potentially hostile space."

"These are already tested, Captain." Tanaka argued. "Just not installed. At the time, it was more important to allow you and your crews as much time with the new ships as possible so all the software, wiring, and control subsystems for the new hardware is already installed on the *Ares*. We will simply be plugging in the new boxes and providing your crew minimal training on their operation."

"Very well." Jackson still wasn't convinced. "Coordinate your efforts with Chief Engineer Singh. I will authorize no changes to this ship until he clears them."

"Of course, Captain." Tanaka bowed his head slightly. "If you will excuse me."

The civilian doctor walked out of the cargo hold, punching an authorization code into the pad by the hatch to gain entry to the ship. It was entirely likely the scientist, who had been instrumental in the design of the *Starwolf*-class ships, had a higher level of access to the ship's systems than he did.

"Excuse me, Captain Wolfe?"

Jackson turned as another civilian that had been aboard Tanaka's shuttle approached him. "Dr. Allrest?"

"Yes, sir." Allrest looked around nervously.

"What can I do for you, Doctor?"

"Is there somewhere we might speak in private?" Allrest asked.

Jackson gestured for the doctor to follow him over to the office, just behind the dockmaster's control room.

"I've come here to give you this," Allrest said once Jackson secured the hatch, handing him a generic looking data card.

"Couldn't this have simply been transmitted, Doctor?" Jackson asked. "Take this in the spirit in which it's intended, but you're a little too important to risk losing in a freak shuttle accident because you were personally ferrying a data card up here."

"My com transmissions are being closely monitored," Allrest said. "I also couldn't risk giving you this while on the surface of Haven, since the CIS has ears everywhere."

Jackson looked down at the data card, now intrigued. "What's on this?"

"The truth about the Phage," Allrest said simply. "And more. I went through great trouble and copied this information at great risk to myself and family, so please take it seriously. I convinced Dr. Tanaka to bring me up under the guise of wanting to see the *Ares* in person so I could get it into your hands. There has been much information on the Phage suppressed as well as secret strategies to deal with the problem that I feel will only draw resources away from the war effort."

"I'm not sure what to say to this," Jackson said. "If what you're saying is accurate, I would assume we now share the risk equally for processing this information. Why trust me?"

"I don't think there is anyone else I can trust, Captain," Allrest said. "You've already proven yourself a man unafraid to make the ultimate sacrifice. Please... just look over the information, and do what you feel you must. Now, I need to get back to the shuttle before it departs."

"Perhaps I should have an orderly give you a tour of the ship, and you can catch the last shuttle back to Jericho," Jackson suggested. "A tour of the cargo dock control room won't be very convincing if someone is aboard these shuttles that can report on your actions."

"Yes, of course." Allrest nodded emphatically. "Thank you again, Captain."

Jackson escorted the scientist over to where an enlisted spacer from the com department met them and began a quick walking tour of the destroyer. The young spacer, taking his job very seriously, was gesturing expansively to parts of the ship as they walked down the main starboard access tube, completely oblivious to the fact his charge wasn't paying him the least bit of attention.

****

"All shuttles have cleared our orbital path, and the dock master is reporting all cargo has been secured," Lieutenant Davis said as Jackson walked back onto the bridge.

He'd secured the data card Eugene Allrest had given him in his personal vault but had yet to view its contents.

"Very good, Lieutenant," he said as he sat down. "Tell Engineering to begin prestart on the main engines. Coms! Signal the *Icarus* to prepare to get underway."

"Aye, sir."

It was only twenty minutes later when Engineering reported the plasma chambers on the main engines were hot, and the com officer verified the *Icarus* was ready to fly. Jackson ordered the formation to break orbit and set a course for the DeLonges jump point, the most direct route to the star system in which the New Sierra Shipyards orbited one of the two inhabited planets in that star system.

As the *Ares* accelerated to transition velocity, Jackson was painfully aware he was also flying toward a potential showdown with a sizable armada of Fourth Fleet ships—with nothing more than two destroyers. He could only hope that the New American captains wouldn't actually fire on a pair of Terran ships.

Chapter 12

"So what has Dr. Tanaka been installing on my ship?" Jackson asked as he picked at the remains of his dinner.

It had been three days since they transitioned out of the Alpha Centauri System, and the warp flight routine was already starting to drag.

"Currently we're installing the control systems for a new type of sensor," Daya said. "It will work in concert with our radar, LIDAR, and optical sensors to give us a better picture of what's in a system. You want the details or the broad strokes?"

"Aim for somewhere in between those two." Although Jackson had studied engineering at the Academy, Daya's technical explanations usually went a bit over his head.

"Well, the long and short of it is that it can detect gravitational waves of objects in a system." Daya tossed his napkin onto the tray in front of him. "No matter how stealthy a ship is, or how dark it's running, everything that has mass will cause ripples."

"How the hell can something be sensitive enough to detect that while being bolted to a starship underway?" Jackson asked skeptically.

"Because it isn't," Daya said. "To set up the system, you deploy a series of twelve satellites that will fly themselves into a formation and deploy a laser interferometer network that can detect gravimetric waves on any axis. The data is then routed back to the

Ares where the computers we're installing now will interpret it and update the tactical computers."

"Clever," Jackson conceded. "They've been using a similar method to map deep space anomalies for centuries. I wasn't aware they could be sensitive enough to detect something as small as a ship so close to a star's influence."

"The latest and greatest from the Tsuyo think tanks," Daya said. "Dr. Tanaka seems to think this is a great advantage, but I'm not so sure. At best, it will give us marginally more warning than our conventional sensors."

"Why do you say that?"

"Gravity waves move at the speed of light, the same as radio waves," Daya said. "Theoretically, in a best case scenario, it will be twice as fast as radar and slightly slower than an optical sensor."

"Yes," Jackson said slowly, "but a radar can't resolve a target at long range with a single pulse, and the degree of coverage we have with the optical sensors is woefully limited. If this gives us at least a warning on what direction we should be looking in, it might not be a total waste. But deploying and collecting twelve individual satellites isn't exactly practical in most applications."

"I told him that," Daya said. "But he lives in a bubble. Real-world applications seem to be a bit of a mystery to him. There's also a new instrument that can more accurately measure the energy output of an object like a Phage ship and a couple other little tweaks and upgrades to the existing systems."

"Begin putting together a training package for my operators," Jackson said. "I want it to be only on switchology. We don't have time for them to learn the theory of operation on a bunch of brand new systems.

They're already overwhelmed just operating the new class of ship. Get the raw materials to Lieutenant Davis by end of first watch tomorrow."

"Yes, sir." Daya tossed his captain a mocking salute.

Fortunately, they were eating in the Captain's Mess alone, so he didn't have to reprimand his friend. Again. The pair sat in silence for a few moments before Jackson gave voice to something that had been bothering him since he'd taken command of the *Ares*.

"Are you as underwhelmed with the level of Tsuyo tech on the *Ares* as I am?"

Daya's eyebrows shot up to his hairline. "You can't be serious. This ship is generations ahead of the old *Raptor*-class—"

"True, it is," Jackson said slowly. "But there aren't really any major advancements, nothing *different*. This ship boasts the best from Tsuyo R&D, but there isn't anything that isn't just a smaller, more efficient version of what we had on the *Blue Jacket*. In some cases, that's not even a good thing. The main engines are more powerful, but their total plasma capacity is decreased from the older MPDs, and they don't respond as quickly. The lasers take less power, but the practical range of the projectors is still so pitiful they're not really useful for anything other than point defense. The list goes on, but the point is that I was expecting something revolutionary in either propulsion or weapons. A smaller fusion warhead with a hardened nosecone was about the best we got."

"I've never looked at it that way," Daya said after a few seconds of silence. "I've been so enamored with smaller reactors, smaller warp components, and improved gravimetric generators, that I didn't really look at them as the same thing we already had."

"It's just something that's been bothering me since Tanaka told me that humans didn't actually invent the warp drive." Jackson waved the thought aside.

"That's something else I was unaware of." Daya now looked quite distressed. "I was taught that the first generation warp drive was a Tsuyo invention from the mid-twenty first century."

"According to the doctor, they found a crashed alien ship in the Solar System and adapted the technology." Jackson idly spun his water glass. "I suppose that's what bothers me: even though everything on this ship is more advanced, it's essentially the same technology, the same science from four hundred years ago."

"Where are you going with this, Jack?"

"I don't know." He let the water glass drop with a *thunk*. "But after four years of living in fear of the Phage and waiting for Tsuyo to open their toy chest and give us a game changer… to find out that there might not be anything like that, it makes one think that maybe humans shouldn't be out here in the first place. Maybe our colonization is a mistake that the cosmos is just getting around to correcting."

"I think maybe you should start drinking again if these are the types of thoughts filling your head," Daya said with some heat. "Do you hear yourself? So you're ready to throw in the towel because you were praying for some miracle weapon that doesn't exist? Grow up. We will win as we always do: through sheer determination and will. Now if you'll excuse me, Captain, I need to see to the new tactical systems being installed on this warship."

Jackson felt his neck and cheeks flush as Daya stormed out of the Captain's Mess. He was supposed to be a pillar for the crew, even those who were personal friends like Commander Singh. Now the engineer would have his captain's doubts bouncing around in his head, and he would likely now look at Jackson's orders through that filter.

He sighed as he pushed himself up out of his seat and headed toward the bridge. Only a few more hours left on first watch, and then he could escape to his quarters and try to get some sleep.

****

The flight from Haven to New Sierra was just over seventeen days, without pushing the ships too hard. For most of the crew, it was simply the boring routine of trying to stay busy. Any and all preventative maintenance that could be done while underway was accomplished. Junior crewmembers were subjected to as much training as their supervisors could manage, and under the stern gaze of Master Chief Green, the ship was cleaned until it gleamed.

For some, however, the days were filled with trying to develop a strategy that would allow them to secure the release of the Black Fleet ships being held at the shipyard with a minimal loss of life and material. Jackson would prefer zero on both accounts, but Lieutenant Commander Amiri Essa assured him that was a completely unrealistic goal.

While the NOVA team leader technically fell under Jackson's authority while aboard the *Ares*, as soon as they disembarked to execute their role in the mission, he would no longer have any say over how the group of elite troops would accomplish their goals.

"Lieutenant Commander, I want to stress that the shipyard is not necessarily a hostile environment," Jackson said as everyone filed into the briefing room. "We want to get the Seventh Fleet crews released and those ships secured, but I'd like to avoid civilian casualties or needless deaths of Fleet personnel."

"Captain Wolfe, I can assure you that there will be no needless deaths," Amiri Essa said in his quiet, measured voice. "However, we may have greatly differing opinions on 'needless.' Those ships are vital to the defense of no less than four Frontier planets. I will not risk mission failure or the loss of critical team members. If the civilian contractors and Fleet personnel stay out of our way, no harm will come to them."

The answer wasn't exactly what Jackson had wanted to hear, but he understood the Lieutenant Commander's point of view. He might have a similar dilemma himself if the Fourth Fleet captains in that system pressed him once the *Ares* transitioned into the DeLonges System.

Others were now packing into the secure briefing room, so he let the matter drop. He'd voiced his concerns, but the NOVA team was made up of professionals that would follow their orders how they saw fit. His input on their end of the operation was not necessary or likely even wanted.

Once the planning session started, it rolled along quickly, and the strategies for the mission were finalized and the details locked down. Of course, it could all change in an instant when they transitioned in and the conditions they were planning for according to the latest intelligence were completely different. They planned for as many contingencies as they practically could, but there was simply no way to be absolutely certain until they laid eyes on the objective.

"If there's nothing else, I believe we have as airtight a plan as possible given the circumstances. I'm not going to mince words." Jackson leaned back in his seat. "The idea of fighting against other humans right now in light of what's happening, or about to happen, along the Frontier is as horrific for me as I'm sure it is for each of you. But without those ships, we won't be able to hold the next system the Phage decide they want. Let's get ready to execute this mission to the best of our abilities. I want to get in and get out without being drawn into a shooting battle with Fourth Fleet. Are there any questions?" Jackson looked around and didn't see any raised hands.

"Then I'll expect zero missteps on this one. Dismissed."

****

"Two minutes to transition, Captain."

"Coms, alert Flight OPS that they'll be launching within ten minutes," Commander Celesta Wright said.

"Aye, ma'am," the coms officer said. "Flight OPS indicates they're standing by."

The *Icarus* was due to transition into the system as close to simultaneously with the *Ares* as they could manage but approaching from a slightly oblique angle from the normal jump point. Both destroyers would go to maximum acceleration into the system, broadcasting loud and proud with active radar and transponders. Then their stealthy payloads would sneak out of the launch bays and utilize the momentum provided by the larger ships to make their respective approaches unpowered.

Despite her fears and self-doubt, Celesta surprised herself by how easily she adapted to being in command of a ship. Although "Captain" was a strictly honorary title, as her transfer didn't include a promotion, she was certainly enjoying being called "Captain Wright."

Her joy was tempered by the circumstances somewhat, however, as she liked Captain Levitt on a personal level, and the only reason she was there was because he had failed so spectacularly. It reminded her that getting a starship safely from one point to another was one thing, but commanding one under combat conditions was something completely different. Her own baptism by fire was fast approaching.

"Stand by for warp transition!" the specialist at the nav station called loudly, his announcement triggering three short klaxon blasts ship-wide that alerted the crew to prepare for transition turbulence.

The *Icarus* shuddered as the warp fields collapsed, and they were dropped back into normal space.

"OPS, locate the *Ares*," Celesta said sharply. "Tactical, full active scan of the system."

"*Ares* has transitioned in approximately twenty-seven thousand kilometers off our port side," the OPS officer reported.

"Very good. Notify Engineering I want the main engines up immediately," Celesta said. "Coms, tell Flight OPS to stand by for our signal. Activate our IFF transponder, and ignore all com requests from any Fourth Fleet ships, New Sierra Shipyards, or either of the planets in this system. Understood?"

"Understood, ma'am," the coms officer said.

"Engineering says ninety-seconds until main engines are available," OPS reported.

"The *Ares* has gone to full power, ma'am," the tactical officer said. "She's approaching maximum acceleration along the predesignated course."

"Thank you, Lieutenant Holt. Helm! As soon as you have engines available, you're clear to begin accelerating on your own course."

"Aye aye, ma'am," the helmswoman said.

Celesta's voice was calm and controlled, but inside her head was a profanity laced tirade as she berated herself. She'd neglected to order the engines started the moment they transitioned from warp, a command only the CO can give.

"Main engines available, all ahead full," the helmswoman called out even as the subtle vibration of the mains running up to full power hummed beneath Celesta's feet.

She was beginning to agree with Captain Wolfe that the new ships were just too soft. She'd flown in luxury starliners that were less comfortable than this new class of warship.

Celesta consulted her status board. "OPS, please ensure the *Icarus* is configured properly for intersystem flight."

"Aye aye, ma'am." The OPS officer flashed her a slightly guilty look.

A moment later, the warp drive nacelles retracted back into the hull. Apparently she wasn't the only one feeling the jitters. This crew had already been kicked in the teeth once when their captain abandoned the *Atlas* during the second battle for Xi'an.

"Coms, put me through on the ship-wide." She stood and moving in between the OPS and Tactical stations.

"Ship-wide keyed to your voice, ma'am," the coms officer said.

"Attention crew, this is the Captain." She hesitated slightly, wishing she'd put a little more thought into her remarks first. "I'm flying you into a situation I wouldn't wish on any crew. For the first time in over two hundred years, there may be shots fired in anger between two groups of humans. I also know that you have some lingering doubts from your last combat engagement.

"I will make you no promises save one: no matter what happens, we will do our duty. We will not abandon the *Ares*. Nor will we leave our fellow Seventh Fleet spacers stranded. Let's settle down, do our jobs, and make sure at the end of this mission, the *Icarus* has earned her wings. CO out." She turned and made a slashing motion across her throat while every pair of eyes on the bridge was riveted on her.

"Ship-wide channel closed, Captain," the coms officer said.

"OPS, when will we be cleared to release our payload?" Celesta asked, all business again after her impromptu pep talk.

"The *Icarus* is just now clearing the debris belt, ma'am. We're ready when the confirmation signal comes in from the *Ares*."

"Go ahead and give Flight OPS the go ahead to open the launch doors," Celesta said. "I don't want any delays from the time we get the signal to the time we release."

"Aye, ma'am."

****

"The *Icarus* has caught up, Captain," Lieutenant Commander Barrett said. "We're ready to launch at your command."

"Coms, how soon until we can expect a message from our Fourth Fleet friends?" Jackson asked.

"The soonest we'll likely receive a query is one hour, fifty-four minutes, assuming they transmit as soon as they detect our transponder signal," Lieutenant Keller said.

"Helm, standby for braking thrust." Jackson never took his eyes off the mission clock that began running the moment the *Ares* transitioned into normal space.

"Lieutenant Commander Essa and Commander Juarez are both giving a ready signal, sir," Lieutenant Davis said from the seat to Jackson's right.

He'd practically had to force her to sit in the seat vacated by Commander Wright and assign another officer to OPS. The replacement wasn't as proficient as he'd spent most of his time in CIC, but Barrett was doing an admirable job of taking up the slack.

"OPS! Give the launch signal," Jackson said. "Tactical, let me know how soon the *Icarus* launches after us."

"Payload is away clean," the OPS officer said. "Launch bay doors closing."

"Helm! All reverse one half," Jackson barked.

"Reverse one half, aye!" the helmsman said

The engines seamlessly redirected the drive plasma through the forward nozzles.

"*Icarus* launched .35 seconds after we did, sir," Barrett reported.

"Helm, full reverse." Jackson continued to watch the clock. "Come starboard 2.11 degrees. Maintain elevation."

"All reverse, aye. Helm answering new course."

The jump point from Haven to the DeLonges System had them descending nearly forty degrees inclined off the ecliptic. There was no point in trying to sneak into the system with a pair of destroyers, so Jackson planned on making as much noise as possible in the EM band and creating enough light pollution with the main engines firing in reverse to hide the fact that the *Ares* and *Icarus* had released a pair of practically undetectable insertion pods carrying two NOVA teams.

Prior to release, the two destroyers aimed the pods at the site where the massive New Sierra Shipyards complex would eventually be, so that, theoretically, there would be no course corrections necessary until the final deceleration burn. Potential obstacles were being tracked by the active sensors on both Black Fleet ships and broadcast to the pods on an encrypted carrier frequency that was disguised as a harmonic from the standard Fleet identification beacon all ships carried.

Another added benefit of the violent braking maneuver was that Jackson could plan out the *Ares's* flight path to allow him to approach the Fourth Fleet ships head on while maintaining the advantages of the "high ground" of outer orbit as well as the velocity he was still carrying from their initial burn.

The *Icarus*, on the other hand, was going to try to sneak away while the *Ares* was still lighting up the sky. Commander Wright had veered sharply to starboard and begun accelerating lightly once the *Icarus* had launched its insertion pod and the *Ares* had begun providing cover. With any luck, the Fourth Fleet ships left securing the shipyards would think that the *Ares* appeared in their system unescorted.

"We're getting standard IFF interrogations, sir. I expect we'll get a hail from one of the ships in-system shortly."

"Very well, Lieutenant Keller," Jackson said. "Alert me the moment you receive something, but send no response."

They didn't have to wait long. The IFF interrogations came from an automated system, and the com messages came in less than a minute later.

"We've received a message on a standard Fleet frequency, Captain," Keller said. "It's been authenticated with the proper decryption key."

"Helm! Zero thrust," Jackson said. "Tactical, passive sensors only... Shut down all active emission sources including the Nav and IFF beacons."

"Aye, sir," Barrett said.

"Coms, go ahead and play the message over the bridge speakers." Jackson leaned back and smiled slightly.

He hoped going dark the instant he received a message would look like a bumbling attempt to hide the *Ares* from the Fourth Fleet commander.

"*TCS Ares, you are unauthorized to be in this system,*" the unidentified speaker began. "*You are ordered to heave to and prepare to be boarded. Your crew will be detained until a representative from your government can be notified. Please respond on this frequency to confirm your compliance.*"

"*Our* government?" Davis asked. "I wasn't aware New America had seceded from the Confederacy."

"Coms, send the following reply," Jackson said. "This is Captain Wolfe aboard the Terran Confederate warship, *Ares*. As we are currently in a state of declared war with the Phage, please confirm your status. Are you no longer a part of the Confederacy? Send."

"Message sent, sir."

"OPS, put a plot on the main display of the *Icarus's* projected course," Jackson said. "Also, tell engineering that we'll be powering up all the tactical systems shortly."

"Do you really think it will come to a shoot out?" Davis asked.

"This is all just posturing," Jackson said. "Right now, we're acting like we're trying to hide. When they message back with another threatening order they don't actually expect us to follow, we'll power up all our combat systems and begin powering down the well at full acceleration. They know they have the numerical advantage right now, but they also know there could be an entire armada sitting outside the system waiting to short-jump in."

"All the while, we're nothing more than a distraction." Davis nodded.

"Exactly," Jackson said. "We've got to sell it better than just sitting in the outer system transmitting insults to them, or they'll begin to suspect the real attack is coming from somewhere else. If we look like we're committing to an engagement, the commanding officer will have no choice but to redeploy his ship to respond. That clears the way for the *Icarus* and keeps them from looking too closely as the troop pods move in."

"We're getting resolution on the ships sitting in orbit with the shipyard complex, sir," Barrett said. "Populating the threat board now."

The main display showed three destroyers and two cruisers flying in loose formation with the New Sierra Shipyards as it swung around the fourth planet in the system.

"That's a lot less than I expected for such a strategically important target." Jackson rubbed his chin. "Our two destroyers are more than a match for that entire formation if the class designators are correct."

"They've had control of the facility for over two months," Davis pointed out. "Maybe they repositioned their ships when their delegates announced New America wouldn't be providing support to CENTCOM."

"No, something else is going on," Jackson said. "Tactical, go full active. I want this entire system scanned."

"Aye, sir," Barrett said.

"I know this is ruining the charade, but I feel like there's a significant piece of information we're missing," Jackson explained. "If they have a com platform in orbit over the third planet while it's on the other side of the primary—"

"New transponder signals coming in, Captain!" Barrett nearly shouted. "Eleven Fourth Fleet warships have just arrived in-system with us."

"And there we are," Jackson said with disgust, "the missing piece."

Chapter 13

The DeLonges star system was a Holy Grail find when humans first began mapping the space around them using Alpha Centauri as an epicenter. Established by the New America enclave, and named for a long-forgotten nineteenth century explorer, the system boasted two planets of similar size and climate capable of sustaining human life: DeLonges and New Sierra. It also had two dense asteroid belts rife with the raw materials needed for starship construction, most notably iron ore.

It was the often overlooked planet of DeLonges that was causing Jackson Wolfe so much trouble. All his planning had assumed Fourth Fleet would mass their forces as close to the shipyards as they could. After all, that's what he would do. Since they were flying into the system from above the ecliptic, he never considered the fact that his counterpart commanding the Fourth Fleet elements would also try a bit of misdirection.

"It looks like the new arrivals were maintaining a heliosynchronous orbit on the far side of DeLonges," Barrett said as his tactical plots updated. "They were stacked up to offer a minimal profile from the direction of the Haven jump point and using the planet to shield them."

"In other words, they knew exactly where we'd be coming from," Davis said.

"Let's all calm down," Jackson said sternly. "It wouldn't take a tactical genius to know that any force CENTCOM sent was most likely going to deploy from Haven. The mission is still a go, so let's analyze and adapt. Have we been able to resolve the new ships?"

"Yes, sir," Barrett said. "Two fleet carriers, four missile cruisers, and five long-haul replenishing ships. I'll have class designators and ship registries shortly."

"Five cargo haulers," Jackson drummed his fingers on the armrest in a rapid staccato. "So their strategy relies on bluffing us with numbers along with the element of surprise by making it look like we've flown into a trap. Tactical, begin tracking all ships and broadcasting the data to both troop pods and the *Icarus*. Let's not show our hand until we're sure what they know. The carriers and cargo ships are no threat, but four missile cruisers can cause us some trouble depending on what they're carrying."

"New message coming in, sir," Keller said. "Text only. It's just repeating the previous order."

"So let's send our response," Jackson said. "Sound general quarters, set condition 1SS, and prepare the *Ares* for battle. Tactical, I want continuous full power sweeps of the system, and don't bother trying to disguise your targeting scans. Nav! Plot me a course further down into the system that puts us in between the two Fourth Fleet forces. Helm, you're clear to engage on the new course, ahead three quarters."

"Ahead three quarters, aye."

"More misdirection, sir?" Davis said.

Normally Jackson would be beyond irritated with an XO that asked so many questions, but moving Lieutenant Davis to this position had been his decision, and with as little command experience as she had telling her to sit quietly wouldn't bring her up to speed any faster. So he took the opportunity to train her on the job while things were relatively quiet.

"More of a distraction," Jackson corrected. "Trying to find the *Icarus* would be difficult while she's running silent, and tracking the stealth troop pods would be even more so, but there's little chance of picking any of them out of all the noise we're broadcasting into the system. Not only that, but I can't imagine the New American commander is that comfortable with a *Starwolf*-class destroyer bearing down on, them despite their numerical advantages. They'll know, as we do, that unless those cruisers are loaded with the most advanced ship-to-ship missiles available, cornering us into an engagement will be costly."

"Another incoming message, Captain," Keller said.

"Read it out loud, Mr. Keller," Jackson said.

Keller read from his display. "Message starts: *TCS Ares*, you are ordered to withdraw from New America sovereign space immediately. Lack of compliance will result in use of force. Message ends."

"Transmit this, audio only." Jackson stood and turned around to face his com officer. "This is Captain Wolfe. According to the Articles of Confederation, section seventeen under reciprocity of military force, any and all Seventh Fleet warships are to be accorded safe passage through any Confederated star system or enclave. Your statement of sovereignty begs the question: do you speak for the New American government in declaring yourselves no longer part of the Terran Confederacy. Be advised I am prepping a com drone for Haven now for my own clarification. *Ares* out."

"Message sent," Keller said with a grin.

"That should buy us a bit more time as they try to figure out a way to walk that back without looking like a bunch of amateurs," Jackson said to Davis as he sat back down. "Helm! All ahead full. Tactical, begin acquiring target locks on all the Fourth Fleet missile cruisers and no need to be subtle about it. OPS, how long until the troop pods will begin their final course correction and decel?"

"Two hours, sixteen minutes, sir."

"Nav, send an acceleration plot to the helm that puts us outside the orbit of the sixth planet, roughly equidistant to both... opposing fleets," Jackson said, catching himself before he said 'enemy' while he studied the tactical display. "Helm, you're free to execute at will."

"Aye aye, sir," the helmsman said.

"We'll still need to find a way to keep their attention focused on us without actually engaging them." Jackson paced the area in front of the command chair. "If we could pull those units away from the shipyards, that would be preferable. Suggestions?"

"I think I have an idea, Captain," Barrett said.

****

"What can you make out, Specialist?" Lieutenant Commander Amiri Essa asked over the "open" channel in the pod.

The insertion vehicle didn't have full time artificial gravity (it barely had heat), so they were all strapped in securely as they cold coasted down the well toward the New Sierra Shipyards.

"It's all a jumble, sir," the specialist first class said from the pod's very basic com station. "Captain Wolfe appears to be trying to draw off the Fourth Fleet units with verbal insults, but I think I'm only getting half the conversation. We may not be receiving the transmissions from the ships near DeLonges."

"Understood," Amiri said. "Time check?"

"Ten minutes, forty-eight seconds to decel," the specialist answered.

The Chief strapped in beside Amiri bellowed, "Final gear check! Weapons safe until after impact."

"I wish you'd use another word for that, Chief," a young spacer said from the back of the pod.

"Oh, I'm sorry," the Chief said contritely. "How about, 'shut the fuck up and check your gear like I said.' Does that work for you?"

"Yes, Chief."

"Cut the chatter," Amiri said conversationally, silencing his entire team immediately. "Chief Lund, please check that the breaching charges are secured before we begin decel."

"Yes, sir." The Chief popped his restraints off and floated over to the armored hatch at the front of the pod to double check that the optional explosive breachers were secured.

"Thirty seconds!" the specialist at the console shouted. "Standby for final decel! Impact with objective hull in four minutes!"

"Lock seats in reverse position!" Amiri called out.

Everyone in the pod swiveled and locked their seats so that their backs were facing the direction of travel, the best way to absorb the impact that was coming.

Thirty seconds later, the disorienting, conflicting pulls of an artificial gravity field formed, just before the powerful retro rockets fired, violently slowing their decent toward the shipyards. The pods were built for stealth and survivability of healthy young special operators, not comfort.

The NOVAs were subjected to forces in excess of ten G's as the motors continued to burn, the attitude thrusters firing constantly to control their decent as they scrubbed off the incredible velocity they'd inherited from the *Ares*.

"Thirty seconds to impact!" the specialist wheezed into his headset.

Everyone in the pod grunted and squeezed their core muscles as hard as they could as the retro motors throttled up for one last, intense burst before the nose of the craft slammed into the hull of the upper shipyard hard enough to snap everyone's heads back into the seat rests. The shock absorbers on the nose did an admirable job of soaking up the last bit of relative velocity, and by the time the team was shaking their heads and taking stock of their bodies, the lights ringing the forward hatch were blinking amber, indicating the pod was anchored securely, and they were clear to breach.

"Weapons hot! Lock and load!" Chief Lund tore his headset off and jammed his helmet on.

"Rat! Position check," Amiri called out to the thin faced specialist at the control console.

"Off target by seven meters!" Rat called back. "We're still on top of that service bay, sir. Clear to breach."

"Give me a go, no-go!" Amiri shouted as he popped his restraints and grabbed his own helmet. After twenty-four "go" calls, he put on his own helmet and cycled the action on his carbine.

"Breach! Breach! Breach!"

At his command, there were a series of muffled *whumps* just outside the hatch, and smoke began curling in through the atmospheric ducts.

"We didn't make it all the way through." Rat's voice came over the team channel in everyone's helmets. "Firing secondary charges."

Whump... whump... WHUMP!

"We're though! Purging airlock and opening hatch!"

The air pumps hissed as they blew compressed air through the forward airlock to clear out the smoke and debris. The hatch popped and swung out of the way. Amiri shouldered his way past Chief Lund and Rat in order to get the first view of where they were. Inside the service bay they'd blasted into, there was the expected dust, a few small fires, and klaxon alarms blaring loudly, but no armed party intent on repelling them.

"Go! Go! Go!" He jumped off the airlock platform and onto the deck of the New Sierra Shipyards. "Colt! Get to that panel and upload the package now!"

At his command, a short, stout specialist sprinted for the command terminal that was beside the entry hatch. He pulled out a specialized tile with a trailing lead and made a hard connection to the terminal. Amiri deployed his team to cover all the entrances and waited tensely. If the codejack program that smart ass CIS spook had given him failed to gain them control of the shipyard's automated defense functions, this would be an unbelievably short mission.

"We're in, sir!" Colt disconnected the lead and navigated through the menus on the tile. "I have command access to most of the subsystems we'll need, but I wasn't able to deactivate the small arms aboard."

"One thing at a time." Amiri walked over to look at the tile's display. "Kill all the alarms on this deck, and seal all the hatches to both Marine garrisons... That should cut down on how many of those apes we'll have to deal with. I also need confirmation that the Black Fleet crews are still aboard their ships."

"Working on it, sir," Colt said.

"Rat, Samson... Cover Colt while he's working the tech." Amiri strode back to the hatch. "I'm taking point. Chief Lund, I want you at the rear. Standard deployment—five man teams and keep your intervals. Colt, make sure you're transmitting updates to the team network."

"Yes, sir!"

"Let's get this done," Amiri said. "If Team Six gets to the objective before we do after the head start we have, I will not be happy. Understood?"

"Understood, sir!"

The last five-man group out of the service bay made sure the heavy pressure hatch was closed and locked. It was a required feature for rooms with direct access to the outer hull to have such a pressure-capable hatch. It was also the main reason Amiri liked to hug the outer hull whenever coming aboard an orbital structure: the heavy pressure hatches were surprisingly resistant to weapons fire.

Leap frogging each other to make sure the side entrances to the outer ring were always covered, the five individual fire teams pressed ahead to make it quickly to their first checkpoint before the personnel on the station could get over their initial confusion and mount an effective defense. The fact they were making such quick progress without seeing so much as a wandering technician told Amiri that they might already be too late.

"Halt!"

The strident, fear-tinged call stopped the trailing team as they kept watch over a side corridor to allow the rest of the team to pass. Crouching in one of the hatchways, weapon trained on them, was a young Marine lance corporal. He was without helmet or body armor, so he'd probably been on a regular patrol when the alarms sounded and not dispatched afterward.

"You don't want to die in this corridor, Marine," the NOVA element leader near the junction called out. "Just toss that carbine out on the deck, and let us do our job. We're on the same team here."

"Stand down you bottom-feeding Fleet scumbag," the Marine yelled back with false bravado. "The rest of my squad is coming up behind you. You're pinned down."

"Don't be a—" the element leader didn't get to finish his sentence as a round from the Marine's carbine slammed into his chest plate, knocking him flat to the deck.

The Marine's eyes widened in fear as it seemed he may have accidentally squeezed off the round, but the other four NOVAs responded immediately. Hardened penetrator rounds fired from specialized carbines peppered the unprotected man's exposed right flank, and one went through his neck. Amiri had been already begun moving back when he heard the first shot.

"Report!" he shouted as he came sprinting back toward the engagement.

"One Marine down, sir," a garbled voice came over his headset. "Specialist Halsey was hit center mass. His armor held, and he seems to be okay."

"Fuck!" Amiri shouted, not caring that it went over the open team channel. "Are there any more station defenders in the area?"

"Unknown, sir. There are none within sight, however."

"Colt, are you able to see personnel trackers on your tile?" Amiri asked.

"Negative, sir," Colt answered as Amiri walked up to see Halsey climbing painfully to his feet and slapping away the proffered hands of his element mates.

"What happened?" Amiri asked, looking down at the Marine's body sprawled out in the corridor.

"He fired first, sir." Halsey rubbed his chest underneath his loosened body armor. "It may have been an accident."

"What a mess," Amiri said. "You and you: go police that body. Don't leave it just laying out there. Get an ID on that young man... He was just doing his job, and we will make sure he's properly honored when this is all over. Halsey, make sure your element doesn't screw around. I want you back in the rotation in the next few minutes."

"Aye aye, sir!" Halsey said. "I'm sorry, sir."

"Don't be sorry," Amiri said. "Just get this cleaned up and get your head back in the game." As he ran back up to where his own element waited, Amiri was both heartbroken and angry. He couldn't fault his men for the reaction that resulted in the Marine being killed, but it was precisely what Amiri wanted to avoid the most. No matter how successfully the rest of the mission went, all anybody would recall is that his men had gunned down a young lance corporal.

"I've gained control of these two lifts, sir," Colt said as Amiri jogged up to his team. "They'll take us down eleven decks, and from there we'll be able to gain access to Master Docking Control."

"Are the lifts being monitored?" Amiri asked.

"The intrusion program has spoofed the station's computer into thinking they're stationary," Colt said. "At least in theory."

"Then let's take two elements down simultaneously," Amiri said. "Same rules as before. Try to minimize the damage and loss of life, but *do not* let anyone impede our progress. Samson and Halsey, your teams are going down first. Colt and I will be last."

With Colt controlling the lifts from his tile, the team made quick work of descending to the lower levels of the shipyards. They'd made entry on one of the upper levels simply because that was the easiest to get to in an unpowered, unguided insertion pod drifting in from the middle of the system.

The upper levels were mostly large bays that contained the automated machinery that fabricated individual ship components and never had many people wandering the corridors. Once they got down into the lower levels that contained the command and control sections and administrative offices, they weren't likely to be so lucky. The fact that agent's program had managed to seal all the hatches closed would help a bit, but there would still be a lot of people that hadn't been in a compartment at the time the command went out.

With one last look around, Amiri climbed into the lift with Colt and three more of his operators to join the rest of his team on the lower level. When the doors opened again, he was relieved to see a calm scene, his NOVAs deployed in a defensive position around the lifts and three Fleet officers in plastic restraints and lying face down on the deck.

"All clear, sir," Halsey reported as Amiri stepped off the lift. "These three were milling around in the area and were detained without incident. No further contact to report."

"Fine. Halsey and Samson, your teams will take point," Amiri said. "Everyone else will fall in behind. Right now, getting Colt to Docking Control is *the* most important objective. We will be going hard and fast to not give the defense force any time to organize. Once there, we'll fortify our position within and wait for the *Ares* to conclude her operations. Clear?"

"Clear, sir!"

"Let's hit it."

****

"Coms, any luck getting through to either battle-group commander?" Jackson asked for the fifth time.

"No, sir." Keller had stayed on duty into second watch and was trying to make contact with the captive Black Fleet ships to let them know to get ready to fly.

"Have you identified any source of interference or signal jamming?" Jackson asked.

"No, sir," Keller said. "It could be a localized interference, or it may be due to the ships still being within the confines of the dock. I can boost the signal strength again if you'd like."

"Don't bother," Jackson said. "We're at almost eighty percent transmit power now. Another boost in wattage isn't going to do anything. Nav! Interface with Tactical, and give me a route that swings us down toward New Sierra. Use the *Ares's* maximum acceleration in your calculations, and cut us in between the two approaching fleets."

"Aye, sir," the chief at the nav station said.

"Captain, the fleet coming from DeLonges has been spreading out into a picket line since they got underway," Barrett said. "If we move between them, we could get caught between the effective firing ranges of the edge of their line and the ships coming from New Sierra."

"Then I suggest you make sure our point defense battery is ready, Lieutenant Commander," Jackson said. "I'm not wasting the time it would take to fly all the way out and around the DeLonges fleet. Nor will I risk giving the *Icarus* away by skirting around the New Sierra fleet. I have to assume Lieutenant Commander Essa has been successful so far, as we've received no alert from the shipyards. That means we need to get word to those docked ships so they're ready to fly."

"Course is calculated to the best of my ability to predict the reaction from the DeLonges fleet, Captain," the nav operator said.

"Tactical, check it over, and then send it to the helm," Jackson said.

"Course checks out, sir," Barrett answered. "I've adjusted slightly to favor more toward the New Sierra fleet to try and stay out of range of those missile cruisers since we don't know what they're carrying."

"Very good," Jackson said. "Helm, you're clear to engage. All ahead full. OPS, inform engineering we may need to run up past the accepted engine output limits shortly."

"Ahead full, aye," the helmsman said.

The soft thrum of the engines picked up to a muted, deep rumble as the helmsman smoothly advanced the throttle to full and began quickly entering his course change waypoints. He would allow the ship's computers to do the actual flying unless the captain ordered quick, sudden action that required him to grab the flight controls and override the predetermined course corrections.

"We're thirteen hours from intercepting the DeLonges fleet's maximum weapons range," Barrett reported. "Tactical computers are monitoring the courses of all inbound ships, and I'm sending the information to Nav for manual course updates."

"Once you're sure everything is updating, I want you off the bridge and in your rack for the next five hours," Jackson told him. "That goes for you too, Mr. Keller. The XO will arrange for relief watches to make sure everyone is rested and ready when we come within range of any potential contact. Lieutenant Davis, you have the bridge for now. I'll be back up to relieve you shortly."

"Yes, sir."

Jackson walked off the bridge and stopped by the wardroom to grab a sandwich and a drink before hustling to his quarters to try and grab a few hours of sleep. He'd been awake and on the bridge since they'd entered the DeLonges System over nineteen hours prior, and his eyes felt gritty from staring at the main display for so long. Despite the stress of the situation, however, there wasn't the gut-churning near-panic he felt during the times he faced off with the Phage. However distasteful, going up against human ships was something he was trained for. He knew their tactics, capabilities, and how to defeat each. For the first time since he'd first fired shots in anger from a ship he commanded, he felt reasonably confident in the outcome of his mission.

****

Despite how long he'd been awake beforehand, his eyes popped open after only four hours of restless sleep, so he took the extra time to grab a quick shower and some strong coffee before making his way back to the bridge. The *Ares* had a terminal in his quarters that had remote connections to both the bridge and the CIC, so he was able to confirm that they were still hours away from any potential engagement before he even put his boots on and made sure his prosthetic leg was fully functional.

"You're dismissed, Lieutenant," Jackson said to the lieutenant junior grade that was sitting in the command seat to fill in for the few hours both he and the XO would be off-duty.

"Yes, sir." He practically leaped out of the seat. "Do you require a status report, sir?"

"Not necessary, Lieutenant," Jackson said. "Report back to your department."

Without another word, the young officer turned and hustled off the bridge. Jackson paced around for a moment, looking over the tactical updates on the main display. While he knew he could never give voice to this without looking like the most petty CO in the fleet, he always hated coming on duty and sliding into the command seat while it was still noticeably warm from the previous officer's ass. It was a peculiar dislike that he couldn't account for, so he didn't bother. Instead, at the beginning of each watch, he made some pretense of checking over all the other stations and speaking to the other bridge personnel before sitting down.

He sat calmly, sipping his coffee while waiting for his acting XO and her replacement at OPS to report for duty. A quick glance at the tactical display confirmed that the Fourth Fleet ships were reacting much the way he'd expected: they planned to use their numerical advantage to nullify that of his far more advanced ship. To sell the deception, he'd committed fully to a hard charge down into the system, knowing that he had a few more advantages his opponents wouldn't be aware of.

"Hello, Captain." Jillian Davis walked onto the bridge, sat down, and logged into her terminal.

"Good morning, Lieutenant," Jackson said. "Who do you have coming up to run OPS today?"

"Ensign Hayashi," she said. "He's our most experienced, and I didn't think a potential engagement with the Fourth Fleet was an appropriate time to have a junior operator up here for training."

"I couldn't agree more," Jackson said. "When he arrives go ahead and help him prep a Jacobson drone for launch. Tell Flight OPS I want it configured for maximum speed and endurance and a full com suite. No weapons and no sensors other than passive navigation. We'll feed it telemetry updates as needed."

"Aye, sir." She rose gracefully as the youthful, full-cheeked face of Ensign Hayashi appeared through the bridge hatchway.

The pair worked for the better part of an hour, both on headsets and talking to specialists and technicians down in Flight OPS to get the drone prepped for launch.

"Jacobson drone has passed its self-checks and is ready for mission parameters, sir," Hayashi said before Jackson had to ask or Davis volunteered the information.

Jackson nodded in approval that the young officer wasn't just sitting back and allowing Davis to do all the work.

"Very good, Ensign," Jackson said. "Nav! Send over the course I asked you to lay out earlier. OPS, I'm sending over a mission profile for how I want the drone programmed. Let me know when it's ready for launch. Coms, tell engineering that we'll be performing evasive maneuvers shortly."

"Aye, sir." Lieutenant Keller rubbed his eyes and tried to shake himself into full alertness.

It took Hayashi another fifteen minutes to get the package ready to send to Flight OPS for review. It was uploaded into the drone with minimal supervision from Davis. Jackson had allotted for three times that, so he sat quietly in his chair, enjoying the sounds of his crew at work around him, while he finished off his coffee.

"Flight OPS reports the drone is loaded into the dorsal launch bay and is ready to fly at your command, Captain," Hayashi said.

"Flight OPS, this is the Captain." Jackson held the button for the intercom. The computer would automatically route the intercom channel to where it needed to go. "We'll be launching the drone while under power. Adjust accordingly, and then launch at your discretion."

"Aye aye, Captain," The voice of Commander Juarez came through his speakers. "Drone launching in thirty seconds. Standby."

"Confirmed drone launch out of dorsal bay two," Hayashi reported a minute later. "Handoff successful. We're getting full telemetry downlink."

"OPS, make sure the drone maintains at least ten kilometers of separation." Jackson did some quick math in his head as he looked over the tactical display again. It would be close if the closing ships were sharp and alert, but he expected them to hesitate. "Go ahead and sound the general alert and get everyone into their restraints."

The klaxon sounded twice before Hayashi's voice came over the intercom. "All personnel, standby for evasive maneuvers. Non-essential crew are ordered into their restraints."

Another ten minutes passed in tense silence as Jackson, not bothering to tell his crew exactly what he had planned, watched the rapidly dwindling distance numbers that were pinned next to each of the closing ships' icons on the main display.

"Helm! Emergency stop!" he barked.

To his credit, the helmsman didn't hesitate for even a second. He slapped the throttles back to the null position, reversed thrust, and shoved them forward again while simultaneously firing all the auxiliary braking thrusters.

Everyone was pitched forward as the gravimetric generators were unable to fully compensate for the violent maneuver. The main engines roared as they ran up to full power. and the *Ares* shuddered as inertia and superheated plasma thrust fought against each other. After twenty-two long minutes, the engines were throttled back, and the normal hums and beeps of the bridge could be heard again.

"Helm answering full stop, sir," the helmsman said.

"Maintain our relative position," Jackson said. "OPS, how's our drone?"

"Still flying straight and clean, sir," Hayashi reported.

"Go ahead and let everyone out of their restraints." Jackson popped his own off and stood. "It'll take the incoming ships fifteen to twenty minutes to fully realize what we've done. Tactical, keep the active scans going. Let me know the instant they react to our move."

"Yes, sir." Barrett shrugged out of his own harness.

"Might I ask what out next move will be, Captain?" Lieutenant Davis asked from her seat.

"For right now, we'll wait to see what they do," Jackson said. "They've been reacting to our charge into the system, so now they'll have to decide whether to correct their course to continue pursuing us or come about and chase after the drone that's about to bisect their formations."

"So the rush down into the system was a ruse?" she asked.

"A feint," Jackson nodded. "Show them one thing, get them to bite on it, then wait until it's too late for them to do anything about it before revealing what you're real plan is."

"Might I know what the real plan is, sir?"

"We need to get in direct contact with those ships tied up in dock," Jackson said. "I also want a high-power relay close to the shipyards to forward any communications from the NOVA teams. Right now, our intel says the crews have been sequestered on the ships with mooring clamps and dock overrides in place, but that intel is weeks old."

"And if those ships don't have crews to fly them?"

"We get our NOVA teams back, and we get the hell out of this system," Jackson said. "I'm not risking the *Ares* or the *Icarus* for sixteen aging warships that may not even be in any shape to fight."

As they waited for the Fourth Fleet ships to react, Jackson received a message from Daya Singh. Apparently, the *Ares* set a new Fleet record by coming to a complete relative stop from .35c in less than five hundred thousand kilometers in open space. Impressive. The crew was becoming more tense, more energized as the potential engagement neared.

"Captain, it looks like both groups are reducing velocity," Barrett said. "Thermals are picking up reverse thrust blooms from every ship, and radar confirms."

"Are they just slowing down?" Jackson frowned, punching in the commands to magnify that section of the main display.

"No, sir," Barrett said. "They're also angling in toward our current position, but not by much."

"Is there any indication they even saw the drone fly through their formation?" Jackson tapped his chin, a nervous habit he'd picked up recently for some reason.

"None that they've shown," Barrett said. "Not even the escort vehicles turned or slowed when it went through."

"Then this isn't actually their strategy. Helm! Maintain relative position. Zero thrust, station keeping thrusters only." Jackson turned to Davis. "We've caught them completely flat-footed. They're going to slow down and angle in to give themselves more time to react to anything we might do, but they're completely defensive right now."

"Could it be because they want to hold us here for some reason we can't yet see?" she asked.

"Possibly," Jackson conceded, "but unlikely. They're giving us too much time to think as well as far too many avenues of escape given our superior acceleration."

"This is the first thing even remotely close to a combat engagement any of them have ever seen, sir," Barrett said. "If they're going through what I did the first time, they're likely just overwhelmed."

"The more we observe their movements, the more we'll know about their intentions," Jackson said. "Continue monitoring all ships, and stay alert for any surprises they may be trying to spring on us."

"Aye, sir."

****

"Jam all the hatches except that one!" Amiri Essa shouted as all twenty-five members of the team piled into the large control room labeled "Master Docking Control."

At his command, four team members grabbed adhesive-backed thermite strips and, after sticking them on one side of the hatchway, slammed the hatches shut onto them. The impact and pressure activated the device, and sparks erupted from the four hatches almost simultaneously as they were welded shut by the intense heat.

"Only one way in or out now, sir," Rat said as they deployed around the remaining hatch in a loose defensive formation that allowed them to cover all the angles of approach while staying reasonably covered.

"Colt! Get to work!" Amiri waved away the noxious smoke created by the thermite strips.

Colt ran up with his tile and, pulling out a different lead than he'd used at their ingress point, established a hard connection with the long, multi-display terminal that lined the bulkhead on the far wall.

"Making connection now, sir," Colt said. "Releasing the docking overrides. They'll have control over all their systems and coms again shortly."

"Let's hope the crews are onboard and are ready to act." Amiri looked at his chronometer. "We've already been here far too long. Establish contact with the *Ares* as soon as you can. I have a feeling our original exfil is going to be a no-go."

"I'm on it." Rat moved to one of the unsecured terminals along the near bulkhead. "Let's hope these guys didn't secure the terminals before we subdued them."

When the NOVA team had approached the control room, there had been a lot of frantic conversation about the *Ares* acting aggressively toward their ships, but they seemed oblivious to the fact they'd been boarded. Amiri introduced himself with a pair of flash bang grenades and ten of his men rushing in to tape their mouths and put them in restraints.

Rat fumbled through the menus of the terminal. "I've dropped the localized jamming on the standard Fleet frequencies, sir. There's a repeating broadcast coming in for the ships in both battlegroups from a drone in high orbit. It's giving them orders and letting them know that we're about to release their ships."

"They should have figured that out already," Colt said. "The overrides have been dropped. All ship functions have been returned to the command crews."

"Rat, can you get me an open channel to the docked ships?" Amiri asked.

"Yes, sir." Rat ran through a few more menus before nodding to him.

"Seventh Fleet commanders, this is Lieutenant Commander Amiri Essa, NOVA Team Four. As you likely have noticed, we're in the process of securing your vessels' release. Please respond on this channel with your status and begin preparing your ships for flight. Time is of the essence, so brevity is appreciated," Amiri nodded for Rat to kill the channel. "Monitor that, and let me know what they have to say."

One by one, all the ships began checking in and confirming their orders, and after fifty minutes, Colt let him know that all but two ships had at least one reactor started and were starting on their primary flight systems. Things were going so smoothly that he wasn't surprised when a few shouts from the corridor beyond preceded small arms fire into the control room.

"Close that hatch!" Amiri shouted.

Now that some of Marines aboard were aware of their presence, it would only be a matter of time before they released their comrades and assaulted the room in force.

"Tech, keep working on getting those ships out of here," he said. "Rat, try to get word to the *Ares* and Team Six—"

An explosion against one of the welded hatches interrupted him.

"Sir?"

"Tell them Team Four is buster," Amiri said grimly. "We're not getting out of here."

Chapter 14

"Captain, NOVA Team Four is pinned down in master docking control," Lieutenant Keller said. "They're releasing all the Black Fleet ships, but they aren't able to get to their exfil point. Apparently the Marines stationed on the shipyard have deployed to keep them from escaping."

"Major Ortiz to the bridge," Jackson said over the intercom, his jaw clenching in frustration. "Coms, try to raise Team Six and get an update from them."

"Do you think Team Six could get them out?" Davis asked.

"I'm completely certain of it," Jackson said. "But I'm not ready to order so many troops to their deaths. The NOVA teams would both lose people, and the Marines would almost certainly be wiped out. We're just trying to get back the ships that are ours, not declare war on New America in the process. Coms, get ready to transmit a secure text-only message to the *Icarus*."

"Standing by, sir," Keller said.

****

Celesta Wright had to read through the new order from Captain Wolfe twice to make sure she was completely certain she knew what he wanted. Any mistake in executing these orders would be an unmitigated disaster.

"Nav, how long until we're in orbit over DeLonges?" she asked.

"At current velocity, we'll achieve upper orbit in sixteen hours, ma'am."

"I need to shave at least ten hours off that time," Celesta said. "More would be better."

"Standby, ma'am." The specialist input new velocity numbers into his calculations. "A full burn for seventy-three minutes will get us there in approximately four and a half hours. We'll need to adjust our course to account for the increased velocity, and it will require a hard braking maneuver to make orbit."

"Helm, make it happen," Celesta ordered. "You're clear to engage the mains and enter course updates from navigation as they come."

"Ahead full, aye," the helmswoman said.

"The clock will start when the engines reach full power, Captain" her OPS officer said. "The thermal bloom from the mains will be visible to anyone looking."

"That can't be helped now." Celesta sat back in her chair. "We were a contingency action that was just activated."

"May I be so bold as to ask what the plan is, Captain?" her XO squirmed slightly in his seat.

"For right now, I'd rather not make that information generally available," Celesta said evasively. "Let's just get this ship into position, and then we'll worry about that."

"Of course, Captain."

****

"We're running this all on timing with a ship on the other side of the system and no open coms," Jackson griped aloud as he watched the main display.

The Fourth Fleet ships had redeployed into staggered picket lines, forming a funnel into an obvious corridor between them. It was such a pathetically obvious tactic that he began thinking they had something else they planned to spring on him.

"There's some slop in the timing though, sir," Davis said. "The com lag will work in our favor on this as long as those ships don't hesitate when they get the call."

"Lots of 'ifs' in there, Lieutenant." Jackson raised an eyebrow. "But we have to be unorthodox since we're only two ships against an armada. Hopefully, this won't end up—"

"The *Icarus* has just showed up on sensors, Captain," Barrett said. "She's lit up like a beacon, full active sensors and all transponders are pinging."

"Good, good," Jackson said. "Commander Wright was able to get into position on time. Nav, get me a course that takes us down on a close pass of the shipyards."

"Aye, sir."

"The picket ships will have spotted the *Icarus* over DeLonges by now," Davis said. "How long until they react?"

"Coms, let me know when the first distress calls come in from the planet," Jackson said, ignoring Davis. They only had to wait around thirty minutes before the first panicked, open channel broadcasts came from DeLonges about a Black Fleet ship attacking them from orbit.

"Helm! Ahead full!" Jackson barked. "Engage auxiliary boosters. Let's kick her in the ass."

"Ahead full, aye!" the helmsman said gleefully, slamming the throttle forward and flipping up the controls for the auxiliary boosters. Jackson was pressed back into his seat momentarily as the deck shuddered from the engines at full power and the solid-fuel auxiliary engines ignited.

The auxiliary boosters were four relatively simple, solid rocket motors mounted in the stern, but unlike virtually every other solid fuel motor, they were able to be throttled. The fuel and oxidizer were pelletized and fed at high speed into the combustion chambers at variable rates, giving Jackson incredible flexibility when needing to augment the *Ares's* max performance acceleration profiles.

"Tactical, feed course corrections directly to the helm," Jackson said. "Let's hit that gap hard. Nav, be ready to jump in and get us in position to fly by the shipyards at the proper speed, altitude, and orientation."

He received a chorus of affirmative responses as he watched the green icon of the *Ares* bearing down on the picket ships at an acceleration that very few people in Fleet knew she was capable of. He smiled tightly as he imagined the chaos taking place on the bridges of the Fourth Fleet ships.

****

"We've been captured by DeLonges's gravity, Captain," Specialist Cortez reported from the nav station. "The *Icarus* is in a stable, high geosync as ordered."

"Thank you." Celesta took in a breath before her next order. "Tactical, bring all weapon systems online, and quick charge the forward laser battery." The lieutenant at tactical looked over his shoulder at her, but to his credit (and hers) began executing the order without any comment or complaint.

"Forward battery is fully charged and primed. All projectors deployed," he said. "Missiles and point defense will be up momentarily, and the auto-mag power bank is at fifty percent."

"Belay that," Celesta said. "Laser batteries and point defense only."

"Aye aye, ma'am. Weapons are deployed and ready, Captain."

Celesta looked around and, while she saw confusion and concern, she didn't detect any distrust in the looks the bridge crew gave her. She allowed herself a fleeting moment of pride that they trusted her and assumed that she was doing the right thing.

"Tactical, give me a firing solution into the upper atmosphere of DeLonges," she said. "I want it terminating out over the ocean and with a zero percent chance of damage to the surface. Maximum power."

"Firing solution calculated and locked in, Captain," the tactical officer said with obvious relief.

"Fire."

The four massive laser projectors that had deployed from the nose of the *Icarus* opened up, their beams invisible in space but wreaking havoc as they intersected the water vapor of the upper atmosphere. She knew the vapor trails would be clearly seen in the early evening over the capital, and the sonic booms of the shockwaves created by the flash-heated water droplets would echo across the continent.

"Keep firing," Celesta ordered. "Adjust your firing solution to ensure the safety of the population. We're just putting on a bit of a show."

"Yes, ma'am."

****

"We're approaching their maximum assumed weapons range," Lieutenant Hayashi said.

"If they wanted to hit us, they would have needed to fire well before now," Jackson said. "But let's keep the point defense active anyway, Tactical. How long until we're through the formations?"

"One hour, twenty-seven minutes," Hayashi said.

"Helm, shut down the auxiliary boosters," Jackson ordered. "OPS, tell engineering to purge the fuel lines and secure the booster engines. Do we have any movement from the opposing ships?"

He'd intentionally not referred to them as the "enemy" during the engagement. He needed to get the Black Fleet ships out of dock and out to the Frontier, but he flatly refused to escalate hostilities with his fellow humans. He just hoped his slapdash plan of surprise and misdirection would keep the Fourth Fleet commanders on their heels long enough for him to minimize the collateral damage.

The *Ares*, still accelerating under full power, shot through the formation of Fourth Fleet ships that had been drifting loosely just outside the orbit of the fifth planet. The helmsman automatically began reducing power and altering their course to intercept New Sierra while the ships they'd just zipped past began to turn and accelerate ponderously toward DeLonges.

"The entire formation is heading to DeLonges?" Jackson asked in disbelief.

"It appears so, sir," Barrett said. "I think they know they wouldn't be able to mount a pursuit given our velocity."

"That makes little sense, Mr. Barrett," Jackson said. "It will take them even longer to get to DeLonges, and they've given us a clear path to attack the shipyards— the only thing of strategic value in this system. Why would they…" He trailed off and narrowed his eyes as he looked at the tactical display.

"Sir?"

"Coms, get in contact with Lieutenant Commander Essa's team," Jackson said. "Ask him if the ship yard's automated defense systems have been reactivated. Helm, maintain course and speed."

"Aye, sir."

It took over an hour to get a response from their query given the communication lag from the distance and the fact that NOVA Team Four was still trying to defend its position inside the control room.

"Captain Wolfe, the automated defenses have indeed been reactivated." Amiri's voice came over the bridge speakers with sporadic weapons fire punctuating his words. "It was done discreetly. My tech had to dig deep to find out, and he is unable to shut them down. The station personnel know we're here, and they are systematically reclaiming control. The Marines are mostly content to leave us trapped in here… for now. Please advise, sir."

Jackson's original plan had been to have his Marines aboard the *Ares* take one of the two assault shuttles over and give the NOVA teams enough breathing room to disengage and withdraw, but with the orbiting facility regaining the ability to defend itself, that was no longer an option. He couldn't even get the *Ares* in close enough without opening fire on the weapons emplacements. Worse yet, the stranded Black Fleet ships now couldn't leave dock without being fired upon.

"Tell him to stay where he is and not to risk any direct contact with the Marines unless they have no choice." Jackson resisted the urge to punch a hole in his monitor. "Helm, all reverse one quarter. Cut our forward velocity by fifty percent, and then go no-thrust. We need some time to sort this out."

"All astern one quarter, aye." The helmsman made the adjustments.

"Coms, send a flash message to the *Icarus*. Tell Commander Wright to wait until the Fourth Fleet ships cross the halfway mark, then stand down and make best time for the Haven jump point," Jackson said. "Tell her not to wait for us. If she doesn't hear otherwise, she's to take the *Icarus* back to Jericho Station."

"Message going out now, sir," Keller said. "Standard encryption via the high-power array."

"What are our options now, sir?" Davis asked.

"Not many, Lieutenant," Jackson admitted. "Not without destabilizing the Confederacy. We could blast our ships out of New Sierra, but that would galvanize the position of New America and Britannia. It'd be plausible they would secede, and we'd be without the two most powerful enclaves on the eve of an all out war with the Phage."

"With all due respect, Captain," Hayashi spoke up. "New America fired the first shots when they denied our ships free passage."

"Understood, Ensign," Jackson said. "But that will matter little if the end result is a fractured humanity before an enemy that cares for nothing except our annihilation."

"Things would go so much more smoothly without dipshit politicians fucking everything up," Chief Green said from where he stood near the hatchway. "Sir."

"Let's all agree that things have gone sideways on this mission and move past that," Jackson said sharply. "Complaining about the situation doesn't solve it. I want options. Can we get our people out without demolishing fifteen percent of humanity's ship building capability? Can they get out on their own? Get your backshops involved, and get me some answers. You have one hour."

Three hours later, and they were no closer to a solution than when they started. The only options were to abandon the Black Fleet ships and the NOVA teams at the shipyard or go in hot and risk damaging an irreplaceable resource, damaging the *Ares* herself, and getting a lot of good people killed. Halfway through the conversation, Jackson knew what his next course of action would be, but they were many hours away from New Sierra still, so he let his crew try and work through the problem, if nothing else, then for an exercise in problem solving.

"Lieutenant Keller, send a com request to the New Sierra government," Jackson said as the conversation hit another lull. "Tell them I wish to discuss the terms of our withdrawal."

"Aye, sir," Keller said.

"So we're going to cut our losses and bug out, sir?" Davis asked.

"We're going to try and agree to terms with the regional government of this system," Jackson said sternly. "New America is still a member state of the Confederacy until I'm otherwise notified. This was supposed to be a discreet intervention in which we would be flying out before anyone realized we'd been here. That plan is obviously scrapped, so now it's time to open official channels and talk this out before someone does something that can't be walked back. We already have a handful of dead troops on that construction platform."

"Sir, a Governor Tellaride is responding to our request," Keller said. "His confirmation codes check out with our database."

"Put him through," Jackson said.

They were now close enough to the planet that there was a significant, but workable lag in communications. The governor had opted for high-bandwidth video coms, and Ensign Hayashi put him on the main display. A video transcript of the conversation would almost certainly be used in the hearing he was sure to be called into for this stunt.

"Captain Wolfe," Tellaride said with a polite nod. "I'd always hoped to meet you one day, obviously under much different circumstances. May I ask why you've now decided to make contact with us?"

"Governor Tellaride, I'd like to speak plainly about this incident so there are no misunderstandings," Jackson said. "I'd like to offer my sincerest apologies for the aborted salvage operation that has taken place in your star system. Currently we are standing down and will negotiate with you directly. As a show of good faith, I'd ask that you also have the Fourth Fleet warships in the system stand down."

Tellaride stared at him for a moment before nodding to someone off screen.

"An interesting choice of words, Captain," he said. "We appear to have different definitions of the term 'salvage.'"

"Recovery effort, if you prefer." Jackson kept his irritation in check. "Whatever the term, let's be clear that we're here to secure the release of sixteen Seventh Fleet ships currently being held illegally in the docks of the New Sierra Shipyards."

"Plainly spoken indeed," Tellaride said. "An argument could be made about the legalities of the situation…" The governor trailed off as someone handed him a tile. Without another word, or even a look to Jackson, the channel was terminated.

"What the hell?" Jackson muttered.

"Com drone has just appeared on sensors," Barrett said. "It came in from Haven jump point."

"Incoming transmissions from the drone addressed for the *Ares*, Captain," Keller reported a moment later.

"Sort and store them, Lieutenant," Jackson said. "They can wait until we see what this is all about."

"Com channel request coming in, sir," Keller said after a few more minutes of tense waiting. "Same address as before."

"Put it through."

"Captain Wolfe, I am Administrator Hoff," an officious looking elderly man said. "Governor Tellaride has been called away on a matter of utmost urgency and asked me to relay his message to you."

"A potential civil war within a Confederate star system isn't the most pressing matter the governor has?" Jackson asked in disbelief.

"We have issued an immediate recall of all Fourth Fleet warships currently in the DeLonges System," Hoff went on, ignoring Jackson. "The security force on the New Sierra Shipyards platform has been ordered to stand down and allow the invading force safe passage to the nearest docked Seventh Fleet vessel. Furthermore, all Seventh Fleet vessels are being commanded to prepare to leave dock. They will be towed out of orbit as quickly as can be managed. Afterward, all Seventh Fleet ships are requested to depart the system. Are these terms acceptable to you, Captain?"

"They are," Jackson said. "We will halt our approach to New Sierra, and I will order my other ship to leave orbit over DeLonges and form up on the *Ares*."

"An appreciated gesture, Captain," Hoff said, almost sneering.

The channel again terminated abruptly but, despite the rudeness, Jackson blew out a sigh of relief.

"Nav, I want a heliocentric course that maintains our current distance and orientation to New Sierra. I want to chase it around the primary star," Jackson said. "Plot it, and send it to the helm."

"Aye aye, sir."

"Coms, issue the recall order to the *Icarus,* and try to get in contact with both NOVA teams. Send all classified com traffic to my office, Lieutenant Davis, you have the bridge."

"I have the bridge, sir," Davis said to Jackson's departing back.

****

"Hopefully this message finds you not engaged in a running battle with a full Fourth Fleet squadron," Pike's voice said from the terminal speakers. "I dispatched this com drone as soon as I found out New America had discovered you'd been deployed to recover the two battlegroups from New Sierra. They'd hoped to goad you into some rash action that could be used as leverage in the Senate. Willington thinks you're too smart for that. I figured I'd better send a message anyway.

"I also needed to tell you that Dr. Allrest has disappeared. I'm actively trying to find him, and the fact that I can't lets me know that something fairly horrible has likely happed to him. I know he thought he was being sneaky—hitching a ride onto the Ares to talk to you—but I'm afraid he's not quite the spy he thought he was. Whatever he gave you must be radioactive… I wouldn't take it as an insult if you were to share that information."

"I'll bet you wouldn't," Jackson said with a snort.

"If my sources are to be trusted, I'm guessing that the regional governor has suddenly decided releasing the Black Fleet ships was in his best interest. I'm including official orders from Admiral Pitt in this packet to get them deployed to the Frontier. The Phage have continued to build up in the Xi'an System and have been spotted in the Oplotom System. It doesn't take a xenopsychologist to figure out they're following the same path as the first Alpha. I've put all the data in there... I trust your judgment on the enemy's behavior more than I do that of our scientific community. I'll deny I ever said that if you quote me, of course."

"Oh how I love these little conversations you sneaky, back-stabbing little bastard," Jackson remarked to the ceiling of his office.

"In all seriousness, Jack... something is going on here on Haven," Pike continued somberly. "People are being extra careful to hide their movements, and behavior patterns established over years of observation are suddenly changing. These aren't coincidences, and unfortunately, they're keeping me running from one end of Terran space to the other instead of keeping tabs on the enemy." Jackson was vigorously rubbing his scalp, glaring at the likeness of the CIS spook that never could seem to deliver good news.

"Keep the *Ares* off the grid, and no matter what, do *not* bring that ship back to Haven. If my suspicions are correct, whoever grabbed Allrest will know that you've been alerted in some way. Getting rid of a starship captain, even one as infamous as you, isn't likely to give them any pause. You'll probably want to keep the *Icarus* out there too, even if orders come in to the contrary. The committee has picked some politically acceptable replacement as CO for that ship, and I think you're better off keeping Wright in that seat. That's all I have on my end. Keep me in the loop on the com drone net's backdoor channels. When this is all over, we're going to sit and have a drink of real Kentucky bourbon, and no, I don't give a shit about your newfound sobriety. Pike out."

Jackson leaned back for a moment and absorbed everything that was said in what was another of Pike's whirlwind messages. When he checked the rest of the inbound messages, sure enough, a recall order for the *Icarus* was included in there as well as orders putting Commander Wright back on the *Ares* as Executive Officer. The rest was some raw data from Pike on Phage movements and what they'd been doing in the Oplotom System.

The first Alpha had already wiped all human life off Oplotom's surface, so there wasn't a lot to defend there, but from what he could see they just seemed to be milling around the sixth planet. He made a mental note to come back to that and dig into the detailed files.

Rising from his chair, he locked the hatch to his office and then went to his wall safe. Inside, underneath a few other illicit items, was the data card that Allrest had given him before they'd departed Haven. Sitting back down, he turned the card over and over in his hand, trying to take a few guesses at how bad the news on it was, before sliding it into his terminal.

As it turned out, his worst fears were wildly con-servative.

The video quality of the message labeled "play first" on the data card was quite poor, and Jackson could soon make out that Allrest was holding a portable camera and sitting in what appeared to be a restroom stall. The scientist looked pallid and in a near panic as he stopped twice just before he started to speak, tilting his head to listen for a moment. All Jackson could make out in the audio was that he appeared to have turned on the basin faucet and left it running as background noise. Jackson just shook his head. Any surveillance specialist worth a damn would easily be able to filter out such a steady noise, but Allrest was a researcher, not a spy.

"Captain Wolfe, I don't have much time, and I don't know who I can trust. I hope that this message, and the accompanying data, will be useful to you. As you're about to see... the Phage are only one front in a war that will determine the fate of the human species."

Chapter 15

"You've expressed to some of my colleagues a frustration in the apparent lack of progress being made in preparation for the coming battle with the Phage," Allrest said, his voice a harsh whisper. "Although that in and of itself isn't much to go on, I have no other options, and my time has run out. I'm putting all my trust in you, Captain, and I am hoping that it isn't misplaced." Allrest was fidgety in the video and Jackson could see the man probably hadn't slept in days. What in the hell had him so spooked?

"In addition to this message, the data card I will have handed you contains a complete record of my research up to this point. This research is incredibly restricted, so I've had to assemble it in pieces over the last few weeks. The data brought back from the second battle of Xi'an and your sojourn into Phage controlled space allowed me to complete my predictive models and in the process, revealed a bit more about the nature of our enemy.

"CENTCOM and Haven don't want it widely known, but despite their seeming refusal to communicate and their acceptance of horrific losses in pursuit of their goals, the Phage are possibly one of the most advanced life forms we've ever encountered. They are not mindless beasts. They possess a terrible and profound intelligence, but it has a significant weakness that could possibly be exploited: they utilize an aggregate processing model to make decisions—the "hive mind" you were previously briefed on—but far more profound than that term would imply." A sound off-screen made Allrest freeze like a prey animal and cock his head, listening for a moment before plunging ahead in an even softer voice.

"Each Phage added to a cluster will increase the intelligence of this group-mind. Larger units, of course, have more brain power than their smaller counterparts. The Alpha you first encountered was unique in that it contained more than fifty times the neural mass of any we've seen since, able to make its own decisions and interpret your actions against it."

"I wonder why we aren't being given this data as it becomes available," a voice muttered in the darkened briefing room.

"Quiet," Jackson said sharply. He'd already watched Allrest's message twice, so now he was watching his officers' reactions as they viewed it for the first time.

"There is also strong evidence that the range of this collective consciousness is finite." Allrest's recorded likeness pressed on. "I can't give you an exact distance, but from what I've been able to tell, it's roughly two-thousand AU. I'm sure I don't need to tell you the issue with that range... It easily encompasses most of our colonized star systems. Part of my research has been trying to find out the exact method of this instantaneous communication and develop a way to disrupt it. It was to be humanity's secret weapon when we finally made a concerted stand against the Phage encroachment.

"What you need to know, Captain, is that I was unsuccessful in my efforts. There is no secret weapon being finalized in a Tsuyo lab somewhere. That was all bluster for the media and the politicians that don't already know. As of this moment, we have no way to disrupt, or even understand, Phage communications, other than the empirical evidence that it exists."

Jackson watched the faces around the table in the dim light, their reactions morphing from initial shock to scowls of irritation to cover their fear.

"There are those who are well aware of how inadequate our efforts have been in trying to understand this strange species," Allrest said, the perspective of the video shifting wildly as he appeared to stand up and look around. "I'm also embedding astronomical coordinates in the data you'll be receiving. These coordinates are likely the most closely guarded secret in Terran space right now, but I don't think you'll be happy when you see what it is. I can speak no further… Look at the data, and please think of a way to utilize it. You and your crew pulled off a miracle once. Maybe you can do it again."

The video ended, and the lights in the room came up slowly. All the officers looked around the table uncomfortably while waiting for Jackson to speak.

"The data didn't contain exact details of what's at these coordinates." Jackson stood to address them. "But from the references in the material and a list of what's been going to and coming from the planet, I can take a pretty good guess. It's a planet that they're simply calling 'the Ark.'"

"While I'm no expert on ancient Earth mythology, I'm guessing it's not simply a reference to a generic boat," Singh said.

"Not that I can tell," Jackson said. "I'm making all of Allrest's data available to those in this room, conditionally for now, so consider it classified— your eyes only. When we have more information, we'll discuss wider dissemination. It seems this planet is a closely guarded secret and a failsafe if the worst happens. They've been moving material and personnel to the planet for the last three years as a lifeboat for the species if we're unable to stop the Phage."

"That seems only prudent," Lieutenant Davis said.

"I would agree if it wasn't for the fact that some of the communications that were included on the data card indicate that the Ark has now become Plan A for a powerful group within the Senate," Jackson said. "They do not feel that we have any real chance against a serious offensive from the Phage. Allrest was privy to quite a bit as he was being actively recruited to relocate to the Ark. In fact, I suspect that he was probably abducted since not even the CIS can find a trace of him right now. From what I can tell, there has been a massive diversion of material and personnel from CENTCOM. It seems like they're more than willing to let the Asianic Union and the Warsaw Alliance worlds fall."

"What do we plan to do with this information, Captain?" Major Ortiz asked.

"We don't have the necessary navigation data to jump directly to the Ark," Jackson said. "We'll have to fly through the Columbiana System and then out from there. Right now, we concentrate on getting the rest of the Black Fleet ships out of dock and heading back to Haven, and then we're going on a little fact finding mission. Dismissed."

****

"Have a seat, Dr. Tanaka." Jackson didn't look up from his tile as the Tsuyo scientist was escorted into the office by Commander Singh and Major Ortiz.

"I am beginning to suspect this meeting request is not social in nature." Tanaka laughed uncomfortably, looking over his shoulder at his unsmiling companions.

"We will be flying into harm's way directly from this star system," Jackson said, ignoring his discomfort. "Obviously you're far too valuable to risk having aboard, and I'm sure Tsuyo would like to get you back as quickly as possible. We'll be transferring you to the *Chesapeake* shortly. You'll be taken directly back to Haven aboard her."

Tanaka seemed to deflate with relief, and a small smile played across his face, confirming Jackson's suspicion the man had no desire to visit the Frontier aboard a combat vessel. Now it was time to drop the hammer while his guard was down.

"However, you will not be permitted to disembark the *Ares* until you do something for me," Jackson said.

"Anything within my capability, of course, Captain," Tanaka said carefully.

"You will take my Chief Engineer, get into the restricted equipment aboard this ship, and disable all the Tsuyo failsafes that allow you to remotely control this vessel," Jackson said calmly.

The progression of emotions on the doctor's face was almost comical. Tanaka was a scientist, not a politician or salesman, and he was simply incapable of keeping the truth off his face.

"I'm not sure I understand what you mean, Captain," he said slowly.

"I think you do," Jackson said. "You were one of the project principles for the *Starwolf*-class and know every bolt, every rivet by name. Please don't make me do this the hard way, Doctor. I'm backed into a corner and I am desperate."

On cue, Ortiz shuffled beside Tanaka, crossing his muscular arms over his equally impressive chest, looking down at the scientist meaningfully.

"You cannot possibly mean to threaten me with physical violence!" Tanaka said indignantly.

"I mean to get the answers I require," Jackson said sternly. "We know that these ships were deployed with systems onboard that would allow remote access to disable our weapons, shut down the drives, or even take control and lock the crew out completely. I want them uninstalled."

This was actually a bluff. The only evidence he had that these systems even existed was a vague warning from Dr. Allrest in the data dump he'd received and Daya Singh's educated guess when he'd tried to ascertain what certain avionics boxes were for when he saw that they had been tied into all their major systems.

"Are you denying that Tsuyo Corporation installed such equipment on this ship? Are you prepared to offer me that lie as a defense?"

The internal battle Tanaka waged with himself in his own mind was playing out plainly on his face, so Jackson sat and waited.

"The fact you have knowledge of these security provisions constitutes a breach of contract between Tsuyo and CENTCOM," Tanaka finally said, deciding to go on the offensive, and unwittingly confirming Jackson's accusations and Singh's intuition.

"Doctor, listen to me," Jackson said gently. "We've long passed the point of contractual obligations and legalities. The fate of the human species is at stake here, and unfortunately I can say that without a hint of hyperbole. There are also elements within CENTCOM and the Senate who may not have our best interests at heart... I have to know I can take this ship, and her crew, into battle without the risk of interference from some politically connected officer with an ulterior motive. Will you please help us?"

Jackson's change in tactics once again confused the doctor, but he was finally able to reach a decision.

"Do you swear on your life, on the memory of your ancestors, that you will do everything in your power to stop the Phage?" Tanaka asked. "Do you promise you'll never quit, no matter the cost?"

"No matter the cost," Jackson said firmly.

Tanaka bowed his head and breathed a heavy sigh before continuing. "I will assist Chief Engineer Singh in the removal of the remote failsafe system," he said. "There are likely some other features of the *Ares* you're not fully aware of. I will work up a full brief. How much time do I have?"

"Thirty-seven hours until the *Chesapeake* is ready to get underway at last check," Jackson said.

"Then we need to get started." Tanaka rose gracefully from his seat.

"Thank you, Doctor," Jackson said respectfully. "Your courage and sacrifice will not be insignificant in the coming battle."

"I have a family on Haven," Tanaka said. "I do this for them. I will be imprisoned or worse if the board learns what I do here. I am trusting you to protect them."

****

Jackson sat staring at the hatch after the three of them had left, feeling some regret for the position he'd put the scientist in. After a moment, he shook it off. He was preparing to fly into a system that was controlled by some of the most powerful people in the Terran Confederacy. He had no doubt that if there was a built-in weakness that the designers had included in his ship, someone there would know about it.

"Coms, get me a representative down on the surface of New Sierra," Jackson said, holding down the intercom button. "Route it to my office."

"Aye, sir."

It was twenty minutes later before the puffy face of Governor Tellaride appeared on his terminal.

"How may I help you, Captain?"

"I just wanted to update you personally," Jackson said politely. "All of our ships will be leaving your shipyards within the hour and will be warping out of your star system as quickly as possible after that. The two Ninth Squadron ships will depart immediately afterward. I regret that this incident escalated, resulting in needless deaths."

Tellaride just glared at him a moment before answering. "You seem to sincerely believe in what it is you do, Captain," he said. "From what I've been able to find out about you, it seems you do not partake in the political games your fellow starship captains do so love.

"We were warned about your arrival long before you appeared at the edge of our system. Word came from Haven itself along with details of which two ships, and which two NOVA teams, would be assaulting the shipyards. That's why we had our forces deployed in such a way as to hide them from your scans when you appeared at the Haven-New Sierra jump point."

"I see," Jackson said noncommittally, his mind racing.

"Embarrassingly, the advantage still didn't secure a victory," Tellaride continued. "Your tactics completely confused our untested and, honestly, unqualified commanders. The only reason I called for the ceasefire was that a com drone appeared with an order countermanding the one that called for us to try and hold the two Black Fleet groups here as long as possible."

"I don't suppose you'd like to offer any more detail as to who those orders came from?" Jackson asked hopefully.

"I don't think so, Captain," Tellaride chuckled humorlessly "This communiqué alone is enough to ensure I will not be in good favor. I may be the head executive in this system, but I serve as little more than a pass-through for decisions made in Columbiana. I respect what you are trying to accomplish, and I felt you at least deserved fair warning: Do not trust anyone on Haven. The Phage have shined a bright light on our complacency, causing the roaches and rats to scurry for cover. Good luck, sir."

"Holy shit, I need a drink," Jackson said to the ceiling, rubbing his temples and trying to digest yet another bombshell that had been dropped on him.

Despite all the evidence to the contrary, he was still having trouble believing that in the face of such a dire threat as the Phage, there were still humans who looked at the situation as an opportunity to gain just a little more power, a little more wealth. He found the entire situation offensive.

****

"Captain, all sixteen Black Fleet ships have broken orbit and are making for the Haven jump point," Lieutenant Davis said as Jackson strode onto the bridge, refreshed after a nap and a hot meal.

Davis was once again sitting at the OPS station, but he decided to let it slide.

"Who's in command of the formation?" he asked instead.

"Admiral Iccard on the fleet carrier, *Chesapeake*," she said. "Flight OPS has also reported that Dr. Tanaka was successfully delivered, and the shuttle is on the way back now."

"What about our Jacobson drone?"

"Already recovered and stowed, sir," she said. "The *Icarus* is thirty thousand kilometers off our port stern and pacing us in orbit."

"Has Commander Singh sent up the encrypted packet for Commander Wright?" Jackson asked.

"I just got it ten minutes ago, Captain," Lieutenant Keller said from the coms station. "Should I send it now?"

"Standby," Jackson said. "I'm also giving you a set of orders for the *Icarus* and another message packet. Send it once you get them both."

"Will the *Icarus* be remaining in the formation when we depart, sir?" Davis asked.

"Negative, Lieutenant." Jackson began going though the incoming department reports on his display. "She'll be heading directly to the Frontier to meet up with the rest of the Ninth while we go and investigate this Ark and find out what in the hell that's all about."

He'd made sure Daya had meticulously document-ed the procedure for removing the remote failsafe control from his ship and packaged it into a tech order that the *Icarus's* chief engineer could follow. After that, he had drafted orders for Commander Wright to take the *Icarus* to the Frontier and ignore all recall orders from CENTCOM. He hoped she'd be able to arrange for the *Artemis* and *Atlas* to also pull all the nefarious black boxes from their engineering bays. Either way, the *Icarus* needed to be close to the front, not sitting in dock at Jericho Station waiting on yet another politically appointed CO.

After he'd taken care of that, he asked Daya to add one more modification to the *Ares* after Dr. Tanaka had disembarked. He wanted to know if someone tried to activate the remote override for his ship. The plan was to program an innocuous looking icon on his display that would let him know if the dummy receiver Daya was rigging up down below received an activation signal. The makeshift box was smart enough that it would actually send back the proper responses as if the ship was answering the given commands.

Dr. Tanaka had been adamant that the system was benign, meant only to be activated in the event that the crew was incapacitated, or if the need ever arose for a single crew to command multiple ships. Jackson had simply nodded indulgently at the designer's explanations. Sadly, Tanaka truly believed what he was saying. No doubt that's how it had been sold to him.

Dr. Allrest had been much the same when he'd first been brought onboard to head up the research effort behind the remains of the Phage Alpha Jackson had destroyed—wide eyed and innocent. Now Tanaka was heading back to a probable bleak future when Tsuyo figured out he'd helped sabotage their newest starships, and Allrest was in the wind, recording secret messages in restrooms before disappearing.

"The *Icarus* is signaling they understand their orders and are ready to depart, sir," Keller said, intruding on Jackson's internal musings.

"Tell them they're clear to execute their mission... and Godspeed," Jackson said. "OPS, inform Engineering that we'll be departing shortly ourselves. I want full engine power available."

"Aye, sir," Ensign Hayashi said, having slunk onto the bridge and slid silently into the seat Davis had vacated. Jackson was amused that the young officer gave the appearance he'd done something wrong when in fact he was still over thirty minutes early for his watch.

On the main display, the *Icarus's* engines flared, and she began to accelerate out of orbit and back up out of the system. Jackson felt marginally more comfortable about Wright taking command of the ship on her own than he did before they flew into the DeLonges System. On one hand, it seemed impossible for her to be ready after such a short period of time, but on the other, he had to admit that she was far more qualified to command a starship in combat than he'd been when the *Blue Jacket* had finally caught up with the alien invader two systems after discovering the destruction of Xi'an.

"Nav! Plot a course out of this system via the Columbiana jump point," he ordered after the *Icarus* had cleared the immediate area.

"Aye aye, sir," the chief manning the nav station said without hesitation.

"OPS, inform Engineering that I'll be needing the warp drive available soon," Jackson said. "Helm, when you get your new course, accelerate along the orbital path at half-power, until we reach .15c."

"Aye, sir," the helmsman said. "Clear for ahead one-half."

"Lieutenant Davis, you have the bridge." Jackson paced behind the forward bridge stations. "Resume normal watches, and keep an eye on all the Fourth Fleet traffic. Alert me immediately if any com requests come in from the surface or any other ships enter the system."

"Yes, sir," Davis said, sliding over into the recently vacated command chair.

****

"How is it that I'm the one constantly getting mixed up in these situations? Am I really that unlucky?" Jackson asked rhetorically as he and Daya sat alone in the wardroom finishing off the evening meal.

"You can't be serious, Jack." Daya's incredulity clearly showed on his face. "It was dumb, blind luck that you were the first one to discover that Alpha chewing up planets, but everything after that has been your fault."

"I'm not sure I see how that's true," Jackson said.

"It was your choice to pursue that thing and take it on with a ship that should have been decommissioned years prior," Daya said. "Since then, these situations don't 'fall into your lap,' as you like to say. They're hand delivered. Everyone is terrified about what is coming, and they hope that they can hide behind you, that you'll have one more miracle to pull out to save them all. If you can't, then they'll have to face reality and stand on the line to face the Phage."

"I think we're corrupting the definition of 'miracle' when describing that first engagement," Jackson said sourly. "If this Ark is what I suspect it is, I'd say the decision has been made long before now."

"What do you think we'll find there?" Daya asked.

"Honestly?" Jackson idly spun his water glass on the hard plastic tray. "I think we're going to find that a few very influential people have betrayed the human species in order to save their own asses."

"I hope you're wrong."

"As do I."

Chapter 16

"OPS, go silent, no emissions of any kind. Have Engineering check the warp drive and get back to you on why that transition was so rough. Tactical, begin a passive survey of the system." Jackson wiped coffee off the front of his utility top. The *Ares* had bucked her way back into normal space just outside of a star system that didn't appear on any official survey reports.

"Aye, sir," Barrett and Hayashi said almost simultaneously.

"I can tell you now that there have been ships with Terran warp drives coming to this system, sir," Barrett said after a few moments. "The dissipating radiation from a transition leaves an unmistakable signature."

"I concur, Captain," Hayashi said. "I would also add that it seems a *lot* of ships have come in through this jump point."

"We'd better clear the area then," Jackson said.

Jump points were locations in space that had been designated as safe for transition, but given the slight variances and inaccuracies of each starship's internal systems, ships coming into a system could miss a jump point by a few hundred thousand kilometers.

"OPS, bring the mains online in low-output mode. Helm, minimum forward thrust and port maneuvering jets only. Get us drifting away from this jump point without giving away our presence."

For the next five hours, the engines gently pushed the *Ares* though space, angling away from the jump point until they'd reached sufficient velocity to clear the jump corridor in a reasonable amount of time. Jackson ordered the engines cut off and allowed the destroyer to continue her drift out of the area while the passive sensors watched and "listened" to everything happening in the star system.

As the conversations tapered off, the bridge crew was left with only the omnipresent whir of the air handlers and the beeps and hums of consoles as they faced another long, dull watch. Jackson wanted to stay near enough to the jump point that on the off chance they were lucky enough to catch a ship coming in, or trying to leave, they'd be able to get a positive identification on it with the passive sensors.

Seven hours had passed before Barrett finally had something to report. "Captain, I've got some preliminary results from our survey."

"Give me the highlights, and then make your report available on the server," Jackson said.

"Yes, sir." Barrett turned in his seat. "In addition to the evidence of Terran ships coming in through this jump point, I've also been able to determine that the fourth planet is inhabited. The light pollution on the planet's dark side is significant, even at this distance. Luckily, the planet is to the right of the primary star relative to us in its orbit, so we were able to detect it."

"Even though I'm a little surprised you were able to spot it at this distance, this wasn't unexpected," Jackson said. "What else?"

"The other oddity is that there are no radiated emissions from artificial sources in this system that we can detect. No beacons, coms, or broadcast signals of any kind. I've already run diagnostics on the equipment to make sure it isn't a failure on our side."

"They're keeping special care to hide this planet, not even allowing radio waves to escape and possibly give them away." Jackson tapped his chin. "We'll respect that... for now. Double check that we're not emitting anything ourselves."

"We're going to have some low grade leakage on the receivers from the local oscillators, sir," Hayashi said.

"Understood," Jackson said. "But that would be almost impossible to pick out of the cosmic background noise."

"Do we risk flying in for a closer look?" Davis asked.

"Not yet," Jackson said. "OPS, have a recon drone prepped. If they can quick turn a Jacobson, go ahead and do that. I'll send you over the load out instructions momentarily."

"Aye, sir."

A little over two hours later, a specially prepared Jacobson drone fired out of the starboard launch tube on a blast of compressed nitrogen, drifting away from the destroyer until a predetermined time had elapsed, and it engaged an auxiliary, low-power ionic jet motor.

"Drone is away, Captain," Hayashi said. "It checked in once with a com laser to confirm that it was operating correctly before going silent. There will be two opportunities along its course for it to engage its main engine and perform a long burn as it approaches the planet."

"Very good." Jackson stood. "Maintain standard watches, no special alerts for now. Tactical, keep a sharp eye for anyone trying a stealth intercept. We can't be guaranteed that our transition went unnoticed. Lieutenant Davis, you have the bridge. I'll be back to relieve you shortly."

Joshua Dalzelle

"Of course, sir."

Jackson nodded to the Marine sentry and walked quickly off the bridge. He made his way to the set of lifts near the aft section of the command deck by way of the wardroom to top off his coffee. He absently nodded to spacers and officers as he walked the corridors, deeply troubled by what they'd found so far.

A backup plan to keep and protect humanity's treasures and knowledge was one thing, but from the grainy images he'd seen on Barrett's display, this "Ark" looked like a full-fledged colony planet. Why waste the resources building something so extensive? And when did they start? The Phage had only been a known threat for a little over four years. There was no way in hell they propped a whole colony planet up that quickly.

That left a few possibilities, and none of them were particularly pleasant. It was possible the planet had been colonized for some innocent purpose years ago, but why the secrecy? The unnamed star system didn't even appear on the official Fleet registry, a fact that was quite suspicious by itself. If it had been built up after the appearance of the Phage, even counting when the Asiatic Union first began losing planets and ships, it still represented an unfathomable diversion of critical resources needed on the Frontier. Either way, the fact they were obviously using such stringent emission security protocols meant that whatever was going on down on that planet likely had little to do with defending the Confederate citizens with their asses hanging out in the breeze along the Frontier.

"You look like a man lost in his own head, sir," Chief Green said from a hatchway as Jackson strolled down the port access tube toward Engineering.

"Just making an unannounced inspection, Chief."

"Uh huh," Green said. "It might be more effective if you were looking at the ship and not out at something in front of you with that glazed look in your eye... sir."

"What brings you down here, Chief?"

"Inspections, sir." Green shrugged. "These fucking sewer maggots think that a couple calls for general quarters is some sort of excuse not to clean the goddamn decks."

His last comment was directed loudly at a pair of junior enlisted spacers who happened to be walking by. They'd slowed in order to greet their captain, but at the sight of Master Chief Green, they averted their eyes and hustled down the tube.

"You heading to Engineering, sir?"

"I am. Care to join me, Chief? They usually have decent coffee and pastries down there," Jackson said.

"I'd be delighted, sir," Green said.

"Maybe you could spring a surprise inspection on the drive techs," Jackson said half-jokingly.

"Not a chance, Cap," Green said seriously. "Commander Singh runs a tight ship down there. He doesn't need me coming in and disrupting his people."

Jackson made a mental note to pass the compliment on to Daya as they were very, very rare from the salty chief. Triply rare when it came to compliments for officers.

During the brief visit in Engineering, Jackson took a perfunctory look at the twin deuterium fusion reactors that powered the *Ares* as well as a host of other systems. He complimented all the spacers in the section, made a fuss about the ship breaking a speed record from the Frontier to Haven and outrunning a CIS Broadhead during the process, and then quietly slunk out of the area as Daya and Chief Green had a friendly conversation that he couldn't quite make out.

The starboard access tube was nearly deserted as he hustled over to the set of lifts that would take him directly back to the command deck. He had to relieve Davis so she could get some rest before second watch started, and he wanted to make sure Barrett wasn't pulling his usual game of lying about how long he'd been on duty so he didn't have to leave the bridge.

As the doors to the lift slid shut, he was momentarily overcome with sadness at the thought of the two young officers. They'd already been through so much ,and he had a bad feeling much more sacrifice would be required before the fight was over.

****

"The drone is now twelve hours overdue, Captain," Lieutenant Davis informed Jackson as he walked onto the bridge just ahead of first watch.

"Overdue for a check in," Jackson corrected. "That could be a host of issues, especially using a tight beam com laser."

"Sir, I have our forward optical sensor's bandwidth filtered and looking specifically for the beam's wavelength," Barrett said.

"We're in space, Lieutenant Commander." Jackson tried to hide his irritation. "If the beam doesn't hit us or refract off something else, it could pass within a few hundred meters of this ship, and you'd never see it."

"Understood, sir," Barrett said, unruffled. "But if we don't respond, the drone has been programmed to sweep the com laser in a grid pattern until we acquire each other. In twelve hours, I have to think that we'd have seen some trace of it."

"What's your working theory right now, Mr. Barrett?" Jackson asked.

"I'm picking up a lot of residual light from that planet that fits the bill for short-range LIDAR," Barrett said, referring to a detection system that worked on the same principle of radar but utilized reflected laser energy rather than radio waves. "I think they've got a detection grid in place, and they saw the drone as it came in for a close pass."

"You think they took out a Jacobson drone that very obviously belongs to a Fleet ship?" Jackson pressed.

"Yes, sir."

"And you agree with his assessment, Lieutenant Davis?"

"Yes, sir."

"Well then." Jackson sat. "Let's go see if we can find the pieces. OPS, reconfigure main engines for normal flight. Nav, plot a course down into the system. Give me the most direct route to the fourth planet. Don't worry about getting cute with any grav assists or bother trying to save propellant."

"Course is plotted and sent to the helm, sir," the specialist at nav reported.

"Helm, engage on new course," Jackson ordered. "Ahead one half with a target velocity of .10c."

"Ahead one half, aye," the helmsman said.

"Nav, how long until we make orbit with our current acceleration profile?" Jackson asked.

"Just over forty hours, sir," Specialist Accari said. "Give me a moment to account for the initial acceleration curve."

"Don't bother, Specialist," Jackson said. "Helm, ahead three quarters until you reach .35c. Nav, we'll need a more aggressive decel profile to make orbit. Make sure the helm has that as soon as possible."

"Working it now, sir. Time to target has been reduced to just over twelve hours," Accari said.

"Lieutenant Davis, you're relieved," Jackson told her. "Bridge crew is now on split shifts. I want the full first watch crew in their seats an hour before we begin decel."

"Aye aye, sir." Davis checked to see how much time she had to get some rest and practically ran off the bridge.

"If any of you need to call your reliefs up from your work centers, don't be shy about it," Jackson said. "I expect everyone to be at their very best when we begin braking for orbit."

A few operators looked at each other and then back to the captain as if to see if they were about to walk into a trap. When Jackson only looked over some reports on his terminal and mostly ignored them, a few grabbed their comlinks and called for relief so they could get some rack time before any potential engagements over the mysterious planet.

Jackson continued reading over the very dry technical bulletins his department heads had sent up as well as the equally mind-numbing readiness and training reports on the crew. Couple that with the steady, soft rumble of the mains throttled up to seventy-five percent, and he was ready for the first coffee of his watch before the second hour had passed.

He had barely made it back to the chair from the coffee machine at the back of the bridge when the ensign sitting at the com station turned to him, her face a mask of confusion. "Captain, I'm getting a video channel request for you personally via tight-beam laser. It's classified 'eyes-only.'"

Jackson frowned at that. They were certainly close enough to the planet for them to reach out with a com beam if they really boosted the power. Maybe they had a relay drone somewhere in the system they couldn't detect with the passive sensors.

"Lock the channel down, and send it to my office," Jackson said. "Lieutenant Commander Barrett, you have the bridge."

"Yes, sir."

Jackson jogged the short span to the small office and activated his terminal, not bothering to close the hatch. He wasn't prepared for the face on the other end.

"Wolfe, what in the fuck are you doing in this system?" CENTCOM Chief of Staff Joseph Marcum asked, his face a reddish purple.

"I was about to ask something similar, sir." Jackson refused to wilt under his superior's glare. "This system seems to not exist on any Fleet survey I can find. Imagine my surprise when I found a fully developed colony world here."

"I'm not even going to ask how you found out about this," Marcum said with disgust. "It was that idiot, Allrest... had to be."

"What's going on here, sir?" Jackson asked. "What is this place?"

"Do you need everything spelled out for you, Wolfe?" Marcum asked, his voice dripping with scorn. "I can never tell if you're the smartest person I've ever met or just another dumbass, lucky-as-hell Earther who doesn't have a damn clue what's going on around him. What do you *think* this is?"

"It looks to me like a lot of resources wasted while two more Frontier worlds are ready to fall, sir." Jackson watched carefully for a reaction from Marcum. He counted until he saw the chief of staff roll his eyes, wrote the number of seconds down on the tile in front of him, divided it in half, and then multiplied it by the constant. It wasn't exact, but it was good enough to roughly range the source of the signal.

"So I guess it's the latter," Marcum said. "You can't possibly be this naive. You know as well as I do that Podere and Nuovo Patria are as good as gone. The Phage will rush into those systems and take them with overwhelming numbers. What good does it do us if half of Starfleet is wiped out with them?"

"So we don't even mount a defense?" Jackson checked his numbers once again and then discreetly keyed in a general alert. He typed in a message to Barrett to signal general quarters but to silence the alarms on the command deck. "Sir, I can't accept that we're just going to abandon tens of millions of people."

"We're playing the long game, Wolfe," Marcum said. "This planet is meant as the final holdout for our species. By now you must have come to the same conclusions we have. We cannot win against the Phage with our current technology and numbers. It takes us half a year to build a destroyer and takes them four weeks to grow an Alpha. We lose a ship, and we're out an entire well-trained crew. They lose a construct and use the remains to build more in a few days. We have no answer for this enemy. Does it really make sense to waste our entire military might in a futile effort to defend a single planet? Or does it make more sense to accept the fact that there will be terrible losses in this war and try to ensure humanity survives at all?"

Jackson hated to admit it, but Marcum had a point. If there was simply no possible way to win, why sacrifice the entire species? But there was also the part of him that knew the Phage weren't invulnerable, and that if Allrest was right, and they were highly intelligent, there must be some threshold after which they decide a fight isn't worth the cost of winning.

"I almost see what you're thinking," Marcum said. "Yes, you've killed a lot of Phage... Has it made a difference? Before you transitioned in, we received word that they were massing in the Podere system in greater numbers than we'd ever seen before in one place."

"I'm not arguing that your point is invalid, sir." Jackson looked at his tile as a message popped up, telling him the crew was at their stations and ready. "But you still haven't answered my question about what this planet is. Allrest called it the Ark, and I can see you're taking special care not to risk radio emissions... so is this an elaborate contingency plan... or a lifeboat for the rich and powerful?"

"Call it both." Marcum shrugged. "When we see how the Phage act after they've taken Nuovo Patria, we'll know for certain what this planet's ultimate purpose will be. We'd always planned on brining the Ninth Squadron here before any real fighting began. Wasting five *Starwolf*-class ships in a blaze of glory made little sense. I tried to have you held up at New Sierra, but you managed to defuse that one far quicker than I would have thought."

Jackson frowned, but not at the thinly veiled insult. Marcum was stalling him.

"You are so easy to read, Captain." Marcum chuckled humorlessly. "Yes, I'm trying to tie you up for a few more minutes, and yes, I'm very close. I can already tell that you won't see reason. You're full of righteous anger and, unfortunately, have maybe begun to believe in your own inflated legend. I'm sorry, but we can't risk you leaving here."

The channel hadn't even gone fully dark by the time Jackson was out of his seat and sprinting for the bridge.

"Full active scan! *Now!*" he shouted as he flung himself into his seat.

Barrett didn't hesitate, bringing the *Ares's* high-power radar array online and scanning local space.

"Contact!" he called out. "*Close* contact! Two unknown ships on an intercept course, forward port side, flying on the ecliptic. Range is just over 1.25 million kilometers."

"Helm, come to starboard forty-five degrees," Jackson ordered. "All ahead full."

"Helm answering starboard turn. Ahead full, aye."

"Tactical, build me a profile on those two ships," Jackson said.

"Yes, sir," Barrett said. "I can tell you they don't match any class of ship in the registry, and they're very big. Battleship-size big."

"A new class of battleship we haven't heard about?" Davis asked from the OPS station.

"Possibly," Barrett answered. "Engine output and power levels are both way too high to be anything but. At least if Tanaka's newly installed sensors are to be believed."

"What are they doing?" Jackson watched the tactical display begin to populate as the active sensors mapped the system.

"They've matched our acceleration and are angling over to maintain a direct intercept course," Barrett said. "We've increased our interval marginally."

"They're herding us," Jackson said. "I'll bet they hang back until whatever other forces they have in the system have a chance to move out and cut us off. Then they'll close the gap and start pushing us into them."

"Incoming com request," Lieutenant Keller said. "Standard fleet frequency, but it's using a high-level CIS encryption. I'll need your approval for this one, sir."

"Is it from one of those battleships?" Jackson asked as he authorized the decryption with a biometric reading from his terminal.

"Negative, sir," Keller said. "Signal origin appears to be from near the fourth planet."

"Put it through."

"Fancy meeting you here, Captain." The unmistakable voice of Pike came over the bridge speakers.

"You certainly get around, Pike," Jackson said. "I hope you're not a player in this little party."

"You know me better than that." Pike laughed. "I caught wind of this little side project and flew in to investigate for my boss. By the way, Marcum has two more *Dreadnought*-class battleships sneaking around to pinch you in."

"I figured as much," Jackson said. "Glad to put a name to a face. *Dreadnought* isn't very subtle, but it's informative. When we're not running for our lives, you'll have to tell me all about how an entire new class of battleship was designed, built, and fielded with nobody knowing about it."

"It *is* an interesting story," Pike laughed. "But for now, I think I'll do a little running of my own. I'm transmitting you a copy of everything I have, and then I'm going dark. One of us should be able to make it out of here. Just so you're aware, there are six of those new boomers in this system right now, and they're surprisingly sneaky when they want to be. See you on the other side, Captain."

"Data stream coming in over the same channel, sir," Keller said.

"Compile and store it," Jackson said. "OPS, prepare a com drone. Copy Pike's information onto it, and then set a destination for Haven, and address it to Senator Wellington. Don't launch it unless I tell you."

"Yes, sir."

"The system just erupted with active radar scans, sir," Barrett said. "Two long-range tracking stations in a shallow heliocentric orbit just outside the fifth planet and both battleships behind us."

"Pike and I forced their hand," Jackson said. "They're going to try to end this quickly."

"Captain, the lead ship is demanding we heave to," Keller said. "We're to prepare for capture and boarding."

"Listen up! These people have no desire to fire upon this ship, nor to kill humans," Jackson said. "But their superiors aren't willing to let us leave this system. They know that CIS Broadhead transmitted a data package from the planet before it fled, so we're now the number one priority, and we can't simply disappear like our spook friend."

"Shall I arm our weapons, sir?" Barrett asked.

"Point defense only," Jackson said. "I don't want to provoke them. Nor do I have any delusions of our single destroyer taking on four new-generation battleships. Are they still pushing us?"

"Maintaining the same interval, sir," Barrett confirmed.

"And we can still only account for four of them?"

"Yes, sir."

"What's bothering you, Captain?" Davis said.

"This strategy would only work if we didn't know about the two ships ahead of us," Jackson said. "They have to know we're now aware of them, so it makes no sense that they're still pushing us along. We still have an open shot of space to the Columbiana jump point and a head start that they can't..." Jackson trailed off, staring at the main display as all the known tracks were continuously updated by the computer.

"Sir?"

"Helm! Come about!" Jackson barked. "Reverse course!"

"Coming about!" the helmsman practically yelped.

"Tighter, tighter!" Jackson urged. "As tight as you can manage without a full stop. Put our nose twenty degrees starboard of that lead battleship."

"Trying, sir," the helmsman said.

The ship began to shudder and moan as the engines and attitude thrusters fought to harness her momentum into a short, tight turn. The *Ares* was considered a nimble ship, able to turn very tightly—at least by astronomical standards. In reality, the turn would cover nearly two hundred thousand kilometers before they were facing back the way they came.

"Turn complete, sir," the helmsman said after forty minutes of fighting the ship's desire to continue straight. "We're twenty degrees to starboard off the lead ship now off our nose."

"All ahead flank!" Jackson barked, still agitated. "Everything she's got!"

"Ahead flank, aye!"

"Tactical, keep an eye for the last two battleships coming in from the outer system," Jackson said. "They'll be in the area between us and the Columbiana jump point."

"Yes, sir."

"Nav, utilize the active array, and make sure we're not going to encounter any hazards. We'll be flying manually for a bit, so call out anything you see." Jackson jabbed the intercom button on his seat. "Chief Engineer, this is the captain. I'm going to need every bit of speed the *Ares* has. You're clear to run her up past the limits if necessary."

"Aye aye, Captain," Daya's voice came back. "Disabling safety locks now and priming auxiliary boosters for ignition. Engineering out."

The *Ares* had now fully reversed her course and was roaring full bore right into the teeth of the once-pursuing battleships. The fact that they had begun braking in the face of such an unexpected move told Jackson they were equal parts surprised and confused, not sure what he was doing nor what they should be doing to counter it.

"How aggressive is the decel of the two ships in front of us?" Jackson asked.

"Relatively mild, Captain," Barrett answered. "They're slowing, but only enough to still be able to continue on a direct intercept without overrunning us."

Jackson looked down at his terminal. The Tsuyo remote override system that used to be on the *Ares* still hadn't been accessed. This surprised him, since it would have been an easy way for Marcum to fully disable the ship without even wasting the propellant to chase him. He either didn't know about the system or didn't have the access codes to the *Ares*. Or he was enjoying playing cat and mouse when he had six battleships, and Jackson was running scared in a destroyer.

"Are the two behind us moving to pursue?" Jackson asked.

"No, sir," Barrett said. "They've broken formation and are accelerating up and away from the engagement."

"They're completely confused right now," Jackson said, "so they're going to try and blanket the area to deny us access to that jump point. Tactical, keep track of where those two ships end up during the redeployment, and that should give you a rough idea where our two hiders are."

"Yes, sir."

"OPS, try to ping our drone," Jackson said. "I'm sure it's probably been hit by a surface to orbit weapon, but let's be sure. If you get a positive response, go ahead and send the destruct codes."

"Aye, sir."

After the frenzied bit of activity, the bridge settled into a tense quiet as the *Ares* barreled toward two battleships of indeterminate capability. Whoever was in command of the battlegroup defending the system was apparently content to just block him from what was likely the only cleared jump point, more than happy to allow him to continue down into the system.

Had Jackson been stuck on the idea of leaving the same way he came in, the strategy wouldn't have been a bad one. The two battleships in front of him could continue to push him down toward the inner system, and even once the *Ares* shot by and was behind them, there was no way to get her turned and accelerating back up out of the well toward the jump point without the four other picket ships easily intercepting them.

"No response from the Jacobson drone," Ensign Hayashi said after another hour had passed. "I'm transmitting the destruct signal anyway."

"Don't bother, Ensign," Jackson said. "Tactical, it looks like the two in front of us are under heavy decel again. Can you confirm?"

"Confirmed, sir," Barrett said. "Measuring a significant negative acceleration corresponding to an increased engine output."

"Helm, come starboard another fifteen degrees, and pitch down thirty degrees." Jackson studied the tactical plots. "Be prepared to fire the auxiliary boosters. OPS, you will give the order to fire the boosters when the *Ares* is within five hundred thousand kilometers of the lead ship."

"Helm answering new course," the helmsman said. "Engines still at one hundred and fifteen percent of maximum output."

"Acknowledged," Jackson said. "If the plasma chambers begin to get too hot, throttle back to within the normal operational range—if Engineering doesn't beat you to it."

"Aye, sir."

"Captain, there's a priority one-double-alpha com request coming from the fourth planet," Lieutenant Keller said. "It's addressed specifically to you."

"Any idea who it is?" Jackson knew Marcum was on one of the battleships, so he assumed it would be some high-ranking civilian official on the other end of the channel.

"Decryption routines confirm that the address is one reserved for the Commander in Chief."

"I see," Jackson said neutrally. "Put it through here."

A sharp double-beep let him know the channel was live.

"This is Captain Jackson Wolfe of the *TCS Ares*," he said respectfully.

"Captain Wolfe, this is President McKellar," the familiar voice said crisply over the bridge speakers. "I think it's time we end this little misunderstanding before needlessly putting anyone in harm's way, don't you?"

"I would like to do nothing more, Mr. President," Jackson said. "However, I am not certain that cutting my engines and allowing half a dozen battleships to close in on me is the best way to accomplish that, sir."

"I understand your confusion, Captain," McKellar said tightly. "But you have to realize, the fact that I'm speaking to you from the surface means this project was sanctioned by the highest levels of government."

"I sincerely hope that's true, sir," Jackson said.

He had to agree that the President being on the surface did lend credibility to the claim that this was something planned and sanctioned by the Confederate government and CENTCOM. Despite his reputation, Jackson was very much an officer that put his faith in the chain of command, and right now, he was being ordered to stand down by the two highest ranking members of Starfleet—including the Commander in Chief. But something just didn't feel right, and his gut told him that nobody on his crew would see the light of day again if he allowed the *Ares* to be boarded.

"I respectfully decline, sir. At least until I have some sort of guarantee that my crew will not be incarcerated or otherwise harmed. Is Admiral Pitt available?"

"I do not answer to, nor take requests from, some lowly destroyer captain," McKellar said, his voice brittle enough to etch starship hull alloy. "*I* am the ultimate military authority any way you look at it, and I have given you a direct order. Do you intend to comply?"

Jackson took his time before answered. His answer would dictate how the ships ahead of him, who were almost certainly monitoring the conversation, would respond. He was yet again taking his career and rolling the dice, but somehow that no longer seemed significant.

"It is with regret that I must inform you that I have no intention of allowing my ship to be boarded... sir," Jackson said. "We will return to Haven, and I will submit myself to CENTCOM authorities on Jericho Station."

"You are relieved of duty, Captain," Marcum's voice broke in on the channel. "Commander Wright will assume command of the *Ares*, and she will make way for the fourth planet of this system, enter a standard holding orbit, and await further instructions. Is that clear, Commander?"

"Commander Wright is not aboard the *Ares*, sir," Jackson said.

"There isn't an order given that you will simply obey without question, is there, Wolfe?" Marcum snarled. "Must be something in your genetic makeup. Lieutenant Davis, you will carry out the same order."

"I am relieving myself from duty, Admiral Marcum," Davis said in a clear, strong voice.

Before Jackson could object to Jillian tossing her career down the same drain his was circling, Hayashi motioned frantically and held up five fingers.

Jackson turned to Keller and chopped his hand across his throat to mute their end of the channel. "Tactical?"

"Both battleships ahead of us have ceased braking and are turning in," Barrett said. "We're being hit with tracking radars from both ships. They're getting a firing solution."

Jackson was vaguely aware of both the CENTCOM Chief of Staff and the President of the Terran Confederacy yelling over the com channel for him to respond. He set that surreal, insane part of the situation aside for a moment and focused on the scenario directly in front of him. Not having any performance numbers on the *Dreadnought*-class battleships was a serious hindrance when it came to devising a workable strategy, but he had to assume that a ship with nearly ten times the mass of the *Ares* would at least be half as quick to accelerate. He hoped.

"Helm, fire the auxiliary boosters," Jackson ordered. "Maintain current heading. Nav, standby to begin giving us course vectors for a warp transition. It will be fast and furious when I call for it, so be ready. Mr. Keller, go ahead and kill that channel."

"Aye aye, sir," Keller said. "Closing the channel the *President* and *Chief of Staff* are still talking on, sir."

Jackson didn't miss the inflection in his voice.

"Those of you that have served with me before will find this situation somewhat familiar." He raised his voice to be heard over the harsh rumble of the mains at full power and the auxiliary boosters firing. "As you heard, I'm about to disobey a direct order from both the President and his Chief of Staff. Anyone not comfortable with that may leave the bridge with no chance of reprisal no matter the outcome. You are not under arrest, you may simply return to your quarters as conscientious objectors. For those who choose to stay, rest assured, I will not open fire on a Terran vessel... even one that fires on us first."

"Permission to return to duty, Captain," Davis said from the XO's station, a small smile playing across her lips.

"Granted, Lieutenant." Jackson nodded.

Lieutenant Keller looked like he was about to get up, looked around, and remained seated although not appearing to be entirely happy about his choice. The rest of the crew were staring at him with a mixture of resolve and, alarmingly, not a little bit of adoration and hero worship. When he'd put them in the same impossible situation before, his chest had swelled with pride. This time, his guts churned as he risked the careers and freedom of his people on something that he might be gravely mistaken about.

"We're with you, Captain," Master Chief Green said simply from his customary spot by the hatchway.

"Very well." Jackson returned to his seat. "Helm, maintain max burn for another ninety seconds, and then kill the auxiliary boosters and throttle the mains back to within the normal operating range. If we haven't given ourselves enough of an edge by now, we never will. Nav, I want a course for a warp transition along our current heading, one light-week… I know we're still deep in the system, so we're just going to have to play the odds. OPS, inform Engineering we will be deploying the warp drive momentarily."

The crew quickly went to work preparing the *Ares* to perform a warp transition out of the system along an uncharted, unapproved path. The risk was minimal, despite how hard Fleet beat the drum about the hazards of straying off the warp lanes. Space was very, very big, and the *Ares* was comparatively very, very tiny. The odds of their warp fields encountering anything with enough mass to destabilize them was incredibly remote, and he was taking extra care by having them enter warp at a downward angle off the ecliptic to avoid most of the perimeter debris that was left over from the star system's formation. The forward distortion field pushed most of the smaller stellar debris out away from their flight path before the ship came through.

"Lead battleship is firing, sir!" Barrett said. "Forward laser battery. Thirty seconds to impact."

"Helm, roll to starboard one hundred and five degrees," Jackson assumed this was a low-power warning blast, but he didn't want to take the chance that they'd targeted his port main engine, so he rolled the ship to let the blast hit the *Ares* on the belly where the thermal shielding and ablative layers had the most coverage. Thirty seconds later, there was a clap and a slight shudder as the laser shot impacted them cleanly.

"No damage," Hayashi reported. "Heat absorption on the hull indicates the shot was less than five hundred terawatts."

"Warning shot then," Jackson said. "Nav, do you have my course?"

"I will in fifteen seconds, Captain!"

"OPS, deploy the warp drive, and handoff command authority to the nav station," Jackson said. "Helm, zero thrust and secure main engines from flight mode. Nav, you may transition us out of here at your discretion."

"Zero thrust, aye," the helmsman said.

"Engineering is securing main engines," Hayashi said. "Plasma chambers purging now."

"Standby for transition!" the nav specialist shouted, triggering an automatic alert that was heard throughout the ship.

A few seconds later, the main display dimmed, and the *Ares* shuddered slightly as she vanished from the system.

****

"You told me he was controllable," President Caleb McKellar said, practically spitting the words out at the display.

"A miscalculation, sir," Joseph Marcum said. "After his experience aboard the *Blue Jacket*, I really didn't think the man would even want back on the bridge of a starship. I figured we'd parade him around to increase recruitment and public support for CENTCOM's budget, but it didn't work out that way."

"I noticed," the President said dryly. "What matters now is what we do next. What options do you have?"

"I need to get in touch with the director of the CIS and find out why a Broadhead was snooping around out here and then we try to track down the *Ares*," Marcum said. "There's little damage he can do at this point. He'll likely return to Haven to make a report to Pitt, and then we can have him apprehended and recall the rest of Ninth Squadron."

"What about the report I'm looking at from Podere?" McKellar looked away from the screen, appearing already bored with the matter.

"I saw that too, sir," Marcum said. "It's as we feared."

McKellar sighed. "Intellectually, I understand and agree with the choices we've made, but that doesn't make it easy when it actually happens."

"I feel the same way, sir," Marcum said. "But the choice was made because it had to be made, horrible as it is."

"Just go get Captain Wolfe, and do whatever you need to do," McKellar said. "There's too much happening now to have a single Fleet officer being such a large distraction."

"I understand, sir," Marcum said. "I'll handle it."

Chapter 16

The *Ares* slammed back into normal space after the short warp flight. So short, in fact, that the opposing fields hadn't fully stabilized before the computer had to begin the very careful process of collapsing them in such a way that they didn't tear the destroyer in half.

"Report." Jackson seemed to ignore the fact that his coffee mug had gone sailing all the way past the tactical station.

"Confirming position now, Captain," the chief at nav said.

"Minor damage reported in Engineering," Hayashi said. "Water leak on reactor two's secondary cooling system. Repairs are already underway, and it won't affect ship functions."

"Let me know when it's been repaired," Jackson said. "I'm assuming there were no injuries as a result of the rough transition?"

"None reported, sir."

"Position confirmed. We're almost exactly a light-week outside of the previous star system, sir."

"Good job," Jackson said. "Now, get me a course that intersects the Ark-Columbiana warp corridor. We need to get back to Haven at best possible speed."

"Aye, sir."

"Won't they be expecting that, sir?" Davis asked.

"This isn't about doing the unexpected, Lieutenant," Jackson said. "They'd have an impossible task in trying to track us down out here in interstellar space, and Marcum knows that. He'll have a com drone heading back to Columbiana now to begin disseminating the order that we're to be apprehended on sight. Our only goal right now is to get back to Jericho as fast as we can and let Admiral Pitt sort this out."

"What if we were wrong?"

"Then I'll be arrested, and hopefully someone will be put in command of the *Ares* that can get her to the Frontier and do some good." Jackson shrugged. "This also isn't about individual careers anymore. Things are happening fast now, and if the Phage aren't stalled or stopped completely by the time they reach Nuovo Patria, all of Terran space is at risk."

"I understand, sir," she said.

Jackson glanced over at her and could see her face pinched into a worried expression.

It was a few hours before the ship was cleared for warp flight by Commander Singh and Navigation had a course that would allow them to ease into the warp corridor without another short jump that the new-generation drive seemed to hate so much. Jackson took the time to walk down to Engineering and inspect reactor two, making sure the coolant leak hadn't posed any health risks to the crew. By the time he'd left, Singh was already opening the bypass valves to recharge the system and test all the pumps.

He'd also stopped by his office to take a peek at what Pike had transmitted to him before the Broadhead and slipped out of the system, but the entire contents save for a plaintext message had been locked down with an encryption he didn't have the key for. He tossed around the idea of giving it to his com department to try and crack, but the accompanying message gave him pause.

Senator, suspicions confirmed. Worse than expected. Data package contains as much detail as I can get. Ares has appeared in-system, so I will use the distraction to bug out.

Jackson assumed the message was to Senator Augustus Wellington, Aston Lynch's boss. He'd never fully understood if Agent Pike worked directly for the Senator, still reported to CIS, or was just a wild card that seemed to appear in places where he was least wanted. Either way, he would not be adding to his list of impressive offenses on this cruise by trying to force his way into a com package that was intended for a powerful senator.

"Captain, our course has been verified and entered, and the warp drive has been cleared for operation," Lieutenant Davis said as he walked back onto the bridge.

"Bring the mains online," Jackson said as he sat down. "Helm, you're cleared for maximum acceleration once main thrust is available. I want transition velocity as quickly as possible."

"Aye aye, sir," the helmsman said. "Mains going hot now."

"Is the plan still the same, sir?" Davis asked.

"Affirmative, Lieutenant," Jackson said. "We'll hop in and out of the Columbiana System and be on our way to Haven just as fast as she can take us."

"Engaging mains now," the helmsman said. "Answering ahead full."

****

"The man is worse than you when it comes to getting himself into trouble." Senator Augustus Wellington snarled, pacing in the cramped main cabin of the

Broadhead. "What in the hell was he doing there in the first place?"

"As best I can tell, he'd received intel directly from Dr. Allrest before Tsuyo's personal goon squad snatched him off Jericho." Pike lounged in a chair as his boss paced back and forth like a caged animal.

"Yes, but *why* was he there?" Wellington snapped. "He gets intel reports every time that ship enters a system. Does he chase every single one of them?"

"I couldn't say, sir."

"It was a rhetorical question, you jackass," Wellington said. "So he goes blazing in there and blows your cover. Now McKellar and Marcum know that *we* know about their dirty little secret."

"Not necessarily, sir." Pike yawned. He'd been unable to get any sleep since as soon as the Broadhead entered the system, the Senator lit up his com panel with orders for him to dock and take him aboard. Apparently Wellington had been waiting for some time for him to show up.

"They have no idea which Broadhead this is. There are seventeen in operation and only ten belong to the CIS… For all they know, it could have been a civilian spy. Either way, it was unlikely I was going to sneak out undetected. Once I landed, they activated an orbital LIDAR array and had space pretty well blanketed. I think one of those new boomers might have observed my entry."

"I guess it's all academic now," Wellington said. "I'm surprised we haven't seen a general alert go out for the apprehension of Wolfe. Marcum must be playing this very close to the vest."

"Or they haven't decided the best way to go about it," Pike said. "They know Wolfe is very single-minded about rallying a sizeable force to the Frontier to try and stop what looks to be a significant Phage offensive. He's not stupid enough to let them board the *Ares* and he may decide to just let them play their games while he goes directly to Admiral Pitt to lobby for more ships."

"He did manage to secure the release of both Black Fleet battlegroups," Wellington said with a nod. "He's been rather aggressive in his attempts to stay out of the politics on Haven. McKellar may be of a mind to just let him go and hope anyone he raves to will just ignore him. Despite everything he's done in the last few years, the old resentments don't die easily—there are still a lot of people in the Fleet who aren't too fond of Captain Jackson Wolfe."

"He's not unaware of that fact," Pike said. "But he doesn't care. He's been looked down on his entire time in service to the Confederate Starfleet. He's quite an odd man in that he's fighting harder than everyone else to protect a group of people who couldn't care less that he even exists."

"Takes all kinds, I suppose," Wellington said with forced disinterest. He seemed to take any mention of the blatant bigotry within the Confederacy toward Earth as an indictment of him personally. "Has the director stopped bugging you about reporting on me now that you've been officially detached to my office?"

"He's not happy about the posting, but he's a political animal. He'll honor the agreement. When I'm sent back to the CIS, however, I'm likely to be thrown into a cell for prolonged interrogation," Pike said. "I'm actually only half-joking about that."

"He can shove it," Wellington said. "He deserves no less for trying to infiltrate my office to being with... what's that?"

An incessant beeping had been coming from one of the terminals on the Broadhead's flight deck. It had been getting louder, but Pike had originally intended to ignore it completely.

"No idea." He groaned slightly as he climbed out of the comfortable seat. "Shit! I guess I have no chance of actually getting any sleep anytime this month."

"What are you blathering on about?" Wellington demanded from where he stood in the ship's small lounge area.

"The *Ares* has just arrived in-system," Pike said. "I take it you'd like me to arrange a meeting?"

"Tell Wolfe to keep to the perimeter, and we'll be docking with him shortly," Wellington confirmed. "And you can sleep on the way back to Haven when you drop me off."

"I wasn't aware I was going back to Haven," Pike muttered under his breath as he brought the ship's com system fully online.

****

"Transponder is active, Captain," Lieutenant Hayashi said. "We should know pretty quick if any orders to detain the *Ares* came out of the Ark System."

"Understood, Lieutenant," Jackson said. "Nav, give me a course that clears the area. I want to fly a wide lap around the edge of the system."

"Aye, sir. Sending it to the helm now."

"Helm, you're clear to engage the main engines," Jackson said. "Ahead one half."

"Ahead one half, aye."

The trip into the Columbiana System had been tense. Nearly twenty-six days of warp flight while being completely isolated, not knowing if they were flying back to be arrested or, worse yet, if a couple of those

Dreadnought-class battleships had decided to make the trip to Columbiana to wait on them as it was the only logical destination for them.

During the long flight, Jackson ran through every conceivable scenario in his head as to why elements of the Confederate government would be hiding on an unknown, uncharted planet under com-silence protocols. The obvious answer was to maintain some semblance of a working government in the face of the first serious push by the Phage into Terran space, but six brand new battleships loitering in the area made Jackson think there may be more to the story than that.

The entire remainder of the Fleet only had three true battleships after the *Dao* had been lost over Xi'an. No matter how he looked at it, he couldn't shake the feeling that the Ark represented a profound betrayal on the part of the people who had sworn to do whatever necessary to protect and serve their citizens.

"Captain, coded message coming in. Text only," Lieutenant Keller said after over four hours of creeping around the edge of the system.

"Send it to my terminal, Lieutenant," Jackson said. Once he entered the decryption key, he could only roll his eyes.

Wolfe, Senator Wellington wants a face-to-face with you. So far no news out of that star system regarding you or your ship. Maintain current course and speed, and we'll come alongside.

Pike

He trusted the quirky CIS spook well enough to know that he wasn't trying to sneak his way aboard just to try and arrest him and assume command of the *Ares*. The fact that he had Senator Wellington on gave Jackson some small amount of hope. It went a long way to confirm what Pike had said earlier... and that Wellington had nothing to do with what was happening in that hidden star system. If the Senator wanted a meeting with him, perhaps he was about to be given some more answers about what he'd found.

"Helm, steady as she goes. Engines to zero thrust."

"Zero thrust, aye," the helmsman said. "Maintaining current heading and velocity."

In the time it took for the Broadhead to come alongside the destroyer, Jackson had already ordered his crew back to normal watches and had a full six hours of sleep. He was now dressed in a fresh uniform and standing down at the port airlock as the technicians cycled the safety locks before opening the hatch.

"Attention on deck!" Jackson snapped.

Senator Wellington was a civilian, so Jackson didn't salute as he crossed the threshold onto the *Ares*, but he was a powerful member of the Fleet subcommittee and a man Jackson had grudgingly come to respect, so at least a little bit of ceremony for the man was in order.

"You honor me, Captain," Wellington said as he recovered from the surprise. "All of you, thank you."

"If you and your aide would follow me, sir, we can go somewhere secure to talk." Jackson lead the pair out of the area while his spacers remained at attention.

"Captain Wolfe, would you be so kind as to order your location beacon off?" Aston Lynch asked, looking bored as he walked along the corridor. "The Senator does not wish this meeting to be public knowledge."

"Of course, Mr. Lynch." Jackson pulled his comlink out and called the bridge to give the order.

After a short trip up to the command deck, Jackson decided to hold the impromptu meeting with one of the most powerful men in the Confederacy in his own office, instead of the conference room.

"Let's get to the point, Captain." Wellington sat down in one of the chairs in front of the desk. "I want to know what the hell you were doing in that system."

Jackson had come to expect such brusqueness from his many encounters with the Senator and understood that it wasn't meant to be demeaning.

"Dr. Eugene Allrest managed to sneak himself aboard this ship before we were dispatched by Admiral Pitt to try and get Black Fleet's two battlegroups away from New America," Jackson began as he opened the wall safe behind the desk. "He turned over information that he felt I needed, information indicating that there were factions within the government on Haven that didn't think the war was winnable. He told me the political drama with New America and Britannia was little more than a contrived distraction to keep the legislative body in upheaval." Jackson pulled the data card Allrest had given him out of the safe before shutting it and sitting in his seat.

"He also gave me this." He tossed the card to Pike. "It contains all of the current research on the Phage, things the Fleet commanders need to know."

"Was there anything else?" Wellington asked.

"Yes, sir," Jackson said. "He told me about the planet they were calling the 'Ark' and said it was vitally important that I know what was happening there as well as mentioning that the much-hyped super-weapon against the Phage doesn't actually exist."

"Little bastard sure spilled his guts," Wellington grumbled. "Why trust you?"

"Likely due to the underserved reputation I've gotten in the public's mind thanks to the dramatic portrayals of the first Xi'an incident, sir."

Wellington just looked at him through narrow eyes. "I like you, Wolfe," he said finally. "I don't have to mince words or drag answers out of you. Even if I'm not going to like them, you just toss it on the table. So we know that Marcum and McKellar are involved, or at least they're the Confederate representatives involved in what's likely something cooked up by the Board."

"Do you really think Tsuyo would be involved with this other than just a supplier?" Jackson asked.

"That's one problem with your aversion to politics, Captain," Wellington said. "You're woefully ignorant of the realities in the Senate... and on Haven in general. Tsuyo's board of directors makes most of the major decisions in the legislature via proxy votes from all the senators they're able to buy.

"In the good old days before the Phage, when we didn't have anything to do but harvest resources, colonize uninhabited worlds, and entertain ourselves with meaningless political posturing, it was all just harmless fun. Now that the species is facing its first serious threat, or at least one that isn't itself, things aren't quite so jolly. So no, it wouldn't surprise me if the analytical bastards have calculated the odds of success and have determined that their best bet is to select those who can be in the lifeboat and leave the rest of us to our fate."

"So the Ark is exactly what it sounds like?" Jackson asked. "They'll hide out there and just hope this new threat blows over or that they can wait it out?

"Or the off chance that the Fleet will be able to hold them at the Frontier," Pike said. "But they won't be 'wasting' resources by shoring up beyond what's already been sent."

The confirmation of his worst suspicions caused a hard, cold lump to form in his stomach. He had to swallow hard before continuing.

"So I take it the people of Podere will not be getting any help to hold off the Phage?" he asked.

The pair in front of his desk shared an uncomfortable look.

"What?"

"Son, Podere is gone," Wellington said softly. "Word came in a week ago that the Phage moved in with four Charlie constructs and wiped them out. There's nothing left of the planet, and Eighth Fleet lost six ships before they called for a general retreat."

This time Jackson could stop himself. He leaned back and grabbed the garbage can, vomiting what little there was in his stomach into the bin.

"That was much the same reaction we had," Pike said without a trace of his usual sardonic humor.

"Please excuse me," Jackson said once he'd recovered.

He knew how the Charlie ships worked on an intellectual level, but to know they'd already been used on a populated planet, a planet with terrified and helpless humans on the surface... it made his head swim, and he felt like he might either be sick again or simply pass out.

"Don't lose it on us, Captain," Pike said seriously. "We need you clear headed and firing on all thrusters."

Never had Jackson felt so inadequate, so out of his depth. "What the hell use can one ship be against something that eats planets?"

"We need a plan, Captain," Wellington insisted. "The Prowler we had in the area has let us know that the Phage armada is slowly mobilizing toward the Nuovo Patria jump point. What practical defense can we offer the millions of people on that planet?"

"With only Ninth Squadron and the two Black Fleet battlegroups?" Jackson asked incredulously. "Assuming they can even get there in time, not a whole hell of a lot."

"What else is there?" Wellington pressed.

Jackson tried to slow the spinning of his mind and really see what options were in front of him. Twenty-one ships from Seventh Fleet simply weren't going to do it, no matter how unorthodox the tactics or how lucky they got.

"We need to deny the Charlies orbit over Nuovo Patria." The wisps of a plan started to coalesce in his mind. "But a simple blockade won't work. We don't have the numbers or the sheer firepower it would take to repel the Alphas and Bravos that will fly in with them."

"That's fairly obvious," Pike said. "So how do we accomplish that?"

"We need to focus on the Charlies themselves," Jackson said. "Every formulaic strategy that's come out of the academy dictates that an inferior force needs to dig in against superior numbers and play a defensive game, make the enemy come to you. While that allows us to choose the exact nature of the engagement, it won't work here. Those Alphas will blow through us like smoke and clear a path to a defenseless planet. If we can take out one or two of those Charlies, then we deny them the use of their primary weapon."

"But the Alphas are capable of wiping out the surface on their own," Wellington pointed out.

"I'm not so certain, sir. From what I've seen, and what Allrest's data confirms, I think that first Alpha was a special type and not normally deployed within large formations. The fact they even bring Charlies at all when they have dozens of Alphas in the same system backs that up." Jackson waved away the distinction between the two known Alpha types. "While that's an interesting side topic, let's not chase that right now and just assume that any Alphas we encounter can't effectively wipe out the surface. If they can, we're screwed anyway so there's no point planning around it."

"Blunt enough," Wellington said. "So where do we start?"

"I'm going to need to override the access protocol on the com drone network in order to gain Fleet-wide access," Jackson said.

"Is that all?" Wellington asked sarcastically.

"For starters."

****

"I never realized how cramped these were inside," Jackson commented from the copilot's seat of the Broadhead. "You spend months at a time in here?"

"Confined spaces are the least of my worries in my line of work, Captain," Pike said.

The pair had left the *Ares* running silent near the edge of the system and had flown down to the com drone platform that was in heliocentric orbit between the fourth and fifth planets, the Broadhead running in full stealth mode for the trip.

"I can imagine." Jackson idly looked over the expansive control and instrument panel in front of him, most of it controlling technology he'd never even heard rumors of.

They remained silent for the remainder of the seven hour flight as Jackson worked on his tile and Pike concentrated on flying a course that avoided coming close to the heavy traffic in the Columbiana System. The capital world of New America had no shortage of

Fourth Fleet warships, civilian cargo haulers, and intersystem mining ships. Jackson had just put his tile away when he saw a single speck of light moving faster against the unmoving stars as they continued down into the system.

"That's it," Pike confirmed. "We'll come in behind it and then give the first override order before our final approach, so it doesn't squawk an alarm at these Fourth Fleet frigates nearby."

"And then we can just dock to the maintenance hatch?" Jackson asked.

"More or less. This isn't even the first time I've done this."

"Really?"

"The best way to intercept a message or monitor communications within a system is to come right to the source." Pike shrugged. "I've spent many, many hours sitting on one of these platforms. It's actually fairly nice inside, and the platform is one of those things everybody knows is there but almost universally ignores."

The platform was simply enormous. It was at least three times the size of a fleet carrier and festooned with antennas and specialized capture and launch apparatuses that snagged, refueled, and redeployed com drones as needed, all without a single human onboard. Most platforms were not so large, but since this one sat in orbit above the capital of the largest enclave, it had to be able to handle the substantial amount of com traffic.

The Broadhead automatically recognized the docking collar near the middle of the platform and guided itself to a soft dock with hardly a bump to announce their arrival. A few seconds later, the computer verified that it had established a hard connection, the mooring clamps were attached, and the airlock was being flooded with atmosphere. Now that his plan was coming up to the part where he would be required to perform, Jackson felt the familiar butterflies in his stomach. He grabbed his tile and followed Pike off the flight deck and down the short, narrow corridor to the ship's starboard airlock.

"Once we do this, we're going to have to get the hell out of here… fast," Pike warned. "I can override the initial security measures to allow you the access you need, but once this thing starts launching drones, everyone in the system will know something is amiss. I can't stop the platform from answering a direct query from any of those Fourth Fleet ships, so if we're not in the ship and departing, it's completely possible they could lock us in."

"We'll be fine," Jackson said with a confidence he didn't feel.

"I know you don't see it, but you have to believe you're vital to this effort." Pike stopped at the airlock to face him.

"No single person is vital." Jackson wanted to stop the conversation before it started. "If I'm good enough to get everyone moving in the right direction, then this won't have been wasted time."

Pike looked like he wanted to say more but just shrugged and opened the airlock hatch. "We'll be going through the crew living area and then directly to the operations terminals two decks up."

He hadn't been exaggerating when he said "living area." Jackson was thoroughly surprised at just how plush the accommodations were as they passed through a well-appointed lounge area. To his left, there were two berthing bays with multiple racks and between those a galley that looked like it could feed fifty crewmembers easily.

"Why bother with all this for a station that was always meant to be completely automated?" Jackson asked.

"Preventative maintenance on a platform this large can take a good sized crew up to a week to perform, and that's if everything checks out and no repairs are needed," Pike said. "I guess the designers figured it was easier and safer to have them live aboard rather than in a docked ship. I also heard rumors that the original intent was for the platforms to be used as a lifeboat in case of an emergency."

"That's fairly stupid," Jackson said. "They wanted a ship so damaged that its crew needed to abandon her to fly up to, and dock with, an irreplaceable com platform?"

"Now you know why you've never heard of it until now," Pike said. "Sounded good on paper until someone without such a myopic point of view mentioned how dumb it was."

The platform was cold, but as they walked through each corridor, the automated systems kicked on infrared heaters in the ceiling so that although they could see their breath in the cool air, Jackson was becoming uncomfortably warm. He was just thankful that the platform had a gravimetric generator, weak though it was, that allowed them to shuffle through the corridors. Despite spending most of his life in space, Jackson was not all that graceful when it came to maneuvering his body in a weightless environment.

Soon they left behind the comforts of the crew living area and were carefully avoiding the sharp angles and overhead obstacles that littered the guts of the platform. The area was built entirely with machines in mind. The engineers were just kind enough to include the narrow, somewhat treacherous, path to get back to the main system interfaces.

"Give me a moment to get past the layered security," Pike said as they entered a cramped control room that was barely large enough for the two of them. "Actually, it'll be a lot of moments."

Jackson waited patiently while Pike painstakingly entered long, convoluted pass codes he was reading off this comlink. There were a few truncated alarms that sounded before he would enter another code and silence it. Just over twenty minutes had passed when he pointed to a universal data jack near the panel he was working on.

"Go ahead and cable up and get the packaged queued," he said. "I'll let you know when to send it."

Jackson uncoiled the hard line he'd been carrying in his pocket and plugged one end into the data jack before attaching the inductive connector to his tile with a magnetic *snap*.

"Ready."

"I'm almost there," Pike said. "The platform is no longer accepting new launch requests, but it's still storing and loading all the incoming com traffic. I'm setting it to launch every drone, maximum coverage. Each drone is loaded with another set of override codes for when it hits the next platform. Go ahead and upload your package."

Jackson pressed the blinking circle and watched as a status bar zoomed by and a confirmation box flashed.

"Load confirmed," Jackson said.

"Here we go," Pike said. "You ready to commit over thirty-six punishable offences with the push of a single button?"

"That's why I came, myself." Jackson grinned. "Let's do it."

Pike made a grandiose gesture to the hooded switch labeled "WARNING: Master Override."

Jackson reached over, broke the soft copper wire securing the hood down, and flipped up the spring-loaded switch, until a loud klaxon began sounding throughout the platform before releasing it.

"That should do it," Pike said even as the echoes of com drones being fired out of the launch tubes reached their ears all the way down in the bowels of the platform. "Now we run. Or… move carefully until we get to a wider corridor. Then we run."

Jackson realized he was well past the point of no return as the rate of drone launches began to slow down. Either his plan would bear fruit or he'd be tried and likely incarcerated in disgrace—or both.

Chapter 17

The *TCS Brooklands* had been flying a slow, lazy arc through the Alpha Centauri System for the last three weeks. She'd been refueled and rearmed at Jericho Station, and then Captain Lee had been ordered into a holding pattern far out in the system. He'd begun to wonder if CENTCOM had forgotten they were still out here, waiting for a destination.

The missile cruiser had been held up at Jericho with no explanation given until they received word that their replenishment had been cleared and then, in a mad rush, her magazines and launch tubes had been stuffed with the newest generation Shrike missiles. During all the frantic activity, the missile cruiser also had a team of engineers swarming through the avionics bays. They updated the software and hardware required to use the new munitions before they were towed out of dock and ordered into one of the boundary orbits far out of the way of all the increased traffic over Haven.

Lee had assumed with the near-panicked nature of the munitions loading that they'd be immediately sent to the Frontier to shore up the defenses of Nuovo Patria, but every inquiry they sent to Jericho came back with the same answer: maintain course and speed, and standby for further orders.

"Captain, we have an incoming transmission," the *Brooklands's* com officer said with some hesitation.

Lee noticed the Lieutenant's trepidation. "And there's something about that you dislike?"

"It's coming in on a reserved, priority channel, sir," the com officer said. "Encryption routine flags it as an emergency message."

"Put it through," Lee said. "If it isn't addressed specifically, play it on the main display."

"Aye, sir."

"This is Senior Captain Jackson Wolfe aboard the *TCS Ares*," the instantly recognizable face on the display said. "This message will be brief, and in the spirit of fairness, I'm going to tell you that it's also being illegally transmitted to every Fleet ship within range of the com drone network. While I hope every CO this message finds will at least listen to it, I won't hold it against anyone who deletes it before CENTCOM and Tsuyo Corporation manage to purge it from the buffers."

Over the next ninety minutes, the destroyer captain laid out a case against ranking members of the Confederate government and senior Fleet personnel that chilled Lee to his core. Although people weren't named specifically in the broadcast, the proof was irrefutable. Secret colony worlds, orders to let populated planets face the wrath of the Phage alone... It was all so much to take in. Accompanying the incredible narrative were videos, images, and sensor logs that corroborated everything Wolfe was saying.

There was also a treasure trove of information on the Phage themselves that had apparently been suppressed, though Wolfe never specified why that was. What made Lee's blood boil was that the data included things like behavioral profiles and predictive models that would have allowed them to devise much more effective strategies and tactics. He wasn't sure how Wolfe got his hands on it, but he was well aware of the man's uncanny success against the Phage, even when seriously outnumbered. Lee sincerely hoped the infamous captain hadn't been sitting on the information himself and was now simply trying to clear his conscience after the loss of Podere.

"As you can see, our leadership is broken. Fear has caused them to turn their backs on entire worlds while they cower under the questionable safety provided by a planet they hope the Phage can't find. On top of this, we've been deceived, possibly from the very beginning, about what's being done to combat this new threat. There isn't a new miracle-weapon coming out of Tsuyo R&D that will allow us to sit back on our bridges and eradicate Phage ships without even scratching our hull finish. If we're going to make a difference, it will be down in the trenches." Lee looked around the bridge and noted the angry set to jaws, the narrowed eyes, and the few who were nodding along with everything the Senior Captain said.

"I don't have the authority to ask you to disregard your orders, but I would remind you that we all swore the same oath when we accepted our commissions. I will be upholding that oath to the best of my ability when I stand between the gathering Phage armada and the planet of Nuovo Patria in the Warsaw Alliance enclave. I hope I won't be alone. *Ares* out."

Captain Edward Lee sat back in the command chair after the video portion of the transmission stopped and only the emblem of the *TCS Ares* remained on the main display. He could feel the uneasy stares from his bridge crew and could hear the strident alerts coming from the com station. No doubt CENTCOM dispatching its own fleet-wide broadcast to minimize the damage and call for Wolfe's head.

He didn't dismiss the possibility that Wolfe was playing the same games as those he accused, but his actions on the Frontier while commanding the *Blue Jacket* earned him a lot of credit, whereas Lee had little doubt the vermin infesting the halls of power on Haven wouldn't hesitate to abandon them all to save their own skin.

"Captain?"

But was Lee ready to throw away everything he'd worked for to follow Jackson Wolfe, a captain whose previous claim to fame had been an almost obsessive compulsion to buck against CENTCOM's senior leadership?

"Captain... we're getting a priority one-alpha transmission from CENTCOM demanding that we update them with our status," the com officer said.

"Demanding?" Lee let out a short laugh that surprised his XO. "More likely they want to know if we watched the transmission from the *Ares* and, if we did, what we intend to do."

"What *do* we intend to do, Captain?"

Lee debated asking for opinions from everyone on the bridge. He debated giving the rest of the crew aboard the *Brooklands* an opportunity to voice their concerns on the ship-wide network. He even debated replying to CENTCOM just to buy himself a little time to think. But the thing that stayed his tongue, the thing that kept rattling around in his head, was the message he'd gotten from Fleet Admiral Pitt concerning his candidacy for the captain's chair of the *Icarus*.

"We don't feel like now is the right time to put you on the bridge of a destroyer."

He had no illusions as to what that meant. As far as Wolfe and Pitt were concerned, he was proficient enough of a CO to drive his missile truck into a system and fire his payload from a distance while the computer tracked and targeted everything, but he hadn't shown the sort of boldness or decisiveness that made them want him commanding a destroyer, down in the thick of it, fighting it out at close range with the enemy.

"Coms, inform Engineering I want the mains hot and the warp drive charged and ready," Lee said calmly. "Ignore all further com requests from Jericho Station. Nav, plot a transition course for the Nuovo Patria jump point. When they write of this moment in history, they will not be able to say that when millions of people were in mortal danger, the *Brooklands* and her crew did nothing."

Lee couldn't hear the confirmation of his orders over the cheering and applause of the rest of the bridge crew.

****

"I'm receiving beacon data from all four Ninth Squadron ships, Captain," Lieutenant Keller said.

The *Ares* had entered the Nuovo Patria System after running the warp drive as hard as Singh dared to allow, all the way from Columbiana, after Jackson had uploaded his pre-recorded message onto the com drone network.

"Good, good," Jackson said absently. "Message the *Icarus,* and tell them I want their gravimetric detection network deployed to the coordinates I'm sending you now. Have all four ships form up on us."

"Aye, sir."

"OPS! I'm sending you the same coordinates," Jackson said. "I want you to plot a location on the opposite side of the system and send our detection grid to set up there. What other ships are in the system?"

"I'm getting a lot of com traffic, sir," Keller said. "Sorting through it now."

"It looks like the entirety of what's left of Third Fleet is in formation in the outer system, and I have two full squadrons from Fifth Fleet and all three operational battlegroups from the Eighth," Lieutenant Commander Barrett answered before Keller could begin counting up transponders. "The tactical computer has been tracking them as data becomes available."

"And the Phage?" Lieutenant Davis asked.

"The *Delphi* reports that half a dozen Alphas and an indeterminate number of Bravos have begun massing beyond the system's outer debris field," Keller said. "The *Icarus* is reporting in that both Black Fleet battlegroups are inbound. They sent a com drone ahead of them with their status and armament."

"That makes the Columbiana debacle not a complete waste," Jackson muttered. "Any CIS presence making itself known?"

"Not that anyone has reported, sir," Keller said.

"Tactical, you're clear to run the active sensors," Jackson said. "Standard power for now. Establish the Link with the other ships in the system as quickly as you can. Hopefully everyone has the correct key codes loaded."

Over the next twelve hours, Jackson concentrated on getting their early warning detection systems operational and negotiating with the other captains to determine how they would coordinate the coming battle. It was a contentious argument, but in the end, the holdouts grudgingly conceded operational authority within the Nuovo Patria system to Jackson and agreed that the *Ares* would fly the flag.

Once that little bit of politics was set aside, Jackson began looking over the haphazard formations floating through the system and immediately started issuing orders to get them in position. There was some balking at the fact he was breaking up battlegroups, which spawned a whole other series of discussions to smooth over egos and get them all moving in the right direction again.

He was splitting up the existing formations to best utilize each individual ship by its type and capabilities rather than just keeping them randomly grouped for convenience. At least that was half of the truth that he told the pouty captains. He also wanted to break up existing chains of command that could compromise his ability to have orders instantly obeyed when issued. He couldn't have a Third Fleet frigate CO calling up to the heavy cruiser in their formation to confirm what they'd been ordered to do.

All while this was going on, and the system was awash in thermal flares of starships firing their main engines to get into position, the Phage continued to amass outside the boundary. They were up to eight Alphas, and there was no way they would attack such a fortified human position with so few of their heavyweights. But there were already dozens of Bravos that could be detected zipping around. If they sent in a few waves of the smaller ships first, Jackson was worried about his total number of available missiles being depleted before the real battle even started. That may be where the *Starwolf*-class ships came in, their superior speed and acceleration allowing them to get in close enough for laser fire and auto-mag rounds.

"It's a shame we don't have any starfighters," Barrett remarked at one of the impromptu planning sessions at the back of the bridge.

"There aren't any starfighters even operational. Not for many, many years now," Jackson said.

"That seems a little shortsighted, all things considered," Barrett said.

"They were never an effective platform," Jackson said. "Couldn't carry enough fuel or firepower to make them worthwhile. They were relegated to orbital defense once starships became fast enough to render them obsolete, but better surface-to-orbit weapons were the last nail in their coffin."

"Well, it'd be better to have something small and quick against those Bravos," Barrett insisted. "Something other than a missile we can't get back once it's fired."

"Let's focus on what we actually do have on hand, Lieutenant Commander." Jackson didn't bother to hide his irritation.

"Yes, sir."

"It's eerie to watch them just sit out there," Davis said. "Waiting and planning, just like us."

"But unlike us, they're gaining intelligence with every unit added and can operate using a single, unified consciousness, and they don't get tired," Jackson said. "That's why I'm debating ordering a preemptive strike now, before they get too many Alphas to risk getting close and before the Charlies show up."

****

"Captain, the *Ares* is requesting a two-way com channel with you," the *Brooklands's* com officer said.

The missile cruiser had been pushed as hard as Lee had dared in order to get to Nuovo Patria in time to be of help. He was more than a little surprised at the sheer amount of Fleet ships within the system. Once they'd established their Link, he was equally shocked to see that the Phage appeared to be simply bunching up outside the system and making no overt signs they intended to attack.

"Put it through," Lee said. "Main display."

Senior Captain Jackson Wolfe's face appeared on the screen. "Captain Lee, I'll try to be brief." He, too, was sitting on his bridge and surrounded by spacers and officers frantically moving about in the background. "First of all, thank you for coming. Your load of Shrikes may prove to be invaluable."

"Anything we can do to be of service, Captain," Lee said.

"It seems we may have a use for the *Brooklands* sooner rather than later, but there is some risk," Jackson said. "So far, the Phage seem to be more than happy to hang back and wait while their forces trickle in. I'm operating under the assumption that once the Charlies appear, they'll attempt to clear a path down to Nuovo Patria."

"A logical assumption," Lee agreed. "What's our mission, sir?"

"I want to kick the hornet's nest and try to elicit a reaction while they're not yet at full strength," Jackson said. "There are still less than a dozen Alphas, so I feel that now is the perfect time to strike, but it will require flying the *Brooklands* quite close to where they're currently sitting."

"And we're not fast enough to outrun them if the reaction we get is a flat out counter-offensive." Lee nodded. "We're here to work, Captain, not spectate. Where do you want us?"

"Form up with Ninth Squadron, and I'll send you the mission parameters en route," Jackson said.

"Confirmed that we're joining formation with the *Ares*." Lee glanced at his display. "We'll be underway momentarily."

"Very good, Captain," Jackson said. "*Ares* out."

"Looks like we're to be the first sacrificial lamb in this battle," the XO said with obvious bitterness.

"Stow that garbage, Mister," Lee said. "The Senior Captain does not throw away lives needlessly. We came here to do a job, and we're going to do it, understood?"

"Understood, sir," the XO replied.

"Nav, plot a course to the trailing edge of Ninth Squadron's formation," Lee said. "Best possible speed. Coms, let Engineering know we're about to fire the mains." He looked around at the fearful faces of his bridge crew and let out a slow breath.

"We've been afforded a great honor," he told them. "The *Brooklands* will fire the opening shots in what will likely be a long and bloody defensive war against a terrible enemy. *We* will be the ones to punch them in the eye first and stand defiantly. Let's make certain that when the name *Brooklands* is uttered for years to come, it's done so with reverence."

"Yes, sir!" a senior specialist shouted out from the back of the bridge, breaking the silence and causing others to follow suit. The decks began to rumble and vibrate as the *Brooklands* got underway and, despite what he'd just said to the crew, his stomach knotted in fear as he flew the ship and crew to their doom.

****

"Data coming in from the gravimetric sensor net confirms that the Phage are still milling just outside the system, moving in relation to the primary star," Davis reported.

Since he didn't really need an XO on the bridge for the new class of ship, Jackson moved her back to OPS so she and Hayashi could split shifts and stay fresh.

"Have the *Icarus* and *Brooklands* completed their maneuvers?" Jackson asked.

"*Icarus* is in position. *Brooklands* is moving up and will be tucked in within the next few minutes," Barrett reported.

"Coms, release the *Brooklands*," Jackson said. "I want her accelerating full bore along the course we've designated. Inform Captain Lee that the *Ares* and the *Icarus* will overtake him before they're anywhere near the target area."

"Aye, sir."

"Tactical, have any new Alphas or Charlies arrived yet?"

"I don't believe so, sir," Barrett said. "However, the Phage seem to be using gravity manipulation in their reactionless drives, and it is causing some interference with the new sensor grids whenever one of the big ones move."

"Understood," Jackson said. "Just keep as accurate a running tally as you can, and make sure it's available over the Link."

"*Brooklands* is now accelerating, Captain," Lieutenant Keller said even as the bright flare of the cruiser's engines passed within a few kilometers of the *Ares* on the way out toward the edge of the system.

"Tactical, track the *Brooklands,* and inform the Helm when to get underway ourselves," Jackson said.

On the surface, it made no sense to send the *Brooklands* ahead first and then run both destroyer escorts as hard as they could go to catch her, but this opening engagement was just as much about provocation as it was positive outcome. By flying a single, slower cruiser out to the Phage, he hoped to make them a little anxious to pounce on it, as it would seem to be a soft target with nine Alphas sitting there, but he was more interested in what reaction two of the fastest ships in the Fleet coming at them would garner. Would they hold fast? Would they break their tight formation and swarm into the system in a frenzy?

Nobody could say for certain, but after exhaustively reviewing Dr. Allrest's data on the flight to Nuovo Patria, Jackson felt eighty percent certain as to what the Phage would do. With the numbers they had available, the "hive mind" of the Phage would be reaching levels of intelligence that would allow them to think and react strategically, rather than as individual fighters. With the new detection grid in place, he would also be able to see how long it took them to react after he and Celesta Wright began their approach.

The *Brooklands* was so slow compared to the smaller, speedy destroyers, that it was nearly nine hours later before she was approaching the point where she would intersect the arc to travel around the edge of the system. The *Ares* and *Icarus* would take a more direct line and, with their ability to change course more quickly, would be in perfect trailing position to make sure the cruiser had cover while making her escape. Jackson was running the crew on half watches to make sure every six hours, fresh personnel were rotated in, so the tension of staring down a silent enemy wasn't resting on the shoulders of a few.

"Standby!" Barrett was calling out as Jackson walked onto the bridge, timing his arrival perfectly. "Ten minutes until we get underway."

"Captain." Ensign Hayashi leaped out of the command chair when he spotted Jackson. "Main engines are hot and ready to provide thrust. We're minutes away from—"

"I heard. Thank you, Ensign," Jackson told the nervous young man.

It had been his first watch in the big chair, and he was obviously terrified of screwing something up despite the fact any movement by the Phage would still give them at least ten hours before needing to be ready. "Tactical, put a countdown on the main display. Helm, when you see zero, take us to maximum acceleration. OPS, make sure the *Icarus* mimics our movement."

"Engines ahead full," the helmsman called out, smoothly pushing the throttle all the way up just as the timer reached zero. Jackson leaned into the surge of acceleration as the *Ares's* engines pushed her ahead harder than could be compensated by the grav generators.

"The *Icarus* went to full power less than .02 after us," Hayashi reported, now sitting back at the OPS station. "Time to vector intercept... four hours, eleven minutes. We'll overtake the *Brooklands* forty minutes after turning onto the new course."

"Tactical, keep an eye out for any movement by the Phage or the *Brooklands* herself," Jackson said. "Captain Lee has been instructed not to risk his ship if the enemy decides to meet this gambit with overwhelming force. He will be turning back into the system and Battlegroup One from the Seventh will come out to meet the initial rush."

"Aye, sir," Barrett said.

Jackson couldn't help but raise an eyebrow as he watched the green line on the tactical display that represented the *Ares's* flight path begin to rapidly overtake the *Brooklands's*. The cruiser was over fifteen years old, underpowered in her prime, and had been given engines with only basic maneuvering in mind. In the limited distance of this attack run, the old girl would never reach her maximum velocity. The two *Starwolf*-class ships chasing her down, however, would come into the engagement so fast they would be required to brake aggressively if the Phage took the bait and entered the system, otherwise they'd simply overfly the *Brooklands* and leave her as an easy target for the enemy.

The next four hours were brutally dull. Despite his years in service, albeit very little of it in combat, Jackson was always taken by the fact that battle in space seemed to be hours and hours of waiting and a few brief moments of pure adrenaline, followed by more waiting if you survived.

The biggest problem was that Terran ships simply couldn't accelerate or maneuver in a manner that made the whole endeavor practical, even within the confines of a star system. The Phage could move about in three dimensions as if gravity and inertia didn't exist, but it took a ship the size of the *Ares* hundreds of thousands of kilometers to change directions or velocity, and even then only in a manner the local conditions would allow.

Even with the available power of the massive main engines, the *Ares* couldn't simply fly away from a planet when in a holding orbit. She'd have to begin accelerating while staying in orbit, until she could achieve enough velocity to break away. What galled Jackson the most was that the ship had artificial gravity and the miracle of the warp drive, so it would appear that Tsuyo R&D had a pretty good idea of how to create, modify, and nullify gravity. It seemed obvious, at least to him, that by now they should have at least been able to adapt the tech to a working starship engine.

"Helm is answering new heading," the helmsman called out after he'd throttled the engines back to bring the ship onto her new course. "Engines back to full power." They were now pointed slightly inward of their desired trajectory, so the engines could keep them from flying wide of their new course from all the momentum they carried from the inner system.

"We've got some movement from the Phage." Barrett sat up straighter at his station as the data came in. "Bravos are taking up a screening position in front of the Alphas, but they're between us as we stand now, not where we'll be when we make our closest pass."

"They'll rotate the formation to keep us blocked," Jackson said. "Are they focused on us or the *Brooklands*?"

"They appear to be entirely concerned with us and the *Icarus*, sir," Barrett said. "The *Brooklands* is still over three AU ahead of us, and the enemy is not positioning any ships to cover her."

"It's just how you said it would happen, Captain," Hayashi said. "How did you know?"

"It's how I *hoped* it would happen, Ensign," Jackson corrected. "This was one of a few responses Dr. Allrest's model predicted, given the size of the swarm we're looking at. From here we can narrow it down even further, as long as they don't have a significant number of ships arrive before we get there."

"If this works, we could take out a huge part of their fleet before the battle even starts," Barrett said hopefully.

"Except that we're only seeing a fraction of their available forces." Jackson frowned. "There should have been at least five times this number here already... as well those Charlies."

"Maybe we'll get lucky, sir," Barrett answered.

"You can't actually believe that, Lieutenant Commander," Jackson said in disgust.

"No, sir."

****

"Incoming transmission from the *Ares*, sir. We're a go for our primary target package."

"Very well," Captain Lee said. "Tactical! Begin tagging and prioritizing targets based on data coming in through the Link. Assign weapons to each target, and do not begin active scans until I tell you."

"Aye, sir."

This was it. Captain Wolfe had been right about everything so far. The Phage were more concerned about the two faster targets than the comparatively slow single target with the low power output that was flying on a course that wouldn't directly intercept them. Although Wolfe had access to data from some of Tsuyo's top eggheads, it was still uncanny how well the man seemed able to predict the enemy's movements and reactions.

"How many weapons per target, sir?" his tactical officer asked.

Lee looked over in irritation, until he realized the lieutenant hadn't been present at all the planning briefings.

"Three Shrikes per Alpha," Lee told him. "Do not target any of the Bravos."

"That leaves thirty-eight missiles aboard, sir."

"I'm well aware of that, Lieutenant," Lee said. "Now carry out your orders."

"Aye aye, sir."

Lee help up a hand when his XO looked like he was about to walk over and dress down the tactical officer for questioning his orders. Everyone was on edge, and some small lapses in discipline could be overlooked. The crew had only seen one battle, and that had been from well outside the periphery while they watched a whole armada of Third Fleet ships get ripped to shreds.

The bridge crew watched the Link data anxiously as the *Ares* and *Icarus* began to slow their mad charges and arm the forward laser projectors. Though laughably out of range, the leakage from the powerful weapons would hopefully keep the Phages' attention for just a little longer.

"Approaching the zenith of our arc, Captain," the OPS officer said.

"Tactical, full active scan," Lee ordered. "Populate the board and unsafe the weapons."

"Aye, sir."

****

"Bravos are still focused on us, Captain."

"Excellent," Celesta Wright said with a confidence she didn't feel.

The hardened nose cones of the tactical nukes the *Brooklands* was carrying were a great, simple innovation that had killed their fair share of Alphas, but they were affixed to the same old slow, unmaneuverable missiles that were easily intercepted or dodged.

"Ma'am!" the panicked shout of her OPS officer broke into her thought. "Twenty-seven Alphas have just appeared on the grid!"

"Calm down!" Celesta snapped. "Give me the information calmly and concisely. Where are the new arrivals?"

"Same distance from the primary star as this formation... sixty-two degrees laterally and fifteen degrees inclined." The OPS officer's face turned bright red at the sharp rebuke.

The formation was at another point just outside the system boundary, but nowhere near where they were operating and much too far away to offer any assistance to the Alphas the *Brooklands* was about to open fire on.

"Coms, get me a command channel to the *Ares*."

****

"Tell Commander Wright and Captain Lee to stay on mission," Jackson said to Lieutenant Keller. "Contact the *Artemis,* and tell Captain Forrest I want her tracking and managing the new arrivals. She has permission to reposition the remaining Ninth Squadron ships as she sees fit."

"Yes, sir." Keller slipped his headset back on.

"The *Brooklands* is spitting out her missiles," Barrett said. "Ten seconds until their main stages ignite."

"Coms, have the *Brooklands* clear the area," Jackson said. "Tell Captain Lee he is advised to tighten his escape vector to avoid the new arrivals, even if it means losing velocity."

"Yes, sir." A now harried Lieutenant Keller continued to talk to four different ships at one time about three different subjects.

"*Brooklands* is accelerating back down into the system," Hayashi reported. "Missiles are now actively homing and flying toward the Phage formation."

"Tactical, give them a light show," Jackson said.

"Aye, sir," Barrett said. "Firing forward laser cannons."

The forward projectors on both the *Ares* and the *Icarus* began firing in a strobing sequence that Jackson hoped would at least confuse the Phage long enough for the missiles to find their targets.

"Phage ships are breaking formation," Barrett said. "Bravos moving to intercept the missiles, and the Alphas are moving back and away."

"The new Alphas that arrived have integrated," Jackson said. "They're now too smart to fall for such a transparent deception. Coms, get me the *Icarus* and—"

"Captain, word coming in from the *Artemis*." Keller cut him off. "Another massive Phage formation has appeared outside the system. The Link should be updating their positions now."

The monitor showed that the other two formations were arrayed so each Phage group could cover a one hundred and twenty degree sector. The small group sitting outside the system was meant to goad him into a rash move, but they'd already planned to move in the rest of their forces in such a way that they cut off any chance of escape.

He'd only committed three ships out of his total force to the first formation, so he wasn't nearly as out of position as the Phage likely hoped he'd be. In fact, despite now being outnumbered, it looked like his forces were already in good position to block any individual group from getting too far into the system, at least in theory.

Jackson had no illusions that the collection of untested crews and outdated warships weren't going to be hard pressed to hold their own against the Phage when they decided to attack in earnest. From what he could see, they were experimenting and studying them as much as they themselves had been studied.

"Detection grid has another group of large ships transitioning in. This one is inside the outer edge of the system," Barrett said.

"Receiving transponder squawks now, sir," Hayashi said. "They're ours. Six ships... Oh wow."

"Ensign?"

"Captain, they're all *Dreadnought*-class battleships," Hayashi said.

"Incoming transmission on the Fleet-wide general frequency," Keller said.

"Put it through," Jackson said.

Could they really be about to fly into a contested system, in the middle of a battle, and try to grab him? Or would they simply order the fleet to withdraw?

"This is Admiral Joseph Marcum aboard the battleship *TCS Amsterdam*." The familiar voice came over the bridge speakers. "I am placing all six ships in this squadron under the command of Senior Captain Jackson Wolfe in defense of the Nuovo Patria Star System. Let's give 'em hell. *Amsterdam* out."

"Well, I wasn't expecting that," Jackson said.

Chapter 19

"Three... no, five impacts confirmed," Barrett said calmly. "Good detonations. One Alpha still appears to be under power."

"So we missed four completely," Jackson said. "Still, better than I thought we were going to do."

"Tactical, confirm four destroyed Alphas and one non-combat capable," Lieutenant Davis said.

She'd come up to relieve Ensign Hayashi just before the *Ares* reached weapons range with the Phage formation as per Jackson's instructions. With her additional authority as XO, he was pleased to see that she took it upon herself to lighten the burden on him and help manage some of the more "mundane" parts of combat, if they could so be called.

"Four confirmed destroyed," Barrett said. "Cannot give any certainty on the fifth, but the four remaining ships are now turning toward us and accelerating into the system."

Jackson watched the tactical display. "I see them."

The gravimetric detection system provided a time stamp on the incoming data, so the tactical computer could tell him how old the displayed data was and where the target likely was in that instant. It wasn't guaranteed accurate, given the advanced propulsion the Phage were using, but it was better than just taking a wild guess like he used to when all he had was long range radar.

Jackson weighed his options as four fresh Alphas, and possibly one more that still had some teeth, turned in toward the *Ares* and moved past the outer edges of the system. The two destroyers could likely take out the incoming ships, but it wasn't a lock that they would be able to fly away without sustaining significant damage themselves, and that wasn't even taking into account what a few dozen speedy little Bravos could do.

"Nav! Get me a course back down into the system that maintains as much velocity as possible to swing us down by Nuovo Patria," he ordered. "Coms, make sure the *Icarus* gets our projected course, and inform Commander Wright that we'll be withdrawing from the immediate area—"

"Fifth target is destroyed, Captain," Barrett smiled. "It looked like it was going to try and join the others, but it exploded right when it began to accelerate."

"Outstanding!" Jackson said. "Coms, pass our compliments to the *Brooklands,* and have Captain Lee rally near Black Fleet Battlegroup Two. Inform him that the rest of his missiles will likely be used to control the overflow around the edges—to keep the main Phage formations away from the planet."

"Aye, sir!"

"New course is plotted and vetted, Captain," Specialist Accari said.

The talented young spacer had been called up from his department by Jackson, specifically to run the nav station during the battle, much to the chagrin of the chief petty officer that normally manned first watch.

"Helm, come onto new course. All ahead full. Take us to .05c and hold velocity," Jackson said, forcing himself to sit down and appear calm, so as not to agitate his crew.

"Ahead full, aye."

"OPS, let me know when we come within two-way com range of the *Amsterdam*," Jackson said quietly to Lieutenant Davis.

"Yes, sir," she said.

He wasn't completely certain what Marcum was doing in the system. The fact that he'd announced himself as *Admiral* Marcum seemed to indicate there had been a major shift in priorities, at least within CENTCOM. Whatever the reason, he was glad to have six brand new battleships sitting in the system, even if he had no clue as to their capabilities.

"Coms, send a discreet message to the *Amsterdam*," he said. "I need to know what they're carrying and a rough summary of the *Dreadnought*-class capabilities."

"Sending now, sir," Keller said.

"We're receiving word from the rest of the fleet, Captain," Davis said. "The Phage are now entering the system from all three points, and more ships are appearing at the edge of our sensor range. Still no sign of any Charlies."

"That bothers me more than anything else." Jackson felt like he was missing a significant piece of the big picture.

For the next few hours, the bridge was calm and quiet as his crew sifted through information as it came in over the Link and monitored the *Ares* while she was diving down into the system at full power. During that time, two Fifth Fleet squadrons arrived from the New European Commonwealth, and the first of the Phage formations met up with the Third Fleet ships Jackson had put in orbit around the sixth planet. The Phage could have just flown by them, but he'd correctly surmised that they wouldn't leave an enemy behind them. The quiet only lasted a little longer as reports from the initial engagements began rolling in.

"We've lost our first ship, Captain," Lieutenant Keller said somberly. "Third Fleet destroyer, the *Palli*."

"Thank you, Lieutenant," Jackson struggled to keep his voice neutral. He knew there would be losses, but that knowledge didn't made losing a whole crew any less horrific. "OPS, keep the ship's log updated with any Terran casualties, and have a com drone loaded and ready to launch at all times."

"Aye, sir."

"We all knew this wasn't going to be a lossless victory," Jackson said to the bridge crew. "We will lose more ships before this battle is done. Let's stay focused, and make sure none of those sacrifices are wasted."

"Captain, the second Third Fleet squadron is bugging out after the loss of the *Palli*." Barrett kept his eyes trained on the positions update on the display. "They're making a run for the Pyeong-on jump point."

"They're not going to make it," Davis said.

The display showed two Alphas and eighteen Bravos that had broken off to pursue the seven Asianic Union ships. There was nothing Jackson could do. Any radio transmission he made would take over ninety minutes to reach them, and the data he was seeing was nearly as old already. For all he knew, the Third Fleet ships were already destroyed.

The outcome was all but inevitable as they watched the data trickle in. The Alphas ran through the formation, seeming to disable each ship before the Bravos swarmed in and finished them off. One by one, the Third Fleet warships winked out of existence on the tactical display. A few pixels switching colors to signify the loss of thousands of lives was vulgar, but it was the reality Jackson had chosen. All the ships in the star system were there at his request, and though they came willingly, the loss of so many weighed heavily on his soul.

"Coms, patch me through to the Fleet," Jackson said. "This is Captain Wolfe aboard the *Ares*. We now have a large hole in our picket line with a Phage formation poised to exploit it. We're outnumbered three to one and spread thin. It is imperative you hold the line. *Ares* out.

"Lieutenant Keller, tell Seventh Fleet Battlegroup Two I need them to move into a blocking position just beyond the orbit of the fifth planet, where that squadron just left a gap. I'll send more help as I get it. Make sure the *Brooklands* holds back near Nuovo Patria."

"Aye, sir."

Jackson had carefully arrayed his limited resources in small formations flying concentric circles with Nuovo Patria as the epicenter. He made sure they were all maintaining their forward velocity since Terran ships didn't have the ability to sit at a relative stop and then accelerate after the faster Phage ships. He hoped that by keeping everyone moving, they would be able to more quickly change course and pursue during individual skirmishes.

Of course, his plan hadn't counted on the fact that no matter how brave the ship crews had been when they'd entered the system, there would be some who would bolt as they got their first real look at an enemy they'd been hearing about for years. After watching an entire squadron flee after first contact, he began to reevaluate what he would actually be able to bring to bear in this battle. The answers he came up with didn't make him feel any better.

"Captain, we're within range of the *Amsterdam* for two-way communication," Barrett announced after a few more hours of easily keeping ahead of their pursuers.

"Lieutenant Davis, you have the bridge," Jackson said. "Lieutenant Keller, send a signal to the *Amsterdam,* and inform them I'd like a private two-way channel with Admiral Marcum. Send it to my office, and do not hesitate to interrupt if something happens."

"Aye, sir."

****

"Captain Wolfe," Marcum said neutrally once the channel had been established. "I assume this isn't a social call, given we're in the middle of a pitched battle."

"I just wanted to make sure I had the chance to personally thank you for bringing those battleships, sir," Jackson said carefully.

"You left me little choice." Marcum shrugged. His neutral, almost cordial, demeanor was strange given their previous interaction. Marcum was certainly a politician first and a Fleet officer a distant second. "A com drone entered the Ark System, and before we could intercept it, the message had already begun broadcasting. It stirred the blood of some of my younger officers, and before I had a full-fledged mutiny on my hands, I asked my flag captain to draw up plans to provide support."

"I see, sir," Jackson said.

"Aren't you going to ask if I'm going to bring you up on charges for that little stunt?" Marcum asked.

"Honestly, sir, I'm not sure I even expect to survive this battle," Jackson said. "We're quite badly outnumbered, and more are streaming in."

"I see that," Marcum said seriously. "Would you like some advice… and maybe a bit of a warning?"

"Of course, sir."

"Use the *Dreadnought*-class ships as a quick-reaction force to shore up any holes that appear in your lines," Marcum said. "It took me a minute to figure out what in the hell you were doing with your formations, but I can see that you've done an admirable job of maximizing your coverage and giving our ships a fighting chance by making sure engagements happen at speed. These battleships are very, very fast for as big as they are, so keep that in mind when deploying them."

"Yes, sir," Jackson said. "And the warning?"

Marcum sighed. "I don't want to be here. More specifically, I don't want half the Fleet here making some idiotic last stand for a strategically insignificant planet."

Jackson began to protest, but Marcum held up a hand to silence him.

"You're a captain and, despite all previous indicators otherwise, a damn good one. But you're sorely lacking in perspective when it comes to the big picture. Part of the deal I made with my captains for showing up here is that on my order, we'll break and head for a jump point if this battle looks lost. I will not risk losing our most advanced starships in a symbolic defeat that won't save the people of Nuovo Patria either way, and when I say our most advanced I mean *all* of our newest generation starships currently here."

"You'll order the Ninth Squadron out of the area?" Jackson asked, somewhat surprised.

Before he could tell the Admiral that he had no intention of complying with such an order, Marcum cut him off. "I will do what I feel I must, Captain. Marcum out."

Jackson wanted to punch his terminal when Marcum's face disappeared from it. Having the six battlewagons in the area of operations had been a huge morale booster and an ace in the hole. Now he was being told they'd more or less flown in as a show of force and that Marcum had no intention of allowing him to utilize the ships to their full potential, despite his grandiose announcement when they'd transitioned in.

"As if this wasn't a big enough pile of shit to begin with." He sighed, logging out of his terminal and getting up a slight groan.

He'd had very little sleep, hadn't had a proper meal in the last two weeks, and his prosthetic seemed to be acting up at odd times. What made him feel very, very tired was the realization that the battle for Nuovo Patria had barely started.

When he returned to the bridge, he saw that things had begun to heat up along all fronts, as the Phage spread out from their three-point incursion and began testing the Terran fleet's resolve. Even though the humans were greatly outnumbered, a lot of that was due to all the Bravos flying around the system. While they were formidable in groups, a single Bravo wasn't much of a match for even their oldest frigate.

Jackson watched the tactical board for a moment before coming to the obvious conclusion that he was unable to manage the battle on the far side of the system due to the delay.

"OPS, group our forces into three sectors, and then give me the listings on my terminal." He slid into his chair.

"Aye, sir." Davis pulled up a new menu to quickly comply.

"Tactical, what are our friends behind us doing?"

"The four Alphas are beginning to close the gap, sir," Barrett said. "The Bravos split off ten minutes ago. I'm tracking them through the grav sensors. I think the Alphas are just going to herd us back to where the rest of the fleet is operating."

"Agreed." Jackson looked over the lists Davis had sent to his terminal. As he'd hoped, the fleet was still well distributed around the planet.

"Coms, I'm sending you three lists marked sectors one, two, and three. We are sector one. Inform Captain Forrest aboard the *Artemis* that she is in command of sector two, and tell Captain Koon aboard the *Myeong-ye* that he is in command of sector three. Make it a general order on the command channel, so that the other COs aren't confused by the switch."

"Yes, sir."

"Make sure Forrest and Koon understand they're still reporting to me and that my orders still stand," Jackson said. "I don't want any freelancing out there."

"Understood, sir," Keller said.

"Captain, the four Alphas pursuing us are breaking off," Barrett said, obviously confused.

"Breaking off to where?" He stood and took a few steps towards the main display.

"Unknown, sir," Barrett said. "We're still far enough away from the main battle that they could be heading anywhere."

"Is there someplace where Phage forces have taken a particularly hard beating?"

"Yes, sir," Davis spoke up. "Battlegroup Two has taken out three Alphas and over thirty Bravos near the sixth planet in sector two."

"Black Fleet!" Master Chief Green shouted, pumping his fist.

Jackson couldn't help himself and smiled at the chief's enthusiasm.

"Coms, tell Senior Captain Fergus that he's doing an outstanding job," Jackson said. "Then warn him that four more Alphas are probably heading his way."

"Captain Fergus asked me to tell you, and I'm quoting, 'We're taking all comers. Tell the Wolfe that any fucking Phage that comes into my skies gets turned to slag,'" Keller said after a moment.

"He seems like a... colorful... individual," Davis said.

"That's an understatement, Lieutenant." Jackson remembeed the times he'd met the over-the-top, bombastic captain from the New European Commonwealth. The small smile died on his lips as he realized that Fergus, and all his crew, may die in this system following him into battle.

As the battle began really heating up, and both sides began racking up losses, Jackson tried to remain focused on the big picture. The *Ares* was still roaring down into the system with the *Icarus* following closely behind, but they were more or less alone in their area of responsibility.

The battle was roughly a constricting sphere that would eventually shrink down to be fought over the skies of Nuovo Patria, and there were ships constantly streaming through sector one, but the two destroyers were neither being pursued nor had any targets to pursue themselves. Why? Could the Phage actually recognize the *Ares* and know that it was a ship that had already taken out a few Alphas singlehandedly? The strangeness of two ships flying alone, unprotected, and being left unmolested was too much for Jackson to dismiss as happenstance.

"Coms, send a fleet-wide message that randomization protocols are still in place, even for stricken vessels exiting the area."

Two more Eighth Fleet ships limped away from their respective engagements. This time, it looked like the Phage had no interest in running down the wounded and were concentrating their forces on the formations putting up the biggest fight. Oddly enough, this left the newer battleships barely straining to pick off the occasional attack by an Alpha or group of Bravos while the two Black Fleet battlegroups were fighting for their lives and had lost three ships already between them.

"Also, message the *Amsterdam* and get them moving over to cover Battlegroup One so they can withdraw that heavy cruiser with the damaged engine."

"Aye, sir." Keller's voice was beginning to leave him after ten hours of near constant talking into his headset.

Jackson still felt like he was being toyed with. The Phage were executing fast, flanking attacks on the perimeter that forced the Terran ships to break orbit to pursue or pull back in toward Nuovo Patria so they could remain in range of the other ships nearby. The result was a continual, and alarmingly fast, shrinking of the picket lines Jackson had tried to set up. Most ships would retreat inward under full power after brief exchanges of fire and now, less than twenty-four hours in, it looked like they'd be within striking range of the planet long before he'd hoped.

"Captain, there are two Alphas that made it through Eighth Fleet's picket line and are heading straight for the planet," Barrett said. "They're accelerating too fast for the Alliance ships to pursue." Jackson looked at the plots on the tactical board for a few long seconds before replying.

"Coms, tell the Eighth Fleet ships to hold their position and to *stop* giving ground," he said. "Tell them we'll deal with the two ships that broke through."

"Aye, sir."

"OPS, get ready to—"

"Two more Alphas peeling off the formation at the edge of our sector, Captain," Barrett said. "They're coming right at us."

Jackson rubbed his eyes and tried to think. This wasn't a coincidence. The Phage knew the *Ares* and the *Icarus* were basically bystanders so far by virtue of being positioned so far away from the main body of the battle. So they rush a pair of ships to the planet and two more at him to try and force a decision. Will he turn and defend himself, or will he continue on to defend the planet?

"Coms, tell Commander Wright she's clear to break away from the formation and engage the two targets approaching us out of sector three," Jackson said. "She's free to use anything at her disposal to keep them at bay. Nav, give me an intercept course for the two Alphas approaching the planet."

"Course ready, Captain," Accari said.

"That was fast, Specialist." "I've had multiple courses being updated simultaneously," Accari said. "One of them was in anticipation that we'd need to break hard for Nuovo Patria."

Jackson nodded his appreciation for the forethought, tremendously impressed with the young spacer's instincts.

"Helm, all ahead flank," Jackson ordered.

"Ahead flank, aye!" the helmsman said, sounding happy to be doing something other than cold coasting down into the system. "Helm answering new course."

"Tactical, begin calculating when we'll have to start braking compared to when those two Alphas will reach orbit," Jackson said. "I want to know how much speed we need to put on or, more specifically, how much we *can* put on before we'll be unable to slow down enough for a high orbit."

"Yes, sir," Barrett said.

The rumble of the engines and hiss of the air handlers was the only sound on the bridge for several minutes as his crew worked furiously to get the ship ready for her first taste of combat since the battle had started. It was a strange change of pace to be in command of the overall battle and not actually have his ship right in the thick of things. Unfortunately, if he was being honest with himself, he'd taken the bait the Phage had dangled in front of him, and in the process, taken himself out of the fight. In hindsight, he should have been more patient or sent two other ships to escort the *Brooklands*.

"What's bothering you, sir?" Davis had been relieved again by Ensign Hayashi and resumed her seat to Jackson's right.

"Besides the horrific losses we're taking?" He instantly regretted his sarcasm. There was no reason to be unprofessional, even in the middle of a pitched battle. "I don't understand what the Phage are doing. Where are the Charlies?"

"Maybe they were unavailable," she said. "We're assuming they take a long time to refuel, or whatever the proper term is. It's also possible they aren't able to take much damage, so the Alphas are sent in first to clear out the system before they make an appearance."

"Not bad, Lieutenant," Jackson said after a moment. "Both of those theories are plausible, but I think the second has real merit. If the Phage knew we were going to draw a line in the sand here, maybe they didn't want to bring in the Charlies too soon and risk them getting hit with a few hundred Shrikes."

"Of course, that raises another problem, sir." Davis frowned and leaned in so she wasn't overheard. "Even if we fight them to a standstill here, we may just be delaying them."

"It's something I'm considering," he agreed. "Unfortunately, I don't think they'll let us disengage all that easily, even if I were inclined to leave the citizens of Nuovo Patria to their fates."

"Understood, sir." She wisely dropped the subject.

The idea that the entire fleet he'd called to the system might be wasted in what would basically amount to a short delay before the inevitable arrival of the planet devouring Charlies wasn't something Jackson wanted to consider. He tried to put the line of thought out of his mind since there was little he could do about it at the moment. He'd committed his forces, and now he would have to see the battle to its conclusion.

"Velocity now holding at .17c," Barrett said. "Helm, cease acceleration."

The helmsman pulled the throttles back. "Engines answering zero thrust."

"Tactical, you have command authority for our braking maneuver as well. Assign two Shrikes to each target, and have the auto-mag standing by," Jackson said. "Coms, try and get in touch with someone on the planet surface, and warn them they have two Alphas incoming."

"Aye, sir." Barrett rubbed his eyes and shook his head.

Jackson looked around. Everyone on the bridge was beginning to show signs of fatigue, but not so much so that he was willing to try and get them any relief. At least not until the two targets directly threatening the planet were dealt with.

"We're ninety-five minutes from our initial decel and just over two hours before we're within effective range for the Shrikes," Barrett said.

"Thank you, Lieutenant Commander," Jackson said absently. He had two windows pulled up on his terminal—one a tactical overlay from the Link and another a direct telemetry stream from the *Icarus*.

Commander Wright was taking no unnecessary chances with an irreplaceable starship and its crew, something Jackson approved of wholeheartedly. Though it seemed she was keeping to the basic doctrine developed for fighting the Phage, she did bring a bit of her own innovation to the table. The *Icarus* had already fired two Shrikes at each of the incoming Alphas, but the missiles had been programmed so that once they'd expended their first stages two of the missiles would stack in closely behind the first two.

Although that seemed like a common sense method to protect the trailing missiles, tactical officers weren't normally fans of it, since, when the lead missile was destroyed, the second would more likely than not impact the debris or be taken out by the explosion. The new generation of Shrikes, however, had an ultra-dense alloy penetrator for a nose cone, and the warhead was a fusion warhead, both of which could survive some bumps as they continued on to the target.

Wright had likely insisted on the stacked formation because she would have correctly assumed the first wave of missiles wouldn't have much of a chance against two Alphas closing such a large gap of uninterrupted space. They'd see the missiles coming long before they were within range of their second stage boost and would easily knock them down.

Once he was certain that Commander Wright had her engagement handled, he quickly scanned through the Link updates to check on the overall status of the battle. The news was bleak. Ninth Squadron was down to four effectives as the *Hyperion* was limping out of the area on one engine, and both Black Fleet battlegroups had taken a pounding, losing six ships between them.

The *Dreadnought*-class battleships were flying by individual skirmishes at high speed and peeling a few Phage units off from the perimeters, but they were largely staying out of the fight, at Marcum's express orders no doubt. The Eighth Fleet units in sector two were putting up a hell of a fight, but they were getting pushed back toward Nuovo Patria, and most of the Third Fleet ships were now flying in the periphery, either unable or unwilling to engage the hoard of Phage units that were slowly but surely compressing the battle toward the planet.

"Helm, begin decel on my mark," Barrett's voice interrupted the relative silence on the bridge. "Mark!"

Almost immediately, the deck began to vibrate, and the soft rumble of the engines firing in reverse drowned out much of the ambient noise.

"Give me an update on our targets." Jackson forced himself to turn away from his terminal. Commander Wright would either be able to handle her fight or she wouldn't, and watching the telemetry link would do nothing but distract him from his own task.

"Target A is holding on the far side of the planet relative to our approach vector," Barrett said. "Target B has placed itself directly between us and the planet, holding station and sitting at an altitude of approximately two hundred thousand kilometers."

"Coms, has Nuovo Patria reported any enemy fire coming their way?" Jackson asked.

"Negative, sir," Keller said.

"Another test," Jackson said softly.

"Sir?" Davis asked.

"These last few movements by the Alphas in our sector make little strategic sense," Jackson said. "I think they're gauging reactions."

"Excuse me, sir, but why would they be playing games and trying to observe behavior in the middle of a pitched battle in which they're taking heavy losses?" she asked.

"Losses mean nothing to them." Jackson waved her off, absolutely certain of what he was seeing now. "The intelligence present in this system deliberately pulled the *Icarus* away and now has a target sitting directly between us and a planet with millions of humans. It wants to see if I'll fire on this Alpha at the risk of hitting the planet."

"It seems they have more than enough examples of human behavior to understand that we value individual life," she said. "Why bother with something so elaborate?"

"I couldn't tell you, Lieutenant," he said. "But let's go ahead and throw them a curveball. Helm! Come to port fifteen degrees. All ahead full."

"Correcting course, aye," the helmsman said. "Engines answering ahead full."

There was a harsh swaying back and forth on the bridge as the thrust was reversed and the power cranked back up to maximum.

"Sir?" Barrett asked.

"As you were, Lieutenant Commander." Jackson stood. "Keep weapons lock on Target B, and calculate a firing solution for the auto-mag that assumes a passing shot with the gun oriented perpendicular to the target."

"Yes, sir." Barrett pulled up a new pane at his terminal to get the computer started on the calculations.

"I know a crossing shot with the cannon is less than ideal, but I'm a little hesitant to start firing nukes off this close to the planet," Jackson explained to both his tactical officer and XO. "It's unlikely a miss or deflection would detonate on the surface, but the EMP from even a successful strike near low-orbit could knock out the power grid. I'd rather not take away anything they might be able to use for their own defense."

"Understood, sir," Barrett said. "So far, the target is maintaining position."

"That won't last for long," Jackson said as the *Ares* angled over, and the engines pushed her out of the original orbital insertion vector. He'd committed the ship, and now it was too late to try and decel. They would be passing the planet while accelerating, and the Phage would know that.

"Target B is reacting, sir," Barrett said. "It's dropping back down closer to the planet and pacing us to make sure we can't get an unimpeded shot."

"As I expected." Jackson nodded. "Adjust firing solution for Target A."

"Aye, sir."

"Helm, come back to starboard seven degrees, and incline ten," Jackson said. "Maintain engine power levels."

"Sir, that will put us within effective range of both Alphas almost simultaneously," Barrett warned.

"Noted." Jackson didn't bother to explain himself further.

"Captain, Battlegroup One is withdrawing," Lieutenant Keller said. "They've taken heavy losses and are less than twenty percent combat effective. The *Tempest* was lost."

"Understood." Jackson tried to maintain a calm exterior. The *Tempest* was the massive fleet carrier that flew the flag for Battlegroup One. That ship had a crew of just over five-thousand spacers and more than a few that he knew personally. "Tell whoever is now in command to exit the area as best they can. I can't afford anyone to fly escort. Randomization protocols are still in effect."

The next hour and a half were tense as Jackson half expected the two Alphas to take their opportunity to rush him while hoping they would do as expected and try to use the planet as a shield. He wasn't completely sure what the Alpha on the far side of the planet was trying to accomplish. So far, it hadn't fired a single shot, and it didn't look like it was making a move to attack the surface of Nuovo Patria.

"Captain, the *Icarus* is reporting that both Alphas have disengaged before they were within missile range," Keller said. "They're now heading back out of the system."

"That makes no—"

"Target A and B are also disengaging, sir," Barrett said in alarm. "They're moving back around the far side of the planet and are accelerating away toward where the rest of the fleet is bunched up."

"I'm open to any wild guesses as to what this is all about," Jackson sneered. Although the planet had been spared any enemy fire, it seemed that he wasn't as adept at guessing the Phage's behavior as he'd let himself believe.

"Incoming message from the *Amsterdam*," Keller said. "Admiral Marcum's personal codes."

"Put it through."

"This is Admiral Marcum aboard the *Amsterdam*. I am assuming overall command of the fleet and ordering a general retreat from the Nuovo Patria System. We have taken unacceptable losses and are no longer able to provide an adequate defense. Break contact, and exit the system at best possible speed. *Amsterdam* out."

"Blunt enough," Jackson mumbled.

Before he could gather his thoughts and address his crew, a flashing on his terminal caught his attention.

"Captain, the *Atlas* and the *Artemis* are reporting a complete loss of control," he said. "Both ships appear to be operating on their own and are moving into formation with the *Dreadnought*-class battleships."

Jackson looked at the flashing light again. Marcum was making good on a promise that Jackson hadn't fully understood at the time. He didn't have to order him out of the system. He had the codes to access the remote override protocols for the *Starwolf*-class ships.

"Confirm that the *Icarus* is still under command of the crew," Jackson said.

"Confirmed, sir," Keller said.

"Tell Commander Wright to change course and put her ship in high-orbit over Nuovo Patria," Jackson ordered. "Nav, I want a course for the *Ares* as well… same destination. Helm, get us there at best possible speed."

"Aye, sir."

Over the next few hours, the indicator on Jackson's terminal lit up no fewer than ten times as the override commands were sent from the *Amsterdam* over and over. After that came the inevitable com requests from Admiral Marcum, but the rest of the fleet was now well outside two-way communications range, and Jackson had little interest in opening multiple messages in which the Admiral would no doubt have nothing constructive to say.

"All Fleet vessels with the exception of us and the *Icarus* are confirmed to be leaving the system, sir," Ensign Hayashi said. "The Link is beginning to break down, but from what I can tell, the Phage are letting them escape with only an occasional shot taken from long range."

"Herding them along." Jackson shook his head. "I assume we'll soon be detecting the Charlies arriving near the vicinity of the Podere jump point."

"What's the plan, Captain?" Chief Green asked from the hatchway.

Jackson addressed the entire bridge crew. "We're going to continue to offer a defense to Nuovo Patria as best we can while continuing to collect data. I have no intentions of throwing our lives away in a meaningless gesture of defiance, but the Fleet has given back as good as it got during this battle, and the enemy is weakened and cautious." He knew his crew had to be exhausted, but they still looked determined and willing.

"There are still two destroyers in this system that are undamaged and fully armed. We'll see if there's a chance to take out one or more of the Charlies when they arrive while picking our engagements with the remaining Alphas. I know you're exhausted and more than a little apprehensive about staying behind, but I'll get us through this. Tactical, go full active sensors, and give me a breakdown of what's left in this system."

"Aye aye, sir," Barrett said crisply.

As the Terran ships limped to the jump points and transitioned out of the system, the Phage forces began to move back down and take position just outside the orbit of Nuovo Patria's second moon, while the two Terran destroyers flew fast and low just outside of the planet's atmosphere. Nerves began to fray as more and more Phage arrived, and yet no move was made to engage them.

During the next ten hours, Jackson was reminded of his first encounter with a Phage ship, a specially built Alpha that had been probing into Terran space. Toward the end, that ship had also tested him for specific reactions, shadowing him for over a day until, under the enormous tension, he could almost feel his sanity slipping away.

This time was different. He was different.

As he watched the Phage drift in high-orbit with the obvious intention of cutting off his escape, a detached calm came over him. He was here, they were here, and whatever was about to happen was going to happen whether he wanted it to or not.

****

"These stims are killing my stomach." Barrett complained quietly as he continued to update the tracks of all the enemy ships in orbit.

"Mine as well, Mr. Barrett," Jackson said quietly. "Any change in their orbital trajectories?"

"No, sir," Barrett said. "Still maintaining a precise altitude of just over five hundred and fifty thousand kilometers. No increase in velocity either."

They'd been awake and on duty for over thirty-six hours, and it was showing. The stims were helping keep them physically awake but did little for the lapses in mental acuity and judgment. Jackson had been rotating everyone out that he could, but he and Barrett had remained at their posts ever since the Phage had surrounded Nuovo Patria and begun their blockade, for lack of a better term.

"We're getting some activity in the outer ring of their formation, sir," Ensign Hayashi said.

He and Barrett had been sharing monitoring duties after Jackson had almost been forced to have the Marine sentry remove Davis from the bridge for an hour of rest.

"What have you got, Ensign?" Jackson asked.

The inner ring of Phage ships had been made up completely of Bravos, still quite numerous after the battle, but the eight remaining Alphas were flying a slow orbit slightly further out.

"The Alphas are maintaining their orbital altitude, but they've increased velocity by fifteen percent and are still steadily accelerating." Hayashi highlighted the data on the main display.

"Coms, call everyone back to battle stations, and send word to the *Icarus* that this might be it," Jackson said. "The Alphas are accelerating to increase their effective coverage and keep us trapped down here. This will either be an attack or the arrival of the Charlies we've been waiting for."

"New contacts!" Barrett almost shouted. "Grav sensors picked them up. They just appeared in the inner system!"

"Calm down and tell me what we have, Lieutenant Commander," Jackson snapped. "Is it the four Charlies?"

"Uh... no, Captain." Barrett squinted at his display. "Eighteen contacts, less relative mass than the *Ares* and strangely low power output detected for as quickly as they're accelerating toward us."

"A multiple of nine… sounds like the Phage, sir," Hayashi said as Davis rushed back onto the bridge, her eyes red-rimmed and her utility top half buttoned.

"I would have to agree if for no other reason than if it isn't the Phage, we have a third player to this game." Jackson looked away from Davis as she tried to pull herself together and get up to speed by looking at the tactical display. "Begin dumping data into three com drones simultaneously, and prep them for immediate launch. If we're seeing a new class of Phage ship, CENTCOM will need to know about it. Tactical, confirm your data with the *Icarus*."

"Aye, sir," Barrett said.

"Alphas are breaking orbit!" Hayashi said. "All eight are moving into position between the planet and the new contacts."

"Nav! Put us in a polar orbit, and increase altitude to one hundred thousand kilometers," Jackson ordered. "Coms, get the *Icarus* moving into the same orbit. Tell Commander Wright I want constant line of sight coverage on the new contacts between the two ships. Helm, you're free to adjust your course as you get it."

The harsh rumble of the mains pushing the *Ares* out of her current orbit shook the deck while Jackson's sleep-deprived brain raced to make sense of what these new contacts were. He doubted they were yet another secret class of Terran starship sent in to save the day. But if they were Phage, why were the Alphas moving to intercept them? Unless there wasn't complete unity within the Phage hierarchy, and this was an opposing faction… and if so, were they likely to still have the same views on exterminating human populations?

"OPS, have our two remaining Jacobsen drones prepped and launched toward where the Phage are about to face off with these newcomers," Jackson said after considering all the possibilities. "Full sensor package, and make it fast."

"Yes, sir." Hayashi pulled his headset back on to talk to Flight OPS.

According to the gravimetric sensor nets, the new ships had an impressive rate of acceleration and were also employing some sort of reactionless drive to move them along. That fact alone made Jackson's heart sink, as he'd been holding out hope that perhaps this was another secret Tsuyo R&D had been keeping under wraps. Now the best he could hope for was an "enemy of my enemy" scenario as possibly a third species was flying into the system to fight the Phage.

"Drones are away, sir. They'll have radar contact with the Alphas in the next ten minutes and will be in visual range in another forty."

"Thank you, Ensign," Jackson said. "Helm, continue orbital change. OPS and Tactical, make sure our sensors are backing up the drones. It's likely they'll get taken out pretty quick when the shooting starts, and we need as complete a record as possible before launching the com drones. Coms, what's the situation on the surface?"

"Tense, Captain," Lieutenant Keller said. "They've been waiting for days for an attack that's yet to come. There's some minor civil unrest, but mostly everyone seems to be holed up in their homes."

"That's as good a place for them as any," Jackson muttered.

"It's a shame we have nothing to offer them for assurance," Davis said.

"It would be an obviously hollow gesture, Lieutenant," Jackson said. "Their ground stations are well aware the fleet has left the system, and only two destroyers stand between them and the enemy."

"Sir! Power output readings are spiking on the eighteen new contacts, well past even what the *Dreadnought*-class ships put out," Barrett said. "They're now accelerating toward the Phage Alpha formation, exceeding eight hundred G's and increasing."

"That's impossible!" someone hissed behind Jackson.

"What are the Alphas doing?" he asked.

"Alphas are spreading out evenly," Hayashi said. "Thermal build up on the leading edges of each ship suggests they're preparing to fire."

"Drones are locking on optical sensors now," Hayashi said.

The main display showed that the *Ares* was climbing up around Nuovo Patria and would crest just as the new contacts came within range of the Alphas' plasma weapons.

"Unknown contacts are now slowing... They're redeploying. Eight are continuing toward the Alphas, and the other—they're firing!" Barrett's running commentary was interrupted as eight of the unknown ships fired laser cannons of such prodigious power that the beams were actually semi-visible on the sensors as they impacted trace gasses and particulate matter drifting through the area.

Jackson watched, mesmerized as the new ships fired their powerful beams well outside what he would consider an effective range for that type of weapon.

"Three Alphas have been destroyed!" Hayashi exclaimed. "Four! Five—"

"The other ten ships have split again!" Barrett called out. "They're taking out the Bravos and taking them out *fast*!"

"All Alphas are destroyed!" Hayashi shouted. "Optical scans are picking up expanding debris, and that's about it."

"Who the hell *are* these guys?" Jackson demanded as the ships ripped through the remaining Phage.

Although a few of the smaller Bravos managed to break orbit and escape using whatever method they used for FTL travel, the crew of the *Ares* sat stunned as the eighteen new ships shredded an entire Phage armada in less than two hours.

"All eighteen ships are returning to their previous, low-power readings, Captain," Barrett said. "Putting up the best visual capture we have of one on the main display."

The blurry image was of a sleek, seamless ship that gleamed silver-white as it passed through the light of the primary star. It certainly had little in common with any Phage ship they'd seen so far, but also did not remind him of any Terran designs he'd ever seen.

"What are they doing now?" he asked.

"They've formed up into two phalanx flights of nine each and are moving into high-orbit over the planet," Barrett said.

"Let's give them a moment before we try—"

"Sir, there's another contact that just appeared in the inner system," Barrett said. "It's enormous… computer is trying to resolve the data now."

"Is it a Charlie?" Jackson asked, confused as to why they would only send in one.

"No, sir," Barrett said. "It's an Alpha, but its profile matches the first one we encountered with the *Blue Jacket*, not those we just fought."

"Incoming transmission, sir," Keller said. "Audio only."

"From the Alpha?" Davis exclaimed, clearly shocked.

"It appears so," Keller said. "Putting it through now."

"*I speak to the leader.*" A raspy, metallic voice made all the hairs on the back of Jackson's neck stand at attention.

"I'm Captain Jackson Wolfe," he said. "Who is this?"

"*I bring warning,*" the voice said, ignoring the question. "*The test is concluded.*"

"What test?"

"Channel is closed, sir," Keller said.

"Target has disappeared from sensors," Barrett said.

"Well that was ominous." Jackson fell into his chair. "What did it mean by test?"

"Maybe the more important question is if we passed or failed," Davis said.

"Another incoming com signal, sir." Keller frowned. "This one is definitely coming from those unknown ships. Short-range UHF radio signal... I can't quite seem to make out what they're saying. There's also a video signal, but the computer can't resolve the format."

"Just put the audio through." Jackson's skin almost tingled from the anticipation.

"Greetings unknown Earth vessel," a voice said in an accent that only Jackson was familiar with, though the inflection wasn't quite right and could almost be called archaic. "I am Colonel Robert Blake, Unites States Air Force. I think we have much to discuss."

"Colonel who from the what force?" Chief Green blurted out as Jackson shook his head in disbelief.

Chapter 19

"*Earth* vessel?" Barrett asked incredulously before throwing a slightly guilty look at Jackson.

"Do you have any idea what he's talking about, Captain?" Davis asked.

"Someone is playing games," Jackson said. "Colonel Blake is a famous aviator from Earth's ancient past. I doubt any of you would have heard of him."

"He was the commander and pilot of the *Carl Sagan*, Earth's first attempt at a faster than light exploration mission." Specialist Accari spoke up. "The mission was launched but never heard from again."

"Very good, Specialist." Jackson nodded. "Our friend on the other end of the com signal sounds pretty spry for a man who would be over three hundred years old."

"Captain, the channel is still open," Keller reminded him. "How would you like me to respond?"

"Put me on." Jackson waited for the double beep. "Colonel Blake, this is Captain Jackson Wolfe of the Terran starship *Ares*... First, let me express my thanks for your intervention on behalf of the people of Nuovo Patria, the Warsaw Alliance, the Terran Confederacy, and my own crew."

"I am pleased to make your acquaintance, Captain Wolfe," the voice of the supposed Robert Blake said. "I'm sure that you're either in utter disbelief of my claim, or you have no idea who I am claiming to be."

"You're correct on both counts, Colonel," Jackson said. "The bridge crew is pretty evenly divided."

"Of course," Blake chuckled. "Perhaps, Captain, it would be easier if I either came aboard your ship or met you on the surface of the planet below us. A quick blood test should at least confirm that I am, indeed, human. We can work out the details from there."

"It is not within my authority to invite you to land on Nuovo Patria, Colonel, so I guess that leaves us one option," Jackson said after a moment. He didn't believe for a moment that the voice on the other end of the channel was who it claimed to be and he was treading carefully. Humanity couldn't afford another enemy with such superior technology. "Would you like us to send a shuttle for you?"

"No need, Captain Wolfe," Blake said. "My ship has analyzed your lateral airlocks and is fabricating the necessary collar for us to dock directly with each other—with your permission, of course. I felt it might streamline this process if you were also able to come aboard my ship."

Jackson looked around at his bewildered bridge crew and shrugged. "Very well, Colonel. The *Ares* will maintain her current orbit. When can we expect you to have the necessary hardware completed and join us?"

"Already complete, Captain," Blake said. "Moving to you now."

"In that case, we will see you shortly at the starboard airlock," Jackson said. "*Ares* out."

"Channel closed, sir."

"Coms, tell Major Ortiz I need him and five of his best to meet me at the starboard airlock," Jackson said. "Lieutenant Davis, you have the bridge. Once I leave, you are to initiate lockdown protocols. Nothing comes in here until we've gotten some answers. If this goes to hell, I want you to order the *Icarus* out of the system. In the meantime, bring Commander Wright up to speed on what's happening."

"Aye, sir," Davis said to his back as he walked off the bridge.

****

"He's completely homo sapiens," Commander Owens confirmed to Jackson just outside the conference room.

Colonel Blake was still seated inside with Lieutenant Davis, along with Major Ortiz and his Marines. The strange ship had docked easily with the *Ares* and revealed that it was only crewed by a single person, despite the fact it was half the tonnage of the destroyer that had a crew of over six hundred.

Owens scrolled through his test results. "There are even markers that confirm he would have come from Earth in the mid twenty-first century, though I can't tell you any more precisely than that."

"So, he's either telling the truth, or someone went through an incredible, and unnecessary amount of trouble to fool us," Jackson said.

"Unnecessary?" Owens asked.

"Their ships defeated an entire Phage armada in less than two hours," Jackson explained. "And easily. The *Ares* and *Icarus* would have been no match for them. If they wanted something from us, they could just take it."

"That's not my area of expertise." Owens shrugged. "I'm just here to tell you that as far as my equipment is able to determine, he's human."

"Thank you, Doctor." Jackson nodded and turned to reenter the room.

"Captain," Blake said as Jackson walked in and took his seat.

"Good news, Colonel," he said. "As far as my Chief Medical Officer can determine, you're as human as anybody in this room."

"That *is* a relief," Blake said with a wry smile. "Tell me, Captain... How long have you been fighting the species you call the Phage? We intercepted their message to you. Highly unusual in our experience. As far as I know, they've never bothered to communicate with a species they've marked for destruction before."

"We'll get to that in due time," Jackson said, still highly disturbed by the cryptic Phage message—their first and only contact with the species to date. "I think a far more interesting story would be how a near-mythological figure from the distant past has swooped in with ships of incredible power and pulled our asses out of the fire at the last possible instance."

"I could say it was a wild coincidence, but that's not entirely true," Blake said. "We'd been tracking this group for a while. I'm just sorry we found them too late to help minimize your losses. How much do you know about the Odyssey Project and the *Carl Sagan*?"

"Almost nothing other than it was supposedly our first attempt at FTL exploration."

"Supposedly?"

"A lot of time has passed, Colonel," Jackson said. "The *Carl Sagan* was never heard from again, and Tsuyo Corporation has erased knowledge of your crew by omission. Most contemporary historical accounts only tell of their first *successful* attempt to explore and colonize."

"Tsuyo Corp is still around?" Blake seemed genuinely surprised. "And still manipulating public perceptions, I see. I guess some things really don't change. But yes, I was part of that first ill-fated mission."

"So what happened to you and your crew?" Lieutenant Davis asked.

"How much time do you have?" Blake joked.

"It seems we have plenty now that you've cleared our skies." Jackson leaned back and gestured for Blake to begin.

The story the colonel told them over the next two hours was nothing short of extraordinary.

Once the astronauts, as they were still so called, were shuttled up to the *Carl Sagan*, the ship began its ponderous, chemically-fueled flight out of the Solar System. The FTL drive seemed to work as advertised, and they transitioned out of the system, just past the orbit of Venus. That drive, not even first generation but more of a prototype, had flown twice before in unmanned test flights to prove the system's integrity before trusting it with forty-eight highly trained humans.

The first two weeks of the warp flight were spent monitoring the drive and making sure the ship's automated functions were performing as they should. This was absolutely critical since, even though they were traveling faster than light, the trip would still be of sufficient length as to require the crew to enter an induced hibernation.

Theoretically, the drive was capable of incredible, almost unimaginable speeds, but the human scientists that had adapted it were no closer to developing the necessary power source than they were twenty years prior. The compact fission reactors aboard the *Carl Sagan* just couldn't develop the distortion fields needed to push past a warp factor of 1.5 at maximum output.

"But something went wrong." Blake shuddered. "We were scheduled to arrive in the Proxima Centauri System, scout around, and then fly home loaded down with enough imagery for Tsuyo's marketing department to use for a decade to justify funding for Phase II of the Odyssey Project. Instead, we ended up adrift in interstellar space. We found out later that something had happened to cause our guidance and flight control computer to reboot. The ship just flew on in a random direction, never alerting us until reactor two finally failed and forced the T-Drive to disengage."

"So your warp drive failed," Jackson said. "Then what? You just woke up and found yourselves stranded?"

"Warp drive? That's actually funny," Blake deadpanned. "We were absolutely forbidden from using that term. Anyway, Captain, no... We didn't wake up. The environmental systems had failed long before we dropped back into normal space. We had all been dead for many, many years."

"Obviously you'll have to clarify that," Jackson prompted.

"We had died while in hibernation, the interior of the ship cooling rapidly from multiple hull breaches that we were told occurred from the shear forces caused by variances that developed between our distortion fields," Blake said. "It shouldn't have been an issue since we'd planned to drop out of... warp long before then. The stasis beds were well insulated, so some of us were very well preserved as the temperature and pressure dropped slowly rather than explosively. Most of us weren't so lucky."

"*Who* told you about the field variances?" Jackson asked, already suspecting where the story was heading.

"Twenty-three of us were so well preserved, and our minds had already been mostly dormant during the induced hibernation, that the Vruahn were able to repair the damage and revive us," Blake said. "Before that, they'd already been able to decipher our languages from studying the remains of the *Carl Sagan*. It was still a hell of a shock when I opened my eyes and had an alien jabbering at me through a translator."

"Twenty-three out of forty-eight," Jackson said. "Tough break, Colonel."

"Indeed," Blake said softly. "I have the ashes of those unfortunate twenty-five aboard my ship. When we began the trek back, I had hoped to be able to return their remains to Earth, ideally to whatever family may exist for each of them."

"About those ships," Jackson gestured at the display in the conference room that was showing the two phalanx formations. "Vruahn?"

"Yes, Captain." Blake nodded. "The Vruahn and humanity now have a common enemy—the difference being that their society has evolved to be so passive that they were unable to even attempt defending themselves. Long story short, that's where we came in. Eighteen of us have been clearing out systems for the better part of fifty years now, while the Vruahn continue to build us better and more powerful ships, but we're still losing ground to them... these *Phage*."

"Wait... fifty years—?"

Jackson was interrupted by Ensign Hayashi bursting into the conference room, his face flushed red and tears standing in his eyes.

"What is it, Ensign?"

"A com drone has arrived from a Prowler in the Alpha Centauri System, sir!" the young officer choked out.

"And?" Jackson asked impatiently.

"Haven is gone, Captain!" Hayashi said. "The Phage... they showed up and completely destroyed it!"

Epilogue

Two months after the Battle of Nuovo Patria

Jackson's blurred vision focused again on the business end of his 1911 .45 pistol, the slide still wet with his saliva. Again, he placed the weapon down and grabbed the near-empty bottle on his desk, tilting it up and draining it. He slammed the bottle down and grabbed the pistol again, convinced that this was the only logical conclusion to his life: a coward's way out for a fool that was responsible for the deaths of billions.

He was dimly aware of his hatch chime chirping away cheerfully as well as the harsh pounding of someone *really* wanting into his office. Ignoring it, he lifted the weapon again and, oddly, felt a pang of sympathy for his poor steward who would have to clean up the mess later.

"Put that fucking pistol down!"

Jackson squinted at the hatchway, now wide open with an irate Admiral Marcum, along with a concerned looking Major Ortiz standing behind him. The mutinous Marine officer must have given Marcum the security override code for the hatch.

The *Ares* had been in high-orbit over the irregularly shaped, rapidly cooling lump of molten rock that had once been Haven for the last two weeks. Jackson had been completely incapacitated for more than half of that time, leaving command of the ship to a distraught Jillian Davis. The hatch closing captured his attention again, and he saw that there were actually two people in his office: Admiral Joseph Marcum and Colonel Robert Blake.

"Admiral, may I help you?" Jackson slurred out. "Forgive me for not standing."

"Captain Wolfe, you will cease this idiotic behavior immediately," Marcum said.

"You know, Admiral... it's not smart to antagonize someone with a weapon." Jackson hefted the pistol. "Especially someone who doesn't really like you to begin with."

Blake and Marcum just looked at each other before the Air Force colonel reached over and, with surprising quickness, plucked the pistol out of his hand, ejecting the magazine and clearing the chamber before setting it back on the desk with the slide locked back.

"Well then..." Jackson stared at the now harmless chunk of steel. "I guess I have no choice but to listen to you, Admiral. If you're here to arrest me, you should know that I was about to make that a moot point."

"Are you about finished, Senior Captain?" Marcum snarled. "You had best unfuck yourself and quick. Your crew can't see you like this. When's the last time you've been out of this room?"

"You can't seriously be contemplating leaving me in command of anything." Jackson swallowed hard as his stomach and the bourbon fought it out.

"Jackson, this isn't anybody's fault." Marcum slid wearily into one of the chairs and gestured for Blake to take the other.

"I was too blind to realize the Phage were playing me." Jackson leaned back. "I pulled all of our forces to one area and left it clear for them to come up and hit us in the worst possible place. They even said so much to me directly."

"You made the hard choice to stand fast when nobody else wanted to even admit we were in a war," Marcum said. "The truth is, Captain, that there would *never* have been a significant force in this system. The politicians would never allow one enclave to have any sort of military presence over Haven. That's why this has been Black Fleet's home for all these years, and no other numbered fleets are welcome. They certainly weren't going to revisit that policy just because a few Frontier worlds were at risk. Haven was always going to fall if the Phage wanted it."

"That's rather defeatist of you," Jackson said.

"My point is that this disaster isn't just one man's fault," Marcum said. "We didn't take the threat seriously, and now billions are dead for it."

"So what happens next?"

"We do what humans have always done: we persevere," Marcum said. "We've debriefed your Earther friend here, although he keeps claiming he's an 'American.' He's got a lot more information on the Phage than we've been able to collect in the last four years, including one very significant vulnerability."

At this Jackson perked up and looked over at the colonel.

"That's right, Captain," Blake confirmed. "There is one thing that could bring the Phage down completely, but my team has never had the resources to exploit it by ourselves. So the question is this: do you want us to leave you alone so you can finish what you were about to do here, or do you want to saddle up one last time and go riding for some payback?"

Jackson gave the officer a small, feral smile. "I'm listening."

Thank you for reading *Call to Arms*.
If you enjoyed the book the story will continue with:

Counterstrike
Book Three of the Black Fleet Trilogy.

Coming Fall/Winter of 2015

Connect with me on Facebook and sign up
for my newsletter to stay up to date on new
releases and other exclusive offers.

www.facebook.com/Joshua.Dalzelle

@JoshuaDalzelle

And check out my Amazon page to see other works
including the bestselling

Omega Force Series:

www.amazon.com/author/joshuadalzelle

Author's Note

So there we have it, the dreaded second act and the even more dreaded cliffhanger. I tried to make it as gentle as possible and looking back it's actually the first time I've ever used that particular literary device in a published work.

This trilogy is very much about Jackson Wolfe and his crew, but in this second book I had to give a little more detail into the politics at play in this universe for things to make sense. My goal was to give enough detail to satisfy any questions you may have without grinding the story to a halt. We are on the brink of all out war, after all.

I know I've said this before, but thank you again for the overwhelmingly positive response to this series. With this in mind I've already started writing "Counterstrike" by the time this book is released so that books two and three come out back to back. For the Omega Force readers I hope to have book eight out towards the end of this year.

Cheers!

Josh

22425894R00213

Made in the USA
San Bernardino, CA
05 July 2015